To Nancy
Best wishes
Helen x

TALK OF THE TOUN

Helen MacKinven

TP

ThunderPoint Publishing Ltd.

First Published in Great Britain in 2015 by
ThunderPoint Publishing Limited
Summit House
4-5 Mitchell Street
Edinburgh
Scotland EH6 7BD

ISBN (Paperback): 978-0-9929768-7-3
ISBN (ebook): 978-1-910946-00-8

www.thunderpoint.scot

Acknowledgements

In finally achieving my dream to be a published novelist, I had a lot of help on my writing journey from my family and friends. Top of the list is my husband Donald, the love of my life, who has always believed in me and supported me every word of the way.

I am also lucky to count Karen Campbell and Anne Glennie as close friends and my unofficial mentors and they continue to be a great source of encouragement and inspiration.

Credit too goes to my sons Ross and Lewis, my wee sister Marie, mum Margaret, best friends Veronica Cully and Gillian Millar, my MLitt classmates and tutor Paula Morris, fellow writers Paul Cuddihy and Margot McCuaig, and far too many long-suffering pals to name here who acted as cheerleaders to keep the faith and keep writing.

A special thank you must also go to Seonaid and Huw Francis at ThunderPoint who have worked hard to make Talk of the Toun a reality.

Dedication

In memory of my gran, Ella,
who taught me the meaning of unconditional love.

Summer of 1985

Chapter One

She was greetin' again.

I've been mopping up her snot bubbles since Lorraine Quinn was four and half. We met at the bus stop outside the Co-op and we've been inseparable ever since. Our mammies blethered while they waited with us for the school bus to St Philomena's on our first day at primary school. The double-decker came down the hill and both mammies shoved us into the queue, telling us just to follow the big lassies. We were cut loose.

One of the primary sevens took our hands but Lorraine started greetin' when her mam waved the bus off. The primary seven lassie handed Lorraine a bunch of roses wrapped in auld newspaper.

'Here, you can have them. Give them tae yer teacher for the class altar.'

Lorraine was the teacher's pet from day one and yet she was bawling again at play time. She was feart to tell the teacher that she'd lost her dinner money and had already eaten her play piece. Lorraine's breath reeked of bacon from the packet of Rancheros she'd wolfed and it gave me the dry boak when I pushed my face into hers.

'You'll no starve. Miss Rankine'll tell the dinner ladies that you'll bring in yer money the morra.'

'Are you sure, Angela? Do you promise that's true? You're no just kiddin' me on?'

I shook my head and after a few more dabs of the blubbery hankie, she stopped sniffing.

'Ah promise.'

Lorraine got her dinner like I'd said she would and I let her sit beside me. Faye and Mandy from our class joined us at our table. They should have been in primary two except that they'd been kept behind for a year and I soon realised why. Miss Rankine was demented with them and they were still on the first Dick and Dora reading book.

But although they were thick, they were able to tell us stuff we needed to know. Mandy explained that every Friday morning, a primary seven would bring Black Sambo round the classes to collect a penny for the black babies. Lorraine looked ready to greet again but Mandy told her to calm down, Black Sambo wasn't a real-life darkie, it was a mechanical bank; you placed your penny in its hand and it put it in its mouth. And we had to save our silver milk bottle tops and paper from the inside of fag packets for the guide dogs. It was easy to understand why weans in Africa might need our pennies but we didn't understand why a dog would need silver paper. We had a lot to learn.

Faye and Mandy showed us the stainless steel pail that sat in the corner and told us it was called a swill bucket. They said it was where we had to scrape our plates when we were finished. Mandy explained that pigs got to eat what was left of our beef olives and gravy, and it was all mixed up together with custard and caramel cake. I pictured manky pigs with muddy trotters sitting on the wooden benches, sticking their snouts into soup bowls of swampy left overs. I never said a word. I was too feart Lorraine would start greetin' again and it was just as well I kept my geggie shut because Faye and Mandy were pointing out older lassies to avoid. These bears would batter us if they decided they didn't like us, for no reason. They would've faced up to Gripper Stebson they were so gallus. So like a tube of *UHU*, we stuck together from that day on and me being a lot bigger than Lorraine seemed to help us because we never did get battered.

'See, ah told you tae listen tae me.'

And who'd have guessed that twelve years later, she still believes every word I say is true? Lorraine has blind faith in me because she knows that I'm her best friend and I'll never let her down. I'm like her guardian angel in disguise. But being seventeen now, I'm not the same wee lassie who started school believing that God had a Big Book in heaven and if you did something bad, you got a black mark next to your name. I'd wake up in a sweat that He had all my sins written down in the

Big Book. Faye and Mandy told me halfway through primary one that it was all a load of guff that the teachers tell you to get you to behave, and it hadn't worked on them.

Of course I don't believe in the Big Book or God anymore, although I still believe in guardian angels. I don't mean the cherub types who sit on fluffy clouds and play wind instruments all day, like the ones Lorraine used to glue pictures of into her scrapbooks. I mean the ones who've been put on the planet to protect their best pals, like me looking out for Lorraine but minus the feathery wings and rosy cheeks.

When she was wee, I'd roll Lorraine's snotters round my hankie until it was as rubbery as the ball of elastic bands Miss Rankine kept on her desk. At least these days, there are more tears than bogies.

This time the cause of her tears was the anti-abortion film that had made her neck all blotchy. She wasn't the only one; the assembly hall was full of lassies greetin'. That was the whole idea and it was no wonder the rector looked so chuffed with himself. Everyone called him Papa Smurf because his name was Mr Murphy and he had a bushy white beard and baw face. At the end of the film, Papa Smurf invited the Pro-Life group, led by sure-to-be-girls'-captain-next-year, Pamela Thompson – aka Little Miss Brown Nose – to go up on stage to talk about their "sterling work demonstrating our faith in action". Pass me the sick bucket.

The whole of fifth and sixth year, even the boys, were there. There were only two weeks left to go before the school holidays and with the exams finished, it was obvious that the teachers were filling in time and were literally using murder to kill off any ideas that we had of a summer of sun, sea and sex. Most of us wouldn't get as far as the beach at Burntisland wearing cagoules as it pissed down, but every one of us could get shagged if we put our minds to it. And I was determined that me and Lorraine wouldn't be coming back for a sixth year as virgins.

Papa Smurf's plan to put the frighteners up us worked. Gavin Malley had to run out of the assembly hall when the film got to the bit where the suction thingymabob hoovered the foetus out. He puked his guts up right outside the double swing doors. The Chinese whispers kicked off and everyone passed it round that when he spewed, he splashed Sister Patricia's suede brogues with chunks of carrot. But I was sitting opposite Gavin in the dinner hall and he'd had a hot dog for lunch so Christ knows where the carrots came from.

In fairness, the ones calling Gavin a total fanny were out of order because the Pro-Life horror movie did show some revolting stomach churning stuff. The worst bit was easily the feet of a ten week old baby. They were held between the fingers of a doctor who said the foetus was developed enough to curl her toes or bend her knees if she was touched on the sole of her foot. And most women have the abortion at about ten weeks into the pregnancy. The tiny feet freaked everyone out, not just Gavin.

It wasn't only the video nasty that was getting at Lorraine. I knew the real reason why she was sucking up snotters and dabbing at her electric blue mascara. She took the film's message personally; stuff like abortion always got her thinking about her wee sister Janine, and whether folk who're born handicapped should have been born at all. That's why she could never drink much at the school discos, the cider made her as moody as the three school Goths and after two half pints the greetin' would start.

It was the one thing that came up time and time again when she got pished.

'Who'll look after Janine if anything happens to my mam and dad?'

'What if they get too old to look after her?'

'Will I ever be able to leave home?'

The questions smouldered at the back of Lorraine's mind and adding Strongbow was an explosive mix. I told her over and over that she should just drink Midori or Biarritz; she complained that she'd look like she was still fifteen. And I suppose she was right, it was only wee fannies trying to act grown-up who drank booze that was cyber green or neon orange and glowed in the dark. By the time you're seventeen you need to be able to handle a starter bottle of cider before a steady stream of Snakebites and anything else you could get your mitts on. Lorraine was a light-weight and was better sticking to shandies. Nobody wants to worry about residential care for the handicapped when you're on a night out. No matter how braw looking Lorraine is, that kind of chat definitely doesn't get the guys buying you drinks. Lorraine attracted guys like flies round shite but I couldn't afford to let her blow my chances of getting off with one of the guy's pals. And we've never got enough cash to buy our own drinks all night.

I don't mind minesweeping the tables at Mystique. I've no problem stealing drink from folk who've been daft enough to leave them on tables while they're up dancing or in the bogs; it's Lorraine who's an absolute crapper. She always worries I'll get battered if I'm caught and she's feart she'll pick up a disease from a clarty glass. I like that I never know what I'm going to end up drinking and it's always a good laugh to see if I can get away with it. I've got the stomach for it, steel-lined; hard core drinking is in my genes, but I can't risk Lorraine downing an unknown concoction. She's embarrassing enough sober. Last Friday she slapped down her Garfield pencil case on top of the bar instead of her purse. The barman knows our group are all from St Paddy's, but there's no need to go advertising it by whipping out a ruler instead of a pound note. It was a total beamer, just like this afternoon in the assembly hall with everyone asking her if she was all right after the Pro-Life film and offering her a Handy Andy. And then to top it off, Little Miss Brown Nose was selling gold pin badges. She jumped out from behind a table covered in rows of tiny feet and like Skippy the Bush Kangaroo, she bounced over to us. Her ponytail swung behind her and my fingers itched to yank it until her eyeballs popped like corks. She's a skinny bitch too. Little Miss Brown Nose stood in our way and shook an auld biscuit tin full of coins right into our faces. She doesn't do subtle; she's the rector's wet dream for school captain.

'They're called 'Precious Feet' and they're the exact size and shape of an unborn baby's feet at ten weeks after conception. And they're only twenty five pence each.'

'Naw, you're okay, we'll leave it Pamela.'

I tried to steer Lorraine around Little Miss Brown Nose; she blocked the corridor and pulled on the badge pinned to the lapel of her blazer. She had a woollen Barathea, like Lorraine, they had to be ordered in especially from Dillon's up the town. My blazer was made from fuzzy felt, the same colour and texture as a pool table and I got mine from McAteers with a Provy cheque.

'You mean you don't support the rights of the unborn child?'

Little Miss Brown Nose rattled the biscuit tin again.

Lorraine sniffed hard and I felt her tug on my sleeve. I pushed past, 'We'll buy one later when we get change.'

I linked arms with Lorraine and propelled her down the corridor as if she was bursting for a pee.

'Don't worry, there's plenty of change in the tin.'

I marched on, ignoring Little Miss Brown Nose and pushed the swing doors open into the foyer. The warm waft of damp blazer, teenage BO and Spicy Nik Naks was a breath of fresh air.

'C'mon, let's get oot of here. If you keep this greetin' up, they'll all start tae think you've had an abortion.'

I knew that would shut her up. A flash of fear made her eyes bulge and she choked on a blob of snot. Lorraine didn't argue and followed me through the packed foyer as we elbowed our way out the side entrance. The smirry rain had cleared and I told her to put her brolly up.

'But it's no even spitting,' said Lorraine, raking around in her school-bag.

'It's no tae keep us dry ya fanny, it's tae keep us hidden.'

'Eh?'

'Jeezo, do ah have tae spell out everything for you? Do you want detention for doggin' it?'

'Naw'.

'Well get yer brolly up so the teachers dinnae see it's us going over the canal bridge.'

I tilted my head up towards the staffroom window I could barely see through the thick fog of smoke. And they had the cheek to lecture us about the dangers of smoking. She got the message and we both huddled in close under her lipstick print umbrella. I loved that brolly. Lorraine offered to give me it when my gran's auld one blew inside out and the spokes snapped. I told her thanks but no thanks, her mam would kill her if she gave me more stuff.

'Make sure you keep ma folder dry,' I said.

I held the oversized plastic bag with my artwork tight across my chest. The art department gave out the bags to anyone who didn't have their own portfolio case. I lugged mine in and out of school under my arm like a ginormous badge telling folk I was arty though not trendy or posh enough to have the right gear.

Little Miss Brown Nose was in my Higher Art class and had a black leather zipped case from Millers Art Shop in Glasgow and a full set of her own chalk pastels and watercolours. It was shit making do with the school's supply of chalks. There was hardly ever any skin-tone coloured chalks left and you had to make do with stumps of random colours. I'd stashed a couple of sticks of the best colours in my bag a few weeks back. It was a worry; once they ran out the game's a bogie and I'd be at the mercy of all the shite left in the art department's stock.

I was never going to be able to put together a decent portfolio for my Art School application without my own watercolours either. And I still had to tell my mam and dad about wanting to apply after sixth year. I'd get round to it, eventually, it just never seemed like the right time.

It was getting harder and harder to speak to them. My mam and dad talked at me, not to me. I'd outgrown them when I was about twelve and we'd lived on different planets ever since.

At least I had Lorraine to keep me sane. We walked arm-in-arm along the side of the canal wall and past the bus bays. In a matter of hours, chaos would return to this corner of the school grounds as pupils pushed and shoved to get on their bus. The hard men from the schemes would sit up the back of the top deck to smoke but if the bus was late they had time to give an unlucky first year the legendary Hanging Wedgie. The ten foot canal wall was perfect to dangle a wee first year from their pants and it was even better if they were wearing cartoon ones that their mam had bought them. This had the added bonus of giving the whole bus queue a laugh at their Spiderman pants while they screamed in agony as the cotton cut into the crack of their arse. The fear of being a victim to the Hanging Wedgie must cause primary seven weans all over Falkirk many a sleepless night before the move to the big school. The teachers turned a blind eye, probably kidding themselves on that it was character building without having to admit that they were just as feart of the hard men as the wee first years.

At this time of day, there was no one else around, and me and Lorraine walked up to the bridge over the Forth and Clyde Canal. The path took a steep left through the Bleachy, a shortcut through an industrial estate where it ended at the back of the town hall car park. The Bleachy gave me the heebie-jeebies and I'd never walked it alone even in daylight hours. Mr Stanners told us in our first year History class that the land opposite our school was once used as a bleach field to let cloth dry out in the sun. It was hard to imagine anything in the area being clean and bright these days. The Bleachy was now a maze of boxy concrete buildings with corrugated iron flat roofs and lock-up garages. Round every corner, mad dogs strained on their leash until their mouths foamed if you dared go near the yards of the garages and workshops that lined the muddy path. We called them Bandeath dugs; they were usually a cross between an Alsatian and a wolf and they came from the Bandeath dog shelter in Stirling. No one in their right mind would buy a dog that looked as pig ugly as these brutes. They weren't pets; Bandeath dugs were tougher than night club bouncers.

The puddles along the Bleachy were always oily and rubbish piled up in corners like multi-coloured snow drifts. It wasn't the devil dogs and the filth that freaked me out. The Bleachy was always dark, even on a sunny day and then there would be the men on their tea breaks, overalls rolled down to their waist, greasy thumb and index finger holding a fag between them and blowing smoke rings. And it was just luck what flavour of abuse we got when we walked past in our cow-pat green uniforms. St Paddy's was the only high school in blue-nose Falkirk that forced the pupils to wear a uniform. I didn't mind; it was better than looking like the tinks that spewed out of Falkirk High wearing sweatshirts and joggy bottoms. The downside was that I'd be as well wearing a T-shirt advertising 'I'm a bog trotting tattie munching Tim!'

On a good day, it was the usual banter, "Gies a flash o' yer tits doll". The green and gold uniform didn't hold the same attraction for all the men; the colour turned the air as blue as their Proddy noses.

'What's that mingin' smell?' There would be a pause for a theatrical snort for a lungful of air and hairy nostrils flared. 'Hang on; ah'd recognise that pishy smell anywhere. Aye, it's a wee Fenian bastard.'

That was another reason for the lipstick brolly, no eye contact sometimes helped reduce the risk of the workmen starting on us. Lorraine and me were lucky. There was only one guy standing outside his garage reading the *Daily Record* and he didn't even look up as we rushed by. The air cleared at the end of the Bleachy and all we needed to do was skirt round the side of Brockville football ground and we'd be back to civilisation.

'So where now brown cow?' asked Lorraine.

I laughed to keep her happy. Lorraine never got anything exactly spot on. God loves a trier, that's what her mam always said when the exam results came in. Rita believed in miracles and still thought Lorraine would be able to go to uni. The teachers weren't as holy.

'We could go tae the library. At least it'll be warm,' I suggested.

'No chance, we've no just dogged school to be back at a desk and surrounded by books.'

'Aye, ah suppose you're right enough. But there's no much else tae dae on a Wednesday afternoon in Falkirk.'

'There's no much to do *anytime* in Falkirk.'

I shook my head and sniggered. Lorraine tapped my shoulder

'What're you laughing at?' she asked.

'You dinnae even ken you're funny.'

'I wisnae joking.'

There was no point in trying to explain irony to Lorraine despite the fact that she'd attempted to sit Higher English.

'The market's on a Wednesday,' I shrugged. 'And you're looking for new jeans for the weekend.'

'Good idea, but we'll need to keep an eye out for my Auntie Mary.'

'Why, is she looking for jeans too?'

The thought of Lorraine's Auntie Mary in jeans was hysterical although Lorraine didn't get the joke.

'Naw, it's 'cause she always goes to the fish van at the market!'

I placed my art folder between my knees and made my hands into binoculars so that I could rhyme off, 'Mary had a little lamb, she also had a bear, I often saw Mary's little lamb, but I never saw her bare.' It was enough to get Lorraine giggling, and it didn't take much.

The outdoor market was set up in the car park outside Coasters. The building had originally been an ice-rink and was now a roller-rink where me and Lorraine used to skite about on a Saturday night before we graduated to the town's nightclub and danced and drank in Mystique. The car park was just as mucky as the Bleachy and I had to dodge puddles to protect my beige suede Tucker boots. I made Lorraine stop at the van selling deep fried doughnuts.

'I wish you could bottle that smell,' said Lorraine plunging her nose into the paper bag of sugary dough. It made me sick that Lorraine could eat as much crap as she wanted and was still a skinny minny; I only had to walk past the chippy to put on weight.

'And then you could wear 'Eau de Doughnut' perfume, instead of that Strawberry Body Shop shite you douse yourself in.'

'Shite? Funny that the bottle's half empty and it wisnae just from me wearing it.'

'Dinnae look at me, ah never touched it. And why would ah want tae stink of fruit anyway?'

'Because the guys'll know you're soft and juicy.' Lorraine stuck her tongue through the hole in the doughnut and I nearly choked on mine. I spat out bits of damp dough to make space for my laugh.

We leaned against the back of the doughnut van and I licked the inside of my paper bag. Lorraine's pure jammy; she has the appetite of a sparrow. I come from a family of big eaters and my dad says it's not my fault, it's the metabolism I was born with and I can't fight against my genes. He keeps telling me not to worry about puppy fat. He calls me his Chunky Monkey and squeezes my chubby cheeks. But it still hurts when I get called a porker when I pass boys in the street and they squeal like a pig. I blame the black babies. When you've been brought up to clear your plate because there are black babies starving in Africa you don't like to waste good food. I finished Lorraine's doughnut off, scrunched the bag up into a ball and lobbed it over the metal railings.

'Did you know that cats can't taste anything sweet?' asked Lorraine.

I shook my head, 'Jeezo, nae wonder you failed yer prelims, you talk a load of mince.'

'It's a scientific fact! I saw it on Tomorrow's World.'

'So says Professor Lorraine Quinn.'

'We're no all as brainy as you, Professor Angela McMenemy. But I've got other assets.'

Lorraine opened her Barathea to prove that her blouse buttons were straining. Her tits aren't as big as she makes out; they just look big on her skinny body. She's been wearing the same size of school blouse since third year. Rita has never noticed, too busy looking after Janine. At least my mam does my ironing. Lorraine has to do a lot of other housework stuff I get away with too and as much as she drives me radio rental, my mam always makes my tea and hangs out the washing.

I ignored Lorraine and walked up one side of the market stalls. I paused in front of a stall selling tea towels with red cups and saucers embroidered on them. 'Not five pounds, not two pounds…' The man's skin looked too big for his face, like the foreskin I'd labeled on my Higher Biology worksheet and yet the crowd of auld wifies hung on his every word as if he was Tom Jones. Their eyes were glued to him as his meaty hands came together – bang and the deal was done. The women breenged through the crowd and waved their one pound notes in the air like knickers they were about to throw on stage. And all for the privilege of buying a couple of rags of cotton. The showman threw the bundles of tea towels into the adoring group; his stock was dangerously low. I wanted to wait to see if it turned violent when the tea towels ran out but Lorraine had already wandered off. I saw her pause at a stall selling jeans and remembered why we were at the market. Lorraine picked up a pair of jeans with white piping down the leg seams and stroked the denim.

'Try them on in the back of the van darlin'.'

The guy had a beard like a balaclava and smelt as if he'd eaten a big plate of Chicken Kiev. He shouldered the door and pulled on the plastic handle. A faded sticker on the back window said,

'DRIVER CARRIES NO CASH. HE'S MARRIED' and some other smart arse had written on the muck splattered rear, '*also in white.*'

I nudged Lorraine's arse with my knee and she climbed inside the rusty Transit. I followed and closed the van's door. Almost shut. Lorraine unzipped her pencil skirt and rolled it down like she was peeling a banana. She lay on her back to yank the stone-washed jeans up over her hips. I sat on my hunkers on top of a pile of dark jeans; the dye from the denim honked, and reminded me of burning hair, just like the time I crimped Lorraine's hair for the school disco in fourth year when she was going through her Cyndi Lauper phase. I left the crimping irons clamped shut a lot longer than I should have and a whole clump of blonde hair came away in my hands. The singed patch was at the back, she never noticed at first and she didn't dare to blame me; I never claimed to be a hairdresser.

Lorraine struggled with the jean's flimsy zip and her peach pair of tanga briefs snagged in the zipper's teeth. We knew Hairy Face was watching. Lorraine's giggles turned to snorts and I guessed what was coming next.

My mam said it was because of Janine that Lorraine was an attention seeker and a show off. Lorraine liked to tell lies too. When I was seven, I begged my mam to let me go to ballet lessons and get a pony like Lorraine. I didn't believe my mam when she said that Lorraine was lying. And yet I knew that she only went to the Brownies at the community centre and I'd never known anybody to have a pony in their back garden. It took me a while to accept that my mam was right, Lorraine was nothing but a drama queen and always performing. I didn't love Lorraine any less; in fact I realised that's why she needed me to wipe her eyes when she came off-stage and the applause died.

'Let's give him a proper show.'

The zipper was pulled free; the teeth had bitten a hole in Lorraine's knickers. Her hands groped for the hole and she pulled the cotton apart. I held my breath at the sound of the knickers ripping. The tear was big enough for her to insert three fingers. The door of the van creaked open an inch or so too.

I kicked Lorraine's thigh, hard enough to push her on her side and her face into a pile of denim jackets.

'Fuck off, that hurt!'

The van door slammed shut. Lorraine rolled on to her back, rubbing her thigh as she tugged the jeans off. She threw them at me and I batted them into the corner of the van. Lorraine slipped her school skirt on and grabbed her school bag.

'So are you gonnae get the jeans or what?' I asked.

'I might've got them cheaper if you hadn't stuck your neb in. I was just having a laugh.'

'You took it too far. And someone needs tae tell you when tae stop.'

I swung the door open and jumped out on to the tarmac. Hairy Face was folding a pair of wide arse jeans into a red and white stripy carrier bag for a wifie but he turned round as we shimmied round the side of his stall. The wifie looked us up and down, tutted then walked off with her skanky jeans.

'Any good darlin'?'

'Ahm no sure, they're a bit tight,' replied Lorraine.

'That's how the boys like them, trust me.'

She rummaged in her school bag for her purse.

'C'mon Lorraine. Chelsea Girl has got new jeans in. Better looking than these shitey market ones.'

'But they'll be a lot dearer.' Hairy Face's beard did nothing to hide his smugness. The mere mention of Chelsea Girl was enough to side-track Lorraine. She shoved her purse back inside her school bag.

'You're right Angela, it's no as if I'm skint.'

'You looked cheap to me when you were lying with your legs open,' Hairy Face sneered.

'Fuck you! C'mon Lorraine, we need tae tell the polis that there's a dirty paedo working doon the market, forcing school lassies tae strip for him.'

Hairy Face shouted, 'Slags' after us as we dodged in between the wifies with their tartan shopping trollies. We didn't notice Lorraine's Auntie Mary in the queue for the fish van.

'Oi, what are you pair doing oot of school?'

'Ah wisnae feeling well so Lorraine's tae make sure ah get hame okay.' I coughed and sniffed on cue.

'And since when did that involve a trip doon the market?'

Her Auntie Mary pulled herself up a full two inches to four

foot ten and attempted to eyeball Lorraine.

'Her mam's run oot of Holy Water so Lorraine asked me if ah could manage a wee detour before we get the bus hame.'

I pointed over to the stall that sold all sorts of crap for Catholics. Along with Virgin Mary shaped bottles of Holy Water, allegedly fresh from the grotto in Lourdes, there were rosary beads, crucifixes, Sacred Heart of Jesus statues, First Holy Communion cards, St Christopher key-rings and mini Pope John Pauls standing in St Peter's Square inside snow-globes. My favourite piece of tat was the Jesus/Mary hologram framed picture.

It was the same as the one my mam had in her bedroom. My dad had bought it for her as a present when she made her First Communion aged nineteen. He'd proposed to her on her eighteenth birthday on the condition that she turned Catholic. My mam told me she'd have done whatever it took to keep her man; she even had to make her Communion with a class of seven year olds from St Philomena's. My gran said it was the first time she'd ever been in a chapel when she went to watch her grown-up lassie dressed in her new trench coat but sitting beside weans wearing mini wedding dresses and white shorts.

My mam must've felt a right tube that day and maybe years later as she watched my dad pick-and-flick his bogies across the living room, wondering if she'd made the right decision.

She'd kept the holy hologram and my dad and I were glad she did. I used to lie on top of her bed to look at it one way to see Jesus and then tilt my head to look at it from a different angle to see Mary. Hours of endless fun witnessing a miracle without stepping over the front door. I picked it up, the stallholder grunted and pointed at the fluorescent orange starburst sign pegged on to the edge of the table, "Nice to touch, nice to hold, but if you break it, consider it sold!" It was hard to see how the plastic frame could shatter but I placed it back down. I could get my kicks for free at home and watch Mary morph into Jesus any day of the week.

'The font at the front door's empty and you know my mam disnae like to leave the house without a blessing,' added Lorraine.

Auntie Mary released her shoulders from her ears and patted Lorraine's arm.

'Rita likes tae moan about you but you're a good lassie really. And there's no many your age would go tae the Handicapped Club every week with her wee sister.'

Lorraine shot me a look. I knew that expression and let it bounce right off my napper. The minute we got rid of Auntie Mary and her breaded haddock, Lorraine asked if I would go with her to the Handicapped Club.

'Nae chance, ah told you the last time that ah wisnae going back again.'

I pushed past a clique of wifies, haggling over the price of mackerel fillets and left the market stalls behind. When I turned to check if Lorraine was following, she stopped in her tracks and did that stupid 'beg like a dog' routine with her tongue hanging out like a rasher of bacon and her hands curled up into wee paws under her chin. I knew, and she knew, that she could play me like a fiddle and by seven o'clock that night we'd both be there with Janine and the rest of the Windae Lickers at the Handicapped Club.

Chapter Two

The Handicapped Club had been running for years and was held every Wednesday in St Stephen's chapel hall. My mam said that the Club was the result of too many late night 'lock-ins' at the Celtic pubs and it meant that everybody was somebody's cousin. Nobody gave you a second glance in Denny if you had slanty eyes too close together, buck teeth and a humongous skull. It was normal to look like a freak in Denny; there was no shortage of Club members.

Janine was a regular at the Club, though it was impossible to tell if she liked going or not. She smiled morning, noon and night, whether she was at the Club or being wheeched round the Co-op in her wheelchair. She always had one of those cheery looks plastered to her face when she had nothing to smile about.

Most folk reacted to Janine's smile by tilting their heads to the side and sighing 'Bless,' with a pat to her head like she was a puppy. To piss the do-gooders off, my idea was to train Janine to meow or bark every time one of them patted her head. But Lorraine was worried that Janine might get carried away and enjoy being a cat or a dog so much it would cause more hassle than before.

There was no way to stop her smiling though and Janine's glaikit face pleased the Happy Clappys at Mass the most. The Charismatic Renewal Group or the Charismaddies as they were known, probably thought that she was smiling just for them when they belted out 'Bind Us Together, Lord'. And I smiled even more when they stopped strumming their guitars and shaking their tambourines.

Janine was smiling when the Club minibus came to pick us up.

'God love her,' said Boaby the driver as he lowered the ramp for her wheelchair. Lorraine and I stood back and let him strap her into the Nut Bus.

'This is the last time ah'm going tae the Club. Ah mean it.'

'Oh c'mon. You know you love getting wet kisses off Sadie.'

I elbowed her so hard she fell off her seat and bumped into her wee sister. Janine just smiled. I kidded on I was choking on a blob of thick puke at the thought of Sadie's slobbery chops.

'Shut it, or you'll be wearing ma tea if ah throw up. And it was Crispy Pancakes.'

Lorraine and Janine both grinned.

We didn't say much more on the way over to Denny. I wanted to talk to Lorraine about the weekend but it was too hard to concentrate on anything with the noises coming from the rest of the Windae Lickers. Thank God Denny is only a couple of miles from Bonnybridge or I'd be diving out the emergency exit door.

The Nut Bus unloaded its cargo at the Chapel Hall door and like a scene from Lourdes we lumbered alongside the procession of wheelchairs and crutches. The first thing to hit me was the stench of stewed cabbage. The hall served up school dinners for auld folk at a weekly Lunch Club and still reeked at seven o'clock at night. We shuffled in and the group took up their usual spots round the room. Sadie was always first to claim the table next to the kitchen's serving hatch. She's a greedy bitch for digestive biscuits and she demanded that Baz the Spaz sat next to her with Janine and Shona on the opposite side.

Baz had been warned the last time that I was there about pawing me but he grabbed me and shouted, "Thit!" while patting the chair next to him, probably hoping for a break from Sadie and a squeeze at me. Sadie growled at him like a rabid dog and took the free seat beside Baz.

Baz had a lisp and wasn't smart enough to get a job as a trolley boy at the Co-op, but he was no daftie; there was no doubt that he knew fine well what he was doing when he groped my arse every time I walked by. Baz the Spaz was not as stupid as he looked.

The unspoken seating plan was as territorial as the stampede for each family's favourite pews at Mass every Sunday. It was as fixed as the Ten Commandments that Lorraine's mam had to sit on the very back row. It was easier to park Janine's wheelchair at the back if she needed to make a quick toilet exit and it had the added advantage of giving Rita the longest walk to return to her seat after Holy Communion. That way everyone at Mass had plenty of time to admire how saintly she was on the way back to her handicapped wean.

Sadie was growling again; there was a commotion at the sight of KerPlunk. Any new toy or game always caused a riot and there would be tears, nothing was surer. Heads were flung back and squeals and howls filled the hall. Janine grabbed hold of the new helper's cardigan and the woman stopped to peer into her moon face.

'What's yer name, hen?'

'Her name's Janine.' Lorraine placed a hand on her sister's shoulder and Janine blew spit bubbles. The auld biddy was lucky that she was in the safety zone of the Club, or else she'd be the victim of one of Lorraine's usual replies. Her most common was the classic, 'D'you want a photie? It'll last longer!' We were used to folk staring at Janine when we took her out, and yet the gawping never failed to annoy Lorraine, no matter how many times I told her to ignore it.

I put on my best crone croak, 'What's yer name, hen?' and pushed my face up into the woman's as Lorraine giggled behind me.

'Enough of yer cheek, it's Mrs. Gaffney tae you.'

'Who're you here with, Mrs. Gaffney?' asked Lorraine.

'Ah'm just here tae help oot 'cause Margaret's no well. And ma grandson gave me a lift so how aboot showing him where he can get a drink.'

We wandered off leaving Janine parked in her wheelchair beside her best pal Shona and the rest of the gang eyeing up KerPlunk. Lorraine bent down to dab Shona's chin with a hankie, and I had to move fast. Shona was pawing me and the movement wafted a whiff of her distinct smell. She permanently stank of warm milk and it always reminded me of the bottles of milk left to curdle in a crate next to the radiators at primary school. It was no wonder that I'd never been able to stomach drinking milk or sitting next to Shona.

At the Club, there was only ever two choice of drinks, watery tea or Robinson's Barley Water juice; we knew the options and we always brought a can of Irn-Bru to share. The auld biddy's grandson was easy to spot, he was actually attempting to chat to Boaby the driver, and everyone, even Janine and her pals knew that was a waste of time. Boaby believed he was a born comedian but his patter was utter shite. He was telling Mrs. Gaffney's grandson one of his many crap jokes.

'The polis came tae ma door and told me ma dugs were chasing folk on bikes. But ah telt him, ma dugs dinnae even have bikes.'

Mrs. Gaffney's grandson groaned but that wasn't enough to put Boaby off. He carried on with his dog themed routine.

'What do ye call a dug with nae legs? Disnae matter, it'll no come anyway!'

Lorraine sparked open the can and the guy turned round, any excuse to break away from Boaby's dire repertoire. He looked older than us, maybe even twenty. And he was as sexy as fuck. Every Saturday night, me and Lorraine played 'Crotch Watch' at Mystique although butt-ugly guys didn't make it worth looking downwards and they automatically got disqualified. The rest of the guys were scored out of 10 for the biggest wullie bulge. The best we'd seen was an 8, this guy was easily an 11. I'd always wanted to do a life drawing for my art school portfolio and he'd make the perfect model.

I'd got within a bawhair of drawing someone in the nudie when I made my wee sister Karen pose for me. I told her to face the back of the chair and straddle it as if she was on a seesaw, I'd sit behind her and she could keep her pants on. I promised to give her money to buy a Wham bar and a sweetie bracelet off the ice-cream van and I knew that was enough to get her to strip. When the icey came up our street each night, Karen never had any money to go out to the van and she'd to ask the driver if he had any broken wafers he was giving away. He smashed them under the counter to save her embarrassment; there was no need to tell her and rub it in, she'd think I was lying anyway. She'd never really trusted me since I gave her a bowl of peach slices and after she'd eaten them I said that they were dead goldfish and she threw up all over her bed sheets. Karen won Bubbles the goldfish on Hook the Duck at the gala day but she gagged every time she looked at the tank on top of the fridge. My mam was feart she'd throw up again and cause more washing so she told Karen that she'd given Bubbles away to an auld neighbour.

And I was sworn to secrecy that my mam flushed the fish down the toilet pan when Karen was out playing.

The peach slice drama was a while ago and when I showed Karen the money for the icey, she peeled off her vest top and stashed the cash for the van's next circuit round the scheme. I never confessed that I missed out the outline of her pants in the sketch; it looked like she was completely in the buff, and as if I'd done a proper life drawing like a real artist. The dream sketching exercise would be Mrs. Gaffney's grandson and his donkey dick. If I put my mind to it, and pictured the scenes in the scud books Gavin Malley had passed round the Common Room, I'd manage a half-decent drawing once I got home.

'Why d'you think a guy like him is hanging about in here?' asked Lorraine.

'Maybe he's no right in the heid either,' I offered as an explanation.

'Well he's no bad looking even if he's a daftie.'

'Christ Lorraine, you'd jump anybody. Even at the Handicapped Club.'

'And dinnae tell me that you wouldn't want to shag him.'

'Fair point, well made. The guy's a total ride. Ah'd sook him tae the root.'

Lorraine licked her lips as he made his way across the hall. He was wearing a denim jacket with a Joy Division T-shirt underneath. The black and white T-shirt had a print of the art work from the band's first album, *Unknown Pleasures* and I was drooling almost as much as Shona.

'Awright girls?'

'Aye, good thanks.'

The hot guy lifted a plastic chair from the stacks that lined the side of the halls and dropped a burgundy one at our table. Excitement at the Handicapped Club was virtually unknown, apart from the time a couple of years back when Father O'Donnell popped in to the hall for a cuppa without realising that his zip was down and he was flashing his washed out undies. All hell let loose and no one was sure whose hand was on the priest's zip first as Margaret, the Chief Helper, launched herself at him, nearly knocking Janine's wheelchair over as she pushed Father O'Donnell backwards out the door. Just before she re-entered the hall, red-faced and flustered, she made the sign of the cross. I told Lorraine that Margaret must've got carried away and given the Father a hand-job while she was zipping him back up. Lorraine didn't laugh like I'd expected; maybe she knew more about mad Margaret or sleekit Father O'Donnell than I did, and her mam was up on all the Parish gossip. And Rita knew all the altar boys and who were the Father's favourites, the ones that always got picked to do the funerals with the bonus pay-off from the grieving family who slipped them a fiver for serving at Mass. I wouldn't be surprised if Father O'Donnell slipped the boys something extra.

And this guy would get tongues wagging too, for very different reasons. We both stared at him; it's easier to strike up a conversation at the Club if you have a member beside you to kick off the chit-chat, a bit like talking to another dog walker at the park. But without Janine with us, we were both as dumb-struck as everyone else in the hall.

'So dae you come here often?' I asked, assuming that the Joy Division T-shirt meant that the guy understood irony. He smirked, though it wasn't enough to tell whether he got my corny joke or not.

'Mrs. Gaffney says you're her grandson,' said Lorraine.

'Aye, Ah'm Stevie Duffy.'

Lorraine had the biggest beamer I've seen in the twelve years since I've known her. Even in second year, when Giovanni Moretti pulled her boob tube down at the chapel hall disco her face didn't go as red.

Stevie held his hand out for Lorraine to shake; she seemed so blown away by him she didn't move, and it was left hanging in the air. I took the chance and stepped forward.

'Ah'm Angela, but you can call me Angi. And this is ma best pal, Lorraine.'

'Angi?' repeated Lorraine.

I ignored her. Stevie didn't accept my outstretched hand and his eyes didn't swivel from Lorraine to me.

'You're no a Denny boy are you? I've no seen you about,' said Lorraine, finally able to re-enter our time zone.

'Ah'm fae Denny but ah've been away for the last couple of years.'

'At uni?'

'Aye, the University of Life. But ah bet a sexy wee thing like you could teach me a thing or two.'

We weren't used to smooth talk; the boys at school could never have pulled off a chat-up line as cheesy as that and still sound hot. And the guys we met at Mystique didn't have the balls; the best line yet was, "Is that a ladder in your tights or the stairway to your minge?"

'So where's the University of Life based?' I asked. His patter wasn't going to dazzle me.

'Polmont.'

'There's only the borstal there.'

'Aye, but it's mair like Butlins except ah was there for mair than a fortnight's holiday.'

'What were you in for?' Lorraine asked.

'Ah was set up by the polis. The bastards are aw Masons. They telt nothing but bare faced lies in court. Trust me; Ah'm one of life's good guys.'

Lorraine snorted until her Irn-Bru sprayed out of her nose. Stevie wiped the lapel of his leather jacket.

'Christ, it's no just the mongols that need a bib!'

Her chair wobbled and nearly tipped over when she scraped it back and stormed off into the bogs. I wanted to ask the guy what he was playing at using words like that but I had to race after Lorraine. She was locked inside a cubicle and I could hear the toilet roll burl round before she ripped off sheet after sheet. I banged on the door.

'Lorraine, dinnae let him get tae you. He's an ignoramus.'

There was no denying that he was a sexy guy, especially around these parts, but he'd crossed a line. I gave the door another rat-a-tat-tat.

No reply. The sniffing was getting louder and I hoped there was enough bog roll to mop it up.

'C'mon oot and talk tae me.'

Still nothing.

'Janine'll start greetin' too if she sees you're upset.'

Nothing but more sniffing.

'Ah'm no moving 'til you come oot. Or do you want me tae go and tell him tae piss off first?'

The sniffing stopped.

'Make sure he's no in the hall or I'm staying in here.'

'Leave it tae me.'

I marched back into the hall, hoping Lorraine's tears would spur me on enough to tell the guy, good-looking or not, that he was an arsehole for making my pal greet. I was saved the bother, Stevie Duffy was gone and I decided to tackle Mrs. Gaffney instead. She was handing Sadie another paper plate of digestives; clearly no-one had told her about the four biscuit limit, and to pay no attention to how many times Sadie banged her fists on the table.

'Where's yer grandson?'

'Stevie had tae head back hame. Why're you asking?'

'Oh nothing, it disnae matter.'

All that mattered was that he was gone and I could calm Lorraine down before Janine started greetin' too. There was every chance that the Nut Bus trip was going to feel even longer on the way back unless Lorraine got a grip of herself.

Lorraine emerged from the bogs looking like she'd been mugged although in amongst the club members, she barely got a backward glance. It took a lot to stand out in a crowd where most of the folk in the room were howling like banshees and slavering down their front.

'We wanna shot!' wailed Shona.

I managed to wrestle the KerPlunk from Sadie's grip to give Janine and Shona a go. Janine didn't seem as bothered as her pal, probably because she was able to play with Lorraine's old KerPlunk. Lorraine had every toy that a child had ever listed in their letter to Santa. Ever. One year she got KerPlunk, Girls World, a Spacehopper, a Mr Frosty Crunchy Ice Maker, a Bagpuss soft toy and a Wendy house and that was just the stuff she got to open after Midnight Mass. Her bedroom had a walk-in cupboard that looked like the store room for the toy section from Kays catalogue. My dad didn't let my mam order anything from the catalogues; he said the prices were a rip-off. Instead, my mam upped her smoking habit from October to save up the coupons from her packets of Kensitas Club. She planned to trade in the coupons for the 'must have' toy for Christmas at their shop in Glasgow. My mam didn't manage to collect enough coupons needed for a pogo stick and she was left with a hacking cough until February.

When I asked my mam why my pal had so many toys she said that Lorraine was spoilt rotten because of Janine being handicapped. I shouldn't be jealous and I should be grateful that my sister was normal. My mam has always talked a load of pish.

I remembered Lorraine's dad coming back from Saudi and building up the Wendy house for us to play in. We soon got bored with making mud pies for Bagpuss and her dolls. Even Tiny Tears didn't keep us interested for long. We went exploring and I found a family of hedgehogs living inside a hedge at the side of their garage. A big fat one with two babies. I made Lorraine roll them over and carry them on a doll's blanket into the Wendy house. We tossed them up and down on the pram blanket pretending it was a trampoline for hedgehogs. We got sweaty inside the Wendy house and went inside to get an ice pole. When we came back, the hedgehog family was dead. Lorraine was greetin' for ages until the ice-cream van came and her dad bought us 99s.

Janine often started greetin' for nothing too; it was obviously a family trait as Rita was always blubbing into a hankie. This time Janine was bawling her eyes out because all the KerPlunk marbles had dropped.

'Shush, or you'll start Shona off.'

Lorraine was nowhere to be seen.

She'd been collecting the used cups and plastic beakers and must've stayed in the kitchen. Boaby shouted that the minibus was ready and Lorraine reappeared, running over to Janine and cuddling her tight. The look she gave me would make anyone think that I'd caused her wee sister's tears. Janine's face lit up like a box of Terry's All Gold when she saw Lorraine and I quickly packed KerPlunk away into its box.

'We wanna shot!'

The best tactic was to blank Shona and we wheeled Janine out the hall in silence. I knew from experience that after a greetin' session, Lorraine needed a bit of space. We used lots of names for Janine and her pals in private, but the 'm' word was strictly off limits. And it was different when I called them windae lickers, Lorraine knew it wasn't said out of badness and I'd never use it in public.

Boaby huffed and puffed as he loaded up his cargo and finished off by turning his head and treating us to his usual corny line, 'Scream if you wanna go faster!' He looked grateful that Janine was smiling again, the only passenger on the Nut Bus who found Boaby funny.

I stroked the back of Janine's hand; she wasn't a good traveler, and Lorraine stared out of the window like the rest of them. Boaby offered to drop me off at the bottom of the main road and I gave Janine's hand a last pat before I bolted out of the side door. I needed to start sketching Stevie while I could still picture his features. Lorraine nodded her head sideways as the Nut Bus accelerated away and the rest of the windae lickers pushed their snouts to the glass and waved with two hands.

When I got home, my mam was in the living room flicking through the pages of Ceefax. The tap, tappity, tap from the kitchen meant that my dad was making another nail picture. I went through to get a drink; Wednesday was the best day of the week because the Alpine man went round the scheme with his lorry to drop off his orders. Some lucky bastards got a whole crate of ginger delivered to their doorstep; we were only allowed a bottle of Cherryade and Limeade, and we rationed our supply carefully. Lorraine's dad bought her a Soda Stream as a surprise on his last visit home. It was hard to imagine having fizz on demand. I poured myself a half glass and paused to listen to the bubbles hiss and to look over my dad's shoulder.

'What is it?' I asked.

'Junk,' he muttered without lifting his head.

'It's good dad, honest. Mam disnae ken what she's talking aboot.'

'No hen, ah meant *a* junk. You ken, like the kind you get in China.'

He took off his glasses and rubbed his eyes; on each side of his nose were wee red marks the size and shape of a finger nail clipping and I wanted to reach out and rub them away. But we don't do touchy feely stuff in our family. We're Scottish. Only lassies like Pamela Thompson or the fannies in the Falkirk Youth Theatre hugged their mams and dads and blew each other air kisses. In the real world, a pat on the back was enough for normal folk; we weren't the cast of *Grease.* There were other ways to show you cared.

'Do you want a cuppa tea, dad?'

It was what they called in my English class, a rhetorical question. I lit the pilot light and set the kettle on the gas ring. The kitchen was only wide enough to have a folding table and me and Karen used to be made to sit at it when we ate our tea. Now that we were older, we took our plates through to the living room so we could watch the telly too. And it meant I didn't miss *Neighbours.*

Apart from Christmas day, when the table was shifted into the living room and my gran brought extra stools, the table sides stayed down during daylight hours unless my dad was working on a nail picture. I edged my way round the table and picked up the pattern my dad was following, I never asked for more information about the weird-looking boats. I didn't need to; I knew what was coming next. I was convinced that he had an asbestos tongue because he was able to drink the tea straight away and launch into his lifelong mission to improve my general knowledge.

I leaned against the sink as he told me that junks were used as sea-going vessels from the 2nd century AD, the same time as the Romans built Hadrian's Wall. I nodded to keep him happy. There was an illustration of a junk sailing with the backdrop of an exotic sunrise on the pattern. It was the kind of place I dreamed about going on holiday to instead of Primrose Valley in Filey. Every year. Maybe that was why folk had hobbies like string art, they knew they'd never look up to the sun in one of these glamorous locations so they kept their heads down and kept busy. The less time to think the better.

My dad sat at the kitchen table for hours hammering tiny wee nails on to a board that he'd covered with off-cuts of material. I could tell already that the nail picture of the junk would be my number one favourite. The background was deep blue velvet and I reached out to stroke it.

'Hoi, dinnae touch it with yer dirty hands.'

He'd spend ages using different silky strings to make a picture. They were a bit like the dot-to-dot books that my gran used to buy me and Karen from RS McColls if she'd had a bingo win.

She either bought us a dot-to-dot book, a colouring-in book or a magic slate. There was nothing magical about trying to draw a picture with a plastic stick on top of a piece of grey acetate. No matter whether you said "Abracadabra" when you rubbed out the drawing and "Hey presto" when your doodles disappeared or "Ta-dah!" it was still shit. You needed a big imagination to believe in the 'magic'. It wasn't comparable to Lorraine's Etch-a-Sketch.

Dad had made string pictures for years and his 'artwork' was all over the house. My mam moaned that they were just dust catchers. But I loved them even though they had gone out of fashion along with bell-bottoms, platform soles and kipper ties. His best nail picture was the big one over the fireplace. The multi-coloured shiny strings made a geometric pattern like Lorraine's old Spirograph set. My mam kept threatening to get rid of them; she was all talk and no action. And dad said he didn't have time to decorate or the money for the emulsion to cover up the ghost pictures left behind on the tobacco stained walls.

I went back through to the living room and my mam was still staring at Ceefax.

'Why're you no watching something?'

'Ah'm reading the news afore *Cagney and Lacey* starts.'

It was her all-time favourite telly programme. She hated all the other cop shows but she adored Cagney and Lacey, they were her idols. I could imagine my mam fantasising that she was the sexy blonde Christine, but she'd need to be Mary-Beth because she's dark haired and a married working mum. My mam called herself a "kitchen assistant"; she was really just a tattie peeler and pot-cleaner at the Royal Hotel. And the only majestic thing about the Royal was the carpet in the bar with its wee crowns dotted about between the beer stains. I'd never heard of anyone actually staying in the Royal but it still claimed to be a hotel rather than a crappy bar serving steak pie, chips and peas in the lounge. My dad hadn't wanted her to take the job, not because the work was soul destroying and the money was rubbish, but because it was a Rangers pub. The supporters' bus left from the Royal every Saturday afternoon and although the place was full of Proddies my mam didn't have many other career options. My dad caved in when my mam pointed out that the back pages of the *Falkirk Herald* weren't exactly jam-packed with adverts for women who'd left school at fifteen without any qualifications and couldn't drive.

But I'd bet when my mam used the scouring pad, she'd be humming the theme tune as she pictured herself as a no-nonsense New York crime-fighter, a ball-breaker, ridding the streets of scum instead of chiselling burnt mince off a casserole dish in a poky kitchen behind the dingy bar.

I suppose she was as much of a dreamer as my dad. And I could tell by the thump, thump, thump that my sister would be upstairs in her bedroom as usual, and practising hand-stands against the wall. She was so stupid that she actually believed that she'd make it to the Commonwealth Games next year. The closest she would get to the finals in Edinburgh was watching it on the telly in her tracksuit. Escapism seemed to be a genetic disease my whole family suffered from.

'How did you get on at the Handicapped Club?'

'Weirder than usual.'

'What dae you mean? Has that Baz the Spaz been touching you up again?'

'Naw, Baz was too busy playing KerPlunk. But a guy called Stevie turned up as a helper and upset Lorraine.'

'Why, what did he dae?'

'He used the 'm' word. And mongol is a total no-no with Lorraine, she was greetin' her eyes oot. What sicko calls folk mongols these days?' I asked.

'That's a bloody sin. But you cannae really blame the boy. He probably disnae mean any harm by it. Ah've telt you umpteen times, it's no right, it's just the way folk are around here.'

'What kinda excuse is that?'

'It's mibbae no the right word tae use but it's only a word. Yer dad still says he gets his fags fae the Paki shop and goes tae the Chinky for chicken fried rice. But he's no a racist, he even cheers on the darkies running in the Olympics.'

'Aye, but he always jokes that they need tae run fast so that lions dinnae catch them in the jungle.'

'You need tae lighten up a bit Angela. Yer dad's patter is harmless, just 'cause he used tae watch *Love Thy Neighbour*, you dinnae hear him moaning aboot nig-nogs needing tae go back tae their ain country, he hasnae got a problem with them.'

Nigger was a shade of brown wool that my gran referred to, although my mam told me when I was wee that it was a bad word. Folk used to call out "Nigger" when Arnold Steel walked past at school. He was the only black boy in Bonnybridge and everyone knew him. But not everyone knew his real name. He also got called Kunta Kinte. I was allowed to stay up late to watch *Roots* when it was on TV so I knew all about slavery. Lorraine said that Arnold was adopted and I asked my mam if his parents needed to buy him like a slave. She wheeched down my Snoopy pants and skelped me six times on the backside but I wasn't being cheeky like she said, I was serious. I had to sit next to Arnold on the school bus once and Lorraine said I should check my hair for nits when I got home. My mam skelped my bare bum again when I got the nit comb out of the bathroom cabinet. She was ahead of her time with her liberal ways.

'You'd think Lorraine would be used tae the name calling by noo though.'

'Naw, she still lets it get tae her. Her mam's worse. You've got tae pretend there's nothing wrong with Janine.'

'It's just her way of coping. And Rita's been called a lot of names in her time too.'

'Cause she tries tae talk aw posh noo she lives in Spam Valley?'

'Naw, that's just her acting like the rest of the fur coat and nae knickers brigade. And ye ken what she's like, if someone's been tae Tenerife on holiday, Rita would claim she'd been tae Twentyerife. She's nothing but a blow-hard. But that's no the worst name she's been called.'

'Well, what kinda names are worse?'

'Nothing, forget it.'

'Oh c'mon mam. What were the names?'

'It's none of yer business. Now wheesht, Ah'm missing ma programme.'

'But…'

'You're like a dug with a bone.'

'Too damn right! Ah want tae ken what you mean.'

'Enough of yer language or yer dad'll be through.'

'Well tell me then, she's ma best pal. And ah've got tae pick up the pieces.'

'God, yer such a drama queen. Hang on a minute.' She pulled a blank tape out of the drawer in the display cabinet, shoved it into the video recorder and picked up the remote, 'Ah better tape Cagney and Lacey.'

I hated the Betamax video recorder and our telly with its wood effect panels. We rented them both from the D.E.R. shop in Falkirk and my mam went in every Saturday to have her weekly payment marked up in the book. Lorraine's dad got her mam a new telly and a VHS video player last Christmas. I kept telling my mam that you could hardly hire any new films at the video shop but she was adamant that Betamax was better than VHS. It was pointless moaning, my mam claimed that it was only posh folk in the bought houses who had VHS recorders. And she was never going to be accused of being a snob.

She settled back in her chair next to the fire and I almost expected her to start with, "Once upon a time, there was a girl called Rita..." like she was going to tell me a fairy story.

'Ah said tae yer gran ages ago that the lassie should ken the truth. And ah suppose you'll want tae ken too?'

Chapter Three

'They're gonnae burst!' shouted Lorraine.

I tried to squeeze my feet into Lorraine's Jelly shoes even though there was no chance that I could crunch up my size seven toes to make them as small as her tiny size fours. The crisscross pattern was cutting into my skin and made wee red lines until my whole foot throbbed. I eased the back of the plastic shoes off and left them dangling, bobbing my sweaty feet up and down making the glitter inside the plastic sparkle in the light.

'Can I get my Jellies back now?'

I kicked the shoes off into the air, one landing on her bed and the other bouncing off her wardrobe door.

'Satisfied?'

It was my turn for the swinging basket chair so Lorraine was sitting on her leatherette beanbag. Lorraine didn't reply or get off to reclaim her shoes; she went back to reading her magazine. We both knew the silence wasn't about the Jelly shoes. I couldn't tell if she was in a huff because I couldn't afford to go out on Saturday night or she was still pissed off about the scene at the Club. None of her mood was my fault and yet she kept flicking through this week's *Just Seventeen* and barely said a word to me.

I didn't know why I had bothered to come to hers if she wasn't up for a bit of banter. Next door, her mam had put on a cassette of nursery rhymes for Janine. I was glad I hadn't eyeballed Rita when I arrived, not after the stories my mam told me, about the other Rita, the one I'd die of shame if she was my mam.

The sing-along tape was driving me nuts. No matter how slow Janine was, it was ridiculous to think that she could still want to listen to baby songs at her age. But her mam treated her like a toddler, not seeming to notice the tiny tits that had sprouted on her thirteen year old daughter. It was impossible to imagine her ever letting Janine wear a bra. Years ago, Rita bought a bundle of old-fashioned sewing patterns in a sale from Remnant Kings and used them to make Janine's flowery dresses. Janine had enough folk staring at her without her looking like Laura Ingalls from *Little House on the Prairie*; the poor lassie deserved a break.

I couldn't stand listening to Baa Baa Bloody Black Sheep any longer. Lorraine was usually full of chat about what had happened at school but tonight she was deaf and dumb. She hadn't even mentioned that Gavin Malley was suspended and he was in her registration class so she must've known more than me. The rumour was that he got reported for pouring a box of Cornflakes out of the top deck window on to a midget woman who was at a bus stop waiting for the X39. And the rector went ballistic because the wee wifie had complained to the school already that every time the bus stopped, the top deck sang out the window, *"Hi ho hi ho, It's off to work we go…"* But Lorraine wasn't interested in Gavin or the dwarf.

'Are you gonnae put that magazine doon, or will ah just go hame?'

'What d'you want to talk about?'

Lorraine tossed the magazine on to her bed. The quilt cover had a Pierrot design and the sad-faced clown was on the matching curtains; she even had a table lamp too. I had the stationery set. And Lorraine had a fitted white wardrobe with a built-in dressing table and velvet padded stool. The wardrobe was chock-a-block with clothes and a mirrored jewellery box that couldn't even shut there was so much in it. I wondered if she still had the necklace I made for her with dried melon seeds when I was ten. Lorraine didn't need to hide her tights and make-up from her wee sister and she didn't still have a Care Bears duvet cover. My mam said there was nothing wrong with the cover and she refused to spend "good" money on stuff that visitors didn't see. And she liked to remind me that the off-cut from a carpet she got from her work was an Axminster that would last for years. And years. My bedroom carpet from the Royal had the same crown pattern; all that was missing were the beer stains and fag burns.

'Did you hear the latest aboot Gavin Malley?'

'Who cares about him? He's a dickhead.'

This wasn't the Lorraine I'd known since primary one. She always loved dissecting our day, picking over the bones of gossip from the Common Room and chewing on the tasty bits. Everyone was talking about Gavin Malley whether they cared or not. Something was up with her.

'Are you still upset over what that Stevie said at the Club?'

'Naw. You were right; he's no worth thinking about.'

'But ah cannae stop thinking aboot him, he was a total shag. You cannae deny that. You would, wouldn't you?'

I'd folded one of my sketches of Stevie and placed it inside my pants, pressed up against my pubes; it was one of the best I'd done but it wasn't for sharing. If Lorraine wanted to picture Stevie bollock-naked then she'd have to use her own imagination.

'No after what he said.'

'Since when have you been so high and mighty? The guy was only joking.'

'Ha fucking ha!'

She scooped up the *Just Seventeen* and began flipping through the pages she'd already read. Her cheeks were burning, and the storage heater was off.

'Dae you want a shot on the basket chair?' I asked.

She didn't look up and all I could hear was Baa Baa Bloody Black sheep on repeat. Sometimes Lorraine was a moody wee cow and was lucky to have me as her best pal. None of the other lassies she was pally with or even her mam went to the bother of writing to Glen Michael's Cartoon Cavalcade to get her birthday mentioned when she was nine. But all that effort was ancient history and I still had to work hard. I hated her not talking and I was even prepared to try one of Boaby's crap jokes, I was that desperate.

'How do you make holy water? You boil the hell oot of it.'

Not a cheep out of Lorraine. The joke was shit although that never usually stopped her from playing along. Sometimes it was best to let her stew. I jumped off the basket chair and let it bang against the wall.

With the bedroom door open, it was impossible to ignore Rita murdering her favourite hymn, *'Immaculate, Mary!'* She was probably still on her knees, cutting round a pattern pinned on top of hideous flowery material. It was easy to understand why Lorraine's dad worked in Saudi, and Lorraine said that the money was brilliant, which was an added advantage. Her mam paused at, "Our hearts are on fire" to shout cheerio as I passed the living room on my way out. I didn't poke my head round the door to say my goodbyes and replied, 'Cheerio, Mrs. Quinn,' through the wall. There was no way I could face Rita until I stopped thinking of her as the Mattress.

The wall mounted font in the porch was topped up with fresh Holy Water. I didn't bother blessing myself; the three females inside the house needed it more than me.

I was almost glad to be back home although I was due at my gran's house by seven. My mam looked out from behind her *Falkirk Herald*.

'Ah thought you'd be at Lorraine's for an hour?'

'So did ah but she's in one of her moods.'

'Ah hope you never caused it.'

'Why do ah get the blame for everything?'

'Dinnae try tae act aw innocent with me. You're usually at the root of the trouble. And dinnae dare say you telt Lorraine that Rita was called the village bike?'

'Are you kidding? Ah'm no stupid! And ah thought she was called the Mattress?'

My mam shook her head.

'Ah told you she got called lots of names. But ah'm saying nae mair aboot it. It's none of yer business or mine. It's true what they say, what goes around comes around. It's nae wonder Rita went aw holy after Janine was born.'

'Why's that?'

'Well, that's what comes of being a loose woman. Janine's her penance and a lot tougher than a few decades of the Rosary.'

My gran was right, converts are worse than the ones born into it; my mam stupidly believed every word of her Catechism book and all the bullshit the priest spouted at Mass. All the original Catholics know that you only follow whatever bits suit you. My gran called them Pick 'n' Mix Catholics.

The thought of Rita being promiscuous was gross. She wore a checked nylon overall to do the housework, she had a better moustache than my dad and her tits hung like spaniel's ears. Rita was no sex goddess by any stretch of the imagination. If ever she had sex appeal, it was well past its sell-by-date, like a slice of foosty bread covered in spots of green mold.

'God love Lorraine, it's a bloody sin what she's got tae pit up with living with her Holy Joe mam and poor wee Janine. She disnae deserve any mair problems.'

'If her mam was a slapper, mibbae Lorraine disnae even ken who her real dad is.'

'You never ken when tae stop dae you? Noo give it a rest and get ready tae go up tae yer gran's, ah've said enough already.'

My mam picked up the newspaper, flicked the folds straight, held it open in front of her and hid behind it. The pages weren't turning; I got the message and left the room.

Karen was surprised to see me back home early too because I caught her on my bed pulling apart my string of fluorescent orange Pop Beads. I had crept up the stairs, sideways on the edges, completely avoiding the squeaky second last step and thrown my bedroom door open. She got such a fright that the she sprang off the bed, scattering the beads everywhere. I grabbed my shatterproof ruler, the sword of the classroom, and swiped at her as she dropped on to all fours to collect the beads.

'Get oot, and dinnae dare come in here again!'

I gave her arse a swift kick as she skedaddled out the door.

My dad banged the bedroom wall, shouting to keep it down. He was busy "meditating" as usual after his tea. This daily routine involved him going under the duvet, shutting his eyes and snoring loudly for an hour before my mam shouted up the stairs that it was six o'clock.

I pulled my night-shirt out from beneath my pillow for my overnight stay at gran's, gave it a sniff and decided it would do another night. I'd agreed to dog-sit for her poodle, Bimbo, who cried like a baby whenever she left the house. The other neighbours in her four-in-a-block had all complained to the Council about Bimbo's whining and my gran was on tablets for her nerves because of the all the aggro. Friday night was her bingo night so I said I'd keep Bimbo company; the dog seemed to like me, probably because I didn't sing to him like my gran did.

My dad said that the only thing that should have to answer to the name Bimbo is a blonde with fake tits. He hated gran's wee white poodle and called it a poofy pet. My dad refused to take him for a walk when gran left Bimbo with us when she went on her holidays to Dundee to see her brother. Dad had a point, it wasn't a good idea to walk a "poofy pet" round our scheme, not unless you wanted battered. It was bad enough getting called a "Fenian bastard" when you walked down Bankier Street without being with a poodle. Any time of the day or night, there were always at least three or four Proddy boys hanging about; the wee ones threw dirt bombs, the older ones launched lit matches at your hair if you went to St Paddy's. And the Bankier Street trainee thugs always had a dog running loose beside them and these weren't pedigree dogs, these beasts were classic Bandeath dugs. Bimbo yapped, tried to shag your shin and was difficult to shake off. The greasy furred Bandeath dogs growled and mounted you from behind. If you valued your life you let him have his fun.

My gran named her dog Bimbo after a Jim Reeves song and she sang the chorus constantly to him, even clapping his paws in time to the tune.

It wasn't surprising that the dog ran away whenever he got the chance. The neighbours must've felt sorry for Bimbo; the gate was always left open. I never sang to him and I always made sure the latch was down. I loved Bimbo but I loved my gran more.

I put my hair in a high ponytail and tipped my school bag inside out to refill it with my overnight stuff. I shouted cheerio and as I walked out the front door, only my mam replied. It took me ten minutes to walk to my gran's and I shut the gate behind me and made my way up the path. I let myself in and found gran and Bimbo watching the telly. She had a tin tray on her lap and was mopping a plate with a buttered slice of Mothers Pride to sook up the oily gravy.

'Och, if ah'd known you were coming early, ah'd have made yer tea. And ah had extra kidney.'

The honk of a dead animal's organs was putrid and was worse than my dad's Hobbit feet after a back-shift. She left a chunk of gravy-stained pie crust on the plate, laid it on the carpet and let Bimbo give it a final lick clean.

'You'll no need tae wash that plate.'

She laughed, as usual, at virtually everything I said.

'Aye, you're a comic.'

Bimbo's chin was tinged brown from the gravy and his tongue

propelled round his black lips catching stray pastry crumbs.

'Looks like yer steak 'n' kidney pie went doon a treat,' I said.

'Between you and me hen, Bimbo's been eating maist of ma meals recently. Ah've lost ma appetite for everything except ma ciggies.'

My gran got to her feet and took her tray through to the kitchen. I'd never paid much attention to my gran's body shape, and yet as she passed the couch I noticed that her trousers were hanging loose across her backside.

'You've lost weight gran. Has this been a while since you've been off yer food?'

'Losing a few pounds will no dae me any harm. Ah've got a couple of new outfits for ma holiday. Ah just wish ah could get rid of this stomach.'

She cupped her hands under her belly like she was holding a beach ball.

'You'd think someone had blown me up with a foot pump.'

Her belly did look like I could stick a pin in it and watch my gran wheech round the room.

'Naw, you look as good as ever gran. It's aw in yer imagination.'

She sucked in her belly as she walked past. I took charge of the remote, settling on *Take the High Road* and batted Bimbo away from sniffing at the crotch of my ski pants. It wasn't exactly the Friday night that I'd choose but I needed the money from my café job to save up for driving lessons. And I could only afford to go to Mystique every second Saturday.

My gran went through to her bedroom to get changed out of her 'working' trousers although she hadn't worked for about ten years since her accident at the Wrangler jeans factory. I noticed that she hadn't put up the framed pencil drawing I'd done of her for her birthday and it was covered with the *Sunday Post*. The drawing was a good example of my cross-hatching technique and maybe worth including in my portfolio submission for Art School. Anybody could see it was my gran even though she'd moaned that I'd added too many wrinkles to her face making it look like it needed ironed. She stayed in a huff for hours; I'd have been safer drawing her Picasso style.

I helped myself to the last handful of Quality Street from a tin at the side of the couch that my gran won in the weekly raffle at the bingo. I gave Bimbo the caramel; it was funny for a few minutes but eventually I had to prize his jaw open before my gran came back through to the living room. The warning that she was on the move again was a spicy cloud of Youth Dew wafting up the lobby. Bimbo coughed and I couldn't tell if it was the caramel or the perfume clogging his throat. I slapped his back a few times and he seemed fine again, until the sneezing started.

'What dae you think?'

Gran birled round in front of the telly to model the latest cardigan she'd knitted.

'It's lovely gran.'

'Aye, ah'll be the talk of the bingo, even if ah dinnae win again this week. There's no many of them can knit a pattern like this.'

I doubted if the result of her complicated knitting would be envied by her pals at the bingo. The cardigan had multi-coloured criss-cross panels up and down the front and was finished off with a length of plaited wool threaded around the collar and tied under her chin with a pom-pom on each end.

'Ah managed tae make it with aw ma odds 'n' ends.'

That came as no surprise; no one would deliberately buy wool in those colours unless they had lost the power of sight.

'And ah'm nearly finished Lorraine's Aran cardigan for the holidays.'

Gran knew we liked to have matching outfits and she'd agreed to knit Lorraine a cardigan the same as the one she'd made for me. I hadn't worn mine yet, I was saving it for the holidays. An Aran cardigan was a much safer option than gran's unique designs and would look good with my baby blue fish-tail skirt. It was only two weeks until the Falkirk Fair when my dad's work shut down and we went for a week in a caravan in Filey. And this year, Lorraine was allowed to come too.

'Brilliant. Ah bet naebody else's gran can knit like you.'

My gran could've burst with pride. Her knitting skills were legendary and her speciality was dresses for imitation Sindy dolls to make into toilet roll covers. She sold them at the bingo to raise money for Strathcarron Hospice and had her photo in the *Falkirk Herald* once with a massive cardboard cheque.

'You're no wrong there hen. You'll need tae get Lorraine tae come up soon so ah can get the final measurements spot-on.'

I paused long enough for gran to suss something was up, not like when I tried to talk to my mam.

'What's up wi' yer face? It's tripping you.'

'It's nothing.'

'Do you think ah came up the Clyde on a banana boat? Look, the bus is no until quarter to, ah'll put the kettle on.'

My gran came back with a cup of tea for her, a glass of Irn-Bru for me and two Kit Kats. It was the standard equipment necessary for one of our heart-to-hearts. Bimbo lay at my feet, licking between my fat toes; it was his Friday night treat.

'Lorraine's went aw weird on me since we were at the Club. She got aw touchy aboot a guy calling her a mongol.'

'Has she got her period?'

My gran was convinced that every mood swing was linked to hormones and she had a calendar showing the moon's cycles. She insisted that I get to know Mother Moon as women are connected to the moon by our blood, our hormones and our souls. It sounded a load of tosh to me although I never argued with my gran.

'She's due aboot the same time as me.'

'Could be PMT. Lorraine's always been too sensitive. But her mam's the same; you're feart tae look at Rita the wrong way.'

'Mam telt me she used tae be called the Mattress. Ah cannae believe it.'

'Aye, that's true, mind you that was years and years ago, long afore yer grandda died. Och, it must be at least twenty years noo.'

My gran hadn't mentioned my grandda and yet I'd already been there for over half an hour which must've been a record time. Everything from moon landings to family weddings could be matched against how many years before or after my grandda died, a bit like saying BC or AD to describe before or after Jesus was a wean, only my gran measured time in BG or AG.

'So what's the story? Mam wouldnae tell me the juicy bits.'

My gran loved to share, everything from a packet of Jaffa cakes to local gossip.

'Rita slept with maist of the fitba team and some of them were married with weans. And then she got pregnant. She had mair than one lumber but the goalie, Tam, stuck by her, even though he'd never been seen winchin' her.'

'Jeezo, ah'm sure Lorraine disnae ken any of this.'

'Ah bet she disnae, nae lassie wants tae ken the truth aboot her mam being the fitba team's ride-on toy. But then again she'd mibbae understand why Rita's such a Holy Joe these days. Mind you, having Janine was enough of a punishment.'

'Who'd think it? Lorraine's mam acts like she's a saint. Ah'm shocked.'

'When you get tae my age hen, you've seen it aw. One day nothing will shock you either, it's one of the few benefits of auld age.'

Considering that my gran had lived in the same four-in-a-block all her life, had worked in a local factory for a few years and only ever went on holiday with us to Filey or to see her brother in Dundee. It was hard to believe that my gran had hunners of life experience but in fairness, she did watch a lot of telly and knew everybody at the bingo. My gran drained the dregs of her tea and stood up, stretching like she did when she tried to copy the Green Goddess's moves on *Breakfast Time.*

'Listen hen, ah'll need tae get moving or ah'll miss the first hoose at the bingo and it's a big money Link-Up game on a Friday night. Are you feeling better noo you've got it off yer chest?'

'Aye, gran, thanks.'

'Nae bother.'

In a whirlwind of activity, my gran tested her bingo dabbers were working on the back of an auld brown envelope, checked her lucky rabbit's foot was in her bag, made sure she had the right bus money and gave her turkey-neck a final squirt of Youth Dew. The final step was to pack a Tupperware dish of home-made potted hough that she'd promised the bingo caller before she could head off for the 27 at quarter to seven.

'Help yourself tae the Quality Street hen. Oh, and ah promised one of the regulars that ah'd dae a reading for her so ah'll be late hame.'

My gran was christened Agnes Smeaton but this name wasn't exotic enough for her, so instead she chose to spell Agnes back to front to create the name Senga. Everyone called her Senga and I only ever saw the name Agnes on bills and official stuff. Years later, she decided that she needed a glamorous stage name when she gave readings and added the more appropriate pet friendly surname of Shepherd. She took her career seriously and she'd sent a postal order away to get business cards printed with gold lettering.

SENGA SHEPHERD, PET PSYCHIC
A guiding light to reach your pets with one-to-one readings

My gran helped folk reach their dead pets on the Other Side after their furry friend had crossed the Rainbow Bridge. She claimed that when our pets leave us on earth, they cross a beautiful bridge made of a rainbow and are fit and healthy again, and wait for us there until our time comes. And she wasn't the only one to believe in this guff as she'd no shortage of mugs willing to pay her to hear Rex's bark one last time. My gran reassured them that Rex was playing fetch with all his doggy pals in heaven's back garden and I didn't slag off my gran's theory as she was good at giving me the odd fiver after one of her readings.

I was tired but I wouldn't go to bed without making sure my gran was home safely. And she always made us a supper and slipped a hot water bottle wrapped in a tea towel under my sheets. I missed being able to coorie-in under the heavy woollen blankets topped off with an orange candlewick bedspread; a cheap Care Bears duvet cover from the market, washed out after years dunked in and out of the twin tub wasn't the same. The weight of the blankets pressing down on me made me feel trapped, in a good way, and every now and then I'd lift the blankets to release the warmth before I'd be locked inside again. I hated my new Bri-nylon fitted bed sheets at home too. They snagged on my toenails and there were bolts of static every time I moved. I didn't see how this was progress compared to brushing your legs against my gran's cosy candy-striped flannelette sheets.

There was nothing but the usual shite on the telly. I was glad I'd brought my sketchpad and ink pen; it was the best way to pass the time and I needed to perfect my series of self-portraits. In school the teacher handed out mirrors to help us study our features. There was no need to get the hand mirror from my gran's bedroom; I'd already filled a whole sketchpad with self-portraits. And none of them resembled the real me. These drawings showed a girl with blue eyes like mine but that's where the similarity ended. This girl's lips were full and pouting, her eyelashes were long and thick, her hair was bouncy and shone. This girl didn't have a double chin, squint teeth that overlapped and Gorilla nostrils; she was worth drawing. She was slim and stunning.

By half ten, my gran was still out. I'd finished my self-portrait, the tin of Quality Street was empty, Bimbo was still lapping his tongue over my feet and I was tormented by visions of Lorraine's mam as a slapper. And as much as it made my insides flip and my brain fizz, I couldn't help wondering if the boys Rita had bedded had been as shaggable as Stevie. And a night with Stevie wouldn't need Bri-nylon sheets to make sparks fly.

Chapter Four

My gran insisted on getting up early to walk me to the bus stop the next morning. She wasn't a morning person and my dad said she wasn't an afternoon or evening person either. But she still made an effort to set her alarm clock although she hadn't enough time to get dressed and ended up tucking her nightie into her 'working' trousers and wearing her slippers.

I'd given up arguing ages ago that she didn't need to wait until the bus came. It was over a year since I started my Saturday job and yet she still wanted to wave me off to work, Bimbo always coming too. Bimbo circled on the pavement and eventually crouched for a crap next to the lamp post. My gran flicked the jobby into a neighbour's garden with a stick she snapped off one of their saplings.

'So you'll be hame for yer tea?'

'Aye, ah should be back by quarter past.'

As if she didn't know by now, it was the same routine every Saturday. We both knew that it was hardly worth getting a bus to Denny and back within the hour but it was better than staying behind in the bakery. And my gran always made up a tray for me with a roll on square sausage, a glass of Irn-Bru, a Kit Kat and an Askit powder for the weekly headache. My head was always nipping after a morning sweating like a pregnant nun in the bakery's kitchen.

The 27 bus appeared, spewing out exhaust fumes and as always my gran slipped me the bus money, knowing the feeble wage Patterson's got away with paying desperados like me. I lurched up the aisle through the smog; the only passenger not smoking was the wean sitting on his mammy's knee. He looked so fed up he could do with a puff of her ciggie. I sat behind them and managed to get a window seat on the pavement side so I could wave to her and Bimbo.

When the driver pulled out of the lay-by, my gran waved Bimbo's paw and the wean in front waved too. My gran looked chuffed at our smiling faces but once she was out-of-sight, I sighed as loudly as the stale bus seat and stuck my tongue out at the wean. He turned back and cooried into his mammy leaving me alone with the thought of another day in the hellhole of a kitchen in Patterson's bakery.

I was the youngest of the six females who worked in Patterson's, so I got the shittiest jobs in the place, literally if the bogs got flooded. There were two other Saturday girls, Trina and Nicole, who had worked there longer and were from Denny. I soon learned from Irene, the manageress, that being from Denny mattered – a lot. Nicole and Trina knew all the customers and Irene never gave me the chance to serve out the front. There was more chance of Nicole or Trina giving the Pope a blow job than them offering to swap roles. I had already worked in the windowless kitchen now for over a year, and everyone seemed happy enough to leave me there, up to my elbows in dirty dish water. The 'kitchen' was a sink unit, a two-ring burner and a cupboard full of cleaning stuff. It was my job to clear the tables in the café at the back of the bakery shop, keep the tea urn and the coffee machine full of water, to wash and dry the dishes, empty the bins, sweep the floor, check the bogs were clean and any other crappy task Irene felt like dumping on me rather than ask Nicole or Trina.

Before the shop opened task number one was always to make the 'home-made' soup of the day. When I'd told Irene on my first day that I'd never made soup before, she just laughed and told me not to worry, it was a doddle. She handed me a packet of powdered mix and a huge pot. It was the same pot that I had to use at the end of my shift to boil wash the day's dirty tea towels. Irene was right; making 'home-made' soup was a piece of piss and didn't taste much better.

'Have you done something with yer hair?' asked Nicole, as she pulled on her Patterson's overall and tightened her red velvet scrunchie.

'Naw,' I answered, too quickly, instantly regretting getting my gran to crimp my hair when she came back from the bingo last night. She got bored half-way through and gave up; I'd tried to salvage it with a dollop of mousse and it still felt like candy floss. And I had to agree with my gran, I had gone a bit OTT with the

Sun-In spray; my hair was quite dry and a bit brittle. I'd tried lemon juice and it hadn't made my hair blonde, just orangey so I'd stepped up my efforts with Sun-In to get a sun-kissed look in time for Filey.

'Well you're needing to. It looks like a bale of straw!'

'Worzel Gummidge has a better hairdo!'

The way they swaggered off anyone would think that they were about to go on stage as backing dancers for Madonna at the Barrowlands instead of standing behind the counter of a bakery in Denny. Nicole was Irene's niece and Trina was Nicole's second cousin, and with everyone being related in Denny, it was only because my dad worked with Irene's man that I'd got the job. I'd wished from day one that my dad hadn't bothered to put a word in for me but I needed the money and I couldn't pack it in without letting my dad down and giving those bitches the satisfaction of driving me out.

'Hurry up with the soup, we're aboot ready tae open,' screeched Irene.

'She'll be too busy trying tae dae her hair,' shouted Trina or Nicole. It was impossible to separate one cow's cackle from another.

The café was always busy from the minute Irene pulled up the shutters; there weren't many other options for eating out in the skanky wee town. I brought down the chairs left on top of the tables by the cleaner and laid out tin ashtrays on each one.

It made no difference whether there was an ashtray on the table or not. Denny folk stubbed out their fag ends into the leftovers of their congealed Scotch pie or dropped them into their empty tea cup. I slunk back to the kitchen and psyched myself up for the stacks of cups and plates heading my way.

As I went through to the front shop with the soup of the day, I heard their high-pitched giggles and nearly dropped the pot of boiling minestrone flavoured water. It was Stevie, and of course both the bakery bitches knew him well by the sound of the banter. I turned back to hide in the kitchen, splashing the hot soup on to my overall, staining it orange and burning my tits but I kept going until I was in the kitchen. Even Sadie from the Club didn't make this much mess. I dabbed my overall with a damp tea towel and the stain spread right across my front. I waited in the kitchen until I knew Stevie was no longer at the counter.

'Aboot time too,' moaned Irene. I filled the soup kettle with the minestrone mix and on my way back I dared to sneak a look through the gap in the swing door. Stevie was sitting in the café and had opened a packet of Benson and Hedges to go with his coffee and *Daily Record*.

Between my frizzy hair and manky overall I was a state and couldn't decide if I should wait until Stevie was gone before I cleared the tables, or be bold and see if he recognised me. I had another keek into the café and then ran my fingers under the tap to finger comb my hair while I made my mind up. For a nanosecond, I tried to forget that Irene was shouting through that she needed the "home-made lentil" when it was ready. If I shut my eyes tightly I could imagine me and Stevie, no one else in the café, just us and our passion. The shutters were down and the lights were still on so that he could see me bend over the table, spread my buttock cheeks and take me from behind doggy style. Hard and fast. I realised I was chewing on my J-cloth and I'd need to add boiling water to the lentil mix before Irene was through to hound me. But I couldn't resist another look at him before I made the next batch of soup. And I made a bolt for the door – fuck it, it was only quarter past nine and Stevie's presence in the café was the most exciting thing that would happen all day.

He was sitting up the back, so his seat was safely out of sight of the main shop. Stevie looked up from his *Daily Record* as I leaned over the table opposite him to load up a tray. I chased crumbs off the table with a J-cloth and gawked at him from beneath my fringe, not sure if the frizz would shield my eyes. He winked. And I was sure he'd see my heart going like the clappers through my overall, and he'd notice the minestrone stain too. I managed to stack the tray with shaky hands but I knocked a half empty Kwenchy cup off the pile of plates and it bounced on the floor. I bent down to pick up the plastic cup; Stevie beat me to it and placed it back on the tray.

'You're Lorraine's pal, eh?'

I could feel the beamer creep right up my neck and singe my ear lobes.

'Aye.'

My nylon overall clung to me like a second skin and I prayed that this morning's squirt of Impulse was still working its magic under my sticky oxters. I rested the tray on Stevie's table and flicked my fringe off my eyes.

'Could ye dae me a favour?' he asked.

'Depends what it is.'

But we both knew that unless he was asking me to give Father O'Donnell a blow job at the Club next week while Mrs Gaffney watched and Boaby the driver filmed us, then the chances of me agreeing to help a gorgeous guy in a Blue Nile T-shirt were extremely high.

'Could you pass on a message tae Lorraine for me?'

'Ah suppose so, what's the message?'

The door to the cafe swung open and Nicole breenged through; I lifted the tray from Stevie's table and made a move towards her.

'So this is where yer hiding? Get back tae the sink, there'll soon be nae cups or spoons left!' She pulled the kitchen door open and waited for me. 'And you better move it, Irene's cracking up oot the front, she needs the lentil soup. Pronto!'

'See ya,' said Stevie and when I looked back to reply, I couldn't tell whether his wink was for me or Nicole, all I knew was that she was smiling back at him like she was constipated, which was one of her better looks.

For the rest of the morning I scraped leftovers into a rancid bin and dunked dishes in grey soapy water. This was no different to any other Saturday shift except that this week I had a fantasy of me and Stevie together to keep me sane and the promise of a roll on square sausage at my gran's.

My gran was waiting alone for me at the bus stop.

'Where's Bimbo?'

'He's too bloated tae walk thanks tae that auld biddy through the wall.'

I struggled to see how the neighbour, who didn't look any older than my gran, could've caused Bimbo's swelling although I was sure that my gran could explain it.

'Ah've telt her a million times that she shouldnae throw bread oot for the birds when Bimbo's oot the back. But does she listen? Naw, so noo ma wee dug's stomach is like a water balloon. It could kill him. And then she'd ken aw aboot it. Ah've got a good mind tae report her tae the SSPCA. That'll soon put her gas at a peep.'

'Or the Cooncil and clype on her for a change.'

'Aye, ah'll go doon tae the Toun Hoose and let them ken what kind of neighbour ah've tae put up with. A dug killer.'

'Will Bimbo be awright?'

'Aye hen, dinnae worry, he's been farting like a Clydesdale for the last half hour so he's well on the road tae recovery.'

I wanted to tell my gran about Stevie but there was nothing much to say. After eating my tea, I rubbed Bimbo's belly to ease out another fart and in jig time, I was heading back to Denny on the 27 to finish my shift. Gran offered to walk me to the bus stop but it didn't seem like a good idea; she'd been in and out of the toilet ever since I arrived. It was enough living through Bimbo's bowel actions without knowing what my gran's problem was too. I didn't want the details, though it was worrying seeing her look so drained and I told her it was safer for her to stay at home. For once she didn't argue.

The afternoon went slower than a week in Barlinnie, but I got a blast of fresh air on my break when Irene sent me next door to RS McColls to get her more fags. On the way back in, Nicole shouted that she'd left a chocolate éclair for me on the kitchen draining board. Irene let everyone have a free cake although they often forgot about me and there was usually none left by the time I got my break after everybody else.

I sunk my teeth into the sticky chocolate icing and a dollop of cream pumped out and landed on my chin as Nicole and Trina appeared.

'Thanks for the éclair.'

'Nae worries, it had dropped on the flair anyway,' replied Nicole.

'Aye, there were a few hairs on it but we ken you eat anything,' added Trina. The bitches turned on their heels, with their laughter and bodies bouncing off the wall as they nudged each other.

The end of the shift was in sight and finally I got the okay from Irene to fill up the soup pot and boil wash the tea towels.

Every week I pictured a different neck when I wrung out the tea towels and this week was Nicole's turn. I imagined her butt-ugly face going blue as I twisted and squeezed the gingham cloth between my hands until it went limp. When I got home each Saturday, to help me wind down, I'd get my sketch book out and think of Nicole or Trina. This week, I'd use felt tip pens to colour the pupils of Nicole's eyes demon red, nicotine yellow for the pus-filled spots I'd cover her face with and liquorice black teeth. My fingers itched to turn Nicole into Hagatha.

But as usual, with the front shop now empty, Irene let Nicole and Trina get away early; at least with the cheeky cows gone I was able to mop the floor in peace and think of Hagatha's portrait. I shouldered the fire door open to tip the dirty water into the drain and that's when I noticed Stevie hanging about near the phone box across from the car park. I slipped back inside the shadow of the doorway for a better look. There was no one inside the phone box and I wondered why Stevie was waiting on the corner.

I ripped off my overall, stuffed it in my bag and pulled out my Impulse body spray. This one was my favourite fragrance and if I got out the door quick enough, I was about to give 'Suddenly Sassy' its biggest ever test. After an all-over generous dousing of Impulse and a smear of cherry lip gloss, I bounded down the stairs like a schemie wean chasing the ice-cream van. There was nothing I could do about my hair.

Stevie was still there. I was on the wrong side of the street for the bus back to Bonnybridge and was paranoid that he'd realise I was walking in the opposite direction. But he wasn't interested in where I was heading, he stepped into my path and held out a scrap of paper.

'Can you give this tae Lorraine fae me?'

It would've been nice if he'd bothered to even ask my name or chat first.

'Nae problem.'

'Ta, you're a real trooper.'

Stevie clapped me on the back like I was one of his drinking buddies.

'Ah doubt she'll want tae hear fae you again after the way you insulted her at the Club.'

'That's why ah want tae see her. Tae apologise. Ah ken ah was bang oot of order. It just slipped oot and ah didnae mean tae upset her.'

'Ah telt her that. Ah ken you're no an arsehole, no like maist of the guys we ken.'

'Cheers.'

And he sauntered off, without another word. All I was left with was a scrawl on a bookie's slip of paper, "Please meet me tonight outside The Railway Inn at 7. I need to talk to you. S."

I'd have to go with Lorraine; I couldn't let her stand outside a pub with a guy she didn't know. And I could maybe get to talk to him too.

It was lucky that I'd already told Lorraine that I couldn't afford to go to Mystique and that we'd be free to meet up with Stevie. All I had to do was to let Lorraine know about our new plans except that when I got home my mam was hogging the phone. My gran was upset that Bimbo still wasn't feeling too good and now had diarrhoea "running out of him like lava". I hovered at the phone table but my mam made no move to hurry up the conversation. When she finally came off the phone, I asked if my gran had the runs too.

'Naw, she never mentioned it. Why?'

'It's nothing probably. Just that she seems tae need the loo at lot and ah think she's feeding her meals tae Bimbo. Ah hope she's okay.'

'Dinnae worry aboot yer gran. Needing tae pee a lot is an age thing. But that explains why poor Bimbo's wee arse is red raw. Yer gran's cooking's far too rich for him.'

There was no danger of Bimbo suffering from 'rich' food by dining at our house.

'Have you noticed that she's lost weight even though she's still got a belly on her?'

'She's always been vain and she'll be trying tae slim doon for her holidays. It wouldnae dae you any harm tae skip a few meals either.'

My mam was great at giving advice and not so good at taking it. Anybody could see that she'd let herself go since she married dad but I suppose that's an age thing too. She went out to the ice-cream van in her slippers and tried to stop runs in her tights with blobs of nail varnish. And her nylon nightdress had a crusty hem after she'd singed it from standing too close to the fire and I didn't dare comment on the state of her.

'Put on another record will you?' I stomped off vowing to buy her a mirror for her birthday in the hope that she'd take a look at herself before criticising me.

'Two minutes, and ah'm timing you!' she threatened as I grabbed the phone and dragged the cord to its limit, shut the door on it and perched myself on the edge of the bath. Rita answered sounding as if she was a receptionist at the doctor's surgery, but she soon toned down her posh telephone voice when she realised it was me.

'She's not in.'

'When will she be back?'

'Oh, did she not tell you? She's been invited to whatshername's house party and she's just going to stay the night to save on taxi money. Are you not going too?'

'No. Who's whatshername?'

'It's Stacey, y'know, the wee fat lassie with the ginger hair? Listen, I'll need to go, Janine's shouting on me. I'll tell Lorraine you phoned.'

The phone went dead. I put it back on the table and locked the bathroom door. It was the first time Lorraine was out on a Saturday night without me. And to Stacey's house, who was known as Ginge Minge, who blamed me for her nickname after a never-to-be-forgotten incident at the Chapel Hall disco two years ago.

Stacey didn't even know what VPL meant and as a friend, I had to explain that she looked like she had four arse cheeks. I used to like Stacey; she was fatter than me, an absolute hound. She'd disappeared into the girls' toilets and after a lot of huffing and puffing, she squeezed round a cubicle door to tell us that she'd whipped off her knickers and stuck them in her clutch bag. Stacey waddled on to the dance floor and didn't remember that she was knicker free until all the boys started laughing. Lorraine told Stacey that the zip was down on her purple satin trousers. Stacey's face lit up like a belisha beacon and Lorraine ran for a paper towel to blot the tears. By the time her dad picked Stacey up to go home, everyone in third year was now calling

Stacey, Ginge Minge. She hated me. And Lorraine knew it.

I had no idea what Lorraine was playing at and there had better be a good reason for getting all pally-wally with Ginge Minge. Lorraine would miss meeting up with Stevie although there was no excuse for me not to still go. And there was enough time for my mam to give me a home perm with the Toni kit I'd been saving for a special occasion.

Chapter Five

There was a distinct whiff of rotten eggs from the perm solution and yet my mam insisted that the smell was in my imagination. I wasn't convinced and sprayed a cloud of 'Suddenly Sassy' and walked underneath it. The hairdo didn't work; I was aiming for a sexy just-out-of-bed look like Madonna's shaggy perm from her 'Boy Toy' phase. But my hair was less curls and more frizz. And there was nothing shaggable about it. My mam said it was because I'd over processed my hair and I suppose she's an expert. I couldn't remember what her natural hair colour was and would need to hunt out old photos to check. For the last few years she'd dyed her hair 'Plum Passion' even though the colour was too young for somebody who was nearly as old as forty and in denial that she was ancient.

I told my mam that I was going down to Lorraine's and I wouldn't be late. I paused at the hall mirror to fluff up my perm and reapply another coat of electric blue mascara – that I'd borrowed from Lorraine – and Heather Shimmer Rimmel lipstick. Lorraine wore the same shade of lipstick; *Just Seventeen*'s beauty page said the frosted lavender colour made lips instantly sexy. My mam poked her head round the door as I was practising my pout.

'That lipstick's hellish. It makes yer teeth look like you're a smoker.'

I waltzed past her. It was best to ignore fashion tips from someone with purple hair and wearing Pop Sox with a skirt. I pulled on my candy pink bomber jacket and lace fingerless gloves.

'Mind and be back for the street lights coming on,' she cried after me as I slammed the door shut. It was a ridiculous thing to say, and annoyingly it was a habit she couldn't break. I'd been going out drinking for well over a year and she still wasn't used to the idea that I was an adult and not a wean anymore.

My gran had referred to me as a woman since I was thirteen

and took my first period. She'd been down for her tea as usual on a Tuesday and I'd come in from school and run straight to the toilet. Me and Lorraine ate our bus tickets daily ever since we had met in primary one and for some reason she'd choked on hers on the way home and I thought I'd peed myself laughing at her because my knickers were damp.

But when I went to check, I saw the rusty stain and knew I'd started my period. I shouted on my mam and begged her not to tell my gran or dad and Karen was too wee and stupid to know anything about periods. My mam promised and left me to rinse out my knickers while she went upstairs to tear up an old bed sheet as a home-made fanny pad. She didn't want to frighten me with a *Tampax* for my first time and had nothing else in the house. When she came back, I folded the strip of bed sheet, placed the wad into the gusset of my knickers and shuffled into the living room as if I was wearing a gigantic nappy. My dad never looked up from his *Daily Record*, even when my gran rushed across the room and gave me a big cuddle.

'Congratulations hen, yer a woman noo.' She shook my hand like I'd won the school dux medal and my dad lifted his paper up like a welder's mask to shield his face. My beamer was so fiery I was surprised that my dad's *Daily Record* never burst into flames. My mam shrugged and whispered, 'You're one of us noo,' as if that was a good thing.

And I did feel like a woman waiting on the 27 to Denny. I was going to meet Stevie to explain why Lorraine wasn't able to come and maybe help set up another meeting for them. If he offered me a drink then I'd have to be polite and go into the pub and chat to find out more about him, for Lorraine's sake.

This was the first time I'd met a man on my own. The guys me and Lorraine flirted with at Mystique were mostly in sixth year at school or we knew their sisters or cousins. Meeting Stevie was on a different level and a lot more sophisticated than going to Stacey's house party in Bainsford. Ginge Minge's pals were all geeks and no doubt Pamela Thompson, Little Miss Brown Nose, would be swanning about thinking she was God's gift. Lorraine would be pig sick when she heard that I went to the pub with a real man instead of spending Saturday night with pussies from school.

Stevie was standing outside The Railway Inn at Denny Cross and he looked up as the bus pulled away. I waved at him but he didn't seem to recognise me as he turned his head away. Maybe it was because I wasn't wearing my overall or I had a different hairdo.

He was about to light a fag when I tapped him on the shoulder. He spun round like I'd zapped him with Luke Skywalker's lightsaber.

'For fuck's sake, what're you doing creeping up on me like that?'

'Sorry.'

'Where's Lorraine?'

He looked round me as if I'd hidden her behind my back; I suppose it was possible.

'She couldnae make it so she sent me.'

'Ah want tae see her, no you.'

'It's okay, you can tell me whatever it is, me and Lorraine dinnae have secrets.'

Stevie blew a cloud of smoke right into my face and I choked back a cough.

'Are you deaf? Ah want tae speak tae Lorraine, no her pal.'

Stevie began to walk away and I pulled on the sleeve of his denim jacket.

'Hoi, watch the merchandise!' He shrugged off my hand, his eyes staring at me like a Bandeath dug ready to attack and tear off an arse cheek. I took a step back and Stevie pulled out a stubby bookie's pen to scribble a number on the side of his fag packet. He ripped off a slice of the cardboard and thrust it into my hand. 'Away hame and tell yer pal tae phone me.'

'Have you got time for a drink?' I nodded my head at the doorway of The Railway.

'That's a man's pub, no a place for young lassies.'

Stevie marched into The Railway without even saying cheerio, never mind thanks and left me standing in the street like a pure eejit. A baldy guy with hair sprouting out of his ears came out the pub and asked me if I had a light. At least he didn't talk to me like I was a silly wean. I couldn't blame Stevie for being pissed off, I wasn't going to take it personally, it was obvious that he was disappointed that Lorraine wasn't with me. But it would be different the next time we met; I'd make sure of that.

There was nothing else for it except to head home. The only snag was if I went back too early it was a dead cert that my mam would start digging for dirt and asking if me and Lorraine had fallen out. My mam's a nosey cow, always wanting to know where I've been and who I've been with as if it's any of her business. She forgets that I'm seventeen, not seven.

Even after waiting twenty minutes to get the bus back to Bonnybridge, it was still way too soon to go home. The sky was the colour of *Hubba Bubba* and it was warm even with just my silky bomber jacket. I went to the park and at the far end there was a gang of neds winding the chains of the swings round the top of the frame. Another lot were sitting on top of the climbing frame eating bags of chips and sharing a bottle of *Strongbow*; none of them were from St Paddy's so it was a death wish to keep walking.

It would've looked better if I'd had Bimbo with me; without a dog I had no reason to be alone in the park on a Saturday night. I made a quick U-turn before they could slag me off or even worse, attack me; it wouldn't have been the first time. It was all Lorraine's fault; we're supposed to stick together. I dived behind a row of jaggy bushes running round the edge of the park and trotted along a path that led to the auld quarry. We all used to play at the quarry during the summer until it got dark and we had to go home when the street lights came on. The sandy mounds were ideal to act out *Planet of the Apes*. Me and Lorraine got to be the astronauts who landed in the desert. And I made Mandy and Faye be the gorillas. They had to kid on that they were riding on horseback, chasing us through the quarry. They always moaned that they didn't want to be apes but they needed to remember it was *my* game so I decided. Sometimes I let Karen join in too; I let her rake up the sand with a bunch of sticks when we messed it up and go to the shop for ice poles for us. It wasn't in the programme but I made her the apes' servant and she was chuffed. It kept Faye and Mandy happy too.

The quarry still looked the same and it was easy to remember the layout of Ape City. I could picture me and Lorraine using old brush handles as horses and squealing, "Giddyup!" It had been a great place to play, until the accident. I hadn't been back since; we weren't allowed to go near the quarry again. Ever. It was a mistake to end up here; it only brought back bad memories although I couldn't resist a look at the dunes.

And that's when I saw him. The dog walker had his cock out. He was running his closed fist up and down it while his collie did a crap. I'd only ever seen a man's cock in photos and the pornos me and Lorraine found at the bottom of her dad's wardrobe. It was much thicker and not as pinkish as I expected a real cock would be.

My friend Billy had a ten foot willy
And he showed it to the girl next door.
She thought it was a snake.
So she hit it with a rake,
And now it's only two foot four.

He kept rubbing his stumpy cock up and down, faster and faster, until his dog ran back to him. It was Arnold's dad. Him and his wife were another pair of Holy Joes who fostered weans that no one else wanted; recently there was one with a club foot and one with a harelip. Some sucker took hop-along and the lassie with the mangled lip but they kept Arnold. My mam said it was because having a black boy was more exotic and some folk would do anything for attention.

My mam was right, Arnold's dad must've known someone could have seen him. The dirty beast paused to kick the dog away and sped up his wanking even more. The dog yelped, the perv groaned and I screamed. No wonder Stevie thought I was a silly wee lassie.

Arnold's dad zipped up and ran off with his dog chasing him. I jogged back towards the park and was glad to see the neds were busy trashing the swings. Two of them were using lighters to melt the plastic seats whilst another was engraving one with a Stanley knife. I managed to snake my way along the path and back out to the main road before they noticed me and shouted,

'Gies a swatch at yer fanny!'

Braver from a distance, I gave them the middle finger, 'Up yours!' and ran, or as close to a run as I could manage.

I was only two minutes away from Lorraine's house and desperate for a pee. Lorraine lived in the Wimpey estate that everybody called Spam Valley and where the weans got a row from their mammies if they used slang words that they learnt in the playground at school. Her 'bought' detached house was in an estate, not a scheme like the one where her mam was brought up in the same kind of terraced council house like mine. Whenever I was asked at primary school to draw a house, my artwork always looked a lot like Lorraine's pebble-dashed bungalow except that I put the door in the middle and I left out the porch, the carport and the ornamental lions that stood each side of the driveway. The lions were supposed to look like stone although up close you could see that they were plastic. It made them easy to lift and I got me and Lorraine to move them up and down the street for a laugh, sit them on top of doorsteps, then ring the doorbell and run. A plastic lion made the Spam Valley version of chap-door-run much funnier but it was much tamer than the game played in my scheme where any Catholic neighbours got punished with 'light a shite'.

There was only one other Catholic family in my street and the Proddy boys loved to play their version of chap-door-run and pick on us. They thought it was hilarious to wrap a dog's jobby in newspaper, set it alight then post it through a Catholic's letterbox. The gang would wait behind the row of lock-up garages for the moment that the neighbour would open their front door and have to stamp out the burning ball of newspaper. The boys would shout, *"Ya smelly fenian bastard!"* when the neighbour realised that their foot was caked in shit. My dad once tried to chase them down the street although the jobby stuck to the sole of his slipper and made him go flat on his arse. It made everything worse; the Proddies practically pished themselves laughing at him sprawled on the pavement. I couldn't face going out to play for weeks. But they knew I was still there, they just had to wait a bit longer.

Nothing as exciting ever happened in Spam Valley and I felt the pressure to keep the lions on the move. Rita never knew it was us who moved the lions round the estate. And even Lorraine didn't know that I picked up auld fag ends on the walk to her house and it was me who stuffed the cigarette butts up the lions' nostrils. The plastic jungle kings stood guard at the driveway, protecting Rita's house, car and the wooden wishing well she'd filled with marigolds. Nobody in Spam Valley needed to park in the street so their window wipers were never yanked off or a key scratched along the side of their cars. Fences weren't allowed at the front of the gardens in Spam Valley; it didn't matter, the folk living there didn't need a fence to keep out Bandeath dugs or litter. No fences permitted was a good idea and the Council should have the same rule in our scheme, it might stop the likes of my dad building one out of old wooden pallets that literally did fall off the back of a lorry. My mam once asked the Proddy boys collecting wood for Bonfire Night to dismantle it and let them borrow an axe. But my dad heard them hacking at the fence and he chased them down the street in his slippers with the sole hanging off and slapping on the pavement like a circus clown shoe.

Spam Valley was a safe haven but there was no point in going to Lorraine's house after seeing the flasher. Rita would be sitting in with Janine and I'd probably get roped into saying the Rosary with them. Lorraine would love to hear about Arnold's dad flashing at me although I couldn't say that I'd seen him at the quarry, I'd have to make it a different location. And it wouldn't be the same telling her tomorrow. I had no choice except to go home and listen to my mam talking a load of shite with my dad tapping away on his nail art in the kitchen and Karen playing her stupid *Wham* album all night.

It was a bit of a walk from the park but I decided that my best option was to walk to my gran's to stay the night and I'd phone my mam to let her know. My gran would slip me a couple of Harvey's Bristol Creams and I'd get my supper made for me and a hot water bottle, in June.

'Who is it?'

My gran had started putting the chain on the door, even during the day. She'd been mugged last year on her way back from the post office. The scummy bastard ripped her purse out of her hands when she opened it to get her house key out. He shoved her against the wall and ran off into the woods across the road from her four-in-a-block flat. My gran knew who it was; he was the alkie that lived round in the Crescent. He'd followed my gran up the road and then pounced when she stopped at her gate. She phoned my mam instead of the polis. My mam screeched down the phone that she had to report it;

my gran said that she felt sorry for the fella because he was ill and needed help, not lifted by the polis. And that the alkie's mam was one of her bingo pals and they'd all snub her if she clyped on him. My gran told my mam to have a heart, every man is somebody's husband or somebody's son, even if he's a wanker. But she kept her wits about her now and carried a Jif lemon in her shopper. She claimed that it was just as effective as pepper spray and it was handy to have it in case she made pancakes.

'Gran, it's me, Angela.'

The door chain slid open and she pulled me inside quickly; her paranoia at night was worse.

'Come in and get a heat.'

The hall stank of meat. I poked my head round the kitchen door and identified the source. My gran was stewing link sausages and the tubes of pork bobbed up and down in a pot of boiling water like four peely wally cocks, just pinker and skinnier than Arnold's dad's dick. It would be a long time before I could face taking a bite into a sausage. I shut the kitchen door.

'Gran, it's roasting in here.'

I knew before I went into the living room she'd have the two bars of the electric fire on.

'It's a true saying, "Ne'er cast a clout till May be out." And you could shoot peas through that jaiket.'

The month of May ended weeks ago but I didn't have the nerve to correct my gran. I wandered through and found Bimbo toasting his baws in front of the fire.

'Is it awright if ah stay the night?'

'Aye, of course it is. Does yer mam ken you're here?'

'Naw. Ah'll phone her. But could ah get a drink first gran?'

She went over to the sideboard and poured out a measure in two sherry glasses.

'Cheers.'

We chinked glasses and I kicked off my shoes. My gran had been sorting out buttons for her latest knitting project and I picked up the tin to rummage around in it. We used to gamble with the buttons instead of coins when my gran taught me how to play cards. I loved raking around in the button box and I'd pretend that they were precious jewels. I took a handful once and swapped them with Lorraine for her 'Funtime Sindy'. The doll had blonde hair and a blue swimsuit although Bimbo chewed her arm off when I took her with me to play at my gran's. I gave the one-armed doll to Karen and Lorraine felt so bad about Funtime Sindy being handicapped that she gave me the buttons back. Everyone was happy.

My gran called it her 'Button Box' but it wasn't a box. It was round. Her buttons lived in an auld tartan tin for shortbread. She kept the button box in the sideboard next to her sewing basket and knitting needles. There was a picture of a piper on the lid standing in front of a loch with a bushy ginger beard and sideburns like Sister Patricia's.

'If you sniff hard enough you can still smell Scotland', that's what my gran told me when I was wee. I used to try my hardest and breathed in until my nostrils flared like a fairy tale dragon. But I could only smell buttons. Most of the buttons were just plastic although I never told Lorraine that before the Sindy swap.

I needed a drink after the flasher incident. I took a gulp of my sherry and raked around in the box remembering the days when we started playing cards with ten buttons each. My gran had a few metal buttons too, though they were hard to find. I dug out a couple. I liked the way you could spin the shiny ones on her wooden table and make them catch the light. I asked my gran about the gold one with the pattern on it.

'It looks like real gold.'

I bit the button and my gran laughed, spraying sherry over the table. She wiped the spittle with the sleeve of her jumper and topped up our glasses.

'Ah wish it was gold! That button came off yer grandda's bowling club blazer.'

I liked the metal buttons. But they didn't have the best stories.

'What about this one?' I picked up a dark brown button that looked like a conker with a brick pattern on it.

'Ah remember yer granddad wanted me tae make him a cardigan he'd seen in one of ma pattern books. He thought he was the bee's knees in it. Never again. That chunky cable pattern was a bugger tae knit!'

She handed me a small round tin. It had pictures of berries on the lid. Raspberries, blackberries and blueberries. I opened it up. It was empty but I could still smell the fruity boiled sweets that my gran had sooked the life out of.

'Ah thought you'd like tae have yer ain button box.'

'But ah havenae got any buttons.'

'We aw start with an empty box. Then life soon fills it up. I'll give you a wee start. Take yer pick of the buttons.'

My mam sewed any missing buttons back on and it was hard to imagine that I'd need to do it myself one day but I reached into the box and raked through the buttons. There were all the colours and shapes of sweeties in a ten pence mix-up. And then I found it, a beauty, a teeny weeny pearl button.

'This is ma favourite. Can ah have this one?'

'Aye hen. You can keep that one.'

'What did it come off?'

'The suit ah wore for ma first wedding.'

'First wedding?'

'Aye, yer grandda wisnae ma only man. Ah was left on ma tod and yer mammy was just a toddler so it made sense tae marry again.'

We'd both drained our glasses and the best bit was I didn't need to ask for more, my gran automatically refilled each one.

'This ah need tae hear. What's the story gran?'

'Ah'll tell you after you've phoned yer mam. Dinnae worry, yer drink will still be here when you get back.'

I nipped out to the lobby and gave my mam a quick call before I settled back into my couch. Bimbo jumped up on to my lap and we waited for my gran to complete another piece in the jigsaw of her life story. I'd trade her story for one of mine, that was the way it worked between us. There was nothing that shocked my gran; I'd seen her stash of Jackie Collins novels under her bed. I'd tell her about the flasher. I might even tell her about meeting Stevie, she'd understand.

Chapter Six

I didn't get round to telling my gran about Stevie. She kept pouring the sherry and wanted to talk about her first husband. I took a glug of my sherry and sat back for a bumpy ride. It was hard to believe that my gran had never shared this story before and if the couch had a seatbelt, I'd have fastened it.

My gran told me that my mam's dad was a really keen fisherman but he was as tight as a camel's arse in a sand storm and grudged paying for a fishing permit. He'd go off with his two pals for an after dark session of poaching at the Carron Valley Reservoir. One night, he took a notion to go fishing but both his pals were working nightshift at the foundry. Undeterred, he set off on his own for his usual spot. On his first patrol of the day, the ghillie found him dead at six in the morning, feet trapped between a pile of rocks and face down in the water, still holding his fishing rod, with the fishing line snapped.

'He must've hooked a monster of a fish. Ah loved ma man but he wisnae just tight with money, he was a stubborn bugger tae and nae doubt he refused tae let the beast go. It must've dragged him oot intae knee-deep water but when he tipped forward he got stuck between the rocks. The problem was, he couldnae swim.'

'Jeezo, gran that's a terrible way tae go.'

'Aye, imagine being pulled under and drowned by an animal withoot arms or legs.' She sighed. 'The one that got away.'

I guessed my gran meant the fish, not my mam's dad.

'His pals fished up at the reservoir for weeks, day and night, it cost them a fortune in permits but they were determined and finally one of them caught a 10lb rainbow trout with a hook still embedded in its mooth. They wanted justice. They brought me the killer fish wrapped in auld newspaper and presented it tae me like a trophy. As a mark of respect ah tried tae eat it but it made ma stomach turn. Ah've never eaten fish since. Yer mam grew up thinking it was just the smell of fish ah hated and that her daddy died when he fell oot of a boat and drowned. Ah didnae have the heart tae tell her the real story aboot the killer fish. It was bad enough but can you imagine what yer mam would've been like when *Jaws* came oot at the pictures?'

'Dinnae cry gran. You ken it upsets Bimbo.'

The dog squirmed in her arms and my gran held on tight. I refilled her sherry glass and gave her a reason to let him go. Bimbo jumped off and dived underneath the smoked glass coffee table to chew on one of my gran's old slippers.

'It wasnae easy tae accept he would never come hame fae that fishing trip. You can see why folk turn tae the bottle or religion when they've gone doolally with stress.'

'Do you think that's why Lorraine's mam's never away fae Mass?'

'Aye, she'd be trying tae make sense of things she disnae understand plus she's got a bad case of Catholic guilt. Ah mind ye telt me she had a wee altar with an Oor Lady statue set up in her bedroom.'

'That's right, and she puts fresh flowers in front of Oor Lady every week.'

'Having Oor Lady staring at you when you're at it must put a fella off his stride.'

'Yuck, ah dinnae want tae think aboot Rita and Tam doing it.'

It was my turn for pet therapy but Bimbo had slunk off to the kitchen after the second glass of sherry was drained. Poodles are the second most intelligent breed of dogs in the world. I'd read that in Karen's Fun Animal Facts book. It was one of the only fun animal facts I could prove as I doubted that I'd ever get to test whether a snake can still see through its eyelids when its eyes are closed or that elephants can smell water up to three miles away but there was no question that Bimbo was brainy.

'Does Rita still make you bless yourselves afore you're allowed oot the front door?'

'Aye, and she has a wooden cross that fits intae the palm of her hand and she walks aboot with it. She says that the cross gives her strength.'

'Ah've heard it aw noo. But can you imagine what she'd be

like if you hadnae saved Lorraine's life? That would've tipped her o'er the edge.'

'Too true.'

The memory of Lorraine's near-death experience was stronger than ever after ending up at the quarry. I'd been thinking about the accident before I went anywhere near the quarry. When it had happened, she couldn't thank me enough and Rita and Tam bought me a necklace with a silver guardian angel pendant. It came in a tiny pink velvet pouch with a white ribbon drawstring. I loved that necklace and never took it off until my mam made me give Karen a shot of it to stop one of her tantrums. The chain got caught up in Karen's hair and when my mam tried to untangle it she pulled a clump of hair out. Karen went bananas, jumping about like an eejit, holding her napper where there was a wee bald spot and the chain snapped in two. I kept the guardian angel in its pouch and my mam promised to get the chain soldered. A week later, she collected the chain from the jeweller's and I ran upstairs to get the guardian angel. The pouch was gone. Eventually, after I'd given Karen a Chinese burn, she admitted that she'd buried the guardian angel so that it could go back to heaven and play with all her other angel pals. She couldn't remember where she'd buried it and my dad made us stop digging after the garden looked like it had been invaded by an army of moles.

At least I had the photo of me wearing the guardian angel necklace and cuddling Lorraine in the *Falkirk Herald* with the caption, *Girl Saves Best Friend's Life.* I was still Lorraine's real life guardian angel, even if she'd forgotten that day in the old quarry. I knew that I never would.

'You'll never believe where ah ended up tonight?'

'Here.' My gran laughed at her own joke and spluttered some of her sherry down her cardigan.'

'Very funny. Before ah came up here, ah accidentally ended up at the quarry.'

'Ah thought you knew no tae go back there?' My gran leaned forward and filled my glass with sherry up to the brim.

'Ah didnae plan tae go.'

I finished the sherry in one go and gran never said a word.

'Dae you still have nightmares?'

'No so much noo. Ah try no tae think aboot it.'

It was impossible to forget. Faye and Mandy hadn't turned up and there was only me and Lorraine playing at the quarry that night. There was no point in playing *Planet of the Apes* with just the two of us so I decided that we'd kid on that we were doing the long jump at the Olympics. I found a stick and drew a starting line in the sand and whistled when Lorraine had to take a run and jump as far as she could. It got boring after a while and Lorraine suggested that we should pretend that we were on a diving board and leap off the sand dunes. I went first and bounced up and down on the edge of the dune as if it was a springy diving board. I practised pulling my knees up to my chest before I was ready to hurl myself off the ledge. I turned round to the imaginary crowd to bow before I took my dive but Lorraine wasn't behind me. She was supposed to watch my dive and use the stick to write my score in the sand.

The edge of the dune was ragged with weeds and I dared to put my toes over the edge like they do on the telly. A massive chunk crumbled under my feet and I slid rather than dived, rolling down the dune all balled up like the hedgehogs in Lorraine's garden. I hoped she'd seen my movie-style stunt.

And when I brushed off the sand and got up on my feet again she was gone. I thought she was hiding behind a clump of jaggy gorse bushes but she was nowhere to be seen. I shouted on her to come out and was angry when she ignored me. I ran a quick circuit near where we'd been playing and couldn't see her anywhere. I was spinning like a whirligig, screaming her name. And then I noticed that the mound of sand where I'd landed looked different. Lorraine must've crawled underneath the dune before I jumped off.

Sand went flying and nipped my eyes as my hands morphed into JCB shovels, scooping up and scattering handful after handful. I scraped at the mound and uncovered a tartan stripe on Lorraine's Bay City Rollers white sock. I moved myself upwards and tunnelled at another lump. This time a triangle of skin appeared and I knew it was an arm. I'd gone from movie stunt queen to game show contestant where the studio audience were screaming "Warmer!" as my hands scratched further up the buried shape. Finally as tears mixed with sand to sting and burn a track down my dusty face, I found her nose and then her mouth. I thrust my fingers inside and hoiked out dods of damp sand. Lorraine's lips were blue and she looked like she'd been eating mud pies. I felt the back of her throat and heard her gasp for air. I was back on the fantasy film screen and gave her mouth-to-mouth like any movie star would. I leaned back to take another breath and she coughed up a gungy dark blob. This was the film's happy ending. It would have been even better if I could've lifted Lorraine and carried her in my arms all the way to her front door. Even guardian angels get weak. I cried for help instead. It wasn't long before a dog walker came running up. And this time his trousers were zipped – there's only so much drama a girl can take in a day. Saving Lorraine's life was more than enough for any blockbuster.

No matter how much I tried to bury the episode, it played on a continuous loop at the back of my mind. But the way Lorraine was acting recently it seemed as if she'd forgotten all about me saving her life and how grateful she should be.

'Ah've got a wee job for you that'll help take yer mind off aw that.'

My gran got up and left the room, bumping into the couch on the way past. I drained her sherry glass; it was for her own good, she looked shattered. My gran used to love late nights but she'd lost her stamina as well as her appetite. I'd asked her to go to see the doctor; she insisted that there was nothing wrong with her and that she didn't have time to fit in an appointment. My gran is a crap liar.

Two minutes later, she came back into the living room carrying a life-sized plastic deer and a Poundstretchers carrier bag. She plonked the garden ornament and the bag on the coffee table and sunk back into the couch.

'No bad eh? Ah found Bambi in a skip ootside a bungalow on the Glasgow Road. Ah heard the woman telling the lassie serving at the Co-op that she's putting in one of they fancy avocado bathroom suites.'

'Ah thought mam telt ye tae stop skip raking?'

'Yer mam worries too much. Ah keep telling her, you die if you worry and you die if you dinnae. And there was nae way ah was gonnae leave Bambi lying in amongst an auld bathroom suite and a mouldy carpet.'

'It's no safe tae be climbing in and oot of skips at your age.'

'Ah'm no buttoned up the back. Ah wait till it's dark but ah take a torch and ma folding stool. Ah'm an expert.'

My gran petted the plastic hind of Bambi before emptying the carrier bag. A naked baby doll dropped on to the floor. I wondered if my gran had been at the sherry before I arrived.

'So what's this job you've got for me then?'

My gran handed me the doll.

'Ah want ye tae take its eyeballs oot.'

'Why?'

'Ah need them for Bambi. Did you no notice that her eyes are missing?'

I'd been too thrown by Bambi appearing in my gran's living room to note that the sockets of the deer's eyes were hollow.

'Ah dinnae want tae think aboot how poor wee Bambi lost her eyeballs. She disnae deserve tae be blind.'

Bimbo came trotting through and sniffed the arse of the plastic deer and got no response; maybe poodles weren't that smart after all.

'But what aboot the doll?' I asked.

'You're as bad as yer mam for worrying. Ah'm gonnae knit a matinee jacket and bootees for the doll. Then ah'll tie a strip of bandage roond its heid and hand it in tae the Children's Ward at the Infirmary. The weans will love playing nurses with a blind baby.'

'Ah suppose you're right gran. It's a win-win situation. Happy deer, happy weans.'

I got a knife from the kitchen and gouged out the doll's sapphire blue eyeballs. They sat in my palm like two shiny marbles. I was sure that deer always have brown eyes but I didn't want to upset my gran. She was already applying UHU to the deer's eye sockets.

'Ah feel like a miracle worker.'

I poured us both a large glass of sherry.

Chapter Seven

I'd memorised Stevie's number and didn't need the scribble on the strip torn off his cigarette packet. And I was going to give Lorraine the message but I didn't get the chance.

She wasn't at eleven o'clock Mass so she must still be sleeping over at Stacey's house after the party. I could've asked Rita on my way out of chapel except that she was too busy showing off Janine's new outfit. The wheelchair was surrounded by a mob of auld biddies that were oohing and aahing at the flowery dirndl skirt and matching blouse Rita had made. It was lucky that Janine didn't know any better.

I hated Sundays. Ever since I made my Confirmation in primary six, I'd been a Reader at Mass. It was all my mam's fault. It came about after Cardinal Doyle made a visit to the parish to do the Confirmations and mingled with the families in the chapel hall after the Mass. Rita shoved Janine in front of Cardinal Doyle and asked for a special blessing. My mam wanted a slice of the action and yanked me away from the Tunnocks teacakes to tell the Cardinal that I was the girl who'd read the first letter of Paul to the Corinthians. Cardinal Doyle told my mam that I should read at Mass again and I'd been stuck on the rota ever since.

I told my mam ages ago that I didn't want to do it anymore but she said that it was a privilege to be a Reader and she'd die of shame if I asked the priest to take my name off the rota. She even asked me to think of my religious namesake, Bernadette, and how I should want to make her proud which only made me snigger at how stupid I'd once been to believe in all that hocus pocus guff.

The story of Bernadette Soubirous, the fourteen year old girl who was famous for having visions of Our Lady in her hometown of Lourdes was my all-time favourite when I was wee. And I chose the name Bernadette as my Confirmation name. Lorraine wanted to pick the same name although Rita made her choose Martha after her nana who was apparently a living saint. My mam said martyrdom runs in Lorraine's family.

I was desperate to visit Lourdes and stand in the same spot where Our Lady appeared to Bernadette. Lorraine went to visit the grotto at Lourdes when she was fourteen with Rita, Janine and loads of other handicapped folk. They travelled there in a Jumbalance which was like a huge camper van with medical stuff in it and wheelchairs clamped to the floor. The journey took something like twenty five hours and Lorraine said it was a hunner times worse than a run in the Club's Nut Bus, but she was just saying that to make me feel better. And she played down the amazing food but I saw a photo of her eating croques monsieur and she tried telling me that it was nothing special and really only a cheese 'n' ham toastie. She's as crap a liar as my gran.

It wasn't the food they went for, but they didn't get a miracle either. Janine was just the same when she came home, Lorraine didn't see Our Lady and Rita broke her toe when a wheelchair ran over her foot. Lorraine brought me back a plaster statue of Our Lady but the head snapped off when I used a red felt tip to draw lipstick on the mouth and leaned too hard. I kept Our Lady's head in my musical jewellery box; it was sinful to bin a saint.

I lifted the lid of the jewellery box and the tiny ballerina twirled in time to *Twinkle Twinkle Little Star.* The ballerina was missing an arm but she could still pirouette. It's easier to love something that isn't perfect. It had to be or the likes of Janine had no chance.

I placed the torn off strip of Stevie's fag packet in the side compartment beside Our Lady's head, a dried seahorse I'd bought on our first holiday to Filey, my First Communion medal and a silver Claddagh ring that Lorraine gave me for my twelfth birthday. I slipped the ring up to the knuckle of my pinkie.

The heart in the centre of the ring was held by two wee hands and topped by a crown. Lorraine told me that the crown was for loyalty and the hands stood for us being best friends. She said that I'd always looked out for her and her heart was in my hands. I'd wanted to get her one for her birthday so we could have matching rings but my mam didn't believe in pocket money. Me and Karen did jobs round the house everyday although my mam said she shouldn't need to bribe us to help out so I never had enough cash to buy anything decent until I got my job at Patterson's.

The silver heart on the ring had gone black and I rubbed it with a bit of spit and the cuff of my sleeve and yet I couldn't get it to shine again.

'Get the door!' my mam shouted over the TV and I heard Karen open it to tell Lorraine that I was up in my room. I threw the ring back in the jewellery box and slammed the lid down to silence the ballerina. Before her footsteps could reach the landing, I snatched up my shoebox of cassette tapes and shuffled them around.

'What're you up to?' asked Lorraine, flopping down on my bed.

'Ah'm busy sorting oot ma tapes before the Charts come on.'

'I've got the new *Duran Duran* single if you want to tape it.'

'Naw, ah'm mair intae *Joy Division*.'

'Since when?'

'Ah've liked them for ages.'

'First I've heard.'

'Ah dinnae need tae tell ye everything.'

I rearranged the tapes in alphabetical order. Lorraine lay back on my bed and picked bits of woodchip off my wall paper. The telly blared below us and there was a constant thump from Karen practising her handstands against her bedroom wall. When I listened really hard, I could hear my dad tapping away with his latest nail picture. But me and Lorraine were as quiet as the ballerina.

'So what did you get up to last night?' She'd lasted longer than I thought. I wasn't going to ask Lorraine first, and we both knew she'd be the first to crack.

'Just went oot for a few drinks.'

'I thought you were skint?'

'Ah wisnae paying.'

Lorraine sat bolt upright, scattering a confetti of woodchip on to the bedroom carpet.

'Who were you with?'

'Just some guy ah met at work.'

'In Patterson's?'

There was no need to shriek as if it was a ridiculous scenario.

'Men are allowed in you ken. And ah'm no stuck at the sink aw day. Irene likes me oot front; ah'm good with the customers.'

Lorraine went silent again. This was the first time I'd met up with a boy without telling her and it was clearly too much for her to take in. I could almost hear her brain sifting through the files of possible suspects.

'Is he someone from school?

'Naw, it was a man. Boys dinnae get served in The Railway.'

'What were you doing in an auld man's pub?'

'It's his local. And it's fine for a quiet drink. But enough aboot ma night, how did Stacey's party go?'

'It was alright. It was just a few folk from school. Pamela Thompson was there with her crowd.'

'And was she selling her Precious Feet badges?' It was hard to keep my smirk from spreading across my face.

'She's actually really nice when you get to speak to her. And abortion isn't funny.'

'Ah'm no laughing. See?' I dragged my mouth downwards and arched my eyebrows; Lorraine wasn't willing to play the game and wouldn't smile back. But I had a much better trick than pulling a stupid face to get a reaction and threw open my jewellery box.

The one-armed ballerina sprang into life and I tossed aside the tarnished Claddagh ring to dig out the scrap of paper. Lorraine moved to the edge of the bed and I thrust Stevie's number into her hand.

'What's this?' She uncurled her clenched fist.

'It's Stevie's phone number.'

'Stevie who?'

'Remember, fae the Club. Ah bumped intae him at the pub last night. He wants you tae phone him.'

The cardboard strip sat on Lorraine's hand and she studied it like a Fortune Telling Miracle Fish. We used to collect them from crackers at Christmas and we believed that the little red cellophane fish had special powers. The fish might squirm and twitch its head and body or twist up its tail and depending on the way it moved or didn't, it would reveal your secrets. I'd never know what the scribbled phone number would tell me about Lorraine because she shredded it into tiny pieces to join the woodchip flakes on the carpet.

'So you're no gonnae phone him then?'

'And I thought you were supposed to be the brainy one. What does it look like?'

Lorraine stood up looking like she was going to storm out of my room; instead she picked out the Claddagh ring from my jewellery box. She held it up so it was level with my eyes.

'Do you remember when I gave you this? Or have you forgotten what it stands for?'

'Of course ah dinnae. And ah remember what you wrote in ma birthday card.'

'Really?'

"Love me now, hate me never, we're best friends forever and ever!"

'So why are you trying to wind me up about this Stevie guy?'

Maybe my gran was right and Mother Moon was mucking around with Lorraine's hormones. She shoved the ring in front of my face. I'd never seen her so angry except for the time I put her name on a Valentine's card to Gavin Malley last year and he turned up at her door. She was mortified when he said he'd bought her a present and it was the best dressed cock in town. He started to unzip his jeans to reveal what he called a Dick Dickie Bow. Rita heard Lorraine scream, saw Gavin's cock wearing a miniature bow tie, doused him with Holy Water before slamming the door and pushed Lorraine to her knees to say an *Our Father, Ten Hail Marys,* a *Glory Be* and ended for good measure on a *Hail Holy Queen.* Lorraine was grounded and missed the school Valentine's disco. I understood why she was pissed off at me that time but this wasn't the same; I was trying to help her hook up with a hot guy, like a best friend should.

'Lorraine you ken ah'd never dae anything tae hurt you. Ah'm just passing on his message. Why dae you no want tae meet up? Ah ken he used the 'm' word but he's actually really nice.'

'He isnae.'

'How do you ken?'

'I told my mam about what happened at the Club and she flipped.'

'Because he called you a mongol?'

'Aye, but it was more because I said he was called Stevie Duffy.'

'So?'

I found it hard to believe that Rita knew a sexy guy like Stevie. She only ever went to the Chapel, the Co-op and the Prize Bingo at the Bowling Club.

'She knows Stevie's dad from when she was our age. He was a great player and the Captain of the football team; she used to go along to all their matches.'

From what my gran said, Rita had offered a lot more than support for the team and would know more than just how good a footballer Stevie's dad was. Rita could vouch for all his best moves on and off the pitch. My gran said the joke that went round at the time was that Rita had her own locker in the changing rooms and gave more cuddles than the team mascot. And that was only the pre-match warm-up; the real action happened long after the ref blew the final whistle.

'My mam said he was really handsome but if Stevie's anything like his dad then he's trouble. His dad got the team banned from drinking in the Royal and even these days he's never out of the *Falkirk Herald* for shoplifting and fighting.'

'Yer mam seems tae ken an awfy lot aboot the fitba team and Stevie's dad.'

Lorraine sat back on the bed and I joined her. I put my arms round her and she slumped into my shoulder.

'It's okay, Everybody kens.'

'Everybody knows what?'

'About yer mam's younger days.'

'What're you talking about?'

'You ken, her putting it aboot with the fitba team.'

She sprang away from me and her face was livid. Lorraine picked up the friendship ring and threw it at me. It bounced off my chin and rolled under the chest of drawers.

'That's a bloody lie! I don't know where you've heard that. My dad was her only boyfriend.'

'Ah'm sorry Lorraine; ah must've got the story wrong.'

'Aye, get your facts right before you start bad mouthing my mam. I'm glad the ring doesn't fit anymore.'

My gran never made up stories so for all Lorraine knew, Stevie Duffy could be her half-brother. Lorraine barged past me, taking the stairs two at a time and slammed the front door behind her.

My mam shouted on me and I traipsed down the stairs knowing that there was no hiding place or escape from her moaning.

'What in the name of God was aw that aboot? Lorraine nearly took the door off its hinges.'

'Nothing.'

'It didnae sound like nothing tae me. Is it boyfriend trouble?'

As if I was ever likely to confide in my mam about anything important. I'd rather sit in a bath of Bimbo's shit than talk to her about the opposite sex. I didn't bother to answer her and bolted out the door before she could attempt to wear me down. Lorraine had already crossed the road but she'd hear me shout.

'Lorraine, come back!'

I chased after her in my bare feet, dodging the broken glass from next door's empty milk bottle and a curl of dog shit. Lorraine stopped at the railings that ran down the side of the path. When we were wee, the railings got used daily like a set of gymnastic bars to kid on we were Olga Korbut. There was nothing worth playing on at Spam Valley and **'No Ball Games'** signs were dotted about on every spare patch of grass with the Neighbourhood Watch saddos patrolling like a landmine would go off if you dared to have a kickabout.

We'd always meet at the railings after our tea. Rita called a meal eaten after four o'clock dinner but everyone round here knew that the meal eaten after school or work was called tea. My mam called Rita a snob and said she had her head stuck so far up her own arse, she didn't know whether to speak or fart.

Me and Lorraine used to sit on the railings, swing backwards upside down, dangle from them with no hands, did it all again and often spewed up our tea leaving the path sprayed with chewed up beans and chips.

Memories of splattering pavements with puke were a long time ago although when I took hold of Lorraine's arm I felt sick all over again. She refused to turn to face me and it felt worse than before with nothing to throw up, just a ball of knotted fear lying in the pit of my stomach.

'Ah'm sorry, c'mon, dinnae be like this.' I kept a tight hold of her. 'We'll always be best pals, nae matter what. Ah made a mistake.'

She tried to pull away and I gripped her arm, enough to bruise her if I had to. 'It was ma mam's fault. Ah thought she said Rita but she must've said Anita. You ken what she's like bitching aboot folk and ah only half listen.'

'Who's Anita?'

'Ah dinnae ken. Ma mam was trying tae tell me some story aboot a woman who was a goer when she was younger. Ah'm an absolute eejit for thinking it might be yer mam.'

'Exactly. My mam's hardly the type, is she?'

'Ah ken, ah'm sorry. Ah made a stupid mistake. Still best pals?'

'I suppose so.'

'So, are you coming back inside? Ma feet are freezin'.'

'Naw, I needed to go anyway. And Pamela's coming round later.'

'Oh, well ah better let you go then.'

I loosened my grip and my rag doll arm flopped by my side. She walked off without a backward glance and I stood on the pavement until she'd disappeared round the corner. I gathered up some chuckies from among the weeds and stored the stones in a hollow I made from pulling up the hem of my T-shirt.

I didn't care anymore about my cold feet or if anyone could see my belly; I wasn't ready to go back inside without Lorraine. I jumped up on to the railing and fired the chuckies at the dog crap until it looked like one of my gran's homemade rock buns. They tasted like shit too.

I ran out of chuckies and there was nothing else for it but to go back inside. My mam opened the front door for me.

'Is Lorraine awright?'

'Aye, she just took a joke the wrong way.'

'That's a pity 'cause she needs a sense of humour mair than maist folk.'

'Eh?'

'Well, you have tae laugh or you'd greet.'

I followed my mam through to the living room and lay in front of the fire. My mam insisted that we plugged in the fire so that the fake coals glowed all year round as a safety measure after my dad came home drunk one night and tried to light the plastic lumps.

'Move back fae the fire afore you get corned beef legs,' my mam warned.

Lazy tartan my gran called it and already there were pink mottled splotches on the skin of my calves which were toasting nicely. And I wanted to feel them burn.

My mam nudged my leg as she bent down to pick up her knitting bag from the side of her chair but I didn't move. She'd taken up knitting after my gran told her it would help with her nerves and she was making a coat for Bimbo, inspired by Joseph's Technicolor Dream Coat. My mam aimed to have it finished for our holiday; the strategy was to catch the judge's eyes when my gran entered Bimbo in the waggiest tail competition. And my gran was going to wear a matching jumper she'd knitted; it was a failsafe plan.

'You'd be in tears morning, noon and night if you had tae live in that madhoose, you dinnae ken how lucky you are,' said my mam picking up her knitting needles to start on the purple section of Bimbo's coat.

I edged closer to the fire.

Chapter Eight

Lorraine didn't even notice that I'd threaded the Claddagh ring on to an old silver chain. I'd polished it up with my mam's Brasso and wore the chain over my collar on top of the knot of my school tie. The shine on the ring kept catching the light as the school bus bounced up and down and Lorraine couldn't fail to see it, but she said nothing. She sat beside me on the bus and kidded on that she was finishing homework; we hardly spoke until the bell went for registration. Me and Lorraine were only in the same class for PE and RE. The rest of the classes were streamed and Lorraine wasn't in any of the top ones. She was still speaking to me; it was strained and would've been worse if we'd had to sit side-by-side all morning. But I was glad we had the chance to be together in RE after lunchtime; she'd never stayed in a huff for long.

As a one-off, the RE class was split into two groups of male and females and Sister Patricia was taking the girls for a special class. She told us that we were, "*reaching a vulnerable age and could be prone to unwelcome sexual encounters.*" The pep talk was more than a year too late for Faye and Mandy. From what they'd told us, their sexual encounters were more than welcome although they were forever clawing at their muffs and complaining that some clarty bastard had more crabs than a seafood buffet.

We all played along with Sister Patricia, desperate not to knock her off her stride and miss hearing a lifelong virgin dish out sexual advice. And even with the frosty atmosphere between me and Lorraine, I knew she'd enjoy the banter.

'Good Catholic girls should avoid wearing skirts with elastic waistbands that are easy to get off,' said Sister Patricia.

A class giggle began to simmer. Lorraine turned to me and sniggered when Sister Patricia got to the part that we should all consider getting our hair cut on the basis that a sexual predator likes to grab ponytails and having long hair only makes things easier for him. Mandy couldn't resist asking, 'Is that why you've always had a crew cut Sister?'

And Faye added, 'Dae you think ah'd be safer if ah tried tae grow sideburns like yours Sister Patricia?'

The hilarity reached boiling point and it was the cure me and Lorraine needed to start talking like true best pals again.

'She's a nutter, eh?' said Lorraine.

'Who, Mandy, Faye or Sister Patricia?'

We were laughing like we always did and I toyed with asking her to come round to mine that night, I had news that was too big not to share. Sister Patricia sent Faye and Mandy to Papa Smurf's office and passed round a worksheet called *Challenges and Choices – Building Catholic Character*. She warned us that the next girl to say another word would be out the door too. Me and Lorraine put our heads down and scribbled down answers that would please Sister Patricia but fool no one else. With Faye and Mandy gone the class settled down with only subdued giggles at the fannyish questions like, *"Why is sexual intercourse called "the marital act"? How does it reflect God's love?"* From what Faye told us about her dad shagging her mam senseless whenever he came home pished, it didn't sound as if there was much '*choice*' in her house. And I'd seen Faye's mam at the Co-op with a black eye and I guessed that was the result of the *'challenge'* in building a Catholic character, at least for some Catholic women.

The bell finally rung and we were free to laugh off Sister Patricia's parting comment that we must always remember that *"God calls us to save our sexuality for marriage and not to use another person as an object merely for sexual pleasure."* It was good that Sister Patricia had never gone past the taxi rank and round the back of Mystique on a Saturday night; it was easier for her to live in a fantasy world where an invisible man perched on a cloud in the sky and watched over us all. And on Planet Patricia she didn't need to worry about the teenagers shagging up against the wall of Mystique knowing that they'd be going to Hell and be tortured for all eternity.

We walked out of RE class together and made our way to the library for a study period. The timetable was a joke, with all the exams finished there was nothing to study for and the teachers didn't know what else to do with us for the next two weeks. We'd been told to research the pros and cons of our career options, as if any of us were seriously going to discover the reality about our dream jobs by sitting in the school library flicking through out-of-date books. I couldn't keep my news to myself any longer.

'Ma dad had a win at the bookies and he got a car for me.'

'A car? It must've been a big win!'

'Naw, it's no brand new but he's gonnae dae it up for me. He's getting it tonight if you want tae come and see it.'

'Brilliant! What colour is it?'

'He wouldnae tell me anything aboot it; he says it's a surprise. Come up after yer tea and see it.'

'Sorry, I've just remembered that I said I'd go to Pamela's tonight.'

'But she was at yer hoose last night.'

'I know but I said I'd give her a hand with posters for the Pro-Life group fund raiser.'

'Dinnae tell me she's roped you intae that? Next you'll be wearing one of her Precious Feet badges.'

It was only when she put her blazer on that I noticed the glint of gold on the baby feet badge pinned to her lapel. I was glad that the library was at the end of the corridor and the crush meant we couldn't keep talking. The pong of the library hit whenever I opened the door. It wasn't just the books – it smelt like the contents of a bulging hoover bag needing to be emptied. Lorraine made a beeline to join the table Pamela had bagsied with Stacey and the rest of her disciples gathered round her.

'There's mair room over here,' I suggested to Lorraine, pointing at a free table near the door.

'No, we can squeeze you in,' said Pamela.

'Thanks.'

I couldn't bring myself to echo Lorraine's appreciation.

'Move up girls,' Pamela ordered and bums dutifully shuffled along the bench. I followed Lorraine and dumped my bag on the floor. Pamela patted an empty space next to her and Lorraine filled it. There was only room for one arse so I sat with one bum cheek hanging off the end of the bench next to Ginge Minge.

The librarian appeared from behind her desk and instructed us all to find a book; it was clear she meant any book. It could be a porn mag or a witchcraft manual for all she cared, as long as we had something with pages in front of us.

The group slowly broke up and made their way to the book shelves, Lorraine staying back and rummaging in her bag. I shifted a couple of the books aside and peered through the gap as Lorraine slipped her hand from her bag to Pamela's and brought out a purse which she hid inside her blazer. Lorraine walked over to a shelf of science books and slid the purse between two book spines. I'd forgotten to breathe and let out a sigh like a burst couch. I snatched up the nearest book and only noticed that it was about Pirates when I returned to the table. I needed to sit down. Everyone else was still swanning around talking in Chinese whispers whilst pretending to choose their book as the librarian patrolled the aisles, shooing us back to our seats.

Lorraine was with Pamela and both had books about working abroad as volunteers. I had to listen to Lorraine tell Pamela about her life-changing experience of visiting Lourdes although there was no mention of folk shitting themselves in adult-sized nappies and being woken by constant zombie wailing. Anybody hearing this edited version would've believed that Lorraine was living amongst us as a reincarnation of Bernadette Soubirous herself. It was enough to make me gag.

Ginge Minge leaned over to read the title of my book and sniggered.

'The History of Piracy? Do you want tae be Black Beard when you leave school?'

It was hardly funny and barely raised a giggle from the others until Pamela added, 'She might as well take advantage of her facial hair.' This was the punch line that they'd all been waiting for and the table shook with laughter, even from Lorraine.

The librarian shushed us and reminded us that we were supposed to be taking notes from the reference books.

'Applicants must have their own parrot, drink rum and not suffer from sea sickness.' Once again Pamela made the group hysterical, not to mention the librarian who was starting to foam at the mouth as the noise level increased.

'Detentions will be handed out unless you settle down!' The librarian's empty threat landed on cloth ears. But it did prompt Pamela to get her pencil case from her bag and I studied

Lorraine's face as her new pal shrieked. The librarian took a hairy fit.

'Right, that's it…'

'Someone's stolen my purse,' cried Pamela.

The gasp from her disciples went round the table like a Mexican wave.

'Oh my God, that's shocking,' bleated Lorraine.

The librarian flew over to the main doors and snibbed them shut.

'No one is going anywhere until this is sorted out.'

A class of first years doing research for their geography project were rounded up with the rest of us fifth years and the school office was called. Pamela sniffed something into Lorraine's shoulder about having the Pro-Life Group's raffle ticket money in her purse.

Papa Smurf arrived and ordered everyone's bag to be emptied. Of course the purse wasn't found and he gently suggested that Pamela had lost it rather than it being stolen, as this sort of thing didn't happen at St Paddy's. Just as underage smoking, drinking, sex and violent beatings went under his selective behaviour radar too. That was the reason why Papa Smurf stayed away from the toilet blocks on his lunchtime school patrols. The only problem he ever acknowleged were the damp paper towels that were thrown up to stick on the ceiling and dried like stalactites, not the real issues lurking behind the locked cubicles.

The bell rang and we all had to move on to the next class with a tear-stained Pamela being comforted by Papa Smurf and guided out of the library by Ginge Minge and Lorraine. It was almost tempting to stay behind and retrieve the hidden purse although it wasn't as appealing as waiting for the next move in the game Lorraine was playing.

I didn't have to wait long. During lunch break, Lorraine ran off saying she was bursting for a pee and shot off down the corridor. I hovered around the foyer waiting for her and even above the noise of hunners of pupils I could hear Pamela's squeals when Lorraine returned waving the purse in the air. The sight and sound grated the ends of my nipples; anyone would think she'd returned with the Golden Fleece. Pamela and her disciples gushed round Lorraine, cuddling and squeezing her tightly. I drifted over and heard that Lorraine saw the purse stuffed inside the bin next to the row of sinks in amongst the used paper towels. They all moved in closer as Pamela opened the purse to see that the cash and the raffle tickets were still inside and no one had stolen the photo of her dead cat.

Pamela kicked off the 'Yays!' and soon they were all high fiving like they were a squad of Dallas Cowboys' cheerleaders instead of a bunch of fannies from Falkirk. If they'd lifted Lorraine on to their shoulders it wouldn't have surprised me. Lorraine might be guilty of being an out-and-out attention seeker but she wasn't a thief so I never expected her to keep the money. And yet Lorraine solving the mysterious case of the missing purse didn't make sense. They were all too hyper bouncing up and down with fake smiley faces to ask the question why nothing had been stolen from the purse. How the purse got from Pamela's bag to the bin in the bogs seemed irrelevant to them. I didn't dare burst their bubble and I didn't hang around to bask in Lorraine's glory for fear of being blinded by her saintly glow. She was welcome to her whoopees.

Chapter Nine

On the school bus home, Lorraine was buzzing for the whole journey. All she kept going on about was how chuffed Pamela was to get her purse back. And of course Lorraine made no more mention of how she'd miraculously 'found' it.

'It was lucky you saw it in the bin. But how dae you think it got there when it went missing in the library?' I asked.

'How the hell would I know, do I look like Columbo? Who cares anyway? The main thing is Pamela's got her purse back.'

'Ah suppose so. Ah thought she was gonnae snog the face off you.'

'Me too, she's a great laugh when you get to know her better. It was a shame you missed Stacey's party.'

'Aye.'

'Pamela won't tell me what it is, but she's thought of a way to thank me. She's gonnae tell me when I'm round at hers tonight.' Lorraine was chewing her bus ticket and I hoped she'd choke on it. Pamela this, Pamela that, I was scunnered listening to her, she didn't even mention me getting the car later on.

'Ah'd be desperate tae find oot too.'

For a moment I'd forgotten that sarcasm went right over Lorraine's head. She'd grown up in a house where she wasn't allowed to say things to Janine like, "*act your age, not your shoe size*", so Lorraine took everything folk said literally. I once told her that gullible was the only word that's not in the dictionary. And she looked it up, and kept flicking through the 'G' pages even after I repeatedly said, "*I swear, gullible is not there!*" Lorraine was still as easy to fool but it wasn't as funny anymore.

'You know me, I love a surprise and I've no idea what she's got planned.'

'Aye, the suspense must be killing you.'

'I know, I've no got long to wait. Why don't you come to Pamela's too? We could do with more help making the posters,' said Lorraine.

So it was a case of *'we'* already. It was impressive how quickly Pamela had sunk her claws into my best pal.

'If ah could, ah would, but ma dad would be gutted if ah wisnae in when ma car arrives.'

'Oh aye, you're getting the car tonight.'

'It's no big deal.'

We parted at the bus stop and I spat my chewed ticket out, finding it too hard to swallow it down.

My dad must've got away from work early because his car was in the lay-by. It was parked next to an unfamiliar car which I assumed was mine although I hoped it wasn't. I fancied turning up for Art School in a Citreon Dyane the same colour as Vincent Van Gogh's favourite colbalt blue. I could see myself driving the 2CV back to the land of its birth one day. I'd park it in front of a roadside café in Paris and it would have a soft top to peel back in the summer. If I was skint, I'd go for a run to the shows at Burntisland instead. I already had a pair of fake tortoiseshell Ray-Bans that I'd got down the market so they'd be ideal for my road trips. And when it was windy, I could use a strip of black lace to tie round my head like Madonna to stop my hair getting all matted like a stray dog's coat. I'd look amazing eating a croissant up the Eiffel tower but if I didn't have the petrol money for a French trip, I'd park at the Links on the Fife Riviera to eat my candy floss.

The heap of shit in the lay-by would never feature in any dreams of driving in Paris or even Burntisland. It wasn't the cute wee car that I'd planned to take me and Lorraine up the town or into Glasgow. We'd heard stories of a nightclub called Tin Pan Alley that was supposed to be amazing and with no way of getting home that late, we couldn't add an exotic stamp to our disco passport. Once I passed my driving test, a car was our ticket to a world beyond Falkirk. But the banger parked outside my house was the stuff of nightmares; if this was my motor, we'd be lucky to make it to Mystique and back.

In a better mood, it could be described as being the colour of a Caramac chocolate bar but today it looked more like a nasty shade of diarrhoea to me. It was a three-door hatchback and the badge on the back said it was a Vauxhall Chevette. There was a frill of rust round the edges like an egg that had been fried too long in the chip pan. I hadn't dared to look inside yet. My dad bounded down the front steps with my mam following him along the path in her fluffy mules.

'She's a beauty eh?'

'So, it's mine?'

'Aye, what dae you think?'

'Is it fit for the road?'

'It needs a bit of work but that's why Geordie gave me it for a good price.'

'Would the scrappy no take it?' asked my mam.

'Away with you. It'll be a great wee runner when ah've done it up.'

'That's no what the tow truck driver said when he dropped it off. Pig in a poke ah bet. Yer so called *pal* Geordie saw you coming when he sold you that rust bucket,' added my mam before clip clopping away in her mules.

'Ignore her.'

My dad threw the keys at me. Even the keyring was naff although I couldn't resist twisting the sides of the tiny Rubik's cube; it was a good excuse to avoid unlocking the car door.

'Get in then!' commanded my dad, nudging me forward. I slid round the side of the neighbour's dyke and put the key in the lock. The door creaked as if it was gagging for a drink. I risked a look inside. There was no carpet in the car.

'Dinnae worry. Ah've still got a bit of that Axminster off-cut.'

My dad's ability to cut carpet had been tested in my bedroom. And the finished job looked like he'd cut the carpet with his teeth. Lorraine was the only outsider that I'd ever allowed into my bedroom.

'You cannae have a carpet with wee crowns on it in a car!'

'Who says?'

'Dad, it'll look ridiculous!'

'Rubbish, it'll give it character.' He said it with total conviction. 'Aw it needs is a bit of TLC and this wee motor will be the King of the Road with its royal carpet.'

It was no wonder I was good at lying, I'd learnt from a master.

The seat pad had a greasy sheen as if someone had wiped their hands on it after a fish supper. But it didn't smell as good as the chippy; it had the same pissy reek as the jakey who came into the café every Saturday morning for a roll on square sausage.

Irene had warned Trina and Nicole not to ask the jakey if his order was "Sit in or takeaway?" He only got the takeaway option because it wasn't fair on the other customers to let him stink out the café and have to sit next to a tramp. And I was to make sure he didn't use the "Customers Only" toilet.

'The car honks.'

'Give it a blast of that pine trees stuff yer mam's always squirting.' This was a regular occurrence when dad let one rip. My dad was weaned on McEwan's export and he believed the telly advert's claim that, *"McEwans is the best beer, the best buy in beer!"* His daily can of ale certainly blew us away. 'It'll be fine, it's just because Geordie let his Labrador sleep in here and you'll get rid of the smell nae bother.'

'It'll take mair than air freshener tae smother this ming.'

'Roll the windaes doon a bit for a few days then. It'll be safe enough roond here.' It would be safe to leave the car with the doors wide open, the key in the ignition, a tow rope attached and a sign taped to the windscreen saying, 'Please tow and go!'

He gave me his best cheeky grin and I uncurled my lip. 'Trust me; this wee motor's a good buy. And it'll be great for getting you tae work and back.' He gave the car bonnet a friendly tap.

'It's probably cheaper just tae get the bus tae Denny.'

'Ah wisnae talking about yer *Saturday* job, ah was meaning when you leave school. A clever lassie like you could get intae the office at OKI. One of ma bowling pals, you ken Big Davey? Well he telt me that there'll be jobs coming up after the summer.'

Because OKI manufactured electronics, my dad believed that it was better than a foundry or workshop; but it was still a factory in Cumbernauld, just cleaner inside. And working in the office didn't make it any more glamorous. Loads of folk from school went to work in the Wardpark industrial estate. I wasn't going to be one of them.

'But FUB said ah should apply tae Art School.'

'Less of the FUB, it's Mr McDougall tae you,' my dad said, giving me a kid on clip round the lug. Every pupil at St Paddy's called the head of the Art department FUB; probably the other teachers did too. He actually wasn't that fat or ugly and he definitely wasn't a bastard, it was a name that started long before

I went to high school and it had stuck. FUB liked me because my artwork was the best in our year and he said I had a real chance of getting into Art School. I could go places, much further than the five miles to Cumbernauld. But the best bit was that he didn't see a lassie from a scheme, he saw me, a talented artist.

'Listen hen, ah enjoy making ma nail pictures but it's a hobby. Ah ken you like tae draw and paint but that's no something that'll pay the bills.'

'It's mair than a hobby.'

'It's awright for the likes of Mr McDougall tae fill yer heid with ideas but he's no living in the real world. What kinda of job could you get after Art School?'

'Ah could be a graphic designer or a portrait painter or an art teacher or…'

'Wheesht, when was the last time you saw any of those jobs advertised in the *Falkirk Herald*?'

'But there are loads of careers with a degree in art. FUB says you can…'

'Look, yer dad kens what's best for you, no Mr McDougall. Ah cannae see you in amongst arty farty folk. And ah wouldnae want you tae be disappointed when you couldnae fit in.'

'You're right dad. Ah'm away inside.'

He nodded, believing the discussion was over. It was the end of it, for tonight, until I came up with a better argument. It wasn't going to be easy and yet I was determined not to end up working in a factory, even if it was in the office.

My dad didn't understand that my art wasn't the same as his nail pictures. It wasn't a hobby like Karen's gymnastics or him going to the bowling club. It was what I was meant to do. All I had to figure out was how to make it happen. My gran was on my side but a better idea would be to get FUB to convince my mam and dad that I was good at art, and too good for OKI.

FUB had entered my drawing of Janine into a national schools' competition. I drew it when me and Lorraine were babysitting and Rita was at the Union of Catholic Mothers annual trip to the grotto at Carfin. Janine fell asleep on the couch and I took the chance to sketch her dressed like a rag doll in a pink gingham dress. Nobody looking at the drawing would ever know that Janine twitched and shrieked when awake as if someone was poking her with an electric cattle prod. Janine was so relaxed that she'd dribbled on to the cushion although I left out the damp stain in my drawing. I didn't sketch her droopy smile either, and it made Janine look like any normal wee lassie dreaming of meeting Spandau Ballet. FUB said the drawing perfectly captured the subject's innocence, and he doesn't even know Janine.

I left my dad cutting up an auld newspaper that he was going to use to trace round the gear box and car seats as a pattern for the carpet. He was confident that he had enough bits of Axminster to fit the front of the car. I didn't want to think of what ideas he'd come up with for the rest of the floor if the Axminster off-cuts weren't enough.

My mam was in the kitchen boil washing my dad's skiddy Y-fronts. She was poking at them with a pair of wooden tongs as they bobbed up and down in a huge pot my gran gave her years ago for making bramble jam but that had never happened. Homemade jam, baking and cooking meals from scratch was only witnessed on telly programmes in our house. My mam worked in a kitchen all day so spent as little time as possible in one when her shift was over. There weren't many things that couldn't be lobbed into the chip pan and my dad had bought her a microwave for her birthday. Some fella had turned up at the bowling club with it under his arm one night and although the microwave didn't ping, my mam was delighted that my dad had bought her something she could use for once. He'd given her a 'Jingle Bells' lacy thong with a tiny bell on the front last Christmas and it went straight under the sink to join the odd socks that she used for dusters. Karen thought we'd got a cat when she heard the bell the first time until she saw our 'waste not, want not' mam cleaning the kitchen window with a duster that had bonus sound effects.

When I went into the living room, there wasn't as much as a squawk of "*Nanu nanu!*" from Karen who was glued to the telly getting bloated on guff with a repeat of Mork and Mindy. I leaned against the fire surround and slipped my dad's packet of Kensitas open. I didn't want to be greedy so I only took two fags. My mam and dad dipped into each other's packets so they wouldn't miss one or two. It would look good to have one lit if I was early and have an extra one for later when I met Stevie. He might even light it for me and pass it from his mouth to mine.

Stevie had agreed to meet me instead of Lorraine; I'd made a detour on the way home from the school to stop at the phone box. Before the pips went, I managed to convince him that Lorraine wanted me to take a message to him. He wasn't keen to meet me and said he wanted to speak to her. I explained that I was in a phone box and the pips were about to go so he had to make a decision quickly. It was his only option; if he wanted to communicate with her, it was through me or he could jog on.

I was even more nervous than the last time we met. I tried using my mam's heated rollers although my hair looked more like a tight Afro than soft ringlets. It wasn't a good start to the night; I had to wash my hair again and nearly missed the bus.

There was a dampness in the air and I could feel my hair frizz up, getting bigger by the second. At this rate, Stevie would mistake me for Hair Bear.

At least I was early enough to light up my cigarette. Me and Lorraine weren't smokers but fags were a vital accessory if you wanted to be taken seriously as an adult. I had toyed with smoking to stop me from snacking although I couldn't afford a forty-a-day habit. Lorraine could eat like a horse but she knew when to stop. She wasn't born with the greedy gene and didn't need a sugar substitute like me so she only smoked when we were at Mystique. And she never needed to buy fags from the machine near the bar; there was always a guy willing to share his packet with her.

It only took a half pint of Snakebite and Lorraine would shimmy up close to a guy smoking, a bawhair away from him and blurt out louder than necessary, 'I could murder a ciggie right now.' And nine times out ten, after a quick swatch at her pumped up cleavage or pert arse cheeks, he'd offer her a fag. I'd seen her take one out of a guy's mouth and add, 'I wanted my lips to be where yours have been.' She smoked all night that time and ended up giving the guy a hand job beside the bins before my dad picked us up. I stuck to stealing the odd fag out of my mam and dad's packets or bought singles from the ice-cream van.

Stevie was already smoking when he arrived outside The Railway. This time I insisted that he took me in for a drink. I tried to nip off the end of the fag the way my dad did but it singed the tips of my fingers and I dropped it in a puddle. Stevie marched on giving me just enough time to scoop it up to dry it out for later.

He ordered a coke for me.

'Can ah have vodka in that?'

'Only if you're paying for it.'

It wasn't the charm I was hoping for although I suppose he wasn't made of money. And it's not as if he was Mr Darcy. This was Denny in 1985, and the modern way was to go halfers, but still. Stevie ordered a pint of lager and led us over to a table round the corner in the shadow of the puggy machine. I took a swig of my coke and wished it was me instead of Stevie who was licking the lager foam from his top lip.

'Did you tell yer pal that ah was sorry?' he asked.

It would've been nice to have a bit of banter between us before we had to mention the reason for meeting up but Stevie was obviously a busy man. And cutting to the chase and being direct is a good quality.

'Aye, but you've really upset her.'

'That's why ah want tae make it up tae her.'

And no doubt he'd want to slip his paw inside her pants while he was at it.

'There's nae need. She'll get over it.'

'You said she had a message for me.'

'Aye, and the message was tae swivel on it.'

I raised my middle finger; instead of unleashing Stevie's outrage he threw his head back laughing and slapped the table with his palm. My glass shuddered and coke spilt over the edge of the table, dribbling on to my white ski pants.

'Ah love a fiery lassie. She'll need tae try harder than that tae put me off.' He downed the rest of his pint. 'Ah've got a message for her. Tell her Stevie Duffy *always* gets what he wants.'

He got out a packet of Benson & Hedges and didn't offer me one; fags are expensive and I couldn't expect him to dish them out willy nilly. I pulled out my single fag, asked for a light and hoped that he'd light mine from his own fag before handing it back to me. I'd stash that fag end in my jewellery box with my other keepsakes. Maybe he didn't hear me because he put his lighter back in his pocket.

I lit up and took a hefty drag, only inhaling a wee bit of the smoke, just enough to keep the smoke in my throat until I closed my mouth. Stevie watched me and I was glad that I managed not to cough. I drew my tongue back towards my throat, keeping it pointing down toward the bottom of my mouth. My mouth made an 'O' shape and I stuck my lips out like I was making an 'oo' sound, imagining I was calling Pamela a stuck up boot.

I pushed a tiny bit of smoke out and made a sighing sound, as if Stevie had shagged me and I was lying flat out in bed. There was a quick burst of smoke as it left my lips. I pushed my tongue forward, still keeping it pointing down, and brought my lower jaw slightly but rapidly up at the same time. I tucked my lips inward very slightly, but rapidly. This put a 'spin' on the smoke, helping the ring stay tight and made it a braw, thick band. Years of practice had been worth it.

'There's nothing attractive aboot a young lassie smoking although ah suppose it helps tae stop you eating.'

I stubbed the fag out on top of the red 'T' of the Tennent's lager ashtray. He looked me up and down, his eyes settling on my thunder thighs before he stood up to go. My white ski pants had a brown stain on them making it look like someone with a bare arse had sat on my knee and left a skid mark behind.

Stevie turned and said, 'Tell yer pal ah like the chase. But she'll never outrun me.' He pushed through a crowd of men slurping at their pints and staring at the darts on the telly. Stevie paused to watch Jocky Wilson haul his beer gut up to the ochie and score a double eighteen.

'See ya Stevie,' I called after him.

'See ya.'

If he liked playing games, all I had to do was make up the rules.

Chapter Ten

The Handicapped Club was cancelled as a mark of respect for Boaby. And there was no-one else to drive the Nut Bus. Rita was waiting with Janine in her wheelchair at the bus stop to tell us the news when we got home from school. It was exciting stuff for Rita and a good excuse for extra prayers, maybe even a DIY Vigil in front of her bedroom altar. Our Lady would be chuffed to get the extra attention.

Boaby had dropped dead in the bookies. Rita was pally with Sarah, Boaby's wife and got all the juicy details when she'd wheeched round to the house with Janine in tow. Rita explained that one look at Janine always helped the bereaved take their mind off their troubles. She called it the power of perspective.

It turned out that Sarah wasn't just counting her blessings; she was counting Boaby's winnings. Sarah confided in Rita that it was a relief that Boaby had at least picked up his bookie winnings before his heart conked out. It was a big win. Sarah planned to use it to add to her collection of Lladro ornaments and pay for a cup of tea and a sandwich at the Bowling Club after the funeral, but it wasn't enough for the funeral guests to sit down to steak pie at the Royal.

Much to Rita's disappointment, Boaby wasn't a Catholic and Sarah was too embarrassed to have his funeral at the Parish Church. Boaby had crashed the Nut Bus into the church wall after joining his pals for a lock in at the Royal one Saturday night. He promised the minister that he'd rebuild it, although after a year, the minister had to get a couple of brickies to do the job and sent Boaby the bill. Sarah wasn't prepared to give the minister the money; the bookie win wasn't that big. And she had her eye on a Lladro of a jester playing an accordion. A clown seemed an appropriate memorial to a knob like Boaby.

The Co-op funeral director saved Sarah's blushes and gave her the idea of a non-religious service. He'd heard that it was called a Humanist ceremony and trendy folk in Glasgow had used the service, but the wacky idea had definitely not travelled out as far as Bonnybridge. Rita said Sarah was just trying to be flash and this was no time to be showing off.

Rita wanted us to go round with her later to see Boaby and keep an eye on Janine while she made cups of tea. Lorraine looked desperate as her mam marched on ahead singing *Ave Maria* and wiping drool off Janine's chin.

'Please Angela, it'll no take long. I mean, it's no as if we can chat to Boaby. I don't want to go either,' said Lorraine.

She knew I'd never let her down so we arranged that I'd go home for my tea and meet them at Boaby's house. Lorraine was panicking about seeing Boaby in his coffin. I calmed her down, I'd seen my grandda's dead body and it was no big deal. My gran decided she fancied a bit of his hair for a locket although she couldn't face going back into the Chapel of Rest, she said the lilies were making her sneeze. Only someone needing a white stick wouldn't be able to see that the flowers were plastic, but there was no point in arguing with my gran. I took her nail scissors in with me to snip off a chunk of the wiry hair; it wasn't easy as they were blunt from years of attacking my gran's toe nails. My grandda used to brag that he still had a full head of hair but he had a bald patch after I'd finished hacking at his napper.

My gran used a dab of his Brylcreem to smooth the lock of hair into a curl. I liked the lemony old-man smell and sneaked the red tub out of my gran's bathroom. I kept it under my bed and rubbed a tiny spot of cream into my hands before I went to bed at night. My grandda liked to say, *"A Little Dab'll Do Ya!"* when he stood in front of the medicine cabinet's mirror. He was right, the tub lasted for months. I should've told gran, and it might've helped her sleep too.

If we'd left it a bit later, we could've avoided the fake weeping and wailing from the hangers-on leaving Boaby's house. A lifetime watching my mam wheedling sympathy from my dad meant I could sniff out sincere tears like a highly-trained beagle. This lot was a bunch of amateurs; they needed lessons from a professional like my mam. We parked Janine in an alcove in the lobby next to the coat stand and stood aside to let the procession of distant relatives and nosey neighbours say their goodbyes to

Sarah. Everyone said Boaby looked at rest. And the new three piece suite was lovely too.

'Thanks,' sobbed Sarah. 'Ah was feart tae tell Boaby that ah'd ordered curtains tae match fae the catalogue. Nae need tae worry noo.'

She stuffed her damp hankie back up the sleeve of her woolly cardi. Living with an eejit like Boaby had taken its toll on Sarah: her hair looked like ripped out knitting and badly needed washing. Sarah's clothes smelt fusty with grief and a snail's trail of snotters crawled up her sleeve. A Doctor Who lookalike was standing beside Sarah wearing a dodgy tweed suit, the only thing missing was a multicoloured stripy scarf. He spoke to Sarah, but she was somewhere else entirely.

The last person in the line-up paused to gently tap Rita's shoulder.

'Who's the fella with Sarah?'

Rita bent down to whisper into her ear. 'That's Graeme Hunter, Mrs Gaffney, he's a Humanist celebrant. And he's doing Boaby's funeral tomorrow at the crematorium.'

Mrs Gaffney nodded politely at Graeme as he shuffled past, saying his goodbyes to the stragglers. He puffed up and stood tall; the pensioner's corkscrew curls shook in disbelief. She muttered loud enough for everyone to hear, 'Have you ever heard anything like it, Rita? Imagine using that fella instead of a *real* priest!'

'I know, it's shocking, not even a minister doing the funeral. Wait until I tell Father O'Donnell,' whispered Rita.

'Ah dinnae ken why they call them humorous funerals, ah bet that Mr. Hunter isnae funny at aw. If Boaby wanted a comedian for the service, Sarah should've got the fella that's the compere at the Bowling Club tae dae a turn.'

'Humorous. You're a comedienne yourself Mrs Gaffney.' Rita's comeback was wasted on the auld woman.

'Can I get you a cuppa tea?' asked Rita, waving a pot under Mrs Gaffney's nose. Rita had on one of those checked overalls the Home Helps wear with a tea towel over her shoulder, as if she was something special.

'No thanks hen, ah cannae abide they cheap teabags Sarah buys.'

I remembered Mrs Gaffney's smug chops from the Handicapped Club, and I'd definitely not forget her grandson's face. Ever since meeting him, I'd been going to sleep with a couple of fingers up my Winnie the Pooh nightshirt and my eyes screwed shut imagining Stevie grinding on top of me. But if Mrs Gaffney remembered me and Lorraine she didn't let on; she was at least sixty odd so her memory was probably gone.

'Have you been in to see Boaby?' asked Rita.

'Aye, ah've said cheerio and God bless, he was a good neighbour. When auld Wullie died and his hoose was lying empty, Boaby was the first tae phone the Cooncil and complain when a Paki family wanted tae move intae the street.'

'And he'll be sorely missed at the Handicapped Club. That man had a heart of gold,' said Rita.

It was tempting to add that a beating heart might have been of more use to him.

'Do you want tae see him?' asked Sarah, shutting the front door behind the Humanist fella and joining us in the lobby. Janine grunted. I once asked Lorraine if her and Janine had a system, one grunt for yes, and two for no. She said I was being stupid, but that wasn't true; in primary five our school trip was to Blair Drummond Safari Park and we'd both seen the tricks the sea lions could do so anything was possible.

Rita nudged us. This wasn't an invitation we could refuse, especially when Sarah had already opened a door off the lobby. The body was laid out in an open coffin on top of the dining room table. Six velour covered dining chairs were lined up along the walls; the fake antiques were as regal as Embassy cigarettes. Sarah stood at Boaby's side and picked at an edge of the table's peeling veneer; we shuffled in and Rita put her arm round her pal's shoulder.

'His dad never made it past fifty either. The Murdochs have poor genes. But you get the body you deserve, eh?'

Sarah had a point. I didn't need my 'O' grade in biology to know that Boaby was a greedy bastard and if he'd cut back on the bevvy, fags and pies he might still be here.

'Too true, the man upstairs makes sure everyone gets their comeuppance. I know better than most,' said Rita, with her eyes on the ceiling as if God himself was looking down to nod in agreement. Lorraine was too busy staring at Boaby to tune into her mam's pity party.

'You need tae stop blaming yourself,' whispered Sarah.

Rita, the martyr, let out one of her well-practised Joan of Arc sighs and Sarah, the widow, comforted her pal. It was no surprise that Lorraine was such an attention seeker after growing up watching Rita in action.

'We've all got our cross to bear.'

Out in the lobby, Janine shrieked. For a minute I wondered if she had heard and understood her mam's comment but that was ridiculous. Bimbo was more switched on. Lorraine went out to investigate and knocked a skanky cat off Janine's lap. The cat shot past her and hid under the coffin. Sarah gave it a sly kick; maybe she wished it was dead too.

I peered into the teak casket and understood why Lorraine had been fascinated by Boaby's waxy face. It had a fake glow and gravity had done its job. His mouth sagged downward into a surreal smile making him look as mad as his Nut Bus passengers. I'd only seen teeth as white on Colgate adverts. The dazzling dentures were at least two sizes too big; even Red Rum couldn't have worn Boaby's teeth.

'He'd be happy that everybody got tae see his new falsers,' said Sarah. 'It's just a shame he never got the chance tae break them in afore the funeral.'

There was an awkward pause; Rita said that the candles were a nice touch. And the room smelt lovely – not even the slightest whiff of embalming fluid. Sarah leaned over the coffin and smoothed out invisible creases on Boaby's polyester pinstripe suit.

'Ah dinnae think many folk recognised him in a suit and with his new teeth.'

'He looks very smart,' said Rita. She didn't mention the make-up smudge on Boaby's shirt collar. The thought of lips going anywhere near Boaby, dead or alive made me itch all over.

Not sure what else to do, me and Lorraine sat on the chairs along the wall, sipping at cups of milky tea Rita had forced on us.

'He hasnae worn his old suit in years and it wouldnae fit over his beer gut. But ah won't have folk talking behind ma back that he wisnae well-turned oot. Ah used one of ma Provvy cheques but ah didnae want tae spend too much. It's no as if he needs tae worry aboot wear and tear.'

The mere mention of Provvy cheques gave me a beamer and Lorraine had the decency not to look in my direction. She was the only one I'd told that my mam used Provvy cheques to kit me and Karen out. She didn't even know what they were until I explained that the Provident gave out loans in the form of cheques that you could use to buy stuff, but only in certain shops.

If you were lucky, the shop had a wee sticker in the window so you knew that they accepted a Provvy cheque although often you got an absolute riddy when you had to ask first before you tried to buy something. At least Galls took a Provvy cheque and I was able to get a pencil skirt as Chelsea Girl was a no-go area. We weren't the only family that needed to get a loan from the Provident: a man called Bill with hairy tarantula fingers went round the scheme on a Friday night collecting the weekly loan payments. Nobody liked to admit they used Provvy cheques and if you ever bumped into Bill anywhere else except your own doorstep, you blanked him.

'Listen, we better get going, Angela looks like she's ready to start greetin',' said Rita.

'Aye, her face is beetroot and ah dinnae want the lassie getting intae a state,' replied Sarah.

Janine was greetin' already. It wasn't the cat or Boaby's fault. And at least she didn't need to use Provvy cheques so I'd no idea what her problem was this time.

'Ah'll get Mrs Gaffney's grandson tae give you a lift. He's in next door with his papa and says ah've just tae chap the back door if ah need him,' said Sarah.

'Ah'll go.'

Lorraine sprang out of her seat like she'd sat on a whoopee cushion. I went to follow her through to the kitchen but Rita asked me to zip up Janine's anorak. The cat was slinking about again so I grabbed a brolly propped up against the coat stand and gave it a good poke in the ribs. Janine laughed at the sight of the cat bolting up the banister, proving she wasn't that daft.

The back door slammed shut. Mrs Gaffney ignored me and

Janine as she walked past us on her way into the dining room to speak to Rita; we were both used to feeling invisible, no wonder I felt a special bond with her.

'Stevie'll take you up the road. He's away tae fill up on petrol,' said Mrs Gaffney.

'Where's Lorraine?' I asked, squinting round the door frame.

'She's keeping Stevie company.'

I'd been made to keep Janine company but she was handicapped. What was Stevie's excuse? And the petrol station was barely a mile away. He didn't need someone to hold his hand or his gear stick. I slid the zip up and down on Janine's anorak, over and over. It was one of many habits she liked; it calmed her down and I could understand why.

In the fifteen minutes it took them to get petrol, I'd zipped up Janine's anorak seventy two times, not counting the four times the teeth stuck in her blouse. I heard her before I saw her, Lorraine's pathetic girly giggle seeping through the letterbox. Janine started clapping her hands and I felt like I was back with the sea lions at Blair Drummond. Rita threw open the front door and made the sign of the cross. Her mam always blessed herself whenever Lorraine arrived back safely from any trip, even the petrol station.

'Stevie's waiting for us,' said Lorraine. She mentioned him by name as if they'd known each other for years, not a matter of minutes. I zipped Janine up one last time and I took it nice and slow, just like my breathing. Rita fussed round Sarah, squeezing the life out of her and telling her to keep her chin up; I wondered which one she meant. Mrs Gaffney handed us our jackets. It was a relief to get outside, away from Boaby's rotting corpse and Sarah's double chinned attempt at putting on a brave face.

'So what happened?' I asked Lorraine as I pushed Janine's wheelchair down the path. Stevie revved up a red Ford Escort with two thick white go-faster stripes running up and over the bonnet and along the roof.

'Tell you later,' replied Lorraine, tilting her head back at Rita fast approaching. Like my mam, Rita had super-human hearing and only the likes of Wolverine seemed to be a match for their sensory powers. I wondered if all mammies were blessed with heightened hearing or if ours had a special gift.

Lorraine jumped in the front beside Stevie, leaving me and her mam bundling Janine into the back seat. I was left to fold up Janine's wheelchair and cram it into the boot. And of course it was me who had to sit between Rita and Janine, straddling the hump in the floor.

The, "tell you later" scenario never materialised and I was dropped at the Co-op at the edge of the scheme. To be fair to Lorraine, she told Stevie to take me right up to my door but I didn't want him parking next to my car, or outside my house. From the road, he'd see the old car tyres my dad had turned inside out, painted white and filled with bedding plants. And there were my mam's precious gnomes. My dad added to her collection at every birthday and the latest one to join the crew was a gnome mooning. She positioned it so that the gnome's bare arse faced away from our house but anyone could see the plastic buttocks from the road and I didn't want that to include Stevie.

I waved them off and Lorraine leaned over to press her palm down on the Escort's horn. It was usually Boaby tooting the Nut Bus horn on a Wednesday night but all I could hear was a Bandeath dug yapping at someone's back door and *Greensleeves* from an ice-cream van touring the bowels of the scheme. Stevie's '**HONK IF YOU'RE HORNY**!' sign in the back window disappeared past the phone box. I was glad that the Co-op was still open; it had been a stressful night and I needed a king-size Mars bar.

By the time I got home, the sugar rush had calmed me down. I opened the front door and Karen landed at my feet.

'Move it will you?'

She was practising forward rolls along the lobby carpet. I hated that carpet and couldn't understand how she could let her face get so close to it. It was jobby brown with fan shaped orange swirls on it that matched the pattern of the Artex on the ceiling. My feet sank into it and not in a good way; it felt furry, probably what a porn star's hairy muff felt like, the same as the bushy ones me and Lorraine had seen in her dad's dirty videos. I dragged my feet through the carpet's thick pile and my toenails snagged on the nylon loops. Never mind a porno film of a lassie dressed like Little Bo Peep and sucking a horse's cock, it should be illegal to sell carpets like ours.

'Ouch!' Karen squealed, rubbing her back after I'd booted her on the way past. It was hardly more than a tap but to hear her moan and crawl on to the bottom step anyone would think I'd belted her with a baseball bat.

'Beat it.'

Karen slunk up the stairs and I paused at the living room door. The telly was always on whether anybody was there or not; it was a no-brainer to guess that my mam would be welded to her chair next to the fire, puffing on a fag and watching the soaps. And there was the tap tappity tap from the kitchen from my dad's latest nail picture so it was safe to swoop on the phone. I dragged the cord round the bathroom door frame and shut the door.

'816233'

'Is Lorraine in Mrs Quinn?'

'Not yet.'

'Oh. Dae you ken when she'll be back?'

'I don't think she'll be too late. Why, is it urgent?'

Urgent for fuck's sake, it wasn't the polis station I was phoning. Rita's life was so dull she probably did kid on she was in an episode of Hill Street Blues.

'Ah just wanted tae talk tae Lorraine aboot a homework question.'

'You'd be better asking her tomorrow on the bus.'

Me needing Lorraine's academic help was as far-fetched as Rita starring as Joyce Davenport and giving Captain Furillo a blow job under his desk. The fact that we weren't in any of each other's classes passed her by too.

'So you think it'll be too late for her tae phone me?'

'Probably, she went for a bag of chips with Mrs Gaffney's grandson.'

'Oh, you mean Stevie Duffy. You're right; God knows when she'll be hame if she's oot with him.'

'What do you mean by that?'

'Just that ah've heard that he's a wide boy but it's probably exaggerated. You ken what folk are like round here for telling stories.'

'Aye, I do indeed.'

Lorraine might be as sharp as a spoon but Rita wasn't and she got the message.

Karen was back in the lobby doing backward rolls this time. I lifted my foot to step over her and press it into the back of her thigh. She groaned loud enough to make my mam appear at the living room door.

'Would you pair give it a break?'

'It's her mam. Ah cannae walk up the lobby withoot her kicking me.'

'Christ almighty Karen, this isnae the place for gymnastics. Noo move it.'

My mam gave Karen a boot up the backside and her mule went flying off. Its fluffy tuft lay next to the skirting board like road kill. I scooped it up and handed it back to her before I had to endure the sight of her tusk-like toe nails straining out of her flesh coloured Pop Sox.

'Thanks hen.'

She shuffled back to the telly telling Karen to go for a bath.

'And mind and soap up yer sweaty oxters,' I said.

I was only trying to help; all those star jumps and roly polies must make her ming but Karen slammed the bathroom door in my face. Upstairs in my room, I tore open one of the emergency packets of Cheesy Wotsits I kept stashed underneath my bed. There was only one choice of album and one track I wanted to hear. I stroked the cover of *Alf* and admired the beauty spot under Alison Moyet's eye. She was a big girl too although it hadn't stopped her becoming a pop star. And she knew how it was for girls like us. I gently placed the needle on to track four, lay face down on my pillow and stayed there until it was teardrop damp, feeling invisible and uncared for.

When Karen shouted on me that the supper was ready, I didn't bother going downstairs, I couldn't face the grease dripping off their chins and put up with their crappy chit chat. Although the smell of deep fried chicken wings was hard to resist and I had to open another packet of Cheesy Wotsits. I listened to Alison over and over again until everyone went to bed and my dad hammered on the bedroom wall that he had work in the morning. And it was a school night.

I must've drifted off; emotional exhaustion is draining. Alison would understand and I bet she'd be surprised that I didn't respond to the call of the chip pan. I wasn't the only one awake. Thump, thump, thump. Karen was bang out of order practising head stands against her bedroom wall at this time of night. I leaned over to chap the wall and there was a girly giggle that made me realise the noise was coming from the other side of the room. My mam and dad's side. The giggle stopped and I had a flashback to my mam telling me the story of the three pigs when I was wee.

"I'll huff and I'll puff and I'll blow your house in!"

She was making the same puffing noises she used to bring my favourite fairy tale to life. I recognised the rhythm too. Tap tappity tap. But it wasn't nails my dad was hammering.

"Let me in, Let me in!"

I wished that I wasn't all grown up now and I was able to squeal like one of the three pigs to drown out her panting and his strangled moans. And on a school night too. It wasn't even my dad's birthday. I was sure I'd puke up cheesy balls.

"Not by the hair of my chinny chin chin."

I took a mouthful of my clammy pillow and curled up the sides of it to cover my ears. I'd run out of emergency Cheesy Wotsits when I needed them most.

Chapter Eleven

My sheet wrapped round me like an Egyptian mummy and I'd barely slept a wink after having to listen to my mam and dad's shagfest. My mam shouted up the stairs that I was going to miss the bus; I told her that I had a migraine and I wasn't going into school. She wasn't bothered as long as I opened my bedroom curtains, she was paranoid the neighbours would call us lazy fenian bastards. Daylight was pishing in the window and yet I somehow managed to nod off and sleep until lunchtime. The added bonus was that sleeping stopped me from eating.

The last week before the holidays was a total waste of time and the teachers didn't want you there either. The only downside was not getting to see Lorraine and find out what happened with her and Stevie. She never took a day off school. Perfect attendance was Lorraine's get-out-of-jail-free card and kept her away from home. I'd probably go in too rather than listen to her mam hoovering and singing hymns. Rita was obsessed with cleaning and waged a war against germs because Janine liked to chew on stuff that she found lying around so everything was wiped with J-cloths soaked in bleach. When I was in primary four, I gave Janine one of Bimbo's rawhide chew sticks. I thought it would stop Janine chewing on the sleeve of her cardigan and she loved its beefy flavour. If she had a tail it would've wagged off and she sucked on the stick until its end was a mushy white blob. I'd done Janine a favour. Rita didn't see it that way; she made me say three hail Marys, skelped my backside and left a burning handprint on my right buttock, something she'd never done to Lorraine.

I wished I had a chew stick now; I was so hungry my stomach thought my throat had been cut. It was only days until we left for Filey and all that I'd managed to lose was three pounds since January. I've got a slow metabolism; I was doomed from the start. But men like women with a bit of meat on their bones; I didn't want to be a stick insect like Little Miss Brown Nose.

It was no use, I couldn't sleep any longer and I got up for a shower. I spent as little time in our bathroom as possible; it was my least favourite room in the house. Lorraine's house had central heating and it was kept on 24/7 for Janine's benefit but all we had was the gas fire in the living room and a wee plug-in heater in each bedroom. The electric heater took the edge off the chill but I still had to wear fingerless gloves to read in bed. My mam claimed the electric heaters made the meter spin faster than a roulette wheel so I was only allowed a blast of it if the temperature was sub-zero. There were often ice fern patterns of frost inside the bedroom windows and the condensation was soaked up with old towels bulging like piss filled nappies on the sills.

The bathroom had no such luxury as heating and it was freezing in the winter. I could cut my breath, square it off, and use the blocks to build an igloo. Even in summer, my mam insisted on keeping the hopper window open for damage limitation. My mam didn't let my dad shit in an enclosed space although it didn't stop him regularly peeing in the wardrobe when he was drunk. She had to throw out a pair of canvas sandals that had a yellow tide mark up the wedge heels. When my dad came home steaming, she'd tie up the wardrobe door handles with a pair of tights. She didn't always remember and we all suffered for it the next day.

There was no denying what went on in this poky hole as the proof of my family's disgusting bathroom habits was everywhere. The carpet was cold and sodden along the side of the bath where my mum and Karen had drip dried. My dad used the showers at work so he was less to blame but his trail was still in evidence. There was a urine singed semi-circle on the carpet round the toilet bowl where he'd aimed and missed. I avoided that patch of carpet and stuck to the central zone. He also pebble-dashed the sink with shavings and there was a permanent spit and splash of caked toothpaste up the sides of the pink sink. I could handle the specks of chin clippings and the white streaks of toothpaste graffiti – it was the bath sponge that really made me boak. The lilac nylon sponge had pubic hairs sprouting from all sides like something Jacques Cousteau would find on the sea bed. Last year in biology class Mr White, or

Chalky as we called him, had shown us a film about sea anemones using their hair to launch a wee harpoon-like thingymabob at organisms that injects a dose of venom into the flesh of their prey. There wasn't a chance that the pubic sponge creature was getting me and I flicked it out of the bath with the hair brush.

Once I was dressed, I gnawed on a Ryvita from the packet my mam had bought me as part of my pre-holiday diet plan. It was impossible to swallow it dry; I spread some peanut butter on top. It left me gasping for a drink of Irn-Bru. There was no denying that Alison Moyet was inspirational but as I couldn't sing for toffee, I wasn't convinced that I'd find it as easy as her to get a shag. I'd hate to admit it but my mam had a point: it was simple, and from now on my new mantra had to be, 'eat less and move more'. But it went against my gran's advice to my mam to "Let Angela be Angela" so I fired up the chip pan and dropped in two eggs. There was nothing to beat a fried egg on a crusty outsider of Mother's Pride with the melted butter running down the sides of your hand. My mam only bought *Flora* margarine, it wasn't the same as the Lurpak butter my gran got in and I'd to visit gran to get a taste of the real thing. Her home-made chips were great on an outsider too. I needed to get out of the house. I'd turned the telly on and it was only the guff that they put on during the day for auld folk, nothing worth watching. And there was bugger all to read. The only book my mam read was the Kays catalogue and all my dad ever read were the racing pages at the back of *The Daily Record.*

There was another option; I'd been working on a painting for my portfolio of the view from my bedroom window and it still needed fine details added. I'd moaned to FUB that I was fed up with the still life arrangements we got made to paint at school. I was never going to cream my pants at the chance of painting an empty wine bottle, a plastic apple or a Doc Martens boot. I wanted to capture real life in my art. The view from my window was of our washing line with my mam's American Tan tights flapping in the wind like kite tails above a beach. There was next door's pigeon doocot made from sheets of corrugated metal like a tower for Rapunzel except there were no princes in our scheme to rescue her or me. Underneath my window was the breeze block coal bunker that I used to lock Karen in. My mam wanted the bunker demolished but my dad avoided the job by claiming it was part of our working class heritage. It did look better than some of the photos of urban sculptures FUB had showed me. I'd asked him how a pile of mangled rusty pipes could be called art. FUB told me I had to learn to look at the colour and texture to make connections to the piece and its setting. And I did; my street was oozing art. All I had to do was look out my window to find my favourite spot for colour and texture, the rhubarb patch. The vampire red veins seeped across the rhubarb's leaves and I imagined them dripping with blood although I was happy to eat the juicy stalks.

My mam used to give us a cup with some sugar in it and me and Lorraine would lick a stick of rhubarb, dip it into the sugar and sook it until our tongues tingled. I loved rhubarb – though only when it was sugary – and I wanted to capture the taste sensation with a painting alive with the magic of the prehistoric looking plant.

But I needed to be in the right mood to paint. FUB explained that it was all about chiaroscuro, the technique of using light and shade and the way I was feeling everything was dark. I couldn't do the rhubarb justice. I needed to get out and talk to someone who actually cared about me more than themselves. And I wouldn't find anyone in this house.

I needed to visit my gran anyway. She'd promised to knit something for the Pro-Life group. It was no problem for her to rattle off a few pairs of bootees and mitts while she was watching the telly. I was planning to go down to Lorraine's with them after she came home from school. Lorraine would be chuffed that we had something to donate to Pamela's collection. Little Miss Brown Nose had posters everywhere about girls up the duff who had no money for baby clothes and stuff. The posters were supposed to make folk feel sympathetic except that I couldn't feel sorry for a lassie that hadn't made her boyfriend wear a rubber Johnny. Stupidity shouldn't be rewarded.

I got my arse in gear and left for my gran's with a couple of Ryvitas topped with peanut butter for the journey. When I turned the corner into my gran's street she was bent over in the middle of the road with her bum in the air. I have never had 'run' as a body setting so the best I could do was to semi-jog to help her. But before I could reach her, she was standing upright and holding a shovel full of orangey fur. It looked like Karen's teddy, Mr Fuzzy Wuzzy, had been a victim of a hit and run and I couldn't work out how her teddy had become road kill outside my gran's front door.

My dad won a bottle of Bells whisky at the gala day tombola although he swapped the bottle with an auld wifie who likes a drink. He wouldn't drink anything orange and my mam had to plead with him to let Karen keep Mr Fuzzy Wuzzy. The teddy and Irn-Bru were the only orange things allowed in our house. My dad liked to rant that he had no use for anything that was, "as orange as King Billy but at least Mr Fuzzy Wuzzy had been stuffed up the arse, unlike the rest of the proddies round here."

Last time I looked, Mr Fuzzy Wuzzy lived on Karen's bed; the closer I got the more I realised that the orange furry shape wasn't the protected teddy, it was a dead fox. The fox's head dangled off the side of the shovel and bobbed up and down in time with my gran's stride.

'What's going on gran?"

'Ah didnae want tae leave her lying there in an oily puddle. She deserves better.'

I followed my gran and the fox up the path to her front door and she tipped the shovel gently on to the path to deposit the dead animal.

'Wait with her will you?' asked my gran.

I couldn't see anyone trying to steal a manky fox and there was no chance of it running away although I stood guard as instructed. Bimbo stuck his nose round the door, sniffed like he'd walked into the boys' toilets at school and shook his head in disgust. There wasn't much we agreed on except that the dog was right: the fox smelt as rancid as the bogs after break time.

My gran reappeared and wiped the fox's face with a yellow duster and combed out the dried mud with a dustpan and brush.

'You'll help me bury her, won't you? Ah could use a hand with the digging.'

I stared at the flecks of muck falling from the fox's coat and shrugged.

'Okay, *fur* enough.'

'It's no funny Angela, show a bit of respect.'

'Sorry gran, ah couldnae resist it. You ken ah'll help but ah'd need something tae eat first.'

'Dinnae worry hen; it takes nae time tae get the chip pan heated up.'

'Magic. And the exercise will burn off the calories.'

'It's a fox you're burying, no a woolly mammoth!'

My gran obviously thought her joke was funnier than mine and was still laughing as she went back inside to get something to ease the fox's pain. I wondered what could make any difference to a flattened fox. The fox had a muddy tyre tread across its neck and I decided to call it Sam. It made me think of Sam Fox, a grubby vixen. My dad brought home *The Sun* from work if any of the other men left the newspaper behind in the canteen. It was always stained with oily handprints and my dad took it with him to the toilet after his tea. My mam made sure she'd ripped out page three so he wouldn't linger over tits that were perkier than hers.

My gran caught up with me in the greenhouse and slid Sam off the shovel on to the trampled earth floor.

'Are you leaving her in here?'

My grandda would've gone ape shit if he'd still been alive. My gran never knew that he kept a .22 air rifle loaded to shoot foxes, rats and pigeons. He'd want to shake the driver's hand for killing the vermin for him. And he definitely wouldn't have allowed Sam anywhere near his precious greenhouse, dead or alive.

'Aye, it's just for a wee while tae keep her warm until we're ready.'

It seemed irrelevant to my gran that the dead fox was already stone-cold as she nipped back outside then returned with the life-sized plastic deer and placed it next to Sam.

'They'll be good company for each other,' she said, patting each animal in turn. I didn't follow my gran back to the house right away; I wanted to take a minute or two inside the muggy warmth of the greenhouse. Before my grandda died, I wasn't allowed inside the greenhouse like the rest of the garden pests he shooed away. It wasn't a real greenhouse with glass and shelves and stuff, it was more of a hand knitted lean-to against the shed. My grandda had made it out of auld wooden pallets and used thick plastic to fill the gaps. I knew now that my grandda wasn't my real grandda and wondered if that's why he didn't want me in his private space. He'd shout at me to keep out and give him peace. Maybe if I'd been his real granddaughter things might have been different.

But my gran always claimed that it wasn't his fault he was so angry with me. It was the cancer that made him so crabbit. And the reason he wouldn't take my gran on holiday was that he couldn't leave the tomatoes. When folk asked where he was going on his summer holiday, he'd answer, "*Hameldaeme*" and some of them took a second or two to work out that it wasn't some exotic location. My gran never found the joke funny. As a typical gadabout, it was easy to understand why my gran hated the greenhouse and was hyper at the thought of going with us to Primrose Valley. I was surprised she didn't take a Stanley knife to the polythene walls and trash it when he died. All that was left of the tomato plant era were the dregs in a bottle of Tomorite and a disembowelled Grow Bag of burst plastic and powdery compost. It would take minutes to wreck it and my gran only needed to give me the nod and I'd start slashing.

The walls of the greenhouse creaked with the breeze from outside and I was cosy as toast with Sam and Bambi and I barely noticed the smell of dead fox anymore. I took down the stool from its hook on the back of the shed's wall. My grandda made it from two planks of interlocking wood and a strip of blue leather; it wouldn't hold my backside these days. I didn't dare to sit on it. I'd been braver when my arse was primary-school small. That's when I'd sneak inside to rub Peter Pointer and Tommy Thumb across the leaves of the tomato plants. I'd lean back against the shed wall, sticking the two fingers up my nostrils and breathe in as deeply as Puff the Magic Dragon. I'd scuff my sandals backwards and forwards but I'd remember to sweep the dusty floor with my hands to cover my tracks before my grandda caught me there.

I often lifted the thermometer off its nail on the door frame but I never chanced touching my grandda's watering can. He always kept the zinc can full to the brim and no matter how thirsty the tomato plants looked I never gave in to them and offered them a drink. Not after the time I pretended to pour it and a trickle of water leaked from the spout. A dark patch appeared on the floor like a blood spatter at a *Cagney and Lacey* crime scene. My mam would've known how to get rid of it except she wasn't there and there was no hiding place. I could've topped the can up from the water butt although he'd know that water was missing from there too. When he found me inside, my grandda pressed his forehead into mine as he ranted at me until it left a dent in the skin. Spits of anger sprayed my cheeks and he warned me that the next time he'd tan my arse. I ran back to the house and my gran dampened a face cloth under the cold tap. She dabbed my forehead until the redness died down and gave me a Kit Kat. But my cheeks still burned.

My grandda wasn't there to shout at me anymore; I was free to splash water all over the place, except that the watering can had been dry for years. I left Bambi and Sam to get to know each other and put the stool back on its hook. I ran my palms over the dirt floor and edged out backwards. Old habits are hard to break.

When I opened the front door I realised my gran was not alone in the house. She was talking to Rab, the new neighbour from upstairs and she hadn't had a chance to light the gas under the chip pan. Rab had conveniently developed a routine of turning up at my gran's at teatime with feeble excuses and hanging around until she offered him a plate of whatever was on the go. It was either Rab or Bimbo who seemed to be eating most of her meals and yet she was still moaning about feeling bloated. My gran might not be eating much but it didn't stop her cooking. Ever since she'd bought the chest freezer with a bingo win, she was obsessed with making extra portions to fill up empty Mackie's ice cream tubs to stock up on soups and stews. She used her bingo dabber pen to label the contents as they weren't always recognisable frozen or defrosted. My gran claimed that at her age, you always had to be prepared for emergencies. Rab had sussed the system and was hoping to intercept Operation Deep Freeze before the lid of the tub was snapped shut on any extra food.

It wasn't just her mince and tatties Rab was after. She'd told me that he was sniffing around her like a Bandeath dug on heat and although he was clean and wasn't a drinker, he was ancient and far too old for her. Rab looked about the same age as her to me but it's hard to put a number on auld folk; once you're old it doesn't make much difference if you're sixty or seventy. Unless you're in your eighties and by that time you're practically dead anyway, there's no need to keep counting birthdays.

'Your gran's stew smelt braw but she says it tastes crap.'

'Well, you can judge for yourself. Ah kept you a bowl of beef and carrot stew with tatties,' replied my gran.

'Thanks, Senga, you're a wee doll. Listen, ah ken ah'm a cheeky bastard, excuse ma French, but is there any pastry tae go with it?'

'Sorry Rab. Ah'm nae good at pastry. Ah keep telling you, ma cooking's rotten. You're lucky that ah've no poisoned you.'

Rab laughed like an asthmatic horse, and I could see why my gran wanted rid of him. She winked at me as she spooned the meal into a tub and sealed the lid shut.

'There you go.' She handed him an ice-cream tub half full with orange and brown shapes in thick gravy with a dod of grey mashed potatoes on the side.

Rab winked at me as he walked past into the lobby.

'Yer gran's no just a pretty face. And it looks like she keeps you well fed too.'

The auld knobhead sauntered off with his tub of mush shouting, "If ah dinnae see you through the week, ah'll see you through the windae!" The front door slammed and my gran burst out laughing.

'The only thing he'll be seeing is the inside of a toilet bowl.'

'Eh?'

My gran's home-made crinkle cut chips were legendary. Granted, some of her meat dishes could be mingin' although I'd still rather eat her cooking than my mam's efforts. And she was good at making pancakes.

'Ah added a special ingredient tae Rab's stew. Ah tried tae warn him that it would taste crap but he wouldnae take ma word for it.'

I followed my gran's eyes down to Bimbo who was sitting at her feet. She tickled him under the chin, lifted his floppy ear and whispered, 'Thanks pal, you're due a ham knuckle fae the butcher's for being such a good boy.'

'Gran, what're you talking aboot?'

I had my fears although I didn't think she'd go as far as adding one of Bimbo's shits to Rab's stew. But it wasn't a wind up. My gran showed me a ripped out page from the *Radio Times* with a skid mark of dog shit covering the list of programmes she'd circled with a red pen. We laughed until my gran needed to change into fresh pants. I turned on the telly while she got changed, not bothering to check the *Radio Times* to see what was on. I shouted through to ask if she'd managed to knit the bootees. A muffled, 'Aye' came back and my gran reappeared, pulling up the zip on her trousers and adjusting her corselet.

'Ah ken you hate exercise but promise yer gran no matter how big you get Angela, you'll make sure yer pelvic floor muscles are strong. You dinnae want tae end up pishing yourself every time you laugh, sneeze or fart. Ah cannae trust ma body and some days ah cannae keep up with the washing.'

It was a good time to change the subject, there was only so much womanly advice I could take in one go.

'Are we eating first, or dae you want me tae start digging the hole for the fox?'

But before my gran could plan Sam's funeral, someone gave the front door a chap then breenged in with a squeal of 'Coo-eee!' At least I knew that it wasn't Rab back for seconds.

'Och, that'll be Jeanette here for her appointment,' said my gran, turning to me then shouting over my shoulder, 'We're in the living room Jeanette. Just come through.'

I guessed it must be one of her clients, although Jeanette sounded too chirpy to be grieving, and I wondered if my gran would let me sit in on the pet psychic reading. I'd asked in the past and she'd said no, it was a matter of the client's privacy. But I was desperate to see my gran in action. My mam had warned me never to dabble with The Other Side but I wanted to know how my gran managed to get folk to stump up tenners by claiming she was communicating with their dead pets.

My gran sat next to Jeanette every week at the bingo. She was one of my gran's oldest pals and they'd known each other since Jesus was a boy. She was wide as she was tall; she plonked herself down on my gran's couch and Bimbo bounced into the air.

'My god, this is no Angela is it?' asked Jeanette, as if I was a cardboard cut-out and not able to speak for myself.

'It must be a year since you've seen her. She's aw grown up noo,' replied my gran.

'Aye, she's a big lassie right enough. She never listened tae her mammy after aw then. You must like yer Irn-Bru too!'

My gran laughed and I nudged her on the elbow.

'Any chance of sharing the joke?' I asked.

'Jeanette still talks aboot the time ah brought you with me tae her hoose when ah was delivering her Avon order.'

My gran had dabbled with being an Avon lady years ago and it was hard to believe that the snaggle-toothed beast that was perched on the couch like a Buddha had ever used any beauty products in her entire life.

'Jeanette asked you if you wanted a drink of ginger and you said, "Naw thanks, ma mammy says that if ah drink Irn-Bru, ah'll get fat like you."'

'It's lucky ah've got a sense of humour,' said Jeanette.

The joke was on me and it seemed rich coming from someone whose backside must have its own postcode. It was tempting to storm out although that would just look childish. And I still wanted to hear my gran doing a reading.

'Has yer pet died Jeanette?' I asked. If she sat on it, the animal would've disappeared up the crack of her arse and been lost forever in Death Valley.

'Aye, ma wee Pussita died a year ago the day.'

I'd have said that it was a lot longer than a year since Jeanette's pussy had any life about it.

'Pussita?'

'She was a shorthaired Bengal cat. She was descended fae the Asian Leopard cat and inherited their stunning spotted markings. Pussita was far mair exotic than the cats you see roaming aboot ma scheme. Ma baby had real class.'

If she was that special, Pussita must've been well pissed off to end up living in Denny. My gran leaned over the coffee table and patted Jeanette's meaty paw.

'Ah'm hoping yer gran can reach her on The Other Side, that's if you're feeling up tae it Senga? Have you been feeling any better this week?'

My gran didn't blink but gave Jeanette the Glare of Death that

Papa Smurf used on first years if he caught sight of them abusing school rules. Her eyes never left Jeanette's and she slowly raised one eyebrow before pasting on a stick-on smile that fooled no one.

'You'll be happy that Pussita kens you're here and is desperate tae speak tae you. Ah'll put the kettle on first, ah'm sure Pussita'll no mind waiting a wee bit longer.'

My gran got to her feet and I followed her through to the kitchen.

'Can ah stay for the reading gran?'

'Naw hen, ah've telt you that it's no fair on the client. They need their privacy.'

'Mibbae Jeanette wouldnae mind?'

'Ah'm no asking her, it's too personal. You've nae idea how upset folk get and ah wouldnae want her hauding back because she's embarrassed.'

'But…'

'Ah'm no falling oot with you aboot this. Noo, c'mon, and ah'll get the knitting for yer unborn baby group afore you go.'

'It's called the Pro-life group. And what aboot me digging the grave? And making me chips?'

'Ah'm sorry hen, ah cannae let Jeanette doon. Ah'll make you chips the next time you're here. And dinnae worry aboot the fox, ah'll ask Rab tae give me a hand with the digging afore he gets the runs.'

My gran disappeared and I was left with Bimbo sniffing round the plate of biscuits my gran had laid out for Jeanette. I slipped Bimbo a custard cream, ate one and stuffed two in my pocket; we were doing Jeanette a favour.

I swallowed quickly as my gran returned with a Woolworths bag.

'There you go, three pairs of mittens, matching bootees and a hat.'

Jeanette appeared in the doorway, she must've sniffed out the biscuits.

'Who's had a wean?' asked Jeanette.

'Oh, it's no anybody we ken, it's for a charity that needs knitting for lassies that get intae trouble,' explained my gran.

'Hmm, times have changed. In ma day there was a way of

dealing with that!'

'Wheesht Jeanette, see you and yer big mooth. Things are different nowadays.'

'No that different, ah still get a chap at the door looking for me tae...'

'Ah'm sure Angela disnae want tae hear that kind of talk.'

My gran was wrong. It actually sounded like Jeanette might have something interesting to say although it didn't seem like I was going to get a chance to hear it. I untied the knot in the bag to find the different sized bootees, mittens and hat inside. They were all knitted with brown wool.

'Should baby clothes no be done in pastel colours gran?'

'Usually, aye but ah needed tae use the Nigger broon wool up.'

'And these unmarried mothers are no in a position tae be choosy are they?' added Jeanette. My gran shook her head and I didn't know if it was at me or Jeanette.

'Tae be honest gran, ah cannae see anybody dressing their new-born in that colour.'

'Dinnae worry, ah'm sure the Holy Joes will find some wean that needs them. They can always use them for the black babies in Africa and they'll no show up the dirt fae the mud huts. They're the perfect colour.'

'But it's too hot in Africa tae wear woolly stuff.'

'Ah bet it gets cauld at night though. Isa at the bingo has been tae Benidorm and she needed tae put on a cardigan once the sun went doon,' said Jeanette as she waddled off with a couple of custard creams in her meaty fist.

It was hard to argue with my gran's logic although I couldn't see Pamela wanting to hand out jobby brown baby knitwear, charity or not. And I didn't expect Lorraine to be pleased either.

'Thanks anyway gran. Ah'll get going and take them roond tae Lorraine's. Ah'm sure she'll be grateful.'

My gran wasn't the only one in the family who could dish out bullshit, dogshit or any other type of shit that was easier than telling the truth. And Jeanette was about to lap up utter garbage like it was warm milk, or a glass of Irn-Bru.

'Here, take a couple of biscuits tae keep you going. And say cheerio tae Jeanette afore you go,' said my gran.

I stuck my head round the living room door, 'Bye Jeanette, say hiya tae Pussita fae me.'

'Ah will.'

'Yer poor pussy, gone but no forgotten. Rest in peace Pussita.'

'Thanks hen.'

Jeanette's fat neck meant she wasn't able to turn around quick enough to see the smirk on my face and realise that I wasn't the biggest joke in the room anymore.

Chapter Twelve

On my way to meet Lorraine after school, I stuffed the carrier bag of knitting under a chip wrapper in a bin mounted on the pole at the bus stop. I was early and it gave me too much time to think about the baby clothes my gran had knitted. She was a serial skip raker and was known to check bins when she was out walking Bimbo. But this one was far enough away from her house for her not to find the bag. And yet I couldn't leave the hand knitting inside the grotty bin. The baby clothes were mingin' and yet my gran made them and she made them to keep me happy. Checking that no one was around, I stuck my hand in, rummaged deep for the plastic bag and pulled it out with a sheet of newspaper from the chip wrapper still stuck to it. The grease from the chips had smeared down the side and some brown sauce had leaked inside on to the knitting, but at least the stains didn't show up on the brown wool. I wiped the bag with a used hankie as I heard the rattle of a ladder against bricks.

'Ah might've guessed a Fenian would be raking the bins.'

It was Iain Kilpatrick, our local window cleaner and the biggest bigot in Bonnybridge, which was why he was known as Sash. I hadn't noticed him up the ladder doing the windows of the doctor's house. Only folk in Spam Valley could afford to pay for somebody else to do their dirty work. But my mam kept threatening to get one round after she fell out the living room window when she slipped on the wet tiled sill. She was flat out on the grass with her hand still inside one of my dad's old sports socks that she used to buff up the glass. She'd squealed *"Help!"* except that none of us could move for laughing; my gran would have pished herself for sure.

Sash wouldn't have cleaned our windows even if he got paid. The bampot was the staunchest blue nose in the scheme and had a union jack flying from a scaffolding pole he'd bolted on to the side of his shed. Sash even got a mob of his Mason pals round and they tore up the grass in his back garden to lay slabs so there was nothing green at his house.

The Rangers bus that left each Saturday from the Royal to take the Proddies to Ibrox or their away games was run by Sash and he lead the singing, long before they boarded the bus. His musical talent wasn't limited to his local pub; he played in a Falkirk flute band and practised with his windows wide open in the build-up to The Glorious Twelfth. I saw him on an Orange walk when me and Lorraine took Janine out for a walk in her wheelchair; he was wearing a bowler hat instead of his woolly bunnet with the Rangers Football Club logo, and he looked an even bigger wanker than usual. Janine started clapping along with the booming drum and Lorraine pointed out the baton twirler who was undeniably cute but he was still one of them. I grabbed the handles of the wheelchair and steered it away. Janine liked any music, she didn't know the difference between a hateful drumbeat and her nursery rhymes sing-along cassette, but there was no excuse for Lorraine. It was a case of them and us and she should know better than to encourage the Proddy bastards.

I hated Sash. I wanted to stab the ugly prick in the eye and watch him suffer. Before Christmas, he'd spat on the back of my school blazer and I didn't realise until I got to school. After umpteen cries of, "Eew", "Yuck" and "Fuckin' boggin", I asked Lorraine why the slagging was worse than usual. She looked me up and down and it was only when she made me spin round that she saw the thick sticky blob. By the looks of it, Sash must've ripped his throat to produce the splatter across my blazer.

I balled up the sheet of newspaper and tossed it back in the bin. A woman with Captain Caveman eyebrows walked past and Sash had the benefit of an audience.

'Ah caught the fuckin' tattie muncher lickin' a chip poke. Dirty bastards, the lot of them, eh?'

Sash flicked his damp cloth as if it was a bull whip, making the muscles in his forearm distort his red hand of Ulster tattoo although I could still read the words, '*Remember the Boyne, 1690.*'

Captain Caveman's sister tutted and I gave Sash the finger as I crossed the road. He had a bucket full of water and he was known to throw it at any Catholics who walked past him. I was taking no chances and for once I was happier to wait for Lorraine at her house, even if her mam was singing, *Just a Closer Walk with Thee.*

But the school bus drove by on my way there and when I turned back, there were only a couple of wee first years getting a soaking from Sash. Lorraine was nowhere to be seen. I quickened my pace, as much as I could, to get to her house. It was my job to look out for her and more often these days I wasn't with her. She'd never dog school without me and she'd have phoned me in the morning to let me know if she was staying off sick. There were unwritten rules; I shouldn't need to tell her to check in with me.

I scoured the pavement for fag ends. It took my mind off where Lorraine could be and why she wasn't keeping me in the picture. I found two under a hedge beside the Bowling Club entrance and screwed them inside the lion's nostrils at the end of the driveway. One of these days I vowed to light them too and watch the plastic lions smoke.

'She's not in,' said Rita when she opened the front door.

'Can ah wait?'

'There's no point. She's gone to Pamela's for her tea and won't be back til the last bus.'

'Oh.'

'Aye and she knows it's Janine's bath night and I need a hand. But does she think about anybody else but herself? Not on your Nelly.'

It was one of the first times I could remember agreeing with the guff that Rita spouted. And she did look tired with more bags than the Co-op under eyes.

'And before you know it, she'll be off living the high life and leaving me and Janine in the lurch.'

Rita made Filey sound as glamorous as Tenerife; I suppose the Primrose Valley campsite was a damn sight better than changing shitty pants. She swiped a hankie from up her sleeve, dipped it into the font of Holy Water on the pine clad porch wall and dabbed at the streak of shite on Janine's inner thigh.

'I don't mind her enjoying herself but I don't like her getting the bus late at night on her own. I hope *He* keeps her safe.'

There was no water left for Rita to bless herself and she had to make do with a dry Sign of the Cross. Her right hand touched her forehead, 'In the name of the Father', then the middle of her heaving bust, 'and of the Son,' and her left shoulder, 'and of the Holy Spirit', finishing on her right shoulder, 'Amen.'

Rita gave me the *Look*, the one all mammies get taught at ante-natal classes, the one that doesn't need to go along with a script, it said quite clearly, *"Don't argue with me"*, and it was all done with the eyebrows. I joined in with the blessing for the sake of Rita's sanity. She literally had enough shit on her hands without worrying about my lack of faith too. But if I thought blessings worked, I'd have prayed for me and Lorraine to be best pals, back to the way it was meant to be.

'In the name of the Father, and of the Son, and of the Holy Spirit. Amen.' Rita gave me a jagged smile. I added, 'Ah guarantee God'll make sure Lorraine gets hame okay,' and this seemed enough to please her.

'Aye, *He* looks after his own. I'll tell Lorraine you came round.'

'Thanks Mrs Quinn.'

Janine shuffled down the lobby on her backside with bulging pull-up pants leaking at the sides. It was a disgrace, she should still be wearing giant baby nappies but Rita insisted that Janine wore pull-up pants like a big girl, as if that made her 'normal' somehow. Janine squealed and snorted at the sight of me standing in the doorway; at least someone was glad to see me.

'You'd better come in; I can't take any more tears from Janine.'

'Dae you want me tae give you a hand Mrs Quinn?'

I didn't stay long, not with the sing-along nursery rhymes droning on in the background, but I waited long enough to pour in the *Matey* bubble bath and hand Janine her bath toys. I made Janine gurgle with giggles when I used the bubbles to make myself a foamy beard but once they dissolved I couldn't compete with a set of plastic beakers that could be endlessly filled, tipped out and refilled and I was free to go. The time spent attaching bubbles to my chin hadn't been wasted: I'd had an idea and the phone box was only round the corner.

I knew Stevie's phone number off by heart. Lorraine thought I was mega clever, she was fooled as easily as Janine but it wasn't that I had a supersized brain; it was much simpler than that. The reason I did so well in exams was that I had a brilliant memory.

That's all there was to it. I could regurgitate facts as easily as spewing up after having cross country running for P.E. The term Cross Country always made me snigger considering all we did was run in a loop around the scheme beside the school, not run through woodland and up hills. The school was in the middle of Bainsford, a scummy part of Falkirk which could be classed as bandit country, but jogging through it still didn't justify the label Cross Country; calling it 'street running' was more accurate. I wasn't supposed to think at school, I was there to learn facts. Nothing else. Once I memorised the facts, all I had to do was write them back down. There was nothing clever about it: numbers or words puked up on to paper got me good grades, thinking for myself didn't.

I fished a ten pence piece out of my pocket and dialed Stevie's phone number. I kept my foot in the door frame to let some air into the phone box and the reek of pish out into the street. Before I picked up the black mouthpiece, I pulled my sleeve down over my hand. Three Orange scumbags from Bankier Street were squeezed inside the box the other night and they were taking it in turns to stick the mouthpiece inside their boxers and rub it against their cocks. Typical Proddy behaviour.

I pressed the coin in the slot and swallowed my heartbeat.

'Hullo?'

The male voice sounded like he had a clothes peg at the end of his nose and I'd no idea if it was Stevie's dad or he had brothers. I was relieved that it wasn't his mam that answered, they all learn the *Look* and how to ask awkward questions like 'Who's calling?' and dads don't give a stuff.

'Can ah speak tae Stevie please?'

'Naw, he's no in.'

The phone went dead and the only company I had was the dial tone and a waft of sour pish.

Lorraine was out. Stevie was out. The only one I had to check on now was Pamela. I didn't know her number and I'd never had any reason to phone her at home but I needed to find out if Lorraine was with her or not.

My mam was on the phone when I got in. Someone must've called her as she never used the phone before six o'clock unless it was to dial 999. She was feart to run up her phone bill so my mam and my gran took turns to phone each other every day just after the big hand moved past the hour. At one minute past six the phone rang in either house. Every night.

I helped myself to a couple of slices of *Mothers Pride* from the bread bin and made a piece on strawberry jam while I waited for my mam to get off the phone. My dad wasn't in so that meant he must be doing overtime and our tea would be later. She'd already browned some mince and peeled tatties which was a shame as I still had a craving for chips. Karen was out the back practising her gymnastics. She'd rigged up two wooden clothes poles tied together for a beam and had balanced it between the wall and the coal bunker. She always stuck her tongue out when she was concentrating and inch by inch, she side-stepped along it. I banged the kitchen window and Karen went arse over tit. I was still howling with laughter when she burst in the back door and slapped me on the back. I grabbed her arm and gave her a Chinese burn and she let out a scream. My mam was sure to hear, but it was worth the risk to keep fighting. I pulled Karen's head under my chin, dug it into her skull and tried to seal her geggie shut.

'Christ almighty, ah go on the phone for two minutes and you pair act like a couple of weans!' My mam was bealing. She flipped over nothing and my dad was convinced she had permanent PMT. It was moany-faced women like my mam that gave my sex a bad name.

Karen rubbed her head and dived in first, 'It was her mam, she made me fall off ma beam.'

'You better no be using ma clothes poles again! Noo get oot there and put everything back where it should be. Ma heart's roasted with all this gymnastics carry on.'

I shoved Karen out the back door, 'Ah ken mam, and she's off her heid kiddin' herself on that she can win medals. She's no even got a real leotard.'

When our primary school started doing the B.A.G.A. awards the PTA. held a jumble sale and cake 'n' candy to raise money for the leotards. Karen had pranced about on her tiptoes in her navy blue leotard, throwing her head back and stretching her arms in the air to show off her set of circular B.A.G.A. patches that my mam had sewn on up the sides. My mam loved to brag that her lassie was the only one at St Philomena's with a B.A.G.A. 1 award that could do the splits and put her feet behind her head. Anyone listening to my mam's boasting might believe that Karen was actually talented.

But when the "*gifted gymnast*" asked for a new leotard for high school, it was as embarrassing as watching Karen get bucked off the Pommel horse on to her arse. There was nowhere in Falkirk that sold leotards in Olga Korbut sizes or took a Provvy cheque. My mam bought a vest top instead and told Karen that she'd sew it into a pair of gym pants; the ungrateful wee bitch started greetin' and begged my mam not to get her sewing machine out. My mam soon shut her up saying that Olga didn't let the lack of a leotard stand in her way of a gold medal and Karen didn't question the source of my mam's inside knowledge of Russian gymnasts.

I crept out to the lobby and flicked through the phone book to find Little Miss Brown Nose's number. I dragged the phone cord into the bathroom and shut the door on it. We had a party line and those selfish fuckers along the road were never off the phone; I was back and forth like a bloody yo-yo waiting to get a clear dial tone.

'Can ah speak tae Pamela please?'

'Who's calling?'

'It's Angela, a pal fae school.'

'Hang on a minute.'

Her mam shouted, 'It's for you, Pammy.'

Pammy? Her mam sounded as much of a fanny as her daughter. Little Miss Brown Nose came on the line and I cranked up my bullshit dial to maximum.

'Hi Angela. Is everything okay?'

I knew she'd be freaked out by me phoning her at home.

'Aye, ah'm fine noo but ah was off school with a migraine.'

'Oh, poor you.'

'Aye, it was a real bummer and ah never got the chance tae speak tae you about ma donation for the Pro-life group, so ah just thought ah'd phone you.'

'Great, what've you got?'

'Some knitting ma gran did. Ah should've given it tae Lorraine tae take tae yours tonight.'

'Lorraine's not here. She was going out with Stevie.'

'So she was, she told me but ah totally forgot.'

'She never stopped talking about him all day. And they'd been to the photo booth at the bus station. They make such a cute couple.'

'Aye, a perfect match. Listen, ah'll need tae go Pamela, ma mum's waiting tae use the phone.'

'Okay, ciao for now.'

'Bye Pamela.'

Ciao for now you smug cow. I felt like a total eejit. Me and Lorraine were supposed to be best pals, and it was the second time in one day that I'd lost my appetite. I raked in the press under the stairs for my shoes. The stink of sweaty feet nearly knocked me on my back; it was almost as bad as the communal changing room in *What Every Woman Wants*. We were all guilty of kicking our shoes off straight into the lobby press so it had a permanent mound of shoes, boots, slippers, wellies and sandals all mixed up and mingin'. At the top of the heap there was an auld pair of gutties with holes in the canvas where Karen's toes poked through and the sole's rubbery edge was frayed. My mam finally caved in and got Karen real trainers for her birthday but she still made her wear them for P.E. and they honked to high heaven. Karen slunk past me on her way up the stairs and I managed to elbow her in the ribs as I opened the living room door.

'Ah'll have ma tea when ah come back fae Lorraine's,' I called to my mam from the door.

'Ah dinnae ken what you two lassies have tae talk aboot day and night. Ah'll keep yer plate in the oven. But dinnae be too late or the mince'll dry up.'

I preferred it like that anyway; there was less fat sliding about the plate if it'd been in the oven for a few hours and it tasted better between a couple of slices of Mother's Pride.

'Mind and save me an onion,' I shouted as I slammed the front door behind me. I avoided looking inside my car as I walked past the lay-by. My dad had started fitting the carpet and he was struggling with cutting round the gear stick. Once it had door-to-door carpets, he'd promised to take me to the industrial estate to practise clutch control and all that stuff. I'd rather pull my teeth out through my nose than be spotted in that rust bucket and I'd make sure that it was pitch black before I was free for a lesson.

I hoped that Lorraine would be back before the street lights came on. That was our childhood curfew and even now I still liked to be home before folk took their Bandeath dugs out for a final piss before bed. And there was less chance of bumping into Paedo Pete the scheme's resident perv. I wasn't convinced that he'd actually touched up any weans but we'd all grown up feart of him because his baw face had been burnt when he was wee and his shiny skin was as red as a baboon's arse.

Paedo Pete wasn't the only ugly mug I had to avoid, the place was crawling with Proddy faces I didn't want to catch sight of. The wee ones were annoying wee shites who'd squirt water at me out of their mammy's empty washing up bottles and sing

"Cathy cats,
Eat the rats,
Two for tuppence ha'penny,
The polis came,
Took their name,
And gave them back a ha'penny."
And I'd reply with,
"Proddy dogs,
Eat the frogs,
Two for tuppence ha'penny,
The polis came,
Took their name,
And gave them back a ha'penny."

They'd scatter and run back home for a refill of tap water. But there were at least three gangs of teenage Proddy boys who roamed Bankier Street and these ones weren't as easily fobbed off. They chanted instead of singing.

"UDA,
All the way,
Fuck the Pope,
And the IRA!"

They knew I wore a bottle green blazer and yellow school shirt so I had to body swerve these thugs, unless I wanted spat on, or shouted at before they decided whether they could be bothered to batter me or not. It was still a bit early for a Fenian bashing although it depended on how bored they were and I wasn't taking any chances. I took the long road down to Lorraine's to skirt round the Paki shop and avoid the gangs. They were lured like moths to the light from the corner shop and huddled under a lamppost or lit bonfires on the waste ground at the edge of the scheme.

I wouldn't ever pass one of their bonfires again. It was years ago now but I can still remember the smell.

I didn't know their names; that's why I knew to avoid them: they weren't from St Paddy's and they stayed in Bankier Street. But I had to walk past them to get to my gran's house.

The Proddy boys had gathered auld bits of wood and rubbish to make a bonfire and one of them was twisting strips of a *Daily Record* and stuffing them underneath the pile the others had made. A wee one came running up to the gang with an armful of dried grass and scattered it round the base. They were experts in building bonfires and I kept my head down as I got nearer, hoping that they'd be too busy to notice me. I remembered the story of Saint Lawrence, the poor bugger who was tied on top of an iron grill and had his flesh roasted a wee bit at a time over a slow fire. I hoped that they didn't get told stories like that at the Proddy school.

The urge to run was as strong as my need to pee but it would've been obvious that I was feart from them. I walked fast with my head down and wished I'd worn a tracksuit so I could kid on I was jogging. My bottle green blazer was like a neon sign that lit up to say, *"Batter the fenian!"*

I'm sure the gang could smell a Catholic from ten feet away because as I got closer they looked up from their smoldering mini bonfire. I felt the first match land on my head. The smell of a Catholic was burning hair.

It didn't matter that I was older now; I wasn't taking any chances that they'd turn on me again. The longer route was worth the extra walk and the exercise would count towards my pre-holiday fitness regime. I didn't want to go to Lorraine's front door again and wait with Rita and Janine but I needed to see Lorraine. It felt like one of Cagney and Lacey's stakeouts except I was working on the case alone. I keeked round the fence to check that Rita wasn't at the window and ran up the driveway, giving the lions a pat on the head. I squeezed along the side of her dad's garage and sat on a pile of bricks. From this vantage point, I couldn't miss seeing Lorraine come home and then I'd pounce, there would be no getting away from me. She needed to face facts; Lorraine shouldn't get involved with Stevie Duffy. He was wrong for her and it was my job to put things right.

Chapter Thirteen

My arse had gone numb. It felt like I was sitting on a pin head and I didn't want to risk stretching out in case the bricks toppled and Rita's nosey neighbours spotted me hiding at the side of the garage. The sleekit cat from next door was prowling about but I had a ready supply of chuckies at my feet to fire at it. And I should have brought some food; if I didn't eat regularly, there was a danger of me fainting. That's why I made sure I ate little and often. The thought of me conked out and lying spread-eagled across the driveway might at least get Lorraine to notice me again. She seemed to have forgotten that it was me who'd given her the chance of a free holiday. Well, technically it was my mam and dad except that she wouldn't be going to Primrose Valley if I hadn't asked them if Lorraine could take Karen's place.

It was hard to admit Karen had beaten me for once; the cheeky wee besom was going on a school trip to Créteil, just outside Paris. For some unknown reason the French town was twinned with Falkirk. The Council was helping to fund an exchange trip to the French school to do a week of gymnastics in their new sports hall and a group would come to Falkirk next year to visit the new Mariner Centre. The wave machine and the fake palm trees were impressive by Falkirk standards, a big improvement on the auld Victorian baths where the swimmers were as ancient as the building and a verruca and a swimming cap covered in plastic petals were compulsory accessories. There was no argument that the Mariner Centre was a hell of a lot better but it wasn't worth crossing the Channel for. The problem wasn't the fancy pool; it was who and what was in it. The new pool was hoaching with pasty natives who bobbed up and down in the mechanical waves as they peed in the water, played dodge the corn plaster and shared their athlete's foot. And if the life-guard brought out the giant ladle there was crowd hysteria when a floating jobby could cause more panic than *Jaws*.

It made me laugh to think of the sophisticated French folk arriving in Falkirk, or Fawkurt as it was pronounced by those born in the town and known as Bairns. They'd find that the local cuisine was a plate of chips at the York café and the most popular wine drunk here was Buckfast. There was going to be some well pissed off froggies when they worked out that there was more culture in a yogurt factory than Falkirk.

Our school raised money with a cake and candy, non-uniform day and a sponsored fancy dress fun run. I made Karen's witch costume out of black bin bags and a pointy hat from a sheet of sugar paper I stole from the art department. And because I'm the arty one, I blacked out her front tooth, shaded under her eyes and drew a mole on her chin with eyeliner. I even managed to stick a few hairs from a doll's eyelashes to the mole, a proper little witch.

My mam and dad were supposed to help towards the total cost of sending Karen's gang of saddos on the sports trip. Karen got a couple of pounds every other week to take into the P.E. department and got it marked up on her savings card. My mam was mortified when Papa Smurf sent a letter saying that the school would make up the difference if Karen didn't manage to save enough to cover the balance. But my dad had a brain-wave when he realised that the school would pay the shortfall; the savings card was torn up and my mam said Karen could get a leotard with the extra money.

Last year I'd asked my mam and dad if I could go on the school trip that Sister Patricia was organising to Rome. There was to be a week of sightseeing and Sister Patricia was bouncing off the walls at the thought of being in the audience when Pope John Paul said Mass on Good Friday. I wanted to have my photo taken with a 'gladiator' outside the Coliseum, eat ice-cream in St Peter's Square and throw a coin in the Trevi fountain. I wanted it all. I knew my mam and dad couldn't afford the trip but I begged them to let me go. They said it was too dear and it would mean that the family couldn't go on a summer holiday. I didn't care, I had to go. And Lorrraine said she would only go if I did. The pressure was enormous.

My mam argued that I'd already seen the Pope when he came to Scotland two years ago so I didn't need to go to Rome. As if a day out to a park on the south side of Glasgow, sitting on a tartan picnic rug, eating eggs that had been boiled until they turned blue and drinking warm Robinsons Barley Water was comparable to a week in Italy's capital city. The Charismaddies strummed their guitars and sang hymns on the bus all the way from Bonnybridge to Bellahouston and we had to walk miles to find where our parish was to camp out. All this effort to catch a glimpse of the Papa's napper as he drove by in his Popemobile while we stood there sweating like a priest in the boys' changing room. We were packed into an enclosure with a quarter of a million other Catholic numpties waving wee yellow flags. And we could've watched the whole thing on the telly sitting on the couch with a packet of *Crispy Bacon Frazzles*.

My mam couldn't understand that the Italian trip wasn't about seeing the Pope again; it was about seeing somewhere else. Rome. Italy. Europe. Abroad. Anywhere that wasn't Falkirk. The Pope didn't need to be there too.

But the next best thing to a foreign trip was Filey. With Karen doing 'la gymnastique' with her silly wee pals there was a spare bunk bed and my mam and dad said Lorraine could come to Primrose Valley. For all the money they had, Lorraine never went on holiday as Rita claimed it was too much hassle. If Janine's routine altered, she freaked out and it was even more embarrassing than usual although if I had their cash, I'd have put up with folk gawking. When I told her she could come with us, Lorraine was hyper. Every night of the holiday would feel like a Saturday night and we'd planned what we were going to wear and all the stuff we could do during the day. I told her about the cracking beach, Aladdin's Cave, the amusement arcade and the Beachcomber café's amazing all-day breakfast, but we'd hardly talked about the holiday since Stevie Duffy came on the scene.

When Stevie's car pulled up, I eased myself forward to keek out from my hidey hole. They were so busy snogging the faces off each other they wouldn't notice a two tonne elephant in the drive, far less a sliver of my phizog poking out from the side of the garage. The street lights were on and I could see the outline of Stevie's hand snake inside Lorraine's school blouse and over her tits. Her eyes were shut and no doubt she was doing the moaning noises we'd practised for years.

Thanks to Lorraine's dad, we'd been coached on the art of faking an orgasm. We found Tam's stash of porn underneath a Fair Isle jumper at the bottom of his wardrobe when we were in first year and home alone one Saturday afternoon. Lorraine's mam and dad were out with Janine at her Special School's Fun Day and we didn't want to go, it was worse than the Handicapped Club. The place was full of folk slavering down their fronts and trying to cuddle you, and that was just the staff. I hadn't set foot in the hell-hole since the Special School's nativity play when the shepherd shat his pants and starting pulling his trousers down on stage. Mary started greetin' and Joseph battered her with the baby Jesus doll. It was carnage and I vowed never to return even though there was a tombola stall and free hot dogs at the Fun Day. Tam and Rita let us stay without a babysitter as long as we promised not to answer the phone or the front door. I'd overheard my mam blabbing on the phone to my gran that Tam got pirate copies of videos when he worked abroad. Me and Lorraine got bored; there was only horse racing on the telly and we found the dirty films when we played hide and seek. We tilted the venetian blinds shut and watched *Rambone*, *Saturday Night Beaver* and *Throbbin' Hood* with eyes bulging, our jaws on the carpet and gasps of horror although none of the films were as scary as an afternoon at the Special School Fun Day.

From my look-out post, I was impressed Lorraine hadn't forgotten the moves we'd learnt from her dad's videos. But she was still a virgin. And just like the porn stars we'd watched any time we got the chance, it was all an act with her. A cock-tease was the best way to describe her. A hand job was the furthest she went and she'd had a finger or two slipped inside her but that was all. She got away with leading on the boys from school or the losers we met at Mystique, but I couldn't imagine a guy like Stevie would settle for a quick grope. He'd want a real woman to satisfy him, not Lorraine pouting and pawing at him. She'd no idea that men want curves; only dogs like bones.

Finally Lorraine lost suction on Stevie's face and the car door opened although she couldn't resist leaning back in for one last peck. The exhaust on Stevie's car roared as he raced through the gears but it wasn't as loud as his stereo. I expected Rita at the door any minute except that Lorraine was quick off the mark and darted inside leaving me wanting to upchuck. The sight of them snogging put me right off my mince and tatties. At this rate, I'd be fading away to a shadow.

When she'd jumped out of Stevie's car it was tough resisting the urge to pounce out from my den and grab Lorraine by the throat. She needed to realise that Stevie wasn't the right guy for her. Unless you were blind or a lezzie, any female could see why she'd want touched up by him, but that wasn't the point. He'd done time in Polmont and you didn't get sent to borstal for robbing sweets from the Pick 'n' Mix at Woolies.

The sight of his hands up Lorraine's top was enough to get me fired up. I had to talk sense into her and I knew I couldn't wait any longer. We'd be on holiday soon, I had to sort this out and there was only one way to put her off him. Stevie was smart; he'd fob her off with lies and she was too stupid to see through him like I could.

It was time to take action but I didn't want to look like a demented stalker always two steps behind Lorraine. I chewed the skin off my top lip and waited a few minutes. Just as if I was out on a casual stroll, I chapped Lorraine's door. Rita appeared with a yellow duster in one hand and a statue of the Sacred Heart in another.

'Is Lorraine in?'

'She's just back but I think she's away for a shower.'

I'd need a shower too if Stevie'd had his mitts on my nipples. If bad boys weren't sexy, James Dean would never have been famous.

'Can ah wait in her room?' I already had my foot in the door like the Jehovah's Witness who toured round our scheme every summer. And every year my dad handed back the leaflet and told God's salesman that he'd seen the light, only the bulb blew. My dad's patter worked on moving the Jehovah Witness along the terrace but Rita wasn't getting rid of me that easily.

'You can speak to her tomorrow at school.'

'It's just that ah really need tae see her tonight aboot oor homework.'

'You'd think the teachers wouldn't bother giving out

homework so close to the holidays.'

'Ah ken but if you're staying on for a sixth year, you need tae start the course work before the summer.'

'But I was talking to your mam at the Co-op and she thought you'd be leaving.'

'Naw, ah'm going tae Art School.'

'To be an artist? Well good for you. And what's your mam got to say about that?'

'Excuse ma language Mrs Quinn but ma mam said that the only artists she kens are piss artists.'

Rita's lips were as puckered as a cat's arse although she couldn't help the hint of a smile creep across her face.

'That's very true. But it's still nice to see a lassie from the scheme trying to better their self. I'll say a prayer to St Jude for you.'

Rita had a selective memory; she must've prayed to the patron saint of tarts to make her escape from the scheme. At least I'd have a career based on more than a talent for spreading my legs. I wasn't one of St Jude's hopeless cases.

'Do you ken what Saint Nicholas is famous for Mrs Quinn?'

'Aye, he's known as Santa Claus too. You'll need to get up earlier to catch me out Angela. I know my saints.'

'Very true, but ah thought you'd ken that he's also the patron saint of prostitutes.'

That wiped the smirk off her smug mug.

'St Nicholas saved a dad having tae sell his three daughters intae prostitution. He threw red sacks of gold doon the man's chimney. Every day's a school day, eh Mrs Quinn?'

The bathroom door lock clicked open and Lorraine appeared with a towel wrapped around her head. I couldn't tell if the cloud of steam was coming out of the bathroom or Rita's ears.

'Angela needs help with her homework.'

Lorraine raised a single eyebrow and I raised both mine in reply. We'd always been able to communicate without words so she knew it was a code for, *"I need to speak to you"* and yet she didn't reply with anything like, *"No problem, come in and we'll go over the homework."* Instead, her eyebrow never moved, just like her lips.

'So could you go over that essay question with me?'

My head tipped to the side and all that was missing was a cheeky wink but still Lorraine didn't play along. With consistently dire grades, there was no doubt that Lorraine would be resitting Higher English next year and the fact that her daughter had bombed the exam must've slipped under Rita's radar. Lorraine was staying on for a sixth year because she could, not because she was academic and only because she didn't know what else to do. Another year of fannying about at school would buy Lorraine more time before the bubble burst and she had to face the real world.

'And we need tae plan oor holiday wardrobe…'

'I'm kinda tired; we can talk it over tomorrow,' said Lorraine.

If she'd given me a bikini wax, it wouldn't have hurt as much. Lorraine was on target to fail Higher English but she wasn't that thick, she knew that it wasn't homework I wanted to talk about and that I never went into school for the last couple of 'help-the-teacher-tidy-up-the-classroom' days.

'And I need to dry my hair,' added Lorraine. Her hint for me to piss off was feeble.

'You look a bit washed out yourself Angela, better get an early night too,' added Rita.

The fact that I hadn't had my tea might explain my Casper the Friendly Ghost face, that and the shock of realising that Lorraine wasn't acting like a best pal at all. She should've been desperate to replay what went on between her and Stevie. There was no denying that she'd knocked me back and I wasn't prepared to beg for a juicy titbit.

'Ah suppose ah'd better get going. See you at the bus stop then?'

'Aye, okay. See you.'

Lorraine tucked a strand of damp hair that hung like a rat's tail down the side of her face. I'd sat through hours of her hairdryer whirring while Lorraine chatted, shaking her mane with her head upside down. Drying her hair wasn't a reason; it was an excuse, and a pathetic one.

As much as I could eat a scabby horse between two mattresses, I was in no hurry to go home. I picked up one of the plastic lions and walked off with it. A dog walker with a face as squashed as her pug gave me a second look, but the folk from the estate were all too polite to give me any hassle unless it was their garden ornament I'd knocked. But a couple of streets later, in the bowels of the scheme, every nosey bastard would ask, "And where the fuck dae you think you're going with Leo?" In the safety of Spam Valley I was left to take Leo wherever I pleased and we needed a seat. It was only later when I stood up that I realised that the bench was wet. I left Leo sitting in a bus shelter at the edge of the scheme; it was too dangerous for lions to go any further. My jacket barely covered my backside; I pulled it down in the hope that no Proddies were out on the prowl, they'd notice the dark stain on my jeans, assume I'd pissed myself, call me a smelly fenian and find it even funnier than usual. But if I was really unlucky, I might bump into someone from my year at school and quicker than you could say a decade of the Rosary, my old nickname would be dug up from the depths of my second year at St Paddy's.

Three years ago, the dark stain was blood on my school skirt. It happened in my French class when I felt the bubble of wetness between my legs. I should've kept a note of the last time I took my period but I'd lost count of the days and I couldn't predict when it would come anyway. The gap was sometimes three weeks and sometimes five. Having my period was enough to make me hate being a woman and it was easy to see why my mam referred to it as the curse. The only good thing about having my monthlies was when Mr Harris took us for P.E.; one wee moan about hellish cramps gave him a pure riddy and I was allowed to stay in the changing rooms with a magazine.

There was no bonus for taking my period in the French class; I knew without standing up that my blazer would never hide the damp patch on the back of my skirt. My insides felt like they'd been swirling round in my mam's twin tub and I was cacking myself thinking about how I could get out of the room without anyone seeing the stain. I never made it to the corridor before I heard, *"Please Miss, what's French for she's got the painters in?"* For the next two years, I was called Auntie Flo by the boys in my year and it only died down when my weight crept up and there was a better repertoire of names to slag me off for the crime of being big boned.

I still got fat themed insults at school and ones starting with

"Fenian…" walking though the scheme but I made it home without any new shout outs of Pissy Pants or Auntie Flo. The night wasn't a complete disaster and I wondered if Leo had made it home safely too.

My mam's stumpy toes poked out of her fluffy mules and were gobbled up by the shag pile rug in front of the fire. She was watching some crappy costume drama on telly and she didn't even look up when I came in. I had to admire the way she managed to tip the ash off the end of her fag straight into the crystal ashtray on the hearth without taking her eyes off the screen. She scored a bull's-eye every time. If there was an ash flicking competition my mam was world class.

'Stick the kettle on will you hen? And give yer dad a chap and see if he wants a cuppa.'

My dad was in his shed at the top of the garden that he'd made from auld wooden pallets he brought home from his work. He'd warned me and Karen since we were wee that it was a no-go zone for us because there were a lot of dangerous tools kept inside. But the only tool that was used in there was powered by my dad's pile of nudie books. I'd found his porn mags and a crispy sports sock when I was looking for a hammer to nail the heel of my Tucker boot back on. The heel fell off again when I stepped off the bus and I had to hobble along the road. I was spotted by a Proddy who shouted after me, "*Hoi, Quasimodo, where're yer bells, ya ugly Fenian?*" When I was a safe distance away, I came back with, "*Is yer hunchback fae sucking yer ain dick? Ya dirty Proddy bastard!*" And then I ran like I was a gold winner in the Olympic One-Legged Race.

I chapped the door of dad's shed and pressed me ear close to the rough wood but not close enough to get a skelf as an earring. It was hard to prove that the heavy breathing on the other side of the door wasn't my dad sawing energetically; I tried not to picture anything else.

'Ah'm making tea dad, dae you want a cup?'

'Aye, ah'm just coming.'

Just coming seemed about spot on when a final grunt seeped through the wooden buffer.

'Okay, it'll be ready in a couple of minutes.'

I hot-footed it down the path and slammed the back door on

an image of my dad wanking. I couldn't bear to see if his face was flushed and confirm my fear. I dropped four teabags into the stainless steel pot and turned the gas down to a peep to let it stew until it was builder's tea, the way they both liked it.

My meal was waiting for me on the kitchen bunker. The congealed mince was sweating under cling film and I quickly slid the dollop on to buttered bread before my dad appeared.

I loaded the McEwan's beer tray my dad acquired from the bowling club with four slices of Mother's Pride oozing mince, a cup of syrupy tea and two Wagon Wheels. My energy levels were low after a long tiring day so I added a packet of Pickled Onion Monster Munch to the tray and sneaked upstairs to my bedroom.

I'd never planned to go into school on the last week of term except that it looked like the only way I could get to speak to Lorraine. I mopped up the mince juice with the crusts and kicked at the pile of dirty clothes; at least the mess covered the crowns on the carpet. There was a school blouse in the heap somewhere but it would need a hefty spray of Impulse to freshen it up under the oxters. I fished out the blouse, sniffed it and shook the can of deodorant. I wanted to give Lorraine a good shake too. Something needed to be done and I wasn't going to hold back any longer.

Chapter Fourteen

I psyched myself up by dancing in my bedroom to *Dead or Alive* playing on Radio Luxembourg.

I was in full spinning mode, pirouetting round my bed when my mam burst in to my room.

'For Christ sake, it sounds like a bull elephant charging aboot up here.'

'Ah was just dancing.'

'You call that dancing? You've made the big light in the living room come loose. Yer dad'll crack up. You ken he disnae like touching electrics after the kettle incident.'

My dad had agreed to shorten the lead on the new kettle but accidentally cut the cable of the iron my mam was using on my school blouse. The electric shock sent his pair of pliers sky-high and they smashed a Pyrex dish of stew on landing. I had to go to school with a blouse that looked like I'd slept in it and with a splash of gravy across the sleeve. There were still skiddy-brown spatters up the wall above the fridge freezer where my mam couldn't reach with her J-cloth.

'Well enough of yer dancing afore the ceiling comes doon.' My mam made speech marks by curling her fingers when she said 'dancing' as her attempt to be sarcastic. It didn't suit her.

'And what's with the uniform? Are you going intae school?'

'Well done Colombo. Ah need tae go in tae see FUB about ma portfolio ideas.'

'You're no still going on aboot Art School are you? Ah thought we'd agreed that if you got the chance of a job you'd take it.'

'You and dad agreed, no me…'

'Listen, ah've no got time for aw this. Some of us have got real jobs tae go tae.'

'Aye, you better get going mam; you dinnae want tae be late and put yer career at risk.'

I made wee bunny ears with my fingers when I said 'career'

to see how she liked being ridiculed. My gesture worked; my mam tutted and slammed the door behind her leaving me in peace to shimmy to *Move Closer.* And if I shut my eyes, I was Phyllis Nelson on tour in Bonnybridge singing for a private audience and there was no competition to keep Stevie's attention this time.

If I didn't get my arse in gear, I'd miss the bus and the chance to speak to Lorraine. I'd no time for breakfast so I grabbed a couple of dry Weetabix to eat on the bus and took the last Wagon Wheel in the packet to keep me going until the interval.

Lorraine wasn't at the bus stop which was not unusual. She was hardly ever early and the normal routine was for me to let the school bus go past until she arrived then we'd get a later service bus. I'd never leave her behind. But Mrs Shaw, the auld hag that crossed the primary school weans was always waving her lollipop stick at me and telling me that I should get on the school bus without Lorraine, as if I'd listen to a wifie with whiskers at the end of her chin. It was obvious that she'd never had a best pal to keep her right.

The school bus pulled up and the mob shuffled aboard, dragging their knuckles with joy at the prospect of another day incarcerated in St Paddy's. I gave Karen's ankle a swift kick as she passed me, necessary to keep her on red alert and the only way to train a dumb animal. Lynne, her geeky pal, saw Karen flinch and gave me her best attempt at a look of disgust which was laughable from a silly wee cow that I didn't care about. I knew Karen's pals called me Evil Edna behind my back. I could understand their logic and was actually impressed that they believed that I was as bad as the wicked TV witch. Evil Edna was always crabbit and spent her days ripping the piss out of the sad bastards living in Doyley Woods. But you only needed to walk past Sash to know that there were worse things to be called than Evil Edna. Karen and Lynne sat in the front seats opposite the driver and as the bus pulled away I gave the pair of fannies a two-fingered salute.

Lorraine was in a car, Stevie's car and it drove straight past me through a puddle that sprayed my legs with dirty water. I wasn't sure if she waved but I was sure that the car didn't stop and that I was soaked.

'Ah telt you no tae wait on her.' Mrs Shaw might as well have cackled "*mwahahaha!*" and waved the pole she used as a broomstick to get home. 'And noo look at the state of you. Quick, take the registration number doon, you can report him for that.'

If there was a boulder within reach it would be difficult to decide where to lob it – at Stevie's car or Mrs Shaw's face. I walked off in the direction of the next bus stop further along the road before I was tempted and any damage was done. The service bus would be another ten minutes, which would give me plenty of time to plan exactly what to say to Lorraine when I finally got to school. I made it into Falkirk by a bawhair and I was just about to go inside when I noticed that Lorraine was still in Stevie's car.

Just as I was about to knock on the passenger window, I felt a tap on my shoulder. I turned to see Pamela's dad drive off in a silver Ford Sierra, leaving Little Miss Brown Nose on the pavement behind me waving Daddykins bye bye. Pamela came from a broken home and I pictured her house lying in bits all over the street. But it didn't seem to have caused her any damage. She was a spoiled bitch and Lorraine said it was because her dad had shagged a woman who worked in his office and his guilt was costing him a fortune.

The most I knew about divorce was from Tammy Wynette's *D.I.V.O.R.C.E.* song on my dad's eight track cassette player. He had another version of the song too. It was part of Billy Connolly's stand-up routine and the Big Yin sang it once on *Top of the Pops*. I remember that they bleeped out the sweary words but I could easily guess them. My dad mastered the song as his party piece, calling himself the Wee Yin; he was only five foot three. But although he was short, he was the biggest man I've ever known, a giant in my eyes. He didn't need a flash car with a spoiler and a red silk hankie poking out the breast pocket of a suit to play the big guy. For the first time, I actually felt sorry for Pamela; she didn't have the best of everything after all.

'Hiya Angela, have you brought in the baby clothes?'

'Ah'm sorry Pamela, ah completely forgot. Ah've a lot on ma mind.'

'No worries honey, you can always bring them to next week's

group meeting. Lorraine's offered to have it at her house.'

'Really? That cannae be right; we'll be away on holiday next week.'

'Oh, I'm sure she said next Tuesday was good for her. And she never mentioned going anywhere special.'

'She must've got the dates mixed up.'

The bell rang and the stragglers who'd slept in for their alarm clock drifted toward the main door.

'Ah suppose we better go in,' I said.

'Yeah, I'll catch you up; I just need a word with Lorraine.'

Little Miss Brown Nose trotted off to meet Lorraine as she poured herself out of Stevie's car. He leaned over to blow her a kiss and I gave him my best fuck-you stare but Stevie didn't meet my eye. The effort wasn't wasted, it was all good practice.

I hung back and pretended to rummage in my bag for some crucial piece of kit needed for a day's hard graft at school. The bag was made from the top half of a pair of faded denim jeans and I'd got it down the market to use on holiday. I knew Lorraine would love it and I'd bought her one as a surprise for her birthday in July. The plan was to watch her go green-eyed when I whipped my bag out at Primrose Valley knowing that she'd be chuffed to bits when I gave her the same bag a few weeks later. But I couldn't wait for the holiday to show off my new bag.

It was hard to look engrossed by the contents of a bag when all that was inside was a slim-line biro my gran got free with a diary from the bingo, my purse, a spare pair of tights, two tampons, Wagon Wheels and a packet of Salt 'n' Shake crisps. Ever since primary one, I'd had crisps for my play piece every schoolday; they were as routine as wearing my school tie, only more satisfying.

My head was half inside my bag and I was still able to see that Lorraine took Pamela's arm and hooked it round hers. I swung the jeans bag high up on the arm to wear it over one shoulder but neither of them caught me in action. The bag hung limp and I double-stepped to catch up with them.

'Lorraine can ah speak tae you? In private…'

'It's okay; you can say anything you need to in front of Pamela. She's in the Circle of Trust too.'

'Aw, thanks babe that means a lot,' said Pamela.

Little Miss Brown Nose lunged forward and wrapped her arms around Lorraine to give her a full-blown bear hug; anyone would think she was a member of the Handicapped Club the way she squeezed the life out of my best pal.

I could be described as a lot of things but glaikit wasn't one of them and yet I had no idea that Lorraine had a Circle of Trust and I was in it, along with Pamela. For all I knew there could be hunners of lassies in her Circle of Trust and I was just one of many. It made no sense; me and Lorraine were a double act. We were like shoes, earrings, or gloves which are no use to man or beast without a complete pair.

'So what's up?' asked Lorraine.

'It's nothing, we can talk later. We better get in, the bell's gone.'

'Angela, dinnae give me that look.'

The fact that my insides were as clenched as a fist meant the Glare of Death was unavoidable.

'If it's about Stevie no stopping for you at the bus stop then that's my fault. By the time I saw you he said it was too late for him to pull in.'

The smell of bullshit nearly knocked me out. I'd perched on the dyke along from Mrs Shaw's spot for the last five years waiting on the bus. Same time, same place every school morning.

'It's fine, dinnae worry. Ah'm sure you were distracted.'

'Who wouldn't be sitting next to Stevie?' chipped in Pamela with a wink and a face that was begging to be skelped until it was red raw.

'Tell me aboot it, ah ken how sexy he is when he wants it. Nae wonder you drove by me,' I said.

'What're you on about? You don't even know him,' said Lorraine.

Pamela tightened her grip on Lorraine as if she was holding a precious porcelain doll. But the cracks were showing already and there was nothing that Little Miss Brown Nose could do to repair them.

'And neither dae you. Ah *telt* you ah needed tae speak tae you in private,' I said, trying hard not to get rattled.

In the distance, Mr Harris was herding the smokers out of

their den behind the P.E. hall and it was only a matter of minutes before he did a final sweep of the grounds and we'd be ordered inside.

'We need to go, c'mon Lorraine or we'll be late for reggie class,' said Pamela.

Lorraine didn't respond to the tug Pamela gave her arm and I could feel her eyes drill right through me, searching for the truth.

'Are you winding me up?' asked Lorraine.

'Naw.'

Her eyes dug another inch deeper into my skull.

'You ken ah wouldnae dae anything tae hurt you but there's something that ah need tae tell you.'

'What's the big drama?'

'Ah cannae tell you here, if we're quick, we could get away before Mr Harris sees us.'

I walked off knowing that Lorraine was sure to follow me and left her to shake off Little Miss Brown Nose. If we went over the canal bridge, we could take the shortcut through the Bleachy and be up the town in minutes. It was too early for the tossers who worked in the industrial units to be cut loose for a fag break so we'd be able to cut through the maze of buildings without being asked to get our tits out or called dirty Fenians.

'So, where are we going?' asked Lorraine.

'How aboot the York café? Ah missed ma breakfast.'

'Fine, but it's a bit early for chips even for you.'

'It's never too early for chips but they dinnae start frying till lunchtime. Although they dae a smashing roll on sausage in the mornings so we're sorted.'

'I might've guessed you'd know the deep fat fryer's hours. Is that all you ever think about?'

'You ken me too well.'

My smile was as fake as my old Sindy doll's and for once I didn't bite back at her for having a go at me. She was wrong though; I didn't just think about food, I thought about how to make sure no harm came to her. That's what true best pals do for each other but I managed to keep my gob shut; I'd have plenty to say once I had her captive in the café.

We walked side by side in silence and avoided talking again

until we'd reached the bottom end of the High Street. The legendary York café was our favourite café in the town and every Fawkurt bairn had grown up queuing for a cone and getting taken for a fish tea as a treat. Chips at the York café were chunky hand-cut ones, more like roast tatties than the French fries from the Wimpy bar and the fish tea came with white bread and butter, a cup of tea or glass of Irn-Bru for the weans. The décor hadn't changed since my gran was a wee lassie and some of the waitresses looked like they'd served at the Last Supper. It wasn't trendy but that's the way folk liked it, with its ointment pink wicker furniture, mirrored walls and a kid-on Tudor style shop front. It was a local landmark and there was always a queue to get a table on a Saturday. And the best bit about having our heart-to-heart at the café was that Lorraine's cousin Frances was a waitress. Lorraine would never cause a scene in front of someone who spread gossip swifter than the *Falkirk Herald.* She'd never actually explained how Frances was a second cousin and I didn't care whether she was a blood relation or not, she always knocked something off our bill and gave us bigger portions.

'Hiya, lassies, no at school the day?' asked Frances as we passed the ice-cream counter at the front door. She patted her stiff hairdo as if she feared it might move; I'd seen her at the gala day on the waltzer and even when the guy spun her car round it didn't budge. Frances bragged that she used a can-a-day of Elnett and I worried that she'd get too close to the deep fat fryer and become a human fireball. She dyed her hair so black it looked blue and it was shaped like a crash helmet. All that was missing was a strap under her chin.

'We're on study leave,' I replied, without worrying that Frances would know that the exams had finished weeks ago. If she was clever, she wouldn't have worked in the York café since she was sixteen.

'It must be great tae be brainy,' said Frances.

'I'm not so sure about that, some folk are too smart for their own good,' replied Lorraine.

I wondered how far Lorraine's eyes were able to drill into my skull before hitting bone.

'Exactamondo! You dinnae want a brain that big or you'll end up with a Tefal Heid.'

Frances spoke with the authority of a medical professor, with a PhD in Utter Bollocks.

'So what can ah get you lassies?'

'It's a shame it's too early for chips. Ah'll go for a roll on sausage and Irn-Bru thanks,' I said.

'Chips are the last thing you should be ordering,' replied Frances.

There was no danger of Frances ever telling Fawkurt customers to *"Have a nice day!"* The waitresses serving the Fonz in the *Happy Days* diner needn't fear for their jobs; customer care was yet to arrive in Fawkurt, if it ever did.

'The chips in here are actually very healthy,' I told Frances.

'York café chips, healthy? Ah've heard it aw noo.'

'Aye, 'cause the larger the surface area tae volume, the mair fat a chip will absorb. So they're much healthier than chips fae the Wimpy.'

'You're a Tefal Heid after aw!' Frances tapped my forehead. 'At least you've got something going for you. But ah bet ma wee cousin prefers tae have the looks. Take it fae me, men are feart fae brainy women.'

'Is that right? Are you talking fae experience Frances?'

Frances winked at Lorraine, 'Naw, ah rely on ma looks like Lorraine. But she'll still be yer pal. Every lassie wants a fat bridesmaid standing next tae her in her wedding photies.'

'There's no need to worry about that happening,' said Lorraine.

I couldn't make my mind up if Lorraine meant that I'd never be a fat bridesmaid or that she'd never get married. My head was mince listening to them.

'Is it a roll on sausage for you tae Lorraine?'

'I'm fine Frances, just an Irn-Bru for me please.'

'Looking after yer figure?'

'Aye and I'm feeling a wee bit sick.'

'Wheesht, you'll be the talk of the toun if folk hear you complaining of morning sickness.' Frances made the sign of the cross. 'It would kill yer mammy if she thought you were up the duff. And she's got enough on her plate with yer wee sister.'

'Dinnae worry Frances, I'm no preggers or slack like some lassies I know.'

Without meeting her eye, I knew that Lorraine was drilling down again but I blanked her and chewed on a candy-striped straw I'd swiped from the ice-cream counter. Frances followed Lorraine's gaze.

'Holy mother of God, ah better get yer order in, yer pal will be eating the cutlery next.'

'I wouldnae put it past her,' said Lorraine.

I bit the end off the straw and swallowed it. The ragged plastic scratched my throat but I ripped another chunk off and spat it out into the tin ashtray. Frances didn't notice and was already bounding down the staircase to the kitchen. Lorraine looked at the blob of spittle and red and white tube as if I'd dropped my knickers, climbed up and shat on the table.

'So what's such a big deal that we needed to dog school to talk?'

I leaned forward and reached my hand over the table to pat her arm. The cheesy moves seemed to work for Little Miss Brown Nose when she was being all pally wally. Lorraine ignored it and crossed her arms; my hand slunk back into my pocket like a Flasher's limp cock without an audience.

'Ah didnae want tae have tae tell you this, but there's something you need tae ken aboot Stevie.'

'What's all this guff about you knowing what he's like?'

'It's the truth. Ah'd never lie tae you.'

'The truth is you cannae get a guy like Stevie.'

'Ah wouldnae want one like him.'

'If it's about his reputation then don't waste your time. I know the real Stevie; he's told me how he ended up in Polmont.'

'So you dinnae care that he got sent tae borstal?'

'He explained it all. It was a case of mistaken identity. I know everything.'

'Lorraine, he hasnae telt you *everything*.'

'And what would you know that I don't?'

'That he tried tae shag me the night you were at Stacey's party.'

Frances was back with our cans of Irn-Bru and plonked them on the table; Lorraine's eyes never left mine.

'There you go lassies. Ah'll be up with yer roll on sausage in a minute so there's nae need tae chew on the table leg.'

Frances's comedy routine was never going to get her a turn,

even at the Bowling Club. And Lorraine kept silent when I opened my can of Irn-Bru and the *fzzzt* caused an orange mist to spray her face. I offered her a paper napkin to wipe it but it hung in the air like a white flag of surrender.

'Say something will you?' Lorraine ignored my demand and stared beyond me into the mirrored wall which reflected two best friends. I balled up the napkin and tossed it on to the table. Lorraine grabbed it and tried to dab under her eyes. It was too late; a single tear spilled over and dropped on to the glass-topped table. I rubbed it away with my sleeve. I was sure it left a smear.

'Why?' asked Lorraine. I took a hefty glug of Irn-Bru, fought the urge to burp and swallowed back a gassy bubble.

'Ah dinnae ken why *he* did it.'

'No, why are you telling me lies again? I'm sick of you trying to spoil everything.'

'You've got it aw wrong.'

'Really?'

'Think aboot it. Who dae you believe loves you mair? Me, who's known you since you were four or a guy you met five minutes ago and has done time in a borstal?'

Lorraine was saved from answering by Frances banging the tray down on top of the table. My roll on sausage smelt amazing and I was desperate to tear right into it but I gave Lorraine the respect she deserved.

'Enjoy. But try no tae swallow it in one go!' said Frances, laughing again at her own crappy joke as she swanned off to clear a nearby table.

'Ah'm sorry Lorraine; ah needed tae tell you for yer own good. Ah cannae sit back and watch you get hurt.'

She hoovered up a dribble of watery snot and dabbed again at her eyes.

'I thought you went to The Railway that night with some guy you met at work?'

'Ah did. It was Stevie. Ah knew he'd upset you at the Club and ah wanted tae tell him what an arsehole he was but he kept buying me drinks. And you ken how greedy ah am if there's free vodka on offer.'

'I know at least that bit's true.'

'Ah'm telling the truth aboot everything. Dae you want tae

hear the rest?'

Lorraine nodded. My roll on sausage was going cold and I didn't dare to take a bite, not while she looked so intense, and talking with my mouth full might spoil the impact.

'Well, the next thing ah knew he was helping me oot of The Railway and intae his car. He parked roond the back of the Taj Mahal and he stuck his hand doon ma leggings. Ah telt him that ah wisnae interested but he forced his fingers inside me and unzipped his jeans. Ah ken you hated him and ah'd never go with him so ah bit his arm and he got the message.'

'So that was it? Because I know you've let plenty of guys feel you up at the back of Mystique.'

'Naw, there's worse than that. The drink must've hit me and ah had a blackoot 'cause the next thing ah knew he had it inside me.'

'It? You mean you lost your virginity to Stevie?'

'Christ almighty Lorraine! Keep yer voice doon will you?'

Lorraine leaned forward and whispered through gritted teeth.

'I thought we'd agreed to wait until it was someone we loved? And it was your idea to make a pact.'

It was true that on and off for the last two years we'd talked about when to lose our 'V' plates. Lorraine could've lost hers umpteen times but I made her promise to wait until she'd met the ONE and then we'd discuss whether the lucky guy deserved the once-in-a-lifetime prize. We'd debated a couple of candidates and I'd convinced her that none of them were worthy of being able to brag that they were the first to fuck Lorraine. So far, I hadn't needed her advice on potential cherry poppers for me.

Playing the waiting game suited us fine; she was as scared as me. Her mam drummed into Lorraine that women should be proud to keep their virginity as long as possible. She told Lorraine that men are ashamed of being virgins and want to lose their virginity as fast as they can. And to always remember that only sluts give it away. It seemed a joke now that it was Rita who preached to her daughter.

'Ah didnae forget oor pact. Ah suppose 'cause he slipped it in withoot me realising that disnae really count, does it?' I said.

'A shag is a shag. But if you're saying he forced you, that's not on, it's rape. And you've been robbed of your virginity!'

'You sound like yer mam, *"It's a woman's greatest gift."* Ah was pissed and agreed tae get intae his car; ah cannae go tae the polis and say he raped me, they'd never believe me.'

'But with Stevie's record I bet he'd get carted straight back to Polmont if you could convince the polis.'

'Mibbae.'

'And he told me he got bullied for having a name like Duffy. Wait until the others find out he's a Catholic and a rapist. They'll shag him and then use their sharpened toothbrushes to slash him to ribbons.'

'You watch too much telly Lorraine.'

'If he's a rapist he needs to pay for it!'

'You're right but ah cannae face reporting him. And it would be even worse telling ma mam and dad. Look ah just want tae forget it ever happened, he never battered me and he drove me hame. Ah'm sorry ah had tae tell you, but you need tae ken what kinda guy you're involved with.'

My roll on sausage had gone cold and the juicy fat that had oozed out the sides had turned white on my plate. My tasty brunch was spoiled and my tears came quicker than Lorraine's but turning on the waterworks helped to reinforce my lies.

'Telling you hasnae been easy, trust me.'

'Why didn't you say something before now?'

'Because ah've hardly seen you. Ah tried tae tell you but you're always with Pamela these days and you didnae seem interested in me anymore.'

A light switched on somewhere inside Lorraine's brain and her eyes bulged.

'I feel terrible for you. Now I know why Stevie wouldn't stop for you at the bus stop. I told him I needed to talk to you about our holiday but he just kept driving.'

'What aboot oor holiday? You're still coming with us?'

Cold or not, I sank my teeth into the roll on sausage; I always eat when I'm stressed so I knew Lorraine wouldn't take offence.

'Too damn right. I need to get away from this shithole.'

'Me and you both after what ah've been through,' I said through mouthfuls.

'I'm sorry Angela. I should've been there for you.'

This time it was Lorraine patting my arm and I didn't pull

away from her.

'Everything awright lassies?' asked Frances as she passed with a tray of dirty teacups, scooping up my empty can of Irn-Bru.

'Never better. We're off on holiday on Saturday,' I replied.

'Lucky for some. Well you ken what they say, if you cannae be good, be careful!'

'We're no stupid Frances. And we ken how tae look after each other,' I shouted after her and winked at Lorraine.

She smiled back at me; the bond had stretched until I thought it might snap but it had pinged back in place as strong as ever.

'C'mon, let's get out of here. We've got a holiday to plan.'

'Good idea, ah'll just get Frances tae put ma roll in a takeaway bag.'

Chapter Fifteen

Since my sobbing session at the café, all the way to the bus stop Lorraine kept asking me if I was alright and was I sure that I didn't want to do anything official about Stevie. I told her not to be daft, it was her that was hurt the most and she wasn't to worry about me.

'Like Frances pointed oot, ah'm a big girl!'

She didn't laugh and had been quiet for a while now. The bus shelter was empty apart from an ugly wean that his mam had leashed with leather reins. Tugging and growling like a caged beast, the only cute thing about the toddler was the lamb painted on the front of his harness. The bus wasn't due for another few minutes and I struggled to get a bit of banter going with Lorraine; it could be a long wait.

'Hey, Lorraine,' I whispered, 'isn't that wee boy the spitting image of Plug fae the Beano?'

'Aye, only a face his mammy could love.'

At last, Lorraine cracked a smirk wide open. The wean looked us up and down and I was determined to get Lorraine laughing. I made my scariest face at Plug whilst his mammy was rummaging in a bag full of messages. Wee Plug grabbed his mammy's skirt and looked like he was ready to start greetin'. The mammy turned round to look at us and we gave her and the wean our best joy-to-the-world smiles, one that would make Sister Patricia proud of her Catholic pupils.

'What a wee cutie,' I said, rubbing Plug's wisp of hair.

'Wee shite mair like, he's no mine anyway. Ah'm just watching him for ma sister.'

'So you wouldnae want to keep him then?' asked Lorraine.

'Ah wouldnae keep him if ah won him in a raffle.'

The bus pulled up; Plug got yanked up the steps by his auntie. We shuffled behind them and managed to squeeze out one last Scary Mary face at the wean. This included my tongue flicking in and out and had Plug greetin' before he got dumped on the seat beside his torn-faced auntie.

'See what ah mean? Ah telt you he was a greetin' faced wee shite,' said Plug's auntie as we passed her on our way up to the back seat. Plug's auntie got a dirty look from a man with skin like the surface of the moon, who stared at her as if she could press an off switch and the wean's howling would stop.

'So are we going back to your house?' asked Lorraine.

'Naw, let's go up tae ma gran's. She needs yer final measurements for yer Aran cardigan. And she'll feed us. Who needs the York café when you can get ma gran's homemade chips?'

'Still thinking about food? Nothing changes.'

Nothing changing was the way I liked things. We didn't speak much on the way to my gran's. When best friends are together there's no pressure to fill the air space; you can relax.

'What if your gran's out?'

'The furthest she'll be is the Co-op; she hardly ever goes oot in case someone's looking for a reading.'

'Does she ever do fortune telling?'

'Ah've seen her read tea leaves but she prefers tae work with animals. Why're you asking?'

'I just wondered if she could see when I'd meet the ONE?'

'Who? The ONE yer going tae marry?'

'Naw, I'm no like my mam, desperate to marry the first guy that shows an interest in her. I'm talking about the ONE who's going to be my first.'

'At least you ken it'll no be tae a bastard like Stevie Duffy. It was tough telling you but ah did you a favour in the long run.'

'That's true. Thanks Angela, you always put me first.'

'Shush, that's what best pals are meant tae dae. Now c'mon let's see if ma gran's nearly finished yer cardigan.'

'Aye, we'll need to get our holiday wardrobe organised.'

Lorraine linked her arm into mine and we walked up my gran's path like a couple heading down the aisle; all that was missing was the Wedding March.

'Oh my God, he's killed a mouse!' screamed Lorraine.

Bimbo was running round the garden with his mouth full of a small brown thing between his teeth. It could be a mouse minus the tail, if he'd already sooked it up like a strand of spaghetti, or it could be a hamster; either way it was boggin'.

'Drop it!' I ordered.

The soggy balled up mess he spat out was one of my gran's Pop Sox. I couldn't bring myself to touch it; I left Bimbo to have another chew to satisfy his foot fetish. Things were back on track with me and Lorraine and I decided to share my good mood and give Bimbo a lick between my toes later. I kept chapping my gran's front door until the bathroom window tilted open and she shouted that she'd be out soon. She must've used more toilet paper than the Andrex puppy by the amount of toilet flushing action we heard.

Lorraine cringed and I stood on my tip-toes to reassure my gran that she could take her time.

'It's only me, gran!'

Finally, three more flushes later, she unclipped the door chain and we burst inside.

'Dogging it again?' asked my gran, wiping a streak of sweat from her forehead. Whatever she'd been up to in the bathroom had taken it out of her.

'Naw, ah keep telling you, we're on study leave.'

My gran used a lot less hairspray but was as easy to fool as Frances.

'When ah was seventeen ah was working full-time!'

'Next you'll be telling us that aw the lassies were married and had weans by oor age,.' I said.

'Some did but ah'm no as daft as you think. Yer grandda got on the bus at Fawkurt but ah made sure he got off at Bonnybridge and didnae stay on aw the way tae Denny. Ah'll stick the kettle on.'

My gran wandered off into the kitchen followed by Bimbo and his soggy Pop Sox mouse locked in his jaws.

'Eh? What's your gran talking about?' Lorraine gave me one of her best glaikit looks. It was looks like that and questions like this that made me realise that Lorraine still needed my guidance. The lassie had a lot to learn and it was a good thing I was looking out for her.

'She means that my grandda withdrew, didnae go aw the way.'

'Euch! Way too much information.'

It was a bit late for Lorraine to clamp her hands round her

lugs, the damage was done.

'Be grateful he's deid and you dinnae have tae look him in the eye.'

'True, but I've still got to face your gran!'

It was back to the banter we'd grown up with and I wasn't going to let anyone, male or female, stand in the way again.

'What're you two laughing at noo?' asked my gran.

'Nothing,' we replied at the same time, in the same sing-song tone and our sniggers revved up again.

'You're some pair. Is this what ah've tae put up with on holiday?'

It was pointless trying to sound serious, I knew she couldn't wait to pack her case and set off for the Yorkshire Riviera.

'Anyhow, ah'm glad you're here, ah need a wee hand sorting oot ma holiday clothes. And you two are up-tae-date with the fashions so you can help me choose what tae take.'

Our knowledge of RaRa skirts teamed up with leg warmers didn't seem much use to my gran and I couldn't see her wanting to borrow our matching **'FRANKIE SAYS RELAX'** T-shirts. And I wasn't going to explain the slogan even though my gran wouldn't have flinched. I could tell her anything but recently our bond wasn't working both ways. She looked tired all the time and when she'd opened the front door to us she'd looked as if she'd gone ten rounds with Mike Tyson.

'Bat wing sleeves are in aren't they? And ah'd love tae get a silky blouse with shoulder pads for the Clubhouse. Yer dad says that Bob Monkhouse is doing a turn one night and ah want tae look ma best for him, you never ken, ah might get lucky,' said my gran, winking at us. The fear in Lorraine's eyes was hysterical; she wasn't used to my gran's patter and probably still had a sick image in her mind of my grandda humping my gran.

'Come through tae the bedroom,' said my gran. Lorraine looked reluctant to follow.

'Dinnae worry, ma grandda's definitely deid, she disnae hide him under the bed. Only her sex toys are there,' I whispered.

In the lobby our path was blocked with a pile of stuff littering the carpet. My gran kept 'stocks' in the lobby press on the shelves above the hoover and carpet sweeper. She preferred to use the carpet sweeper to save electricity and the hoover was just for good. There were lots of things she kept for 'good' like her newest corselette, embroidered hankies, and she always had a vanity case packed for an emergency hospital visit with a 'good' nightdress, pants and slippers.

'What's going on here gran?'

'It was high time ah gave this press a good clear out. Ah needed space for mair toilet rolls. Jeanette got them cheap at the cash 'n' carry.'

My gran insisted on gifting a toilet roll along with the knitted dresses worn by the fake Sindy dolls that she made into toilet roll covers for charity. Her logic was that the 'lady of the loo' couldn't be appreciated without displaying the full beauty of her dress if the legs weren't stuck inside a toilet roll tube.

There were multiple tins of processed peas, pink salmon, fruit cocktail, oxtail soup, prunes and packets of jelly cubes stacked in tower blocks next to the skirting board. My gran kept stocks of tinned peach slices just for me. My mam stopped buying them because the only fruit my dad ate was fruit pastilles and Karen wouldn't eat peach slices any more.

In amongst the tins, there was another tower made from boxes of medical rubber gloves. I picked a box from the top of the pile and pulled a pair of gloves out. 'Where did these come fae?'

'Rab upstairs, he used tae be a porter at the Infirmary and has tonnes of medical stuff. He handed them in.'

'Handed them in, very funny gran, ah like it.'

'Like what?'

Her reference to hands was lost on my gran and Lorraine; it wasn't worth explaining the joke to either of them.

'But why did he give you hunners of rubber gloves?'

'They're handy tae have; you never ken when you'll need a pair.'

I resisted the temptation to mention anything to do with hands and gloves again.

'Would you like a box tae take hame Lorraine?'

Lorraine looked at me for guidance. She was on her own this time.

'Thanks anyway Mrs Smeaton but I dinnae see me having much use for them.'

'Ah wisnae meaning for you, ah was thinking that yer mam might use them for cleaning up Janine if she has a wee accident.'

Bimbo saved Lorraine from further embarrassment by dropping the Pop Sox mouse at my gran's feet.

'Ah, so that's where it went. Ah was trying on sandals for ma holidays and it disappeared.'

My gran kicked off her slipper and slid on the damp Pop Sox, wiping Bimbo's slavers off by rubbing her foot on the back of her 'working' trousers. Lorraine sounded as if she was trying to swallow a cat's fur ball.

'Talking of holidays, we need tae get you measured up for yer Aran cardigan. Ah'll try on ma new bathing suit later.'

Lorraine stood on Bimbo's foot in the rush to bolt past the open bedroom door and into the living room where my gran kept her knitting bag. The bed was covered with tops, cardigans, blouses, trousers and skirts laid out in coordinated combos and a Kermit-green halter neck bathing suit hanging from the wardrobe door.

'Wow, gran, the lifeguard'll see you nae bother in that wee number!'

'Too right. And the best thing is that it's got a secret control panel tae pull in ma tummy. Anybody would think ah was expecting twins.'

My gran stood side on to the mirror and held her belly, as if she could feel a heartbeat inside.

'You look fine gran. Just suck it in the way ah do.'

'Thanks hen, if you've got it flaunt it, eh? And you just watch yer auld gran in action and you'll learn a trick or two.'

It was a relief that Lorraine was out of earshot. She'd run away screaming at the thought of my gran hitting on guys at the beach and I was feart she'd change her mind about coming on holiday with us. There was no option for me; one way or another I'd be in Primrose Valley this time next week to witness my gran parading around in her bathing suit. The male population of Filey deserved to be warned. And armed.

Chapter Sixteen

The roof rack sagged under the weight of my gran's family-sized suitcase; the pavement was blocked with black bags stuffed full of sheets and towels, and a huge cardboard box loaded with essentials to save my mam having to shop for food. She had no plans to spend time cooking either, judging by the Smash potato mash, tins of Fray Bentos steak pie, corned beef, beans and tomato soup. We knew from experience that she couldn't buy silverskin onions, McVitie's digestive biscuits, Salad Cream or Irn-Bru at the campsite's mini-market. And my mam only drank the Co-op's own brand of tea bags; she was taking no chances of getting caught short of vital food stuffs when in a foreign country.

'Ah didnae hear the siren.'

'What're you havering on about?' asked my dad.

'You'd think we were hunkering doon for a nuclear war instead of going on holiday.'

I tried to wedge my ghetto blaster into the car boot; my dad lifted it back out.

'We need the space for food. Ah'm no paying those rip-off prices again this year.'

'Yer dad's right. The lassies behind those tills should wear robber's masks. And the freezer section is a disgrace, how's a family meant tae rustle up a week's worth of meals fae packets of burgers and blocks of Neapolitan ice-cream?'

No one answered my mam, we'd all heard the same moan before and would hear it again when she needed to get fresh milk and bread from the shop.

Primrose Valley was designed for genuine holidaymakers. There was a chippy, a restaurant, a café and snack bars but my mam and dad hadn't grasped the idea of eating out and relaxing their normal routine. My dad had bother with his false teeth and didn't like to eat in front of other folk; the only time I'd seen him eat in public was at my grandda's funeral although he refused the steak pie and only took the lentil soup.

My dad asked my gran to walk up and down the street with Bimbo until he did a crap, he wasn't prepared to have a shit-stop before we got to Southwaite services and he was champing at the bit to hit the road. My mam was desperate too, she liked to get to Filey, unpack, have our tea, get the dishes done and be ready for the first house of the bingo. It was a tight schedule.

I took my ghetto blaster back up to my bedroom and shut the door behind me. It was going to be great; all the aggro with Lorraine being upset about Stevie was almost forgotten. She'd refused to take his phone calls or see him again and when he turned up on her doorstep and Rita realised that he was Stevie Duffy, she chased him down the street with a mop still dripping with dirty water. And the best bit was that Lorraine hadn't ran back greetin' to Pamela. I made her promise not to say anything to Little Miss Brown Nose about what had gone on between me and Stevie. Lorraine and me were as tight as ever and the holiday was going to be mega and wipe out thoughts of Stevie and Pamela for good.

My dad was still rearranging the holiday stuff inside the car boot; my mam had taken up position in the front seat and my gran had reappeared with Bimbo. She tapped the passenger seat window and my mam rolled down her window. 'Naw', she answered before my gran had even opened her mouth.

'But you ken he likes tae see oot the front. He'll whine aw the way tae Filey if he has tae sit in the back.'

'He can look oot the side windae and if he's no happy, he can stay with Rab for the week.'

'Ah'd rather drink the car's battery acid than leave ma baby with that bampot.'

'Well, just get in then and remind him that he's a dug. And he's *your* dug so he can sit on *your* knee.'

'He's no just a dug, he's a member of the family.'

My gran slammed the car door shut and Bimbo jumped straight on to my mam's knee. The dog had balls of steel. I was waiting until the last minute to get in and was hoping that the blink of sun playing hide 'n' seek with the clouds would turn my legs from ice blue to milky white. Scottish sunshine was a rare thing and although it was the last week in June and my nipples could cut glass, I was determined to wear my Club Tropicana neon vest top.

'Wagons roll!' cried my dad, same patter, different year.

But before we could head south, we had to drive to Spam Valley to pick up Lorraine. My dad tooted the car horn as he passed Lorraine's house and did a huge loop round the estate rather than park in the drive. The car was as moody as my mam and it didn't always go into reverse gear, so to save us having to get out and push, my dad avoided reversing it. By the time we did a circuit of Spam Valley, Lorraine was waiting out on the pavement with a beast of a suitcase and matching red vanity case. Her mam's face was like a well-skelped arse; she stood with her arms crossed and with Janine clinging to her leg.

'Christ, we'll never get aw that in,' said my dad.

I got out, Lorraine grabbed me and we spun round in circles as if we were back in primary seven and had won a game of netball against the Proddy school.

'You'll need tae leave the wee red case behind hen,' said my dad, loading Lorraine's monster case on to the roof rack.

'But it's all my make-up and hair stuff. I cannae go without it.'

'Ah'll keep it on ma knee,' I said, 'cause Lorraine'll need tae sit with a carrier bag on her lap.'

'And she'll need to sit in the front,' added Rita, nodding at my mam to shift her bahookie.

My mam leaned across the empty driver seat, looking ready to chin Rita.

'Why's that?'

'She's a poor traveller. Unless you want her throwing up from here to Filey, you'll need to let her get the front seat.'

It was hard to tell if it was Bimbo or my mam who made the growling noise. It seemed too deep for a wee dog, I'd put my money on my mam.

'You never said a word about travel sickness,' my mam muttered under her breath as she climbed in the back seat and threw Bimbo on to my gran's lap. A Datsun Cherry was never designed for six buttocks cheek-to-cheek; there wasn't enough room between us to squeeze out a fart.

It was true that Lorraine couldn't travel further than Falkirk without being sick and it was surprising that I'd forgotten the time she'd puked into my hood when it was standing room only on the X37 to Glasgow. The driver had to make an emergency stop in Cumbernauld when folk complained that her second batch of vomit was running down the aisle.

'Don't forget to kiss your Saint Christopher,' said Rita, gesturing at her scraggy neck. Kiss my sugar white arse would've been a reasonable reply. To keep the peace, Lorraine pulled the silver medal out from her cleavage, puckered up and gave the tiny saint a quick peck, smudging him with Heather Shimmer lipstick. Her mam dabbed her eyes with a hankie and lifted Janine's hand to pump it up and down like a rag doll waving in Toy Town. Janine blew spit bubbles, the way she did when she was nervous. A bubble of panicky air popped on her chin and Rita used her damp hankie to wipe off the blob of saliva. Lorraine's sniffs were getting louder and I tapped the back of her head.

'What're you greetin' for? We're off on holiday!'

'I don't like leaving Janine, that's all.'

'You've no left her locked in a cupboard for a week; she's got yer mam with her.'

Lorraine twisted round in her seat and kept her voice low, 'That's what I'm worried about. You know what her temper's like when she gets crabbit with Janine.'

I'd witnessed the flashes of rage and frustration when Rita forgot I was in the background. I'd seen shoes being jammed on to Janine's feet and slapped back on the floor, spoons of food rammed into her mouth until she choked, put to bed with hands pressing down on her shoulders until they left red marks. Spied through a slither of open door, Rita's gritted teeth couldn't hold back demented outbursts and she sang hymns to calm Janine, or herself, down. And this was just the crazy stuff I did see. No wonder Lorraine was in tears.

'Dinnae worry hen, it's only a week we're away,' said my gran.

I was glad that Lorraine faced out the front window and didn't see my mam and gran share a wide-eyed look; maybe I wasn't the only one who knew what went on when Janine was left with Rita. My mam had warned me to pace myself and at least wait until we were on the motorway but this was an emergency. I tore the bag open and passed Lorraine the travel size bag of toffees; it was hard to keep crying if your jaws were busy.

Lorraine settled in the front chewing a caramel with her Chelsea Girl poly bag on her lap. I'd have kept that plastic bag for special and wanted to switch it for one of my mam's Co-op carrier bags for her to puke into. But I said nothing because I could hardly breathe between my mam and my gran. At least Lorraine's sniveling had stopped although Bimbo had started sniffing; he was already in holiday mode and had his nose in my crotch. I didn't let it bother me, the main thing was we were off and Bonnybridge was in the rear view mirror along with everything else that was shitty about home.

Stopping at the services on the M6 at Southwaite was the official start of the holiday. We couldn't afford to eat in the restaurant and I knew not to ask; my mam had made up cheese rolls that my dad insisted we ate on the move to save time. But we always stopped for a wander round the shop, bought nothing and went for a pee. My gran gave me and Lorraine money to have a go on the puggies after our trip to the loo. The coins ran out without as much as three cherries in a row never mind three gold bars and my gran still hadn't come out of the toilets.

The ETA to Primrose Valley was at risk. Each time the automatic glass doors slid open, I got another waft of travel tension from outside. My mam paced up and down the car park dragging Bimbo on his lead and my dad drummed his fingertips on the bonnet, I marched back into the bogs with Lorraine trailing behind me. There was a queue of females snaking up to the sinks with a wee boy clutching his shorts and hopping up and down. I dared to cause a riot and edged past the line to shout over the hand dryers at the row of locked cubicle doors.

'Are you okay in there gran?'

'Aye, but ah wish ah'd packed a cork. Hopefully that's the tank emptied noo. But ah might need a wee while longer, just tae be sure, ah dinnae trust these farts.'

Lorraine was used to embarrassing scenes involving bodily functions but at this she about-turned and left me. In fairness, she was supposed to be on holiday. Eventually my gran's door swung open and she squeezed between the queue of bursting bladders to wash her hands. We found Lorraine scooping up the ten pence she'd won from the fruit machine and we made our way back to the car, where my mam, dad and Bimbo were already inside with the engine revving. The only one not sucking the life out of a fag was Bimbo.

Everyone was grateful that Lorraine had made it past Carlisle without filling the Chelsea Girl bag with vomit and the only whiff inside the car was holiday spirit. Nothing was going to spoil the mood, even when Bimbo dragged his arse along the back seat and dislodged a dangle berry. Lorraine didn't notice, my dad shook his head and my mam kept her lips buttoned as my gran flicked the nugget of shit off the seat and out the door, no harm done.

'There's no even a skid mark,' said my gran.

Bamboozled as ever, Lorraine got back in the front of the car, checking the seat pad first, and didn't ask for an explanation; it was a relief that she'd known my family since she was four. And yet my mam still felt the need to give her the, *"you'll have tae take us as you find us"* speech but I suppose she hoped to reach Primrose Valley before issuing warnings about sitting on dog crap.

'Okay folks, only another hunner and fifty miles tae go,' said my dad. 'We'll fly doon the M6 and next thing you ken, it'll be, cabin crew, doors tae manual.'

Only my dad laughed; the rest of us sat in silence and sooked the aniseed balls my gran passed round. But a cheer went up when we passed the ***'Welcome to England'*** sign at the side of the motorway and my gran waved Bimbo's paws in the air. He didn't look impressed and went back to licking his balls. My dad was wrong that we'd be there in no time – he needed to pull into lay-bys five times to let Lorraine heave into the bushes and my gran insisted that Bimbo got to stretch his legs while we stopped. On the last stop-off, my gran bent down to clip Bimbo's lead on and let out a wet fart. I cringed.

'Gran! Lorraine disnae want tae hear that.'

I protested as if this was the first time I'd ever heard her let one go, although after Southwaite Lorraine already knew what my gran's arse was capable of.

'She'll hear a lot worse through the caravan walls so she'll need tae get used tae it.'

'Aye, and she might come fae Spam Valley but she farts like the rest of us. *"Where ere ye be let the wind gang free"* is ma motto, yer gran's quite right,' said my dad.

It was a poor show that they couldn't make an effort on holiday and in front of a guest. Just because they'd known Lorraine forever and she was used to the horrific sights and smells from the Handicapped Club didn't mean they could fart freely. This was supposed to be a break from real life for me and Lorraine; the only word to describe them was selfish.

'My timings are all buggered up noo, ah'll miss the bingo if she keeps this up,' said my mam.

I held Lorraine's hair back from her face and hoped that she was too busy puking up her guts to hear my mam badmouthing her and the plan to let rip wherever my dad and gran pleased. *"Take us as you find us"* shouldn't mean she had to accept that I was the only one in my family who wasn't an ignoramus.

Lorraine upchucked until she was empty and didn't ask my dad to stop again until she saw a sign saying:

Malton
North Yorkshire's Best Loved Market Town

'Any chance of getting a look round the stalls?' asked Lorraine.

My dad ignored her and accelerated past the town but my mam explained, 'It's no like the market in Fawkurt, there's nothing worth buying. This market just sells real food for fancy cooking.'

'Real food?'

Once again it was obvious that Lorraine didn't really know us at all. I wanted to explain that my mam meant fresh fruit and veg, not frozen stuff covered in breadcrumbs or batter but she beat me to it.

'Posh vegetables,' said my mam.

'What're posh vegetables?'

Anything other than tatties, cabbage and turnip was classed as posh veg in our house. I'd need to have a word with Lorraine that it was pointless keeping a conversation going with my mam and expecting any sense.

'You ken, like avocados.'

'Dae ye boil them?' asked my gran.

'Dinnae ask me, ah'm no a chef!'

My mam's attempt at a joke was as bad as my dad's piss-poor patter; no one found it funny or pointed out that an avocado was a fruit. It was a blessing that she didn't dabble in cooking exotic food. I passed a bag of lemon bonbons round and we sucked in our cheeks and sat in silence again until we reached the campsite entrance.

As my dad dropped down the gears to take the turn into Primrose Valley, my gran clapped Bimbo's paws in time and joined in with my mam singing, '*We're all going on a summer holiday*'.

My dad's knuckles went white gripping the steering wheel and I hoped their double-act wouldn't make Lorraine puke again. Lorraine had to live with Rita's mad hymn singing but the sound of my mam and gran repeating the same few lines, over and over while swaying from side to side was hardly a welcome break. The car slowed down to ten miles an hour and it was good to see that the place was hoaching with folk who didn't know my family. But it was safer to lean over my mam's lap, roll up the window and pray that the sound of their Cliff Richard medley was trapped inside. And I was grateful that Lorraine had no way of escape either. We parked opposite the main building and my mam trotted over to Reception to collect the key for our caravan.

'This place is massive,' said Lorraine, scanning the acres of static caravans beyond the car park; it was impossible not to be wowed by it. Primrose Valley wasn't a few rows of clapped out caravans dumped in a field or perched on the edge of crumbling cliffs like some shitty sites. This wasn't just a caravan park, this was a holiday village, an indoors and outdoors all-action entertainment complex, and for once I'd have someone with me to make the most of it. Never was I so glad that Karen was a gymnastics geek and would be doing a handstand in France rather than bugging the hell out of me in Filey.

As if the drive down wasn't embarrassing enough, my gran was waving out the window like she was on the Nut Bus. An auld man wearing a cowboy hat with eyebrows a sparrow could nest in waved back at her. He was driving what was called the 'Primrose Puffer' and the chancer grinned and winked at my gran as he passed our car. He'd teeth that looked like a row of

Werther's Originals that had been sooked for hours, and despite them being yellowy brown, my gran would be impressed; she always was if a man still had his own teeth.

The Puffer was actually a tractor and trailer poorly disguised as a train and it travelled round the campsite to take folk up and down to the beach for free. The wee train was always mobbed with weans wanting a ride on the Puffer and although I felt like a pure fud when I was a passenger the shame was worth it to save the trek.

'Looks like ah've got lucky before we've even got the keys tae the caravan,' said my gran, nudging me in the ribs. It was hard to believe that my gran had hit on a guy before me and Lorraine; maybe she was right and she could teach us a thing or two.

While we waited for the keys, my gran got her camera out and made Bimbo pose wearing her new hot pink sunglasses. Lorraine was impressed by Bimbo's patience but he knew as well as I did that it was best to smile for the camera and keep her happy.

My mam reappeared and her retarded grin filled the windscreen as she dangled the keys like she'd won the caravan on *Bullseye* along with a matching speedboat. When my dad drove past a brand new static and parked next to our home for the week, I half expected Jim Bowen to appear on next door's veranda and tell us to, *"Come and have a look at what you could have won!"*

A sign was perched on the window ledge and faced outward:

"Home Sweet Caravan"

Even Jim Bowen couldn't have managed to fake a *"super, smashing, great"* reaction to the heap of shit my mam had booked for us. Her smile vanished leaving behind a face that could curdle milk.

'This is what happens when you book a holiday advertised in the *Sunday Post*,' said my dad, pushing the door open to reveal a 70s time capsule. 'This van must be as auld as their readers.'

'There's many a good tune played on an auld fiddle,' said my gran. I wondered if she meant the van or the Puffer's driver but I didn't dare to ask.

'It'll be fine, it's only for putting oor heids doon,' said my mam, the self-appointed cheerer-upper.

Lorraine crunched up her face and wiggled her nose like Samantha from *Bewitched*; all that was missing was the tinkle of a xylophone to add the doodle-oodle-ooo sound effect. My mam flung the nearest window open to release the stale soup of air; it was as thick as my gran's lentil soup and I'd swear I could see it waft away in a green cloud.

'The main thing is the telly's working,' said my dad, flicking through the channels and adjusting the volume.

'God forbid that we'd need tae speak tae each other,' said my gran.

'We'll never see you anyway, the bingo's on day and night here,' replied my dad.

'Suits me.'

'Suits me too. But mind, *"Don't come knockin' if the caravan is rockin"*'.

'Aye, you should be so lucky.'

My mam ignored their banter; she was busy opening up every cupboard door in the kitchen area. Lorraine was busy too, prizing Bimbo from her shin and was more concerned with the dog trying to shag her than picturing the horrific image of my mam and dad going hard at it. She didn't realise that Bimbo had saved her from throwing up again; I'd toss him a chew stick later as a reward.

Next on my mam's arrival checklist was to turn on the kitchen taps to make sure we had running water; anyone would think we'd arrived in North Africa not North Yorkshire. She then moved on to the living room area and lifted all the ornaments from the built-in units and placed them on the highest shelf. Last year Karen was so excited when we arrived that she did a cartwheel indoors; any normal person's reaction would be to punch the air and cry, "Oh ya beauty!" not crash into a display of ornaments and smash a crystal owl to smithereens. My mam spent the rest of the holiday scouring the shops for a replacement owl and had to search as far as Bridlington; the best match she could get was a swan. She was taking no chances this time although it was hard to see how anybody could damage a miniature brass kettle, iron, cannon, spinning wheel and pair of clogs.

My gran filled the kettle and I gave Lorraine the nod to follow me to our bedroom at the back. The door of my mam and dad's bedroom was open; Lorraine's leg couldn't have given him any satisfaction as Bimbo was humping one of their pillows, the first of us to get any bedroom action.

'I dinnae fancy lying on that,' said Lorraine, pointing at the stained mattress of the bottom bunk bed. 'I'll need to take the top bunk.'

On the wall next to our bedroom window there was a framed cross stitch with the message, *"Well behaved children welcome. The rest will be made into pies"* sewn in pastel coloured threads. I wondered how many weans without a sense of humour had lost sleep over the warning, and if the embroidered words made wee ones piss the bed and sweat buckets. It might explain the yellowy patches. The overlapping circular stains looked like the Venn diagram I drew once in biology filled with the names of carnivores, herbivores and omnivores. This one was made up of overlapping sets of sweaty pee-the-bed holidaymakers.

Our usual caravan was fully booked when my mam phoned up so we'd taken the chance of hiring the *"superbly appointed fully equipped luxury caravan situated within easy reach of both the on-site facilities and the beach"*. Whoever wrote the advert must've choked on the reek of bullshit as they put pen to paper.

'And thank God my mam made me pack my slippers,' added Lorraine.

She looked down at the purple and orange carpet with its swirly pattern. It didn't quite manage to disguise the shape of a dried up splash of an unknown liquid; a tuft of carpet fibre could provide vital evidence in a case for Cagney and Lacey. It was best not to think about who or what had been in the bedroom before us.

And there was the mingin' smell to deal with. I opened the window, praying Lorraine hadn't noticed the fusty aroma. It transported me back to one of my biggest fears, the changing room at *What Every Woman Wants*. This wasn't actually a room; it was a curtained area where every female in Falkirk stripped to their undies to try on cheap clothes. It wasn't just the humiliation of changing in front of strangers that was dire, it was the fact that the constantly packed 'room' stank of stale sweat and cheesy feet, and our tiny bedroom had that same rank rotten hum.

'Ah ken it's no great but ma mam's talking sense for once. We'll hardly be in the caravan and it'll be dark when we get in after the Clubhouse, so you'll no see the state of the place.'

Lorraine didn't look as convinced as I hoped. 'And where would you rather be right noo, back hame listening tae yer mam singing *"Kum bah yah ma lord"* tae Janine? Or on holiday with yer best pal?'

A reality check was enough to ditch the whinging; I knew which buttons to press. To complete her mood swing, I pushed my hair over to one side of my face and pouted.

'What the hell are you doing?' asked Lorraine, smiling at my best Madonna impression.

'Never mind bloody Cliff Richard, we've got a much better theme tune.'

I wished my dad had managed to squeeze in my ghetto blaster and I could've had the music to back my singing.

Everybody spread the word
We're gonna have a celebration
All across Filey
In Primrose Valley
It's time for the good times
Forget about the bad carpet, oh yeah
One week to come together
To release the pressure
We need a holiday

Lorraine could hardly stop laughing at my new lyrics but managed to join in the chorus.

We danced on the spot; there wasn't room to move anywhere else. But we didn't need the Clubhouse disco, we were already in holiday mode and things could only get better.

Chapter Seventeen

She knew I was right, the holiday was going to be brilliant. Lorraine phoned home to tell her mam that she'd arrived safely and Rita thanked St Christopher for delivering us safely to Filey as if the man himself was listening in on a party line. And then her mam had whined about Janine being on to her fourth change of clothes since coming home from morning Mass. Her mam had gone down into the Chapel hall for a cuppa tea with the rest of the Holy Joes who hung around the priest like love-sick groupies and Janine had a glass of orange juice. But the drink had run right through Janine and every pair of pants she'd worn was beyond saving and needed bagged and binned. It was more than enough information for Lorraine to forget about the caravan's stinks and stains; it was a palace compared with the mess Janine could produce.

The phone pips went and Lorraine claimed she'd no more coins. Rita was ranting about next door's cat tipping over the bin, ripping open poly bags and scattering shitty knickers all over the garden as the phone line went dead.

We walked back to the caravan the long way so that I could show off the highlights of the holiday park and I pointed out the motorised bumper boats and canoes for hire. A dad shouted at his wean to give it some welly and the bumper boat shot off in search of some poor bugger who was about to get a soaking. Lorraine didn't seem that impressed; we had a boating lake at Callendar Park in Falkirk too. Our local 'attraction' had swan-shaped pedal boats with white paint flaking off the wings like dandruff; the giant plastic birds were as pathetic as the Primrose Puffer kidding on it was a train.

I knew it was hard to compete with our local leisure centre, the Mariner Centre, but I continued my tour with a keek through the glass walls of the campsite's indoor swimming pool. A cute guy with a bulge in his speedos waved at us, which never happened in Falkirk. It didn't need a wave machine to be a better pool.

'What dae you think?' I asked.

'Of him?'

'Trust you tae notice his budgie smugglers. Ah was talking aboot the pool!'

'Aye, it's good having an indoor pool 'cause my mam said the weather will probably be crap.'

'Mibbae she's said a prayer for us tae the Sisters of the Holy Umbrella.'

Lorraine laughed and tripped on a tree root that had burst through the path. A man with bloodhound jowls lunged to catch her and break her fall.

'Watch yourself hen, you could've given yourself a sair one there.'

I'd forgotten to tell Lorraine that there was always loads of Scottish folk on holiday in Primrose Valley, so there was no fear of lingo problems and it was another good reason why Filey beat the likes of Benidorm.

'Thanks,' said Lorraine.

'Nae bother. You can buy me a drink later in the Clubhouse.'

The man's jowls wobbled as he winked at Lorraine and turned off down one of the rows of caravans.

Lorraine looked at me and raised one eyebrow. We reached our caravan in a heap of giggles.

The minute we stepped in the door, I could see that my mam was more harassed than usual; she claimed that the stressful drive meant that she couldn't face making a meal.

'Ah'll treat everybody tae whatever they fancy fae the chippy,' said my gran, diving into her handbag and fishing out her purse.

'Put yer purse away,' replied my mam. It was the same old battle: my mam acted all affronted and adamant that she couldn't accept my gran's offer until finally she'd surrender to my gran's insistent 'Ah'm buying!' bombardment and the cease-fire meant there was peace again, until the next time.

My mam went in search of the *Daddies* brown sauce from our box of essential food supplies and my gran produced a bundle of banknotes rolled up with an elastic band. The only time I'd seen a wad of cash that thick was at the Falkirk market when one of the stall holders gave you change back. My gran peeled off a fiver and winked at me as if she'd just pulled off a bank job; I wondered if she knitted balaclavas as well as toilet roll covers.

Whispering in her ear I asked, 'Where did you get aw that money gran?'

'It's the charity money for the hospice.'

I was glad that Lorraine was out of earshot and sitting on the caravan steps flipping through a *Just Seventeen* that she had bought at Southwaite. Before the holiday I took it for granted that Lorraine knew my family well and there would be no surprises, but within hours of leaving home I realised she didn't have a clue what they were really like. It was a worry.

'You mean the cash fae selling the toilet roll holders?'

'Aye, and ah've been crocheting blankets for folk in wheelchairs too. They're snapped up at the bingo, ah can hardly keep up with demand.'

'But you cannae keep the money.'

'Do you think am an eejit? Of course ah'm no keeping it!'

'What're you two whispering about?' asked my mam. She'd emptied the kitchen cupboards and was busy washing all the mugs, plates, bowls, glasses and cutlery in water hot enough to kill bacteria and melt human skin. My mam was paranoid that the caravan was jumping with germs after I filled a glass with Irn-Bru and she noticed a lipstick mark round the rim left by the Ghost of Holiday Past. There was a squeal; I assumed that it was the shock of the dirty glass but it was because I was already drinking the rationed Irn-Bru within minutes of arrival. The rule was to pace ourselves with no more than a half glass a day or our supplies wouldn't last until the end of the week. She had a point: running out of Irn-Bru was a big deal.

'Ah said, what're you two whispering aboot?'

Standing at the sink, my mam had her back to us but she wasn't easy to ignore.

'Nothing,' said me and my gran at the same time.

'One's as bad as the other,' muttered my mam, snapping off the Marigolds she'd brought from home and stuffing the kitchen scouring pad into the open mouth of a ceramic frog sitting on the draining board. I wondered what holiday dramas the frog's bulbous eyeballs had seen over the years and the tales its big gob could tell.

My mam unpacked the black bin bag full of our bed sheets and marched off to make up the beds. Her mission was aborted; the snoring coming from her bedroom meant that my dad was 'meditating' just like he did at home after work every night and it was a no-go area. Her cleaning radar homed in on the bathroom zone instead and once she was safely out the way I turned back to my gran.

'Listen hen, ah've earned that money and all ah'm doing is borrowing it. Once ah've made mair blankets then ah'll top up what ah've used and replace it, okay? Or dae you think yer auld gran disnae deserve a nice holiday?'

It was hard to argue with my gran's logic and I didn't want to fall out with the only other person I loved as much as Lorraine. I might call Lorraine my best pal and I gave her the title she deserved, but my gran was my best friend too; she knew me better than I knew myself.

'Dinnae worry gran, you'll soon pay back the money. Once word goes roond the bingo, folk'll be dying tae get their hands on one of yer crocheted blankets.'

'Ah feel bad enough about the hospice, there's nae need tae rub it in.'

It took me a few seconds to realise that my gran thought I was making a sick joke about terminal patients.

'Gran, ah swear ah didnae mean it like that.'

'You ken what your trouble is m'lady? Afore opening yer mooth you should make sure yer tongue is connected tae yer brain.'

She was right. I'd lost count of the things that popped into my head and then jumped feet first out of my mouth.

'You ken me too well.'

'So you'll be wanting a fish supper then?'

'Too right and mind and ask for plenty of salt and…'

'Vinegar.'

Lorraine let out a yelp as if Bimbo had bitten her on the arse but he was still at my feet pushing his fuzzy tongue between my toes. She'd come inside to go to the toilet but my mam was standing in the doorway with something furry sitting in the palm of her hand and a J-cloth ready to be whipped into action in the other.

My mam sidestepped to let Lorraine pass her and joined us in the living room. 'What a big feartie yer pal is. It's just a hair ball ah pulled oot the shower's plug hole but you'd think ah'd thrown a deid rat in her face.'

'You'd think she'd be braver,' said my gran.

'Why's that?' I asked.

'Well she's grown up seeing aw those disabled weans. There must've been scarier sights than a wee hair ball,' added my gran.

'Tae be fair, it's the size of a hamster; it'd freak me oot,' I said.

'Rubbish, ah've shaved mair off ma legs,' said my mam. She wasn't wrong; in between shaves Chewbacca couldn't compete with her hairy legs.

My mam placed the tip-of-her-toe on the pedal to open the kitchen bin, the lid sprang up and I half-expected a Jack-in-the-Box to appear. With one swift flick, my mam used her index finger to kick the hair ball from her palm and scored a goal into the mouth of the bin.

Lorraine went straight from the bathroom into our bedroom and slammed the door shut. I hoped the toilet flushing had drowned out my mam and gran bitching about her; I was glad Bonnybridge was over two hundred miles away because storming off home wasn't an option. And yet I kept my eye on the door in case Lorraine reappeared with her suitcase.

'Right, ah better head off tae the chippy,' said my gran, getting to her feet and grabbing her handbag. From a side pocket, she pulled out her favourite Kiss Me Coral lipstick and guided it across her thin lips. It was a pity that she hadn't read Lorraine's copy of *Just Seventeen* or she'd know that orangey shades make your teeth look yellow. I had to admire how she could fill in her lips without a mirror although by that age she should know every inch of her face. She mwah-mwahed her lips together and seemed pleased. Maybe it was the lack of a mirror that meant she didn't realise that the lipstick bled into the lines round her mouth, or maybe she did and accepted it after years of sucking on a fag. My gran always told me to be true to myself and not to worry what others think, and no one could argue that she oozed confidence, even with wonky lipstick and smoker's teeth.

'You and Lorraine can give yer gran a hand at the chippy,' said my mam.

'Naw, you're fine hen, ah'll get the Puffer there and back.'

I went to speak to Lorraine but she was lying in bed with her face covered by her pillow. I wondered if she was 'meditating' too and thought it was best to give her a bit of peace; it was hard work being with my family for any longer than an hour. I couldn't blame her but at least she'd be able to escape at the end of the week. I took Lorraine's *Just Seventeen* into the loo with me and balanced it on top of the toilet roll holder while I peed. I wasn't the only one who used the toilet as a hidey-hole – the plastic loo roll holder was dotted with fag burns. The Ghost of Holiday Past was a heavy smoker.

To take my mind off waiting for my fish supper, I read the *'Dare to Bare Guide to Your Best Bikini Body'*. I also memorised the entire A to Z of Summer Beauty, noting that there was still time to tick off 'V' from the list and add "Va-va-voom nails" with the Heather Shimmer nail polish Lorraine had to match her lipstick. It was too late though to buy a new bathing suit that followed the rules of "*Which Shape Suits You?*" although I could try hoiking up the straps of mine to give it the sexy high cut legs look. And I'd take the chance of ignoring 'Z' for 'Zzzz': no matter how essential sleep was to boost my "*health and well-being*" I didn't come on holiday to lie any longer than necessary in a piss-stained bunk bed. My bum was numb by the time I got to the horoscope page and there was still no shout that food was ready. It was time to investigate.

'Ah'll need tae put the oven on tae heat up; they suppers will be stone cauld by the time she gets back. Dae you ken she'd the cheek tae wave at me when she went by in the Puffer?' said my mam.

'She's just passed again,' I said, pointing out the window as the tail-end of the Puffer disappeared round the corner. My gran sat behind the driver's cabin, yapping at the back of the auld cowboy's head with Bimbo bobbing up and down on her knee and the fish suppers cooling by her side.

'Yer gran takes the biscuit! Ah'll need tae get ready and forget tea; if ah dinnae get a move on, ah'll miss the first session of the bingo.'

My mam decided that her and my dad couldn't wait any longer for my gran.

'She must've got lucky.' I said.

'Enough of that talk, ah've still tae eat,' said my dad, kidding on he was gagging.

My mam ignored us and chanced her arm to suggest that her and my dad could get chicken in a basket at the Clubhouse.

'It's supposed tae be oor holiday,' pleaded my mam.

My dad wasn't convinced and looked pained at the thought of dusting off his wallet and dining out.

Me and Lorraine decided to hang back until the bingo was finished to give us time to drink our carry out. My gran bought it for us out the Co-op before we left and she'd kept it hidden in her suitcase. She agreed to buy the booze but only got us a half bottle of vodka so that we didn't get too pished. I didn't want to argue, it was enough to get us started and keep the holiday mood topped up.

There was no danger of my gran's holiday spirit drying up. Finally back with the fish suppers, she Tigger-bounced into the caravan all fired up from her jaunt on the Puffer. My gran claimed she was too excited to eat and instead she had a quick wash that she called a 'bird bath'. She burled round the living room in her new outfit and me and Lorraine oohed and aahed enough to keep her happy and set her on her way. We waved Bimbo's paw at her as she left for the Clubhouse and at last we had the caravan to ourselves, peace to get stuck into the voddy and after a shower we'd be transformed into disco divas.

We gulped down a voddy while we curled each other's hair with Lorraine's tongs and back combed it at the roots to make it as big as Tina Turner's. I wanted to wear my baby blue fish tail skirt but Lorraine thought we should keep our pastel coloured outfits until we got a tan. I had to admire her optimism and agreed to wear our stone-washed denim mini-skirts with our fluorescent vest tops. While Lorraine touched up her make-up, I sneaked into my mam's room and brought back her bottle of Anais Anais. From above our heads, I squirted the perfume into the air and it fell on us like smirry rain.

'Blessed Sisters of the Holy Umbrella, we ask for only showers of sacred perfume and for God's sun tae shine upon us. Amen.'

We clinked our glasses of voddy and downed the dregs.

'This skirt keeps riding up my thighs,' said Lorraine.

'That's no the only riding oor thighs will get this week,' I replied. My banter didn't make Lorraine laugh as usual; instead her top lip formed an Elvis curl.

'Don't you think you should be careful after what happened with Stevie?'

Before I could top her glass up with coke, Lorraine took a swig of neat vodka. Her face screwed up as if she'd sucked on a lemon but you couldn't blame her for not adding Panda cola to her voddy and wanting to get blootered quicker.

'Ah'm no gonnae let that put me off. And the good thing is that ah'm no a virgin anymair so it wisnae aw bad.'

'I don't know how you can say that after what he did!'

'He did me a favour. We dinnae want tae go back tae school after the summer and still be virgins, dae we?'

'No everyone's done it. Pamela's waiting until she's in a serious relationship.'

'Lorraine, wise up, all the good-looking lassies have already been shagged umpteen times. Pamela will be the only virgin in sixth year along with aw the other rejects that no guy'll touch. Unless you and Pamela want tae join Sister Patricia in the convent, the sooner you lose it the better.'

'I suppose so.'

'You ken ah'm talking sense. We'll be fighting them off with a stick. Now, c'mon, let's get oor arses doon tae the Clubhouse.'

The place was mobbed; it was a struggle to find the table my family had claimed as theirs for the night. And yet above the noise of glasses slamming on tables, cutlery clattering off plates, chit-chat passing around pals, laughter filling cupped palms, music pounding off walls, dancers high-kicking and whooping, I recognised my mam's cackle. It was a relief that they'd hooked up with other Scottish folk and their table was full: no space for us, easy to get steam boats, out of sight.

The disco wasn't due to start until after the cabaret; the exact time depended on whether or not the mob beat the comedian into submission with heckles. It was a game my dad had never dared to play again since three summers ago when he shouted out that the comedian was rubbish. The comedian replied, '*If I wanted to get the opinion of an asshole I would have farted.*' My mam was mortified; she slapped a lifetime heckling ban on my dad.

Our plan was to find a table upstairs; the top level formed a balcony over the rest of the Clubhouse and was ideal for spying on all the action. I let my dad know where we'd be and told him we'd check in with him every hour or so. Their table was already chock-a-block with glasses drained of beer and Bacardi; it wouldn't be long before they couldn't see where they were, never mind where me and Lorraine were hiding. It was shaping up to be a good night already. My dad insisted on buying us our first drink and suggested something not too strong; he'd promised Rita he would keep an eye on us.

'Thanks Mr McMenemy, I'll take a Midori and lemonade,' said Lorraine.

'Aye, we dinnae want tae end up drunk dad.'

We held back our Mutley sniggers until my dad left us to it and although the Midori was as alcoholic as wine gums, the bright green concoction did add a touch of sophisticated glamour. It worked. Like wasps around a picnic, the guys eyed us up and they were definitely a better bunch than the losers that hung about Mystique.

'I like him with the fair hair,' said Lorraine.

Two guys gave us the once over. It was obvious why Lorraine would be after the one with blonde streaks. He was tall and wore a cream suit with the sleeves rolled up, a black T-shirt underneath and had on stripy canvas espadrilles with bare feet. Guys from Falkirk always wore white sport socks; they could never pull off a Miami Vice look. He wasn't my type, too smooth and shiny for me although there was no denying that this poser had style. His pal was far rougher round the edges, not in a butch way, but a couldn't-give-a-shit way. If Lorraine decided that the Don Johnston wannabe was hers, I'd have to make do with his side-kick.

'So here I am, what're your other two wishes?' asked Miami Man.

'Did you hear that one Angela?' laughed Lorraine, nudging me with her elbow. Unless I'd gone deaf, of course I'd heard his pish patter and I'd bet he'd a whole catalogue of cheesy one liners at the ready.

'Now that I've broken the ice, can I buy you a drink?' said Miami Man.

'Thanks, we'll have a double vodka and coke.'

Lorraine lapped it up like warm milk and practically foamed at the mouth; at least he was buying the drinks.

'I'm Danny by the way, and that's my mate Brian,' said Miami Man. He nodded at his pal and signaled to him with a slick hand gesture of his palm outwards and two fingers upright, then a 'V' and a 'C' with his thumb and forefinger. This was a tried and tested routine and Brian needed no verbal instructions whatsoever; he raised a rubbery thumb. Lorraine was easily impressed and gave me another nudge in the ribs. At this rate, I'd be black and blue before the end of the night.

'I'm Lorraine and this is Angela.'

'Ah prefer Angi.'

Danny didn't so much as turn his head an inch in my direction. Up close, he wasn't as glossy; there were definite hints of wrinkles under his eyes. If he was a model in my art class, I'd draw those lines in with cross hatches to show his face had seen a bit of life.

'Are you girls on holiday?'

Why else would two Scottish lassies be drinking in the bar of a campsite in North Yorkshire in July? Don Johnson could sleep easy; his role as Sonny Crockett was safe, there was no danger of Danny ever playing an undercover police detective.

'Aye, we just arrived earlier,' said Lorraine. 'And we're here for a week of sun, sea and s…seashells.'

Danny laughed. 'There's no guarantee you'll get sun. But two out of three's not bad and if you stick with me there might be an extra 's'.'

I choked on the corny chat up line and badly needed another drink. Although he'd been battered by the ugly stick, I was pleased to see Brian return from the bar and slide the tray on the table. He sat down opposite me, sighed, gulped his pint and let out a garlicky belch. He said nothing and yet he said it all. Me and Brian were spectators in a sport that we weren't fit enough to compete in. All that was left for us to do was to cheer on the favourite contenders. Danny would assume he was odds on that he was going to score tonight, but for all her talk of losing her virginity, I knew Lorraine was called a cock tease by the guys at Mystique and all that Danny was likely to get was a hand on her rug, a classic case of all talk and no action.

Danny was certainly out to earn more than a sly grope. He was working hard to impress, buying her doubles, stroking the back of her hand and making her giggle with his attempt at a Scottish accent and pathetic "*Och aye the noo*", when she asked for another drink.

'Eeeh-bah-gum, yer pal's patter is so original,' I said to Brian, loud enough for Danny and Lorraine to hear; I got a response from no-one. My sarcasm was wasted, it didn't make Lorraine laugh or bring her back to planet earth. It was time to break up the lovefest; I needed to save her from Danny the Fanny before he made a complete arse of her.

'Are you coming tae the toilet?' I asked her. She didn't bother to face me.

'I'm no needin' the now.'

'But yer make-up needs touched up.' I knew that would get her attention and sure enough she grabbed her clutch bag and shimmied her way out from behind the table, managing to jiggle her tits in Danny's face at the same time. I grabbed her arm and dragged her towards the ladies' toilets; she lurched forward and leaned across the sink, her breath fogging up the mirror as she checked for signs of smudging. A cigarette butt was lodged in the plug hole and I flicked it out to free the sink full of murky water, which drained away with a gurgle of relief.

'You better slow doon with the double voddys,' I warned.

'You're just jealous 'cause Brian isnae buying you a drink.'

'Ah'd rather buy ma own than owe him anything. And ah hope you realise that Danny'll be looking for something back for aw the booze you're hoovering up.'

'He's no like that.'

'They're aw like that. And guys his age expect you tae go aw the way.'

'He's only 22.'

'Mair like 32, or he's had a hard paper round.'

'I don't get you. One minute you're telling me I need to catch up with you and shag someone and now you're going all serious on me.'

'It was just a bit of banter. You've always said you want tae wait for the ONE so dinnae dae anything you dinnae want tae, okay?'

'You worry too much about me. I can look after myself.'

Lorraine reapplied her Heather Shimmer lipstick, pushed past me and banged her elbow on the paper towel dispenser on the wall. She staggered out the door without waiting for me and zig-zagged her way between the tables; I didn't follow, needing a few minutes to myself to decide how to play out the rest of the night.

The disco was due to start after the cabaret and I was keen to show off the dance moves I'd practised with Lorraine. We'd rehearsed a whole routine, our hips bumping together as we sang along, to Maddona.

Brian didn't look like the boogie-on-down type. He was a big lad, as they call them round this way, and I guessed he was no John Travolta. Rather than forcing him on to the dance floor and embarrassing me, I had a better idea that would suit us both.

I made my way back to our table; Lorraine and Danny were a bawhair apart and were practically eating each other. It made me hungry just looking at them. Brian was shredding his beer coaster into confetti and didn't notice me either.

'Hey Brian, dae you fancy getting some chips?'

His eyes turned on full beam and Brian knocked back the last of his pint; it was the most animated I'd seen him all night.

'Okay, I'll buy you a bag of scraps.'

Romance was not dead.

The fish supper my gran had bought me was a distant memory; I was ready to sample the local delicacy of leftovers of batter called scraps. It was a shame that Scottish chippies were too classy to sell scraps, they were damn tasty and Brian was even more excited than me.

Zebedee couldn't have sprung up quicker than Brian. I'd hardly spoken to him so it was hard to tell if his enthusiasm was at the thought of leaving the Clubhouse, sampling the chippy's specialty or being alone with me. If he was expecting some action in exchange for a bag of scraps, I hoped he didn't like vinegar; it nips like buggery if you're fingered by a guy who's eaten chips. Kebab sauce fingers sting too.

I tapped Lorraine on the shoulder to let her know that we were going to the chippy and I'd be back soon. She grunted that she'd heard me but didn't unlock her eyes from Danny. On the way down the stairs, Brian announced that he needed a slash; I told him that I'd wait for him in the main foyer. As I reached the bottom of the stairs, my dad walked back into the Clubhouse and explained he'd been outside for a breath of air, which really meant he needed a break from my mam and gran. He wasn't amused that Lorraine wasn't with me; I'd broken one of the golden rules.

'Ah thought ah telt the two of you tae stick together at aw times.'

'Dad, ah'm only going next door. And Lorraine's still inside the Clubhouse.'

'Well straight back after the chippy.'

'Ah'm seventeen, no seven!'

'That's why ah'm worried.'

'There's nae need tae be.'

The call of an ice-cold pint reached my dad and I managed to shoo him away before the mens' toilet door opened. Brian juggled his balls back into place and I wondered if he'd washed his hands.

'Was that old man mytherin' you?' asked Brian. I was touched that he was bothered and I was tempted to see what he'd do about it if I complained about my dad.

'Naw, he's ma dad.'

'I thought you two girls were here by yourselves?'

'The game's a bogie,' I mumbled. Brian didn't hear me; he'd already set off for chips on his own.

I'd scored an own goal. A sexy girl on holiday had no room for their mam, dad, gran and poodle on a winning team. And yet it wasn't over until the final whistle. I shouted after Brian, another shot at the ball.

'Ma family is here on holiday too but me and Lorraine have a separate caravan.'

He stopped and turned back. Result!

''Appen we could go there then and make a chip butty?'

'Ah dinnae want the place stinking of chips; ah'd rather sit on a bench up at the boating lake.'

'Reet, and there are plenty of bushes up there.'

Romance was dead.

Brian had a limited supply of conversation and he'd obviously used up his quota getting served at the chippy; he never uttered another word until after we'd left with a bag each of scraps. I wandered off in the direction of the boating lake but soon realised that the deep fried smell of Brian was gone. He wasn't following.

'Are you coming?'

'Sorry, I'm gunna have to go back to my van. I think it's the bevvy. My friggin' guts are bubbling. Tarra.'

It certainly wasn't his personality that was bubbly. Brian broke into a jog with his arse cheeks clenched and I waved him off. He still had his bag of scraps to eat when he got off the toilet so his night wasn't completely ruined.

'Nae worries,' I called after him and kept walking until I reached the swing park.

My scraps were cold but still crispy. I sat on one of the swings, funneled the crumbs down my throat and tossed the empty chip bag into the sand pit. I pushed off and soon got into a steady rhythm.

My heel slipped out of my sandal and I tossed it into the air. Me and Lorraine used to keep a running score of who kicked their shoe the furthest. The grand total was 35 to me, 17 to Lorraine. We stopped competing when my school shoe bopped Janine on the napper and gave her a black eye. I gave Janine the rest of my Toffos to chew on, and it stopped her greetin'. Rita cracked up about the shiner but it wasn't my fault; Lorraine should never have parked the wheelchair right in front of the swings.

I'd always known that Lorraine is a liability, and it was time I rescued her from Danny the Fanny. I collected my sandal and trudged back to the Clubhouse. The crowd at my mam and dad's table clapped like circus seals as the glitter-bombed drag queen pranced around the stage in white stilettoes and black fish nets. According to the poster, the drag queen called herself Donna Matrix and from where I stood it seemed that my gran had caught her eye. It wasn't surprising, my gran's penciled-in eyebrows and Princess Di chalk-blue eye shadow matched Donna's.

My gran's hand shot up when Donna asked for volunteers to join her act. I refused to wait and see if she got picked. I managed to give my dad the nod that I was going back upstairs and he gave me a thumbs-up. It was hard to tell if his signal meant he was glad I was safe or relieved that Donna had found another victim from the audience. My gran slumped back in her seat and took a slug of her brandy as Donna air-kissed her new best friend.

As I sauntered past the bar, I expected to see Lorraine's face still attached to Danny's. At our table, their faces were replaced by a couple of tarts whose bleached hair was fried, dried and petrified into crimped side ponytails. Their caked-on pan stick was thicker than Donna's stage make-up; the drag queen was fresh-faced in comparison. The pair of hounds were trying to act stylish with their matching cocktails; one picked her teeth with the wee parasol from her Pina Colada, and the other jiggled the plastic monkey swinging from the rim of the glass. I asked the tarts if they knew where Lorraine and Danny had gone; one gave me a couldn't-give-a-fuck shrug and sucked on her straw, the other blanked me and stirred her cocktail with a flamingo swizzle stick. I knew where I wanted to poke it.

Lorraine and Danny were nowhere to be seen on the top level. I hung over the balcony, scanning the lower levels for Danny's tiger striped hair and Lorraine's fluorescent vest top but there was no sign of them. I doubted that they would go anywhere near the oldies down below or that they'd both gone to the toilet at the same time.

There was no way that I could tell my mam and dad that I'd lost Lorraine on the first night. I bought myself a voddy and hoped that she'd turn up again soon; I took sips rather than swigs. The only one perched on a bar stool, I felt like one of those outcast lepers from Sister Patricia's R.E. stories. All that was missing was the bell. The disco was due to start any minute and I'd look even sadder sitting alone while the tarts went downstairs to strut their stuff. The finale of the cabaret drifted up and over the balcony; rising above the mob's laughter was my mam's pissed screech. There was nowhere safe from embarrassment.

I toyed with going out to look for Lorraine but where would I start searching? Primrose Valley was a shagger's paradise with a five mile beach, a jungle of bushes and a bed in every caravan. I was sure she wouldn't go down to the beach in the dark; the fear of the dunes and the memory of her near-death experience was still strong. But she could be pressed up against a wall or flat on her back anywhere. I'd be farting against thunder trying to find her, and the only option was to sit it out. It was just a pity I didn't have the cash to get pissed while I waited.

I nursed my drink until all I could do was crunch on the half melted ice cubes. By the time the DJ announced the last dance, I was crapping myself that I'd have to go home without Lorraine. I leaned over the balcony; my mam and dad downed their drinks and said their loved-up drunken goodbyes to their new forever friends, the ones they'd promise to keep in touch with after the holiday and who wouldn't get so much as Christmas card.

It was a now or never moment. I bolted down the stairs two-at-a-time, which was asking a lot of my body, and managed to catch my gran shuffling out behind my mam and dad.

'Gran, Lorraine's away tae the toilets then we're going tae the chippy.'

'Yer dad said you've already been.'

'Aye, but it's the sea air, it's making me hungry.'

'And ah suppose there would be laddies going with you?'

'That'd be telling gran.' I gave her a wink.

I turned to go, although I'd no idea where, but my gran grabbed my arm and pulled me close. 'Noo promise me, you'll keep yer hand on yer ha'penny.'

'Nae need tae worry gran, ah can look after myself and ah'll keep an eye on Lorraine.'

'That's what ah like tae hear. Have a good time but make sure you two lassies stick together.'

'Ah will. Listen gran, there might be a big queue at the chippy so tell ma mam and dad no tae wait up for us.'

'Hen, they're both steaming, they wouldnae be able tae wait up if they tried. Yer dad's claiming the drive has taken it oot of him and yer mam's saying it's the excitement that's wiped her oot. But they've no mentioned the beer and Bacardi they guzzled aw night. Ah'll wait up for you. Just dinnae be too late.'

'Ah won't gran. Once ah've had a bag of scraps, ah'll be straight back tae the caravan.'

'Just watch oot for the vinegar; if ma memory's right, it disnae half sting if it gets in the wrong places.'

Chapter Eighteen

As always, my gran was right; there was no sign of my mam and dad when I keeked through the slit left between the curtains and knocked on the caravan window. The telly was on and my gran was busy dealing with her teeth. She dropped a Steradent tablet into a glass of water; the white disc fizzed and covered her falsers with bubbles. I didn't want to knock too hard and give her a fright; I took off my sandal and used the heel to gently tap the glass. The curtain wheeched open and I was the one who got a fright as my gran pressed her gummsy grin up against the glass, eased open the window and whispered into the darkness, 'Where's Lorraine?'

'She left the Clubhouse withoot me.'

'Tae go where?'

'Ah dinnae ken. She was with a guy called Danny the last time ah saw her.'

'Hells bells, ah thought ah warned you tae stick together. Right, wait there and ah'll be oot the noo.'

I hoped she put her teeth back in before we went out, it wasn't fair to scare anyone else and without her falsers, she lisped like Baz the Spaz. My gran disappeared from view and sleekit as ever, Bimbo took the chance to chew on one of her slippers. He showed no respect for the slipper; with the fur lining and satin bows it was easy to assume that they did nothing except keep my gran's feet cosy. Bimbo didn't realise that her slipper was also a piece of sporting equipment, similar to a discus and I was a champion thrower. I'd more chance of competing at the Commonwealth Games than Karen and this latest pair had seen a bit of action. I first knocked Rab's cat flying with one when the manky brute crapped on my gran's front step. Rab called the bloated ball of fur Major Tom and it shat its body weight without worrying where it dropped a batch. It was a monster but thanks to my slipper throwing skill, my gran's size five regularly floored Jabba the Cat.

Major Tom's daily dumps were a problem my gran thought she could solve. She saw it on the telly that apparently lion shit works a treat; little cats don't like big cats. Although I'd decked Major Tom with a slipper, he could never be described as a wee pussy but my gran assumed that he would still be feart of a lion. I wasn't convinced; there were scarier beasts than a lion roaming round the scheme. Her plan was to take a trip to Edinburgh Zoo and ask a keeper to fill an old ice-cream tub with lion dung. She felt it was the kindest way to keep Major Tom out of her garden; I didn't tell her that her slipper already had a world-class success rate.

My gran reappeared with her shoes on and the sure-fire slipper fell from Bimbo's mouth, the pink satin bow dark with slavers. I tiptoed along the veranda; inside the caravan my gran lisped something about taking Bimbo out for a last pee before the door clicked open.

'Ah dinnae ken why ah bothered sticking ma heid intae yer mam's and dad's bedroom. They're both oot for the count. Yer mam's snoring like a pig and yer dad's beer fart brought tears tae ma eyes.'

She trotted down the steps as if she had a plan. I'd no idea which way to go – paths zig-zagged all over the camp site.

'How're we gonnae find her gran?'

'We'll start back at the Clubhouse and work oor way up and doon the main paths.'

For a massive place, it was surprisingly quiet. The only noise close by leaked from a caravan where an after cabaret crowd had gathered to get stuck into a carry out of home measures and with no fear of a call for last orders at the bar. It felt like we were in a cop show and should be shining a torch in big wide arcs across paths and into bushes. And we shoud've let Bimbo breathe in Lorraine's scent from her nightshirt and he'd snuffle into bushes. But this wasn't the telly and the thought of what we might find hidden gave me the heebie-jeebies.

A dog walker wearing a Newcastle football top stopped to let his rat on a leash have a sniff at Bimbo's arse.

'You havenae seen a girl with long blonde hair have you?' asked my gran.

'Nah, sorry. I've just stepped out with the wife's mutt.'

The guy tugged on the chihuahua's diamante lead and turned down a path before anyone else saw him with the poofy pet; it made Bimbo look butch. We walked off but turned when he shouted back at us,

'Hang on a minute, when I closed the curtains I did notice a lass run ahint the van. But I'm not sure she was a blonde, I'd usually notice that.'

'She's no a natural blonde and her roots need done,' I said.

'Never mind her, which way did she go?' asked my gran, drawing me a dirty look.

'Doon that way I think.'

He pointed along a row of caravans that went on as far as the beach, which is far enough away to need the Puffer to drop folk off.

'When did you see her?'

''Bout half hour ago, I'd say. But I can't be sure.'

In that time she could be anywhere, and there was no telling if it was Lorraine or not. It was the only snippet we had though and my gran was already hoofing it down the path.

'Wait up gran.' She only ever moved that fast if she was worried that she'd missed the bus to the bingo.

'Mibbae if you stayed away fae the chippy, you'd be able tae keep up with yer gran.'

Folk often say things they didn't mean when they are stressed but it still hurt, especially coming from my gran. It wasn't my fault Lorraine had gone missing in action and yet my gran was giving me a hard time. It was typical that I had to suffer for my best pal's stupidity. I'd never go off with a strange guy, no matter how much I fancied him and it was no excuse for my gran to slag me off, even if she was worried about Lorraine. I was freaked out too but I didn't tell my gran that her crocheted cardi looked like mice had chewed holes in it. And it was too tight round her bust and the buttons looked like they were about to ping off and take someone's eye out. I said nothing to upset her and proved how mature I was.

I followed my gran and Bimbo up the path until we came to a crossroads. She stopped at a floral display in the middle and I called out Lorraine's name.

'Wheesht, there are weans sleeping.'

'Who gives a stuff? We need tae find her.'

'Aye, but if you keep that up you'll wake the whole site. And all hell will break loose if folk think something's up. Afore you ken it, the polis will be here.'

'Well we cannae go creeping aboot in the dark all night.'

'You're right, we'd be better off waiting at the caravan. She might even be back by noo.'

We looked down the four paths leading from the crossroad, but there was nothing to see except the glow from caravans with tellies still on. All we could do was turn on our heels and set back. We walked in silence with bad vibes keeping us company, my gran looking well scunnered and making everything seem worse. Bimbo tried to sniff a wet patch next to a bench and he practically got choked by his lead when my gran kept marching on. As we rounded the corner on the path leading to our caravan, I could make out Lorraine up ahead – she was alive, and in one piece. Everything was going to be fine. I couldn't help myself; I shouted out her name and did my best to break into a run.

I grabbed Lorraine from behind and spun her round for a hug. Her head was down, her body was rigid and her arms stayed limp by her side. My gran caught up and Bimbo's wagging tail slapped Lorraine's leg; she was statue-still and her zombie eyes stared at the ground as if she was counting blades of grass. I tilted her chin up and when our eyes locked, the tears tumbled; her mascara was already smudged across her cheeks. She found her inner wolf and let out an almighty howl; anyone would think she was auditioning for a horror movie.

'C'mon hen, let's get you inside.'

Patting Lorraine's arm, my gran hushed her like a baby and together we gently guided her up the stairs and into the caravan.

'Shush. Please Lorraine. If you dinnae stop greetin', ma mam and dad'll hear you,' I whispered.

'Angela's right, there'll be a helluva scene if you wake them up.'

At last my gran was back on my side, a team again. She switched the kettle on and we sat at the kitchen table. I pulled Lorraine in tight; it seemed to help comfort her and had the added bonus of muffling her sobs. I ignored the snotters on the shoulder of my new vest top.

'You need tae keep the heid and try tae calm doon, there's nae problem that cannae be sorted oot o'er a cuppa tea,' said my gran. I'd the feeling that Lorraine was going to prove her wrong. I'd noticed the rip at the seam of her denim skirt the minute she'd fallen through the caravan door. At first I assumed she was hammered, but this time was different. I'd seen her stagger home drunk before but never in a state like this. Had something bad happened because I wasn't there to protect her?

Bimbo sniffed at my leg and I wondered whether he could smell my guilt as toxic fumes that clung to me. The lies I'd told her about Stevie forcing me to have sex with him hadn't just finished the relationship between Lorraine and him; my dishonesty had meant she'd put herself at risk to keep up with her best pal's fictitious sexual experience.

Bimbo tried to get up on Lorraine's lap but she pushed him back down to the floor and he landed on his side. He let out a yelp and without giving Lorraine a row my gran slid a cup of milky tea across the table. I prized Lorraine off me and urged her to take a drink, but she shook her head and sucked up a plug of snot.

'Ah looked for you everywhere,' I said. 'Where did you go?'

Nothing except more sniffing and shaking. My gran lifted the overhead cupboard and pulled out a scratchy blanket, the kind a horse wore on its back. Lorraine wrapped the hairy blanket round her shoulders, so numb she didn't feel its wooly roughness.

'Leave her be, she's in shock,' said my gran. 'Drink up Lorraine, you're safe noo.'

Lorraine slurped at the tea and continued to shiver.

'When you've finished that, go wash yer face and then we'll talk.'

'I want a shower.' It was the first time she'd spoken since we'd found her wandering outside.

'Sorry hen, but it might waken them up.' My gran tilted her head in the direction of my mam and dad's bedroom. 'And trust me, the state they're in, they're better off staying in bed. Angela, go and get Lorraine's nightshirt.'

I wasn't sure I should leave Lorraine's side; my gran made my mind up for me and elbowed me off the padded bench seat. I crept through to our bedroom and heaved Lorraine's case out from under the bed. She'd hung up her going out clothes in the skinny wardrobe but the rest of her stuff was still packed in the neat piles. I peeled off layer after layer of T-shirts, vest tops, shorts and undies until I found her nightshirt at the bottom of the pile. The lilac nightshirt had a picture of a teddy bear and the slogan, *"I'm beary special"* across the front. I already knew that she was special; it didn't seem as if Danny did.

I bit down on my pillow, pretending that it was Danny's face, raging that she'd come home in tears. This was supposed to be a holiday of a lifetime for us and that wanker had ruined it on the first night. The bedroom walls were cardboard thin and it would've been easy to punch a hole in one. I remembered the time my dad came home from the Clubhouse and got his feet caught in his jeans trying to strip for bed. Me and Karen heard the crash and then his elbow poked through the wall next to the bunk bed. It was stuck there long enough for me to grab one of Karen's felt tips and draw a face on it. Karen fell off the bed laughing; it didn't take much to amuse her. But when my dad saw my doodle, it turned out his funny bone was faulty; his hand was still able to swing when he clipped me round the back of my head. Karen peed herself laughing.

I resisted the urge to knock lumps out of the wall and took another bite at the pillow before I could face Lorraine again. Even with the horse blanket round her shoulders, Lorraine still shivered with both hands wrapped round her mug of tea. She looked more like a mountain rescue team had airlifted her off Ben Nevis rather than having danced the night away at the disco. Although the truth was I had no idea where she'd been or what had happened to wipe her out.

I lightly placed the nightshirt on her lap; she didn't look up from the bottom of the mug. My gran prized her frozen fingers from the mug and held her hands within hers as if she was about to lead a Happy Clappy prayer meeting.

'Ah have tae ask you, did he hurt you?' whispered my gran.

Lorraine shuddered.

'You need tae tell me. It's important.'

I couldn't bear to listen to Lorraine's reply. I needed chocolate but I was too stressed to move. I've always believed that me and my gran were tuned into the same frequency, and she claimed to have a sixth sense. I wasn't surprised when she told me that there was a bar of emergency fruit and nut in her handbag, I was glad to leave my gran to deal with Lorraine's answers. I dipped into my gran's bag on the ledge above the couch, peeled the wrapper off and snapped off a chunk. My gran leaned in close to Lorraine and I couldn't make out what she was saying. But I heard Lorraine's reply without any trouble; my teeth clamped on to the square of chocolate and crushed an almond in two.

'I should've taken your advice, not hers.'

My gran turned to face me, eyes as wide as a toddler on their first trip to Santa's grotto.

'The chocolate was meant for Lorraine, you're no the one in shock.'

'Sorry.'

I could've argued that I'd had a hellish night too, but instead I handed the rest of the bar over. Neither of them took it from me so I broke off another square.

'What dae you mean aboot listening tae me instead of Angela?'

Lorraine finally lifted her head and gave me the evil eye, the same hard look we'd practised since primary school. We saved the evil eye for folk who pissed us off, not each other. My gran waited for me to give some sort of answer but my mouth was full of fruit and nut. She turned back to Lorraine. 'Ah telt you tae keep yer hand on yer ha'penny. Are you saying that he took advantage of you?'

'That's one way of putting it.' Lorraine pointed a trembling finger at me. 'But you said I should get it over with.'

'Did you?' My gran's neck swivelled round like a periscope.

'Ah didnae think she'd actually go through with it. It was a joke. Ah'm sorry!'

'Joke? Ah cannae see Lorraine laughing. And neither am ah. Get tae bed.'

I was seventeen and in a handful of words thrown at me my gran erased a dozen years and I was a wean again. I knew not to argue and there was nothing else I could say. Sorry wouldn't give Lorraine back her virginity. But it was worth a try.

'Ah'm really sorry, ah didnae mean…'

'Just go.' Lorraine cuddled into my gran's shoulder; anyone would think she was hugging into her own gran, not mine. The whole scene was wrong, tonight wasn't meant to play out like this. Lorraine was supposed to come back with the juicy details of being with Danny, I'd share my time with Brian and together we'd build up a story of holiday romances. My gran would wait up to have a laugh with us and make us a toast an cheese for our supper. But sometime after me wolfing down a bag of scraps and Brian getting a bad case of the trots, everything went tits up.

I slunk off to my bedroom although I kept the door open wide enough to let snatches of their conversation drift through the gap. My gran asked her whether Danny had taken precautions. There was mumbling from Lorraine; I caught the phrase, 'withdrawal method' and needed to bite on my pillow again.

'God love you. That takes years of practice. And it still isnae 100% safe. Angela wouldnae have a mammy if it worked every time.'

I wondered if my mam knew that she was the result of a dribble on the end of my grandda's willy. An accident. It made it sound exciting, like something out of the ordinary had happened. I couldn't help thinking that if my mam was lucky to be born, she should've done something special with her life. Although I suppose if my grandda had slipped out from my gran in time, I wouldn't be here either. On the plus side, the world of gymnastics wouldn't have to suffer Karen's pathetic attempts at sport.

At least I wasn't going to throw away my chance of a life worth living. Once I'd finished sixth year, I'd be off to Glasgow Art School and leave all the losers from the scheme behind. Lorraine could share a flat with me in the west end and we would have parties every weekend or go to Tin Pan Alley. I'd help her find a job, there was a huge Top Shop in Argyle Street and she'd love working in fashion. And she'd get a staff discount on cool stuff for us. She could end up as Top Shop's international buyer and dress their windows. It would be amazing and when we came home to visit, everybody would be jealous of us because we'd have a life they could only dream about. We wouldn't let our dodgy genes hold us back. We had a future; all I had to do for now was get us through the next year and we'd never look back.

But first, I had to help Lorraine into her *'Beary special'* night shirt. She tottered through to our bedroom and swiped the night shirt from my hands. We'd changed in front of each other since primary one – she was the only one on the planet who'd seen me semi-naked – but she took the nightshirt into the bathroom and locked the door.

There was water running and I realised that Lorraine had ignored my gran's order and turned the shower on. My gran wouldn't give her a row, who could blame her for wanting to wash the night away? Not that having a shower would be a pleasant experience, since the water coming out was more of a trickle than a spray and the slimy curtain wrapped around a wet body like a giant squid. It wouldn't matter tonight though, Lorraine wouldn't care about the clingy curtain and my mam and dad wouldn't hear the feeble dribble of water.

My gran was reckless too and lit a fag inside, sticking two fingers up at the **'No Smoking'** stickers dotted round the caravan like markers for an orienteering trail. I sidled up the couch beside her and raised my eyebrow at the tower of ash ready to topple; my gran cupped her hand and flicked the ash into her palm.

'Ma nerves are shot tae hell,' she said. I knew the feeling and was tempted to ask her for a fag too but decided that'd be chancing my luck.

'Dae you think Lorraine'll be okay?' I asked.

'Depends when she had her last period. Dae you ken when it was?'

'Ah dinnae ken when ah had mine; so ah've nae idea aboot Lorraine's.'

'Ah just thought that with the amount of time you spend together you'd have menstrual synchrony.'

'Eh?'

'Ah've telt you aw this before. The Moon and Mars control the menstrual cycles and it's a fact that close friends have similar sun and moon positions in their horoscopes. So you and Lorraine should have astrological harmony.'

I couldn't concentrate on my gran's Mother Moon guff after all the drama. I just wanted Lorraine to scrub clean whatever happened with Danny. Why couldn't we wake up tomorrow and make a fresh start on our holiday?

'But everything will work oot okay, won't it?'

'It's all doon tae destiny hen, you cannae fight that. If yer name's on the brick, it'll hit you.'

When Lorraine poked her head out the bathroom door, she looked like the brick had already battered her on the napper; it didn't seem as if the shower had helped.

My gran jumped to her feet and I had to barge past her to get to Lorraine first. It was the free toilet my gran was after, and by the expression on her face she couldn't have waited much longer. It looked like her insides were strangling her and her heavy breathing made her sound like Darth Vader. She hadn't eaten her chips and that was the third time today that I'd seen her run to the loo, not to mention her session in the bogs at Southwaite. And yet even with bouts of diarrhoea, her belly still looked like she was smuggling a space hopper out of Woolies. If I wasn't so worried about Lorraine, I'd be concerned about my gran. It felt as if everyone wanted a piece of me, and I didn't want to spread myself thin. I had to prioritise; my gran could look after herself. It was Lorraine who needed me more than ever.

Chapter Nineteen

I wanted to comfort Lorraine but my gran had warned me to leave her well alone and let her rest. Lorraine didn't sleep and neither did I; every time she tossed, turned and whimpered it shook the frame of the whole bunk bed. I bounced up and down on my marshmallow-soft mattress; any other night, I'd have joked that it felt like she had someone up there with her but tonight I said nothing and covered my head with my pillow, dotted with bite marks.

The morning light seeped through the tissue-thin curtains and for once it was a relief to get up early. Lorraine had eventually gone still; she finally crashed out but I couldn't lie underneath the weight of her mood any longer. In the kitchen, my gran was already moving around so I slid my cover off and gently eased the bedroom door open. It was doubtful that it would wake Lorraine up; right now she could beat my mam in a Snore Off competition.

'Cuppa tea?'

'Thanks gran. And can you stick on a couple of slices of toast?'

I squeezed passed my gran to nip into the loo. The bath towel was still sodden from Lorraine's late night shower and I wondered how much of it was damp from tears. I'd have to make sure Lorraine troweled on an extra layer of make-up today; nothing got past my mam, she'd notice puffy eyes and interrogate us until she wore us down. The Gestapo could've used her skills.

'Is Lorraine still asleep?'

'Aye, she hardly slept a wink aw night.'

'Poor lassie, but no matter how knackered she is today, make sure you keep her busy. It's the best way,' said my gran as she buttered my toast. 'That's why ah knit; it stops me dwelling on dark stuff.'

It was hard to see how knit one, purl one would chase away demons, but I wasn't up for a debate. My gran's logic always won in the end.

My mam stoated out from her bedroom, rubbing crusted mascara from her stubby lashes, a yawn revealing a furry tongue.

'Stick the kettle back on will you mam?' she asked my gran. She might look rough but I wasn't fooled that her radar was any less efficient. 'So where did you two get tae after the disco?'

'The chippy then straight up the road. Eh gran?'

'Aye, ah locked up once they were hame safe. Did you no hear them shout good night? Or were you too drunk?'

'Ah wisnae drunk, just merry. It's the sea air that knocks me oot for the count. It does it every year.'

My mam unpacked the Kellogg's variety pack from the box of messages she'd brought with us; we were only allowed the mini boxes of cereal on holiday as a treat and it was even better that Karen wasn't here to fight over the Coco Pops.

From the kitchen, we all heard my dad let a fart go that could launch a balloon. My gran shook her head in disgust. Lorraine couldn't have slept through that and sure enough a few minutes later she stumbled into the kitchen. I thought my mam was rough but she was fresh-faced compared with Lorraine who looked like she'd gone ten rounds with Giant Haystacks. Lorraine shuffled into the toilet, my mam too busy eating her box of Corn Flakes to sniff out trouble.

Bimbo licked my mam's bowl clean and my dad surfaced from the bedroom to make his way to the fridge.

'Christ, ma tongue could sand floorboards.'

He scratched his arse as he drank the milk straight out of the carton and my gran plopped five eggs into a pot of boiling water. I sighed; eggs were the last thing my dad needed to add to his rancid beer fart mix and we'd all suffer for it later. It was a blessing that there was no sign or sound of Lorraine leaving the bathroom to share the joy of a family breakfast.

'Ah hope she's no going tae hog the bathroom aw week. If she disnae hurry up, ah'll need tae go behind those bushes,' said my dad, pointing outside at an innocent clump of greenery. I was sure a shiver of fear shook through their leaves. At least he hadn't peed in the wardrobe like he often did when drunk at home, although it was early days.

'You will not! We'll get thrown off the site if you're caught.'

'Naebody bothered on the way hame last night.'

'That's 'cause everybody was steamin' said my mam.

'Except you,' added my gran.

'You sunk a few brandies yourself!' said my mam.

'Aye, well ah was just being sociable,' replied my gran. 'You should try it some time.'

Thankfully Lorraine was still locked safely inside the bathroom. I was so used to the banter and insults ping-ponging back and forth that it was easy to forget how my family could cause an embarrassing scene before they'd even got dressed. By the time the bathroom door creaked open, my gran had stormed off in a huff with Bimbo under her arm, my dad had bolted into his bedroom with the empty milk carton and holding his crotch and my mam had bitten a fingernail and used it to pick out bits of Corn Flakes from her teeth: a scene of domestic bliss.

'You'll need tae shake a leg Lorraine, we'll be heading doon tae the beach soon,' said my mam, chewing a morsel of corn flake she'd rescued. Lorraine looked as if she'd rather douse herself with petrol and set herself on fire.

'I'm no feeling too good,' mumbled Lorraine.

'Tae be honest, ah'm feeling a bit fragile myself; ah think the English pub measures must be bigger than we're used tae at hame. Ma heid feels like it's full of doors and they're aw banging.'

My mam drained the boiling water from the pot of eggs and left them to cool for our picnic; she was a woman on a mission. 'We could all dae with a bit of fresh air, or we'll never be fit for the Clubhouse tonight.'

'Mam, if Lorraine disnae fancy the beach, we'll just hang aboot here.'

'Nae chance. We came here tae spend time together as a family. And ah promised her mam we'd give her a nice holiday. It could be pissing doon the rest of the week so we're having a day at the beach.'

'But mam…'

'But mam nothing, the pair of you've got the rest of the summer tae stay indoors.' She turned to Lorraine who was hugging a cushion. 'And you look like a washed oot dish cloth, a bit of colour in yer cheeks will dae you good.' Her glare spun round, I wasn't getting off with a direct hit either. 'And it's a known fact that a tan makes you look slimmer. So away and get ready.'

My mam was maybe right, getting Lorraine up and running was probably best and I didn't fancy being stuck with her on my own with nothing to say that could help make her feel any better. Lorraine didn't seem to have the fight in her and plodded back to the bedroom as my gran burst in the door dragging Bimbo behind her.

'You'll never believe who ah've just met?'

'Naw, but ah'm sure you're gonnae tae tell us whether we want tae ken or no,' said my mam, packing the five hard boiled eggs into a Tupperware tub along with sachets of salt and pepper she'd pocketed at Southwaite. She'd also stashed a week's worth of tomato sauce sachets which wasn't a bad haul considering we hadn't even eaten in the café.

'Ah bumped intae Big Davey. He's doon here with his wife and three weans. They're staying in Row 13. Ah telt him we'd be at the Clubhouse tonight if they wanted tae join us.'

'Great. He plays bowls with yer dad. Ah'll mibbae get a chance tae get roond the shops in peace if they go tae the Bowling Green in Filey.'

The importance of quality family time was quickly blown out the water now that my mam had a better idea. She shouted through to my dad who was emptying the piss filled milk carton down the bog.

'Dae you hear that? Big Davey is in Row 13!'

'Ah didnae realise it was this week he was coming. That's magic, he's got a great job as a supervisor at OKI, he'll be able tae buy us a round or two at the Clubhouse.'

The poor guy was shafted before he'd finished unpacking his suitcase. I left them to the excitement of trapping one of their own and risked joining Lorraine in our bedroom. She was lying on the top bunk instead of under the covers which was a promising sight.

'Listen, it's probably a good idea tae get oot. The beach is miles long, we dinnae need tae sit anywhere near them.'

There was no reply, just a sigh that could split a heart wide open. I reached up to stroke her arm but she batted it away.

'Please Lorraine, if you come it'll shut ma mam up.'

'Why don't you shut up and leave me alone?'

I worried that Lorraine's growl would get louder. My mam could hear the grass grow and would be through any minute if she thought we were arguing. At home, even when I whispered, *"Ah hate you"* at Karen, my mam's super-powered ears picked up the slightest signal of any aggro and her slipper was slapping arses before we knew she'd come into the room.

'C'mon, stick on yer sunglasses and you'll look fine. And there's always an ice-cream van parked at the beach.'

'So you think a 99 is all it'll take to make me feel better?'

She leaned over the side of the bunk bed and was glaring at me. 'And you're supposed to be the clever one?'

She didn't push it any further. I was chuffed to see her get off the bed and put on her denim shorts and spaghetti strapped top. It was progress. I yanked on my denim shorts too but decided on a T-shirt; it was dangerous to let my 36Ds swing free and my white bra had gone grey after I accidentally chucked it into the washing machine along with a load of my dad's work clothes. Lorraine could get away without wearing a bra and she was able to put her hair into a French plait without even looking in the mirror. All I could manage was a ponytail and I didn't chance asking her to do a plait for me. We packed our bags for the beach in silence; it was enough that she had agreed to go and I guessed that twenty-four hours in my mam's company had convinced her not to challenge the almighty force of She-Ra. Karen gave my mam the nickname She-Ra when she threw her weight around acting tough, although it showed what a numpty Karen was because my mam wasn't glamorous enough to be compared to the cartoon character. We'd done Celtic history in school and Atilla the Hun was butt-ugly – that hound would've been a better match for our mam but the nickname would've taken too much explaining to Karen.

My gran and Bimbo were already gone when we joined my mam and dad in the living room.

'She's feart she misses the Puffer,' said my mam. 'Me and yer dad are just gonnae walk tae the beach. Are you coming with us?'

'I'd like to have a shot on the Puffer,' said Lorraine.

Any other time, I'd slag her off for being a big wean and I wondered why she seemed so keen to ride on a tarted up tractor.

'Okey-dokey. See you doon there,' said my mam.

Lorraine followed me along the path to the stop for the Puffer but when I turned to speak to her she'd veered off to the right.

'It's this way!' I called but she marched on. I jogged up behind her and grabbed her arm. 'Where're you off tae?' She pulled away and kept going.

'I'm going home.' Lorraine was walking in the direction of the campsite entrance leading on to the main road.

'Dinnae be ridiculous! You cannae go hame.'

'I can and you can't stop me.'

'How're you gonnae get back? You cannae just jump on a bus tae Bonnybridge fae here.'

'I'm no stupid. I'll phone my mam and she'll come and get me.'

I tugged on her arm again and she stopped to face me.

'Dinnae be so selfish! What're ma mam and dad going tae say if you just disappear? They'll kill me.'

'That's typical! All you ever think about is yourself.'

'That's no fair Lorraine. And never mind aboot me, what aboot yer mam? How's she going tae get doon here with Janine in tow? It's no fair tae give her aw this hassle. And how're you gonnae explain why you've cut the holiday short?'

'That's my problem. No need for you to concern yourself.'

'Look, ah ken you're upset aboot last night, and ah've said ah'm sorry, but you shouldnae take it oot on me. Ah'm the one who spent hours looking for you. Dinnae blame me 'cause *you* left the Clubhouse with Danny and left me with his pal.'

There was a rumble on the road behind us then a squeal of, 'Stop!' We both spun round to see my gran sitting in the front row of the Puffer and waving Bimbo's paw at us. The driver pulled the Puffer into the side of the grass verge and tipped his Stetson at us.

'Jump aboard ladies.'

My gran shuffled along the bench to make room and the rest of the passengers waited patiently for us to climb up. Her cheery face seemed to melt Lorraine's determination to go; either that or she didn't have the balls to delay the Puffer. Lorraine squeezed in beside my gran and Bimbo and we bounced along the road to the top of the steep hill down to the beach. I made it clear to my gran that we planned to sunbathe alone.

'Disnae make any difference tae me, ah'm no going tae the beach anyway. Johnny is due a break after the next two circuits so ah'm staying on and going for a cuppa with him.'

The auld cowboy had a name and my gran had wasted no time in getting up close and personal.

'He keeps the Puffer in a garage but he's done it up like a saloon in a western,' added my gran.

'With a bar?'

'Naw, screw the bobbin, he wouldnae be allowed tae drink and drive. He's decorated the garage with stuff he's collected o'er the years, like cow hides and kid on wagon wheels. But it's got a wee seating area for taking his breaks.'

'That's cosy,' I said.

'Aye, he's nicknamed the place Saddle Sore. Ah cannae wait tae see inside it.'

Whoa there cowboy; Johnny boy was obviously a smooth operator, full of patter and he even had a customised shagging pad to lasso desperate old women.

'Saddle Sore? Is this wise gran, you ken nothing aboot this Johnny character. And this den of his could be well dodgy.'

'That's just yer dirty mind working! It's only where he rests his backside after a shift in the Puffer.'

'Really? Are you sure?'

'There's nae need tae worry aboot me; ah've been roond the block a few times, ah can look after myself.'

'He sounds like a total chancer tae me.'

'You've got him aw wrong. In ma line of work you need tae be a good judge of character and ah saw right through him. He's heartbroken and ah can help.'

'What's that got tae dae with you going roond tae Saddle Sore?'

'Ah'm doing him a favour, that's aw. His Jack Russell crossed over the Rainbow Bridge a while ago so ah've offered tae contact Amigo for him.'

'What happened tae Amigo?'

'Johnny reversed the Puffer o'er the poor wee thing.'

'Oh my god, should he be allowed tae drive the Puffer?'

'It wisnae Johnny's fault. A wean dropped a Funny Feet ice-cream lolly in the parking bay and Amigo jumped oot of

Johnny's cab for a lick. But Amigo had a bad hip and wisnae quick enough off the mark tae avoid the Puffer crushing him.'

'So he was flattened licking a foot-shaped ice-cream? What a way tae go.'

'Aye, Johnny's been having nightmares aboot pink feet chasing him. He thinks it's Amigo's way of blaming him so ah need tae reassure him that his wee pal is happy on the other side.'

Lorraine's eyeballs rolled but at least she kept her geggie shut; the last thing I needed was my gran to be in a bad mood too.

'Well, say hola tae Amigo fae us.' I winked at Lorraine. She didn't react other than to turn on her heel and march down the hill to the beach, and I was just relieved that she was further away from the campsite's phone boxes.

We stopped at the end of the path to suss out a decent sunbathing spot. The beach was already hoaching, as if all the caravans had been turned upside down to tip the folk out, leaving them sprawled across every inch of sand. I scanned the length of the beach but it was hard to find my mam and dad among the crowd. There were weans everywhere, running back and forth to the water's edge to refill buckets and pour the dregs into moats round sandcastles that dads had masterminded. Others just wanted to dig a hole in the sand to Australia and the rest were jumping the waves or queuing for a cone at the ice-cream van.

Hiding behind candy striped wind breaks, men slept underneath newspapers and women shooed wasps from picnics. Teenagers were spread-eagled on beach towels with ghetto blasters pumping out Radio Lux and in the middle of it all I spotted our tartan rug with my mam and dad lying side by side. They weren't sunbathing, they were snogging. My breakfast toast shot up and stuck in my throat. I tried to force the dry lump back down but it was like swallowing a cat's fur ball. Lorraine hadn't noticed the gruesome sight and I steered her in the opposite direction towards the ice-cream van. I desperately needed a 99, my sugar levels had nose-dived with the shock of seeing my mam and dad groping each other in public.

There was a sign up at the end of the path with the beach rules.

NO MOTORISED VEHICLES
NO LITTERING
NO DOGS
NO FIRES
NO ALCOHOL
NO GLASS CONTAINERS

There was no mention of **NO PARENTAL PAWING IN PUBLIC** and surely that was much more anti-social than any of the other no-nos. I was in dire need of something to wash down my disgust and joined the queue for the ice-cream van.

'Can't you go five minutes without food?' asked Lorraine.

'Oh c'mon Lorraine, that's harsh. It's nearly an hour since ah had ma toast. And ah'm on holiday.'

I could've explained why I had the taste of bile in my mouth but I didn't want her to see my mam and dad in action; one of us feeling the need to puke was enough.

'I'll find somewhere for us to sunbathe,' said Lorraine and she walked off, thankfully further away from the sickening scene. Watching her traipse across the sand, I noticed she was walking funny; it made me wonder if Danny had her hurt last night. I didn't want to bring it up again and was only happy that she was still here and still talking to me. After five minutes the queue for the ice-cream van had barely moved; a group of greedy bastards were ordering double cones, choc ices, sweets, crisps and juice. It seemed like a lifetime ago when I queued for broken wafers off the ice-cream van at home. And yet I was still living in the same street, doing the same things with the same folk. Something had to change soon or I'd go radio rental. At least the end was in sight and my life could actually begin. Only one more year at school to put my portfolio together and then I'd be off to Art School. Me and Lorraine would have our own flat and we'd be partying every weekend. The uni was in the trendy west end but then again maybe I'd want to stay nearer the Art School and if Lorraine got a job in one of the big shops she'd want to be close to Sauchiehall or Argyle Street. There were lots of decisions to be made although it didn't really matter where our flat was, we could use the underground to get all over the city, wherever we fancied. Not stuck in a shit hole with nothing to do but eat, sleep, work and watch telly. My mam and dad existed like hamsters on a wheel; their sad little life wasn't for me and Lorraine, we would do more than exist, our motto would be to love what we do and do what we love. All I needed was to get Lorraine back on track and the plan would take shape.

By the time I got served, Lorraine was sitting with her back against a sand dune with her *Just Seventeen* covering her face. She looked as if she might be sleeping. I didn't want to disturb her after she'd had such a tough night but it was a shame she wasn't awake; I had to eat the 99 I'd bought her before it melted. It'd been a hellish start to the holiday. I opened my can of *Fanta* to wash down my Mars bar and hoped that the sugar rush would calm me down. I tilted my head up to the sun and screwed my eyes shut and through the thin layer of skin dots darted around in squiggly lines, my eyelids filling with kaleidoscope patterns. The effect only lasted for seconds, long enough to block out the real world where my gran was off talking to Amigo on the Other Side, my mam and dad were playing tonsil hockey and Lorraine was breathing heavily next to me. There was no one else on the beach except me.

'So this is where you're hiding?'

My dad's shadow blocked out the sun and the light was gone. Lorraine stayed with her magazine shielding her face, a smart move.

'Ah've just been talking tae Big Davey and it's aw sorted.'

'What're you talking aboot dad?'

'A job. For you. Great news, eh?'

I choked on my Fanta, as he kept rabbiting on. I heard the words but they made no sense. Within five minutes of chatting to a pal from his bowling club, my dad had arranged for an interview at OKI for me, although Big Davey promised him that it was just a formality and as long as I showed up for a quick chat with the Office Manager, I had a job. And that was all that was needed to set a match to my dreams and watch them burn.

'You've wasted yer time. Ah keep telling you that ah want tae go tae Art School!'

'Angela, we've been through aw this before. Ah'm no saying you're no allowed tae draw or paint anymair but naebody gets tae make their hobby their job. Life disnae work like that and the sooner you wise up the better.'

'Ah'm no going for an interview.'

'You are. As long as you're living under ma roof, you've got nae choice. End. Of. Story.'

Chapter Twenty

After my dad stormed off, Lorraine wasn't interested in helping me find a way to avoid working at OKI. She had a cheek to accuse me of being self-centered. My brain was in overdrive and it was hard to concentrate with a pair of brats playing up on the grass behind us. They were whacking each other with mini golf clubs and every time their plastic sticks connected with a body part, their squeals made me want to flatten their faces into the sand.

With all their bouncing up and down, the sand underneath the ragged edge of grass had fallen off in a chunk that landed right behind Lorraine's head. The little shits were so noisy, I didn't realise that it was Lorraine screaming. The boys tumbled on to the beach, kicking up a sandstorm as they ran off, they'd dropped three feet on to their arses but it was more likely that Lorraine's squealing made them fill their pants. I almost felt sorry for the boys, they weren't to know what had freaked Lorraine out. One look at her terrified face and I understood that she wasn't on a beach in Filey; she was back at the quarry in Bonnybridge, a wee lassie fighting for breath under a collapsed sand dune. But her best pal saved her.

'It's okay, you're fine. Ah'm here.'

I hugged her tight. It was good to feel this close again and I didn't care that people were staring at us; I couldn't blame them for gawking. Lorraine sounded hysterical and no one except me knew the reason why she was shaking, but at least she'd stopped screaming. A busybody stood up from behind her wind break to ask if Lorraine was alright.

'It was a wasp, but it's gone noo. Thanks.'

This seemed enough information to stop the rubbernecking. A few shook their heads at Lorraine's outburst and I resisted the urge to give them the one fingered salute.

Lorraine eased herself out of my grasp.

'You made me sound like a right fanny.'

'Well, what did you want me tae shout across the beach? That you had a flash back tae a near death experience? Would that have sounded better?'

She made no reply, she knew I was right. It was hard work protecting her all the time. All these years I'd been there for her, day in, day out – it was a full-time job. I'd put up with her constant moaning about her mam and Janine, helped her with schoolwork, done her hair and make-up, listened to her go on about boys she fancied, held her hair back when she threw up, let her use my razor to shave her legs. And then there was the fact that I'd saved her life. I wondered if Lorraine knew what unconditional love actually meant. My gran taught me that love is an action, not a feeling.

'I want to go home.'

'Please, dinnae start aw this again. How many times dae you want me tae say that ah'm sorry?'

She grabbed her magazine and stuffed it into her straw beach bag along with her towel.

'You don't understand.'

'Ah dae. But you're safe. Everything's fine noo.'

'Naw, everything's no fine. This whole holiday has been a nightmare.'

She'd raised her voice and the wobbly tone would soon have the nosey bastards asking what was up again, and unless there was a wasp's nest nearby I was snookered for a good excuse this time.

'Dae you no think you're being a bit of a drama queen? We've only been here twenty four hours and okay, last night could've been better but we've got the rest of the week tae make up for it. Forget aboot Danny.'

Although she didn't scream the sobbing was just as embarrassing.

'You're making a show of yourself. Let's go back tae the caravan.'

'I've told you, I want to go home.'

She took off across the beach, another attack of sand clouds to piss everyone off. A cry of someone bawling, *'For fuck's sake!'* didn't slow her down; I'd never be able to keep up with her in my flip flops. I grabbed my stuff and bundled it into my bag, making sure I didn't lose sight of Lorraine. The last thing I needed was for her to go missing again; there was no way I could explain that to her mam. There was more to Lorraine's reaction than a disastrous date with Danny or a childhood traumatic memory; she'd completely lost the plot.

Sister Patricia had taught us the prayer for loss:

O blessed St. Anthony, the grace of God
has made you a powerful advocate in all
our needs and the patron for the restoring
of things lost or stolen.
I turn to you today with childlike love and
deep confidence.
You have helped countless children of God
to find the things they have lost, material
things, and, more importantly, the things
of the spirit: faith, hope, and love.
I come to you with confidence; help me in
my present need.
I recommend what I have lost to your care,
in the hope that God will restore it to me,
if it is His holy Will.
Amen.

But when we were in a hurry, if we'd lost our keys, library card or lipstick, we went for the high-speed, no nonsense version that Lorraine's mam used round the house.

Saint Antony, Saint Antony,
listen listen,
you better come quick,
'cause somethin's missin'.

I said both prayers for good measure; I was taking no chances of losing Lorraine, not just in person but the bond between us. Sister Patricia always told us that sincerity moves mountains so I repeated the prayers as I followed her zig-zag path between the folk littering the beach. It was a relief that Lorraine skirted round the spot where my mam and dad had taken up residence; it was obvious now that she was heading straight for the phone boxes.

'Lorraine wait up!' I shouted and she stopped ahead of me, not because I'd roared at her, but because my gran and Bimbo were blocking her path. My prayers had been answered; I knew

I could rely on my gran, she would save the situation. Bimbo was in my gran's arms and she passed him over to Lorraine before scurrying off into the main complex. The handover gave me enough time to catch up with her; Lorraine lowered Bimbo to the ground and let him sniff the arse of a Labrador tied up outside the launderette.

I staggered up to her panting and patted her on the shoulder. She jumped as if I'd used an electric cattle prod.

'Where's ma gran gone?'

'She needed the toilet.'

This was promising, it was a good sign that she was talking to me and she'd stopped crying. It was dangerous pushing her but I needed to sort this out before my gran came back.

'Lorraine, ah hate seeing you upset but ah honestly dinnae ken what the big deal is. Ah ken it didnae turn oot great between you and Danny, but dinnae let him spoil oor holiday.'

'It didnae turn out great? That's putting it mildly!'

'But ah thought you liked him.'

'I did.'

My gran waved and made a bee-line for us; Bimbo pulled at his lead trying to drag Lorraine to join his mammy.

'Whatever went on, you ken you can tell me.'

'What difference will it make? You weren't that bothered after what happened between you and Stevie.'

'That wisnae the same. But you said that Danny didnae hurt you either.'

Lorraine's head dropped. I wanted her to tell me what was wrong but my gran was within earshot. And yet my gran knew about last night's carry on and she was the best person to help me deal with Lorraine. Maybe Saint Antony was hovering around after all.

'I've told you, I'm going home.'

'You cannae. It's no fair on everybody else.'

My gran flapped a piece of card above her head like she'd won a full house at the bingo. It was impossible to ignore her and impossible to get any more out of Lorraine.

'Because ah've got a golden ticket, ah've got a golden twinkle in ma eye.'

My gran jigged in front of us and hummed the theme song to

Charlie and the Chocolate Factory, stopping mid-tune when she got close.

'Ah wish ah had a mirror. The pair of you have faces that would turn milk soor.'

Neither of us said anything, I didn't know how to explain Lorraine's mood and she didn't seem keen to throw my gran a line.

'Well? Spit it oot. Have you been arguing?'

'Naw. We're fine,' I said.

Lorraine drew me a stinker as if everything was my fault. Anybody would think I'd made her go off with Danny and tipped a mound of sand beside her.

'So what's the golden ticket for gran?'

My gran flashed the card again, our crabbit faces forgotten.

'It's a VIP cabaret ticket for Bob Monkhouse tonight. And ah can get as many as ah need tae get us a table up at the front.'

'How did you get yer hands on that?'

'Johnny gave me it for getting in touch with Amigo.'

'And how is Amigo?'

'He's made lots of new pals. Ah could see him leaping fae cloud tae cloud with his wee wings fully formed noo and his hair flowing in the wind.'

I resisted the urge to point out that Jack Russells don't have long coats; I suppose she was allowed to use poetic license considering the whole scene she described was a load of guff.

'And Amigo's dodgy hip disnae bother him anymair so he's able to run free with aw the other pets. Johnny's happier noo that he kens a piece of his heart lives in heaven.'

My gran tipped her head back to look up into the sky and we followed her gaze. I half expected Amigo's tail to be dangling over the side of a cloud as he gave us a two-pawed wave while we stood like a bunch of fannies down below.

'It's a pity you didnae have one of yer poems tae give Johnny.'

My gran dug into her handbag and produced a used envelope stuffed with paper.

'Ta dah! Ah always carry a supply; you never ken when you might be called tae comfort a dog lover.'

When I was younger, I spent hours helping my gran copy out poems which she gave out to her clients as a parting gift at the end of their session. I still wrote them out for her if her stock was low and there was nothing on the telly when I was visiting. I knew them all off by heart and my favourite was the one that spells GOD backwards.

When God had made the earth and sky,
The flowers and the trees,
He then made all the animals,
The fish, the birds and bees.
And when at last He'd finished,
Not one was quite the same,
God said, "I'll walk this earth of mine,
And give each one a name."
And so He traveled far and wide,
And everywhere He went,
A little creature followed Him,
Until its strength was spent.
When all were named upon the earth,
And in the sky and sea,
The little creature said, "Dear Lord,
There's not one left for me."
Kindly the Father said to him,
"I've left you to the end,
I've turned my own name back to front,
And call you DOG, my friend."

There was also 'From Your Pet in Heaven' that my gran gave folk. Either no one seemed to question the fact that their pet now had the ability to put pen to paper, or they accepted that my gran had channeled their thoughts to write:

"To my dearest family, some things I'd
like to say.
But first of all, to let you know, that I
arrived okay. I'm writing this from the
Bridge, where I dwell with God above.
There are no more tears of sadness here,
just eternal love."

And my gran was insistent that they got great comfort from the last lines,

"And when it's time for you to go, from that body to be free. Remember you're not going...you're coming here to me."

I asked her once if anyone had ever compared letters and noticed that the wording was identical. She was horrified at the suggestion, as if she was unaware that everyone got the same letter. My gran assured me that the readings are confidential; her clients are sworn to secrecy and agree that what happens in the session stays in the session.

'So Johnny's feeling better then? Or dae you think he'll still get bad dreams aboot the pink feet chasing him?'

'He's only got tae worry aboot me chasing him noo.'

My gran laughed; it was too scary an image for me and Lorraine to coax a smile on to our faces.

'Dinnae look so disgusted. You'll be my age one day too.'

Lorraine walked off in the direction of the phone boxes.

'What's up with her?' my gran asked.

'Lorraine wants tae go hame. She's away tae phone her mam.'

'That'll be right!' My gran tugged Bimbo's lead and marched off to hunt Lorraine down; everything was going to be fine now. I followed in awe of the mighty force that was my gran.

'Put the phone doon hen.' She stepped inside the phone box and tapped Lorraine on the shoulder.

Lorraine replaced the phone in its cradle as if she was replacing a gun in its holster. A phone call to her mam with the real reason why she wanted to come home would be just as devastating as firing a bullet into Rita's heart.

'Whatever is bothering you, upsetting yer mammy isnae gonnae solve it. Noo let's get you back tae the caravan and we can sort this oot.'

The way Lorraine turned obediently it made me think my gran did have special powers; if she was able to talk some sense into Lorraine, then talking to dead pets must be a piece of piss.

In silence, we walked back to the caravan. The minute my gran opened the door, Lorraine burst into tears again and threw herself face down on to the couch. This was really going to test my gran. We stood over Lorraine and gave her a wee shoogle, but she kept her face buried in the cushion and pushed our hands away.

'Ah think Danny must've hurt her after aw,' I said.

'Is that true?' asked my gran. 'Because we can go tae the polis.'

'He didnae hurt me,' Lorraine mumbled. 'Brian did.'

I sank to my knees on the floor beside her and gently lifted her head out of the cushion.

'What dae you mean? Brian was with me. We went for chips.'

'That must've been before he came back to their caravan.'

'But where was Danny?'

'I told him he didn't need to get dressed again to walk me home so we said goodnight at the caravan door. Brian must've been hiding somewhere close by; he followed me and pulled me into the bushes.'

'Oh my god! The dirty bastard. Did he force himself on you?'

'Aye. And he didnae use a condom either.'

'Right, that's it, we're phoning the polis.' My gran's fist banged the table, Bimbo darted out from underneath and shot off into our bedroom, as nervous as I was.

'It's a waste of time. I'm sure Danny said that him and Brian were leaving later today. They could already be gone. And I don't even know their second names or where they live.'

'That's no for you tae worry aboot hen. Even if they've left the site the polis will still be able tae track him doon.'

'I don't want the police involved. My mam said she'd kill me if I fall pregnant before I'm married.'

I was on one side and my gran was on the other with Lorraine in the middle, and we both squeezed her tightly. It was a sandwich with misery as the filling and a huge dollop of fear spread on top alongside my side dish of guilt. My gran whispered into Lorraine's ear that everything would be fine and not to worry. There was no mention of my gran's usual warning to me, that only the good girls get caught.

Chapter Twenty One

Lorraine's suitcase was packed and although my gran had tried to talk her out of it, she was adamant that she was going home one way or another. She had plenty of spending money so that wouldn't hold her back although I found it hard to believe that Lorraine would have the savvy to work out a route from Filey to Bonnybridge all by herself, cash or no cash. But then again I'd seen her cadge lifts home often enough from Falkirk, only this time I was sure she'd no intention of using her charms on men, not after last night. I couldn't help be impressed by her determination; but it was another sign that she didn't need me as much these days. I decided not to walk her down to the phones boxes; she was a big girl now.

My gran insisted that Lorraine should have a story ready that wouldn't upset her mam. It was obvious that my gran didn't know what Rita was really like; any reason for needing to make a mercy dash would have her reciting Novenas all the way down the M6.

Lorraine's greatest fear was of playing pregnancy roulette after the double whammy with Danny and Brian. But as Lorraine couldn't remember when she had her last period, and Brian hadn't withdrawn, there wasn't much my gran could do to reassure her. All Lorraine kept repeating was, *"My mam'll kill me."* No one disputed the fact that Rita was indeed a nutter but she wasn't capable of murder. I made my point by reminding Lorraine that Janine wouldn't be walking, or shuffling, the planet if her mam was truly capable of killing. It didn't help; in fact it made things worse. As if I didn't feel bad enough about the way things had turned out, she screamed at me to "Shut the fuck up!" and didn't care that my gran witnessed the outburst.

My gran asked me to go to the amusement arcade to change pound notes for coins so that Lorraine could phone home. I couldn't be arsed with the walk and the only advantage was being cut loose from the tension, but it was a relief to get away from

Lorraine's grim mood and the least I could do to help.

The sun was splitting the trees and yet there were still a few peely wally bodies inside Aladdin's Cave, too addicted to the glow from the machines to trade it for the real thing. Humongous speakers blasted out *'Legs'* by ZZ Top; the after-dark rock song seeped out into the sunshine, too loud for daylight hours. I pushed my sunglasses up on my head and squinted inside the entrance to the arcade.

A whippet-thin boy fed a stack of coins into the slots of the Penny Falls; I paused to see if the sweeper would push the teetering pile-up of brown pennies to crash over the edge. Not this time; the penny slipped on top of the others. The machine was a greedy bastard, and the boy didn't let it go hungry. The beeps and bloops of the machines grew louder as I moved further into the darkness. Within the Cave, the *Space Invader* lit up as a teenager with skin pitted like a lunar landscape gripped a joystick with bloodless knuckles. He stared at the screen with the concentration of a brain surgeon and I wondered what it would take to get his attention. A fire alarm would be wasted inside Aladdin's Cave; crackling flames and clouds of smoke probably wouldn't make much difference either, certainly not to the woman my mam's age perched on a stool with arse cheeks like blancmange spilling over the sides. She sucked on a fag before yanking the arm of a fruit machine; nothing less than the promise of a row of three gold bars would be able to tempt her out of the building.

I made my way over to the Change booth in the corner to swap the notes for coins; it sat next to the *Star Wars* cockpit. Karen tried the game last year and loved it. I'd never fancied climbing inside; it had as much appeal as a dingy under-stair cupboard fitted with disco lights. I could think of better things to do than make my ears bleed with the sound of star-fighters roaring past to launch explosions and laser fire until the shit-your-breeks boom when the *Death Star* was destroyed. I couldn't see the attraction although some loser jerked around inside, lost in space firing laser cannons at the same time as being bombarded with fireballs, his idea of fun. There was something about the chipolata fingers steering the on-screen ship that made me creep closer. There was no mistaking the smell of greasy chips that clung to him. It was Brian.

I bolted, out of reach of the Death Star and Brian. Daylight blinded me; I flipped my sunglasses down and ran. Behind me the cockpit's sound effects gave Han Solo a voice and he shouted after me in triumph.

There was a queue at the Beachcomber's till. I stood in line to get the coins, behind a group of weans ordering Slush Puppies and constantly changing their minds and asking for Blue Raspberry instead of Cherry instead of Cola… I hoped the wee shites got brain freeze. Their fannying about gave me too much time to think. In running away from Brian, I wasn't sure who had escaped.

What's done is done was another of my gran's favourite sayings; I didn't understand why she wanted Lorraine to go to the polis. Faye told us her mam once tried to report her dad for coming home pished and shagging her so hard she was left bleeding. After the polis left, Faye's mam got battered for clyping on him and letting the whole scheme know he was a drunken arsehole. Who would believe Lorraine's story if she went to the polis? She'd been drinking underage and wasn't forced to go to Danny's caravan; I didn't need to be a lawyer to know the case would be a joke. And Rita would die of shame. Lorraine had to move on; this was real life, not Cagney and Lacey.

The coins clinked in my pocket, mission accomplished. All that mattered now was getting back to the caravan and helping Lorraine. When I burst through the door, she'd disappeared into the bathroom to freshen her make-up. I took the chance to get a bit of one-to-one time with my gran without Lorraine hogging her.

'Dae you no think she'll be awright?' I said.

'Ah hope so. The poor lassie's got herself worried sick that she'll fall pregnant. And after what happened tae her own mam, ah'm no surprised she's uptight.'

'But she disnae ken aboot her mam being called the Mattress.'

'True, but she kens how obsessed Rita is aboot her Holy Joe image. An unmarried mother for a daughter would get everybody talking. And they'd soon remember Rita's own shotgun wedding tae the only boy in the toun who never fired his pistol anywhere near her.'

'Stop, that's way too much detail!'

I covered my ears with my hands.

'Sorry hen. The thing is, Tam might no be Lorraine's real daddy but she kens how much shame it would bring her mammy if she brought mair than a stick of Scarborough rock hame with her.'

I couldn't help wonder what would happen if Lorraine had been unlucky, after all the stuff she'd spouted to me about Pamela's Pro Life Group and wearing a Precious Feet badge on her blazer. It was easy to be anti-abortion when it didn't affect you and there was nothing at stake. It was a hassle to have Janine as a sister but Lorraine loved her and wouldn't have wished that she'd never been born. And even if Rita had been known as the Mattress, she'd at least faced the consequences of sleeping around and kept Lorraine. But would Lorraine also believe that bringing an unplanned baby into the world was the right thing to do if she had a choice?

My gran ordered me to wheesht when the toilet flushed. I panicked that even though we'd been whispering and weren't near the bathroom, Lorraine might have heard us bad mouthing her mam. If I was Lorraine, I'd be glad of the ammunition. It would be impossible for Rita to give Lorraine a hard time if she had the facts up her sleeve that her mam was no saint herself. Listening to my gran and mam talking about Rita shagging the whole fitba team, it made Lorraine look like an angel. Everyone knows that the best form of defense is attack and if we wanted to protect Lorraine we had to arm her with the knowledge that her mam had once been a slapper and was in no position to criticise anybody. Lorraine felt I'd let her down and this was a way to help to make up for things. I weighed up the risk that it would make her feel worse; I decided that it would be worth it in the long run. If Lorraine was pregnant then at least she'd be able to make a choice without Rita intimidating her. We had a pact to look out for each other and if I dropped the bomb and made her start greetin' again, Lorraine would eventually understand that it was a case of tough love.

Lorraine crept out of the bathroom. She'd touched up her make-up; it had been a pointless effort, she didn't look any perkier, and I wasn't feeling too bright-eyed either. I'd rather sit in the car pulling off my toenails and wait for the end of the week than hang about with my mam and dad. The more I thought of being left behind, the more I realised that I had a duty to stick by Lorraine and I should offer to go home with her. There was every chance that she might need me by her side if Rita turned nasty. I'd seen her mam being rough with Janine often enough to know that she was capable of worse behind closed doors. It was one of the few benefits of being a big-boned lassie, no one messed with me for fear of getting battered. If I had to physically defend Lorraine then I'd do whatever it took to protect my best pal. There had been plenty of times in the past when I'd felt like walloping Rita and giving her a good slap. It was a win-win situation. All I had to do was sound Lorraine out about going home with her.

'Ah've got plenty of coins for the phone,' I said.

Lorraine gathered up the tower of ten pence pieces and slipped them into her purse. She put on her sandals and didn't thank me for the coins or ask me to come with her to the phone box. It was an ideal time to convince her that I should go home with her and I could tell her all she needed to know about St Rita's teenage years. I'd also make sure she kept away from the amusement arcade and avoided bumping into Brian.

'Ah'll just nip tae the loo before we go,' I said.

'You're going nowhere with me,' replied Lorraine.

My gran said Bimbo needed a walk, she'd keep Lorraine company and I should wait in the caravan. She probably wanted to make sure Lorraine didn't bolt off and do something stupid. I'd never seen Lorraine so demented. It was embarrassing. And without me getting the chance to talk some sense into her and keep her out of Aladdin's Cave things could get worse.

'So what're you going tae tell yer mam?' I asked.

Lorraine ignored me and my gran jumped in with a reply.

'She's going tae tell her mam that she's feeling hamesick and is missing her and Janine.'

My gran made it sound like the script was carved in stone and Lorraine knew it word for word.

'That sounds pretty lame tae me.'

I turned to Lorraine expecting her to agree but she didn't back me up at all. 'Yer mam kens how desperate you were tae get away and noo you're trying tae make her believe that you cannae last a week withoot her!'

My gran shook her head as if I was the one with the daft ideas.

'You've a lot tae learn.' She spoke to me like I was a stupid wee lassie. It was bad enough being talked down to by my mam, but I was miffed to hear my gran speak to me like that; she was the one person who I relied on to respect me as an adult.

'Mammies only hear what they want tae hear. If Lorraine tells Rita that she's missing hame, then she'll be that chuffed, she'll no question it,' added my gran.

Lorraine nodded obediently. To watch the two of them, anyone would think that Lorraine was her granddaughter; it was as pathetic as Lorraine's feeble excuse.

'A seventeen year auld claiming she's hamesick is ridiculous. Plus, why would her mam be happy for Lorraine tae cut her holiday short? It disnae add up.'

My gran sighed and again made me feel like a wean that didn't understand what the grown-ups in the room were talking about.

'Your gran's right. My mam'll maybe put up a bit of an argument but she'll be secretly pleased. And she never wanted me to go in the first place,' said Lorraine.

'She should want you tae have fun and no be so selfish.'

'And you call being raped fun?'

'That was a low blow. You ken ah didnae mean that but running back hame won't change what happened. And what am ah supposed tae dae here on ma tod?'

'So you expect me to forget about last night so I don't spoil your holiday plans? Pamela was right to warn me. She says you're a user and me and Stevie would still be together if I'd asked him for his version before believing your story. Was it all lies?'

'She's nothing but a shit stirrer and a stuck up…'

'Forget it. I'm not listening to you slagging off my pal.'

Lorraine picked up her purse stuffed with coins and marched out of the caravan.

'You cannae help yourself can you? You've always got tae push it too far,' said my gran.

She hurried to clip Bimbo's lead on and catch up with Lorraine, leaving me alone with my gran's box of Maltesers. My gran couldn't deny that she'd been nippy with me, she'd understand that scoffing the Maltesers was comfort eating and wouldn't mind if I finished them.

The giggling oozed through the caravan walls along with a loud thud. Something or someone banged against the door, my heart skipped a beat and I froze, glad that it was broad daylight or I'd have shit myself. The door flew open and my mam and dad fell inside, still sucking the faces off each other. They were so busy having another game of tonsil hockey that they didn't hear me gag on the last Malteser.

Before I could scream, 'Pack it in!' my dad slipped his mitt up my mam's polka dot sundress. I coughed like an Alsatian tied up with a frayed piece of rope in a scrap yard and they jumped apart. If the sight of them snogging hadn't been so sickening, it might've been funny. I was too stressed about Lorraine to laugh at anything, even the thought of my mam and dad indulging in sun, sand, sea and sex.

'Jesus Christ, you frightened the life oot of me!' bawled my dad, wiping my mam's slobbers from his top lip with the back of his hand. 'What're you doing hiding inside?'

'Hiding? Ah'm hardly curled up under the table. Ah'm just sitting minding ma own business.'

'That makes a change,' said my mam.

'Why're you no at the beach? And where's yer gran and Lorraine?' asked my dad.

'Ah've eaten them.'

'That wouldnae surprise me.' My mam stood with one hand on her hip, the other waggling a finger under my nose. 'You've mowed yer way through a whole packet of Wagon Wheels.'

'So where are they then?' asked my dad, drumming his fingers on the window ledge.

'You'd better sit doon.'

'Dear God, there's no been an accident has there?' asked my mam.

'Ah telt you we were off our heids bringing Lorraine with us. Rita will go berserk and Tam'll kill me if anything's happened tae his wee princess,' said my dad.

'You said you didnae mind Lorraine coming on holiday,' I said.

'That was just to shut you up. You've inherited yer mam's

nagging gene.'

'Charming. You've got a bloody cheek. A minute ago ah was yer hot babe and now ah'm just an auld nag. Ah'll tell you something, you can forget getting yer nookie again for the rest of the holiday.'

'Ah never said anything aboot you being auld.' My dad then aimed his annoyance at me. 'See what you've done!'

'Ah've done nothing! But as usual everything's ma fault. Nae wonder ah want tae leave hame.'

'Dinnae start aw that again.' My dad shook his head. 'So are you gonnae tell us where they are or just keep moaning?'

'Lorraine's hamesick and gran's away with her tae phone her mam.'

'Is that it? You can make a drama oot of hee-haw. Rita'll tell Lorraine tae pull herself together and that'll be the end of it,' said my dad.

My mam tapped my dad on the shoulder as if she was challenging him to a fight outside.

'You think ah'm a nag? Ah wouldnae be surprised if Rita's made her feel guilty aboot leaving her alone with Janine. That's her style. And she's far too protective, Lorraine's no a wean anymair. Ah'll phone Rita and tell her the lassie needs a break. It's no as if we'll let anything bad happen tae her. She's safe with us.'

'Naw mam, dinnae bother. Lorraine's determined tae go hame.'

'But she's no even been intae Scarborough yet. And ah thought she'd want tae go tae Flamingoland and see Cuddles.'

'Mam, she's no gonnae change her mind just tae see a killer whale splashing aboot and soaking weans.'

My dad shook his napper in disgust; he didn't believe in keeping animals in captivity and always switched channels if Johnny Morris was on.

'For crying out loud. Stuff Cuddles, yer mam bought extra packets of Smash and tins of Fray Bentos. She even bought tins of fruit cocktail and Angel Delight tae pander tae her.'

'Yer dad's right, ah dinnae want her telling Rita that we didnae lay on a nice spread. Ah should've known a caravan holiday wisnae good enough for Princess Lorraine.'

My mam paced up and down the length of the caravan with

her fists balled. At least Rita was more than five hours away; there should be plenty of time for my mam to have a good rant and a chance to cool down. When I pissed her off, I'd learnt that the best strategy was to keep shtum and wait until she'd got it out of her system and exhausted herself. I hoped that five hours would be enough.

'So Lorraine's expecting Rita, with that wee mite Janine on her hands, tae come aw the way doon here tae take her hame?' added my dad. He'd just poured the equivalent of a can of petrol on a bonfire, as if my mam needed stirred up.

'She's been spoilt since the day she was born. If Rita claims tae be living by the Bible, these days anyway, it tells you, "spare the rod and spoil the child". Did you ken that it comes fae the Bible?' asked my mam.

'Aye, fae the Book of Proverbs, you've telt me before.'

She'd told me umpteen times. Me and Karen had the Bible's advice rammed down our throats anytime my mam tried to justify our arses being skelped. Now that we were older, she'd moved the whacking up our bodies; we were more likely to get a slap round the chops than the buttocks. It was far more dignified, especially in public.

'And noo ah've got tae go shopping and get ripped off doon at the mini-market!' She swiveled to face my dad whose eyes bulged like a frightened rabbit. 'And you might need tae drive me intae Filey if ah cannae get another Fray Bentos.'

'Why's that?' asked my dad.

'Ah'll need tae feed Rita and Janine after their long drive. Ah cannae just offer her a cuppa tea. And she might be in a bad mood.'

'Maybe a wee voddy would be a better idea then?' suggested my dad.

'The only thing she drinks these days is communion wine. That's the root of her problems; if she got stuck intae a carry oot on a Saturday night like normal folk she would be mair forgiving on a Sunday morning. Instead she waltzes intae Mass with her nose in the air and a pole up her arse thinking she's better than the rest of us nursing oor hangovers.'

'Listen hen, there's nae point in getting yer knickers in a twist, you brought loads of food. Ah could hardly get the boot of the car shut. And ah'm sure ah saw a tin of Campbell's meatballs that you could add tae the Fray Bentos.'

Considering my dad had known my mam for nearly twenty years, I'd have thought he'd have worked out how to handle her by now. And that pointing out the obvious wasn't the way to go if he wanted her to be reasonable. But it was too late for logic, my mam's worryometer dial was cranked up to the max and nothing my dad said would save her.

'Are you off yer heid? If ah try tae bulk up a Fray Bentos with a tin of meatballs, ah'll be the talk of the toun.'

'Christ on a bike, what a palaver.'

'You dinnae need tae tell me that!'

'Ah'm away tae see if Big Davey's up for a pint.'

My dad stomped out of the caravan leaving me as the only viewer of the Mad Mam Freak Show; I wished he'd taken me with him. My mam flung the door open to shout after him.

'Aye, it's awright for you. Ah'm stuck here trying tae sort this bloody fiasco oot.'

My dad kept walking and I was held captive as she yanked cupboard drawers open as if somehow the ingredients for a cordon bleu meal hid behind a tin of evaporated milk.

'Ah've got it! The perfect follow-up tae a quality steak pie.'

I didn't want to ask what my mam's light bulb moment was but I knew better than my dad that it was best to play along. And he'd pay for bailing out to the pub; she had an elephant's memory and the arse to match.

'Got what?'

'Two packets of chocolate Angel Delight. That'll be mair than enough for seven of us if ah water the mix doon. Aw ah have tae buy is four oranges. Rita'll be blown away when she sees her pudding.'

All that my mam needed was a pair of pom-poms to jump up and down squealing, "*Angel Delight! Rah! Rah! Rah!*"

'Mam, you'll need tae help me oot here. What're you havering on aboot?'

'Ah saw it on *Pebble Mill at One* when ah was off work after ma hysterectomy...'

My mam relived her "*trials of being a woman*" lectures at any given opportunity. With younger women, she dished out advice on bloating, vaginal discharge, breast tenderness and child birth, maybe to avoid scaring them with what lay ahead. For any wifie over forty, she wallowed in tales of heavy periods, fibroids and her all-time favourite conversation topic – the hysterectomy. Should she ever fancy her chances on *Mastermind*, she was unbeatable on her specialist subject – why it's necessary, how it's performed, different types of hysterectomy, recovery time and the possible complications of the operation.

'And? Why dae you need oranges?'

I wasn't going to let her get started about how the operation knocked the stuffing out of her and how she felt less "*womanly*" than before. I'd heard it all before.

'You cut an orange in half, scoop oot the segments and then add them tae the Angel Delight. The showstopper is that you let the mixture set inside the hollowed oot orange instead of a bowl. Wait till Rita sees ma Chocolate Orange Surprise, that'll give her something worth talking aboot!'

'It sounds amazing. Ah'm sure Rita'll be impressed.'

'Aye, if ah can get the oranges. Yer dad might even need tae drive intae Scarborough if Filey's got none.'

'You're probably right. The closest ah've seen tae fruit in the mini-market are chocolate bananas.'

'True. Yer dad better no come back bevvied.'

'Why don't you nip intae Filey yourself?'

'Ah've got enough on ma plate. And ah've never driven further than Fawkurt. Naw, yer dad's in the bad books as it is so he can get his arse intae Filey or Scarborough if need be.'

I had to get out of the caravan, away from my mam; she was doing my head in and I wanted to go find my gran and Lorraine. I couldn't understand why they'd been at the phone box for so long; Lorraine would've been quicker posting Rita a letter. My mam was too busy counting out cutlery to notice me slip out the side door; I took my chance and bolted, swiping a packet of salt 'n' vinegar Ringos on my way past.

Down at the complex, all the phone boxes were empty; there weren't many other places I could think where they might be. When she went to the bingo in Denny, my gran liked a go on the slot machines at the interval; Aladdin's Cave was worth a try. I edged past the entrance, feart that Brian hadn't left for home yet and was still doing battle inside the *Star Wars* cockpit instead of being halfway to Hull.

But through the gloom, all I could make out were two wee Scottish boys feeding coppers into the *Penny Falls*. The pennies clattered into the silver collection dish and the weans squealed, *'Gaun yersel!'* as they bent down to dig out their winnings.

The Beachcomber café was mobbed with pensioners chewing on meringues and picking coconut flakes out of their teeth. I gave the café a quick scan, my gran wasn't one of the OAPs testing the chomping power of their falsers. There was a chance that I'd missed them on the way back to the caravan but Lorraine didn't know any of the shortcuts and my gran always stuck to the paths to stop her heels sinking in the grass. I'd no idea where else to look for them; the only option I had was to return to the caravan. I prayed that my dad was back from the pub and I wouldn't be alone with my mam as she whipped up Angel Delight recipes and bored the arse off me. If my dad needed to hunt for oranges, maybe me and Lorraine could go with him, it would pass the time and save any awkward conversations between us. Every time I opened my mouth, I seemed to piss Lorraine off; I didn't know how to suggest me going home early too without her going ballistic.

"Seesaw Margery Daw
Johnny shall have a new master.
He shall earn but a penny a day
Because he can't work any faster"

A mammy sang the nursery rhyme as she pushed her wean backwards and forwards on the play park's iron rocking horse. The toddler needed a pee and squealed, the horse needed oil and squeaked and the mammy needed singing lessons and screeched. All three were drowned out by the chug, chug, chug of the tractor. The Puffer's next stop was much further along the road but Johnny slowed the tractor right down to walking speed alongside me.

'Alright pet?'

He leaned out from his cab window. It was a relief that the only passengers were an auld couple; thank God no one else witnessed the ancient cowboy talking to me as if we were pals, or worse, related.

'Aye, ah'm fine.'

I kept on walking. He shouted again.

'Wait up will you love?'

Johnny twisted in his seat to face the auld dears sharing a tartan travel rug. If their legs were as wrinkled as their top halves, I was grateful they had the decency to hide them under the checked blanket. There were 5mph max signs dotted all over the campsite, surely some could be swapped for:

'NO SHORTS TO BE WORN BY OVER 50s'

And spare us the sight of saggy knees and rumpled tortoise skin.

Johnny signaled with two fingers in the air, raised his bushy eyebrows and mouthed "Two minutes"; the couple gave him a cheery thumbs-up as a reply. It wasn't as if they were on a tight schedule between connecting flights but I wished they'd grow a pair of balls between them and demand that Johnny kept his arse in the seat, got the Puffer back in gear, do what he's paid to do and just drive. But of course there wasn't a peep out of the auld muppets. Johnny was free to jump out of the cab, walk over the grass verge and harass me.

'Howdy!'

He'd taken this cowboy bullshit too far, my gran needed her head examined for going anywhere near this nutter.

'Just in case you're looking for your grandma, she's in my garage with your mate. I call it the Saddle Sore saloon, just my little joke.'

'Aye so ah've heard. What're they doing in there?'

'They needed somewhere quiet to talk privately and my saloon's ideal.'

He pointed at a breeze block garage with a corrugated iron roof. The only hint of the Wild West inside was a pair of bull horns mounted above the wooden doors.

'You'll find them in there.' Johnny tipped his Stetson hat at me and parted with a 'Nice talking to you.'

He really should've added 'Ma'am' at the end. And it seemed a shame that he couldn't mount a trusty steed instead of a clapped out John Deere tractor doing a piss poor impersonation of a steam train, it might've improved his act.

I skirted round the crazy golf's fence, not sure whether I actually wanted to find my gran and Lorraine after all. Johnny turned the Puffer round for his repeat circuit and waved at me, still pointing at the garage as if I could miss the three foot bull horns. It was hard not to be miffed about Lorraine and my gran having a heart-to-heart. Lorraine was supposed to confide in me, not my gran, it wasn't fair. I was used to her being needy; what I hadn't expected was that Lorraine would be such an emotional vampire, not only sucking the life out of me but even draining my gran's good nature dry.

I was prepared to constantly prop up Lorraine but for her to spoil my gran's holiday showed her up as utterly selfish. It seemed as if my mam was right about Lorraine being brought up to be a brat. And although I assumed I knew Lorraine inside out, her true colours were hard to ignore.

The more I thought about Lorraine's behaviour, the more it made me angry. I psyched myself up to storm inside and catch her off-guard. The magnetic pull of the open door drew me closer but the sound of Lorraine laughing and her squeal of, 'No way, you're kiddin' me on!' made me stop dead.

It was weird to hear Lorraine giggle without me there and in my gran's company. I knew more than anyone that my gran had hunners of stories that could make someone laugh or greet to suit their mood. And yet it still surprised me that my gran had managed to save Lorraine from drowning in her own self-pity.

I edged closer to the door. They sat side-by-side, cosied up on a couch made of patchwork squares of brown and white cow hides. Like an armed robber clocking the joint before it got dark, I slunk out of sight; all I needed was a SWAG bag, a balaclava and a stripy jumper, although horizontal stripes aren't good for big lassies with curves.

'Aye, ah ken you're shocked but it's aw true, no a word of a lie. Remember that ah knew yer mammy long afore she reserved her seat at Mass.'

I couldn't hold back a second longer, I burst through the door. They managed to peel their eyes off each other to face me, the perfect example of two's company, three's definitely a crowd.

'You'd make a better door than a windae Angela. Come away

in, you're blocking the light.'

My shadow cast a fat blob across the floor. I could picture Johnny standing in the doorway imagining that he'd walked into a real saloon, not a manky garage, and he'd challenged the local hard man to a shoot-out at high noon. Taking a step forward, I cast my eye over the room's décor and resisted the urge to slap my thigh with a shout of, *"Yee haw!"* To get any further, I had to duck under a massive stars and stripes flag. Next to me on the wall was a photo of a scrawny Jack Russell wearing a red and white bandana. I assumed this was Amigo, before he was flattened.

'So what's so funny, spill the beans?'

My gran patted the space beside her on the cracked leather couch but I stood where I was; my arse cheeks would never fit into the tiny strip of cushion.

'Ah was telling Lorraine that her mam wisnae always the angel she makes herself oot to be these days.'

Lorraine didn't seem devastated; I guessed my gran had held back details of Rita being a serial shagger. And the knockout blow that her mam didn't want Lorraine to get involved with Stevie Duffy just in case he was her half-brother. Whatever tale my gran had shared was obviously a mild one so I dared to ask:

'Well? Tell me too.'

'You'll never believe it; you know how my mam's always lecturing me about my reputation, that *everybody* knows if a girl does *everything* with *everyone*?' said Lorraine.

'Aye.'

'And to keep myself pure because no man wants damaged goods? Wait until you hear this.'

'C'mon, stop winding me up and tell me!'

'Awright, ah'll repeat the story but this stays between these four walls,' said my gran.

My gran couldn't trust Lorraine to make the story sound as juicy as it was hyped up to be; she leaned forward and looked both ways as if folk from Bonnybridge were hiding behind the six foot cardboard cactus in the corner and would report back to Rita.

'Ah was at the bingo one Saturday, it was afore you two were born, and ah went tae the one in Bonnybridge for a wee change because the prize money was better than at Denny.'

'There was a bingo hall in Bonnybridge?'

'Aye, but it's long gone, it was knocked down years ago tae make a car park for the Co-op. Noo, stop interrupting, will you? Anyway, ah wisnae sure of the bus times and ah was feart ah'd miss ma bus hame so ah took a shortcut through the park. That's when ah saw Rita although ah didnae recognise her fae behind; it could've been any lassie. But when ah slipped on an empty crisp packet and fell flat on ma face, ah let oot a scream. And so did Rita when she knew she'd been caught straddling a laddie on the chute.'

'The chute?'

'Aye, he was lying on his back at the bottom of the chute and Rita was riding him like Red Rum. Well she was until ah appeared. Of course the laddie jumped off and…'

I wanted to stick my fingers in my ears and chant, *"La, la, la, la, la. I can't hear you, I'm not listening."* It was too late though; the thought of Rita shagging a boy on the same chute that me and Lorraine had slid down our whole childhood was mingin'. I felt queasy.

'Enough! Ah get the picture.'

Lorraine sniggered at me cringing; it was worth it to see her lighten up a bit, a chance to get us back on track.

'Dae you remember that time on the spider's web roundabout when ah was sick?' I asked.

'How could I forget? You made me push you faster and faster and then sprayed me with butterscotch Angel Delight. And the puke was the colour of diarrhea! I've never been able to touch Angel Delight ever since.'

I made no mention of my mam's plans to transform a packet of the powdery stuff into a blow-your-mind dessert; at least it was a different flavour and colour.

And even though she hadn't forgotten that I'd pebble-dashed her in pudding, Lorraine still grinned. A one-to-one with my gran seemed to have worked; all I needed to know now was whether or not she was still hell-bent on going home or if my gran had managed to talk her into staying.

'So was yer mam in when you phoned?'

It was a stupid question; unless she was at Mass, Rita wouldn't go very far with Janine in tow.

'Aye, she had Sarah round for a visit. They're sorting through photies of Boaby for the Handicapped Club noticeboard.'

'Why? Surely everyone kens by noo that he's deid?'

'It's a memorial montage, a kinda tribute to him for driving the bus all those years.'

'What, a wall of Boabys? Mind you, ah bet it'll be popular, they'll be the only boabies Mrs Gaffney and Margaret have seen in years.'

'Ah doubt the same could be said for Father O'Donnell,' muttered my gran.

She must've heard the rumours too; it was an open secret that Father O'Donnell had favourite altar boys. I sniggered at the idea of pictures of cocks decorating the Chapel Hall walls and the bamboozled auld helpers trying to remember what to do with a boaby. And then there was the image of Boaby's boaby in the centre of the display. Sometimes being artistic was more of a curse than a blessing.

'It's no funny; my mam says they can't get anyone else to drive the bus.'

'Dinnae tell me that you're surprised? Who wants tae drive aboot with folk slavering doon the back of their neck and screaming every time the door shuts?'

'Mibbae you could dae posters tae recruit a new driver?' suggested my gran.

Ever since my gran gave me an alphabet stencil set in primary four, she'd come up with poster projects for me. I'd made posters for lost pets, a prize bingo, a carol concert, a jumble sale, a Teddy Bears' Picnic, a coffee morning, Santa's grotto, a silent auction, a pub quiz, a sponsored walk, an Easter Bunny hunt, a Beetle Drive…But my gran preferred not to advertise her pet psychic services. She firmly believed that she only wanted business from word of mouth recommendations to keep it exclusive, so only folk she knew from the bingo passed on her details.

'You'll need tae make a **'WANTED! A NEW BOABY. APPLY WITHIN'** poster. You'll get a lot of interest if ah stick them up at the bus stop ootside the bingo,' said my gran. As always, she laughed loudest at her own jokes but as Lorraine joined in too, it seemed a good time to ask *the* question.

'So is yer mam coming tae take you hame?'

'Aye, and she's bringing Sarah with her to help out with Janine.'

'Could Sarah no babysit?'

'My mam says since she lost Boaby, she needs company.'

'There's only so much you can dae on yer own withoot a boaby.'

My gran slapped her thigh cowgirl style and laughed so hard there was no noise coming out. Johnny would've been impressed. I tried to ignore my gran's hysteria and turned to Lorraine.

'There's nae going back then? You're definitely leaving?'

'Aye, my mam'll be on the road by now.'

'Dae you want me tae come back with you?'

Lorraine's face crumpled like a used teabag.

'Are you joking? You think I'd want you to come with me?'

'Of course. If you go, ah go.'

'Your gran tells the best jokes.'

'Ah'm no kiddin'. There's nae point in me being here withoot you. And we always stick together.'

'Not anymore.'

Lorraine sprang up from the couch and walked off, ducking underneath the stars and stripes flag and slammed the saloon door shut. Bimbo shuddered at the bang and I petted him before I grabbed the door handle to follow Lorraine.

'You need tae let her go,' said my gran, gently pulling me back to sit on the couch.

'But gran, she's needs me…'

'She needs you tae accept that she's no the wee lassie you rescued at the quarry. Lorraine's aw the woman she'll ever be and you're no responsible for her.'

'Ah cannae just let her go, ah ken she thinks ah let her doon last night. Ah need tae make it up tae her. What if she's up the duff and…'

'Would you haud yer wheesht? You're yapping at me a hunner miles an hour. There's nothing for you tae worry aboot. Ah've had a good blether with her and she kens ah can help her if it comes tae that.'

'It'll take mair than a cuppa gran! How can you help?'

'And ah thought Lorraine was the naïve one of you pair. You ken Jeanette?' My gran paused and I nodded, desperate to see how her pal fitted into the scenario. 'Withoot going intae any of the gory details, let's just say that Jeanette can help lassies who get theirselves intae bother.'

My gran paused again; she realised that I needed time to work out how a fat auld woman that I'd known since I was wee was able to deal with unwanted pregnancies.

'And ah've let Lorraine ken that the option is always there if she needs it.'

'So you're telling me that Jeanette fae the bingo does abortions?'

'That's one way of putting it.'

'Ask Lorraine's new best pal Pamela and she'll give you another word for it, and it's called *murder*. Lorraine believes in aw the pro-life stuff we get rammed doon oor throats at school. There's nae way she'd ever have an abortion; she even wears a Precious Feet badge.'

'Listen hen, take it fae me, it's one thing sticking a badge on yer jumper but it's a different story when you've got everything tae lose. You might call it an abortion; ah call it helping lassies in their time of need.'

'But she's always said she'd never have one.'

'Needs must when the devil drives. You'd be surprised how many lassies swear blind that they couldnae go through with it. Aye and they're the same ones who turn up at Jeanette's door begging her tae help them.'

'So you dinnae think it's wrong?'

'Who am ah tae judge what other folk dae with their lives? It's no for me tae say what's right and wrong. And with Lorraine's family history and no knowing a thing aboot who she was with last night she'd be safer letting Jeanette deal with it.'

'Ah doubt if her mam could cope with another Janine.'

'Rita would cope; she'd be mair of a martyr than ever.'

'Very true, two handicapped weans in the family would get her an audience with Cardinal Doyle and an express ticket tae heaven. Saint Rita would love it!'

'Aye, it's a pity that there's a Saint Rita already.'

'Are you making this up gran?'

'Naw, do you remember that yer mam took me with her tae the Chapel's Centenary Quiz Night? Ah knew there was bound tae be holy questions so ah studied a book of Saints fae the library. The real Saint Rita was the perfect wife and mother, our Rita's got a lot tae live up tae, she'll be hoping that Saint Peter disnae mention her teenage years when he meets her at the Pearly Gates.'

'She'd have a cheek having a go at Lorraine if she did fall preggers.'

'Rita's got mair faces than the toun clock, she's yer typical Pick 'n' Mix Catholic, and she makes it up as she goes along tae suit herself.'

My gran got to her feet and clipped Bimbo's lead on.

'C'mon hen, let's get back tae the caravan; with Rita on her way yer mam'll be stressed oot and ah'll need tae try and calm her doon.'

'How did you guess?'

'Ah dinnae just see things on the Other Side.'

I didn't believe she had a special gift; her trick was that she knew folk better than they knew themselves.

Chapter Twenty Two

My mam tore off a square of tin foil she'd found at the back of the cupboard and wrapped it around her face sponge.

'Just lucky some sad folk like cooking when they're on holiday, eh?' she said. 'Mind you, ah'd have taken the foil hame with me, there's at least three quarters of the roll left.'

My gran bobbed her head up and down like the nodding dog Karen gave my dad once for Father's Day. It was hard to tell the breed it was supposed to be; the wee dog sat on the parcel shelf of the car with a gold chain round its neck; over the years I'd picked off chunks of its velvety coat and now it had patches of raw plastic all over its body, although it still looked happy, the only one smiling round here.

Lorraine was packing her stuff. I'd left her to it, the bedroom wasn't big enough for two of us and an open suitcase. As the clock's big hand crept round, my mam got more wound up by the minute, and it was unbearable. My mam decided that "nibbles" were essential to welcome her guests on arrival; she must've seen the idea on another episode of Pebble Mill at One. The only 'Nibbles' I'd ever seen was the rabbit from number seven; the weans from the scheme still talked about that bunny.

Nibbles was eaten by a Bandeath dug whose taste of freedom on its first day out of the pound was a mouthful of white fur. Chunks of Nibbles were spread across our garden, the wee boy from next door chased his screaming pals up and down the street with the head of Nibbles on the end of a stick before another dug ran up and swiped it. The bloodied stick, dripping with rabbit guts kept the weans squealing and the game carried on until my mam went to the front door and shouted at them to, "Shut yer geggie!" Her roar was enough to make the weans scatter, they looked as if they were at a wedding scramble, chasing coins thrown from the window of a bride's limo, only this time there were no coppers left lying in the gutter, only the red tipped stick, flung to the ground like a giant Swan Vesta.

'Ah've heard of Baked Alaska but never Baked Face Sponge, what the hell are you planning tae make with that?' asked my gran.

'It's no going in the oven!' my mam cried. She'd the nerve to raise her eyebrows as if it was perfectly normal to wrap a nylon face sponge in tin foil.

'So what're you doing with it then?'

My mam sighed; my gran wasn't the weird one though, and she'd asked a reasonable question.

'Ah've no got a tattie and ah need something tae poke ma cocktail sticks intae tae serve the nibbles.'

'Ah see,' replied my gran, as if the plan was now so obvious.

'Thank God ah brought a family jar of silverskin onions and two blocks of cheddar with me,' said my mam.

She mopped her brow for maximum effect: there was no crisis, my mam was in luck with Operation Nibbles. My dad ate a jar of silverskin onions a week. Every night, at every meal, he had three on his plate, five at the weekend as a treat, along with a puddle of Salad Cream. We never traveled far without a jar or a bottle and because he liked two buttered McVitie's digestive biscuits sandwiched between cheese and strawberry jam before bed my mam always had supplies. As part of his daily bedtime routine, my dad poked at his teeth with a cocktail stick, so with the sticks and food in stock my mam already had all the vital ingredients for Operation Nibbles to hand. No wonder she was chuffed.

She speared the oval onions with the cocktail sticks and added a cube of cheddar to each end until the foil covered face sponge had the body of a space-age hedgehog.

'What dae you think? Smashing, eh?'

'Rita'll be impressed,' my gran winked at me.

'Aye, very classy mam.'

I winked back at my gran. It wasn't a good idea to be too far from Lorraine in case she needed me but my mam's ridiculous preparations were driving me doolally. I needed to get out of the caravan. My mam was busy cutting the last slab of cheese into cubes; I escaped through the side door and sat on the steps of the veranda.

Lying with my back on the wooden floor I stared up at the

sky and the bald sun poking its shiny napper in and out of a fluffy snood made of wooly clouds, pulling apart until all that was left were wispy strands.

In the last term of art class, we'd studied Monet's work; Mr McDougall said I'd miss a trick if I didn't have a go at the impressionist style and try a seascape or landscape with my pastel chalks over the summer. Just in case I got the chance, I'd packed my art stuff although I thought I'd be living it up with Lorraine and never get round to opening my sketchpad. I sat up; the holiday mood had changed as quickly as the sky view, a breeze brushed my bare legs and the clouds galloped like horses at the one thirty at Aintree. It seemed as good a time as any to try and capture the scene and it would keep my mind off Lorraine's problems, and how I'd caused them.

Beyond the row of caravans a line of washing strung between two trees flip flapped and a field of wheat rippled like a fresh bed sheet before it was tucked in at the corners. The scene had potential except that in the foreground a wean's brow creased with concentration as he pedaled up and down the path on a Chopper, steadied by his dad whose forearm flexed a red hand of Ulster tattoo and chest muscles straining underneath a cutoff T-shirt that looked sprayed on. Monet painted a poppy field with a woman in a bonnet trailing her sun parasol and followed by a child holding a posy of wild flowers; my landscape was a far bigger challenge.

If I half shut my eyes, I could create a new view; I could blot out the father and son and the Y-fronts drying on the washing line, I could imagine Laura Ingalls brushing the tips of the wheat as she walked through the golden field near her farm in Walnut Grove. But I was on the steps of a caravan in Primrose Valley and although the name made it sound romantic and picturesque, it was nothing like *Little House on the Prairie.* And there were no poppy fields. It wasn't a simple time when Lorraine didn't need to worry about unwanted sex with boys from Hull and whether wearing a Precious Feet badge would make a difference in her decision making.

And yet I remembered that the storylines from *Little House on the Prairie* had been about racism, alcoholism and drug addiction, that even Laura Ingalls lived in a world where there were problems. It was the same but different and it didn't matter whether you lived in a wooden farmhouse in the country or a terraced council house in a scheme.

What I couldn't understand was how Lorraine going home would help solve her problems. Shite things happen to folk from Walnut Grove too, Laura Ingalls would tell Lorraine if she could get her to listen. Running home wouldn't wipe out what went on last night but it seemed too late to change her mind or go home with her. I was stuck here, and I'd be bored by day and suicidal by night. The only bonus I could think of was that I'd have more time to do some work for my portfolio.

I slipped inside the caravan to get my chalks and paper. My mam was cutting the crusts off a pan loaf and didn't notice me. Bimbo's stare never left the chopping board on the off-chance of some stray crumbs. My gran had been put to sleep by my mam's wittering and her slack jaw had left a snail's trail of drool on a cushion. I hurried back outside and was glad that the meathead dad and his wean on the shooglie Chopper were gone and with the Y-fronts blanked out, it was as close as I would get to a view fit for Monet.

I took the Prussian Blue stick of chalk and dragged it across the paper, smudging it with my finger. Next I used the white chalk, but it was impossible to recreate the fluffiness of the clouds on a flat surface – the sky was lifeless, the galloping horses were lame now. At least when I smoothed the lines of ochre chalk it hinted at the wind playing Chinese whispers across the field. I sat back to study the landscape. The piece was missing something; it needed a figure to give a sense of perspective and scale and I almost wished the father and son hadn't disappeared. But in the distance I could make out the perfect silhouette that wouldn't look out of place in an impressionist painting, a man taking a shortcut through the field, zigzagging his way through the waist-high wheat. I grabbed my charcoal pencil and sketched. As the figure got closer, it was clear that the man was pissed. And it was my dad.

He straddled the fence like it was a bucking bronco, stopping for a second to balance himself before he went for the dismount. He made it off the fence and staggered forward with his arms searching for an invisible wall to guide him. I only ever saw my dad drunk in daylight hours at a wedding or a funeral, although there were plenty of those within his large family. It would've been funny if Lorraine was with me but sitting on my own it was embarrassing. My dad bounced off the side of a caravan three doors down, making a grab for the handrail up to its door.

'Dad, no that one. We're up here!'

I waved my arms in semi-circles until finally he reset his homing radar and lurched towards our caravan. He flopped down next to me and let the little energy he had left seep out of his body like a balloon deflating.

''S me.'

'Ah ken it's you, what other man would be sitting on the steps of oor caravan?'

'You've got an answer for everything haven't you? You've always been too smart for yer own good.'

I didn't bother to reply or argue. How was it possible to be too clever? My mam and dad were happy to brag about my great exam results and yet at the same time my intelligence threatened them. It must be hard not to be jealous of someone, even if I was their daughter. They weren't that stupid; they could see that I was going places that they could only ever dream of. I tried my best not to pity them.

'What're you up tae anyway hen?'

It would've been too easy to rip the piss out of him but however tempting it was, I resisted the urge to wave the sketchpad under his nose.

'Ah'm doing a pastel drawing of the landscape.'

I pointed to the fields to make sure I didn't need to explain that too. My dad's head rotated in slow-motion following my index finger, his eyes narrowing as if he failed to see the massive field he'd just walked through.

'What? You're drawing somebody's Y-fronts drying on the line?'

It was difficult to tell if the booze had affected his brain or if it was the lack of an artist's eye that meant he couldn't see the beauty of the countryside beyond the washing line. It was easier to show him the sketch.

'Aye, it saves me buying postcards.'

'Very funny. Seriously though hen, it's brilliant, you've got a real talent.'

'Thanks dad, it's hard tae get the movement of the wind in the wheat.'

It wasn't too late to persuade my dad that I should apply to Art School. He knew I was good and maybe all it would take was to get Mr McDougall to talk to him about me staying on at school next year. My mam and dad listened to teachers. Mr McDougall could make them understand that they had no right to deny me a chance to be somebody and do something special. If I got accepted, I'd be able to walk up the same stairs as world-class artists and loads of art students became famous; I could even end up on the telly like Robbie Coltrane. Being bigger built hadn't held him back.

'Mibbae you could dae one of them, whatdayacallit? Aye, a muriel once you've started at OKI.'

'Dad, you're steamin' so you'll need tae try a bit harder than usual tae explain yourself. And they're called *murals!*'

'Ah met Big Davey at the pub and he was telling me that they've got a new canteen.'

'And? What's that got tae dae with me?'

'Ah ken you're keen tae keep doing yer drawing and stuff so mibbae ah could have a word with him tae let you paint something on the canteen walls.'

He patted me on the back so hard it winded me.

'Leave it with yer auld dad; ah'll fix it for you.'

'Thanks dad.'

What else could I say? The man didn't have a scooby about art or about me but he tried his best and I couldn't fault him for that.

'Ah'm away tae meditate, so that ah'm fresh for the visitors. And you can start thinking of ideas for the muriel.'

'Good idea, dad. You're full of them.'

Fresh for the visitors? Sober would be better. My dad managed to get to his feet and keeked through the window before slipping inside. My mam would kill him if he embarrassed her in front of Rita and if she got a whiff of the booze off him she'd be kicking off any minute.

Through the net curtain I watched my mam come out from the toilet just as my dad shut his bedroom door. It was impressive that my dad was pished but still realised it was best to sneak in while my mam was out of sight and my gran snored on the couch. My gran clutched the cushion the way I did when I had my period and held a hot water bottle tight across my belly. I crouched down below the scalloped hem of the curtain. My gran's face was supposed to be at rest; instead it was distorted like one of the gargoyles at Stirling Castle. I wondered if I should tell my mam that I'd noticed my gran seemed to be in pain a lot these days, or would my gran accuse me of being a wee clipe if my mam mentioned it? And gran always said that *"Auld age disnae come itself!"* She wouldn't want me worrying my mam for nothing; she was hyper enough about Rita coming without me adding to it.

I gathered up my chalk pastels and sketchpad. The drawing was promising. It needed a bit of work on the sky and added detail to the trees but it was a decent effort at a countryside scene and was different to anything else I had for my portfolio. Although what was the point if Big Davey had already lined up an interview for me next week? Tearing the page out of the sketchpad, I scrunched it into a jaggy ball and booted it off the veranda. The crushed up colours landed under the car behind one of the wheels, ready to be flattened the next time my dad reversed the car. Maybe the added design of a dusty tyre tread would make the artwork better; a real art student would make something special. It was tempting to wait, to smooth out the creases and turn it into an abstract piece. But what kind of art? I didn't have a clue what I'd do with a crumpled page of chalky smears and a grubby print of rubber. Maybe dad was right, I wasn't creative or trendy enough to belong at Art School, it would be a waste of time for the likes of me. I went down the steps and screwed the paper ball into the ground with my foot until it was beyond saving.

There was nothing else to do and nowhere else to go except inside. I hoped Rita, Sarah and Janine liked silverskin onions; my mam had piped Primula cheese on to Ritz crackers and placed an onion in the centre of each dollop.

'What've you been up tae?' asked my mam.

'Nothing, sunbathing on the steps.'

My mam didn't notice my sketchpad and box of pastels or

wasn't interested. Either way it suited me fine.

'Wise move, ah promise you, a tan will make you look thinner.'

'That's a load of bollocks.'

'Mind yer language, and none of that when Rita comes.'

'How else dae you want me tae describe yer theory, bullshit? Ah dinnae ken how you can stand there with a straight face and expect me tae believe that brown skin will knock three stone off me.'

'And ah thought you were supposed tae be an artist. It's a well-known fact, the darker the thing, the smaller it looks. If you paint a room dark, it makes it seems smaller. Same thing with skin, everyone kens that.'

'Ah'll take the sun tan lotion then.'

'Trust me, it works. But cooking oil is better.'

It was pointless arguing that the benefit of an optical illusion wouldn't outweigh being burnt to a frazzle with Crisp 'N' Dry. I had to hightail it, I couldn't stand being trapped in '*Home Sweet Caravan*' with a blootered dad snoring loudly and a stressed mam talking shite. All I needed to do was check on Lorraine before I could skedaddle but before I reached our bedroom door, my mam grabbed me from behind.

'Lorraine asked me tae let her sleep until her mam came. It's probably best tae stay oot of her road with the mood she's in.'

'Ah'm sure ah can hear her moving aboot in there. Ah'll just…'

'For once would you dae what you're telt? Leave her be. Ah dinnae want you upsetting her again afore Rita arrives. Why don't you take Bimbo oot for a walk and get some mair sun?'

Bimbo lay sleeping across my gran's feet like a pair of furry slippers. I swiped his lead off the kitchen unit, snapped it on to his collar and although he was mid-stretch, I dragged him towards the door. I was about to slam the door behind me □ it wasn't as if my gran or dad would wake and I highly doubted that Lorraine was asleep – when my mam waved a pound note in my face.

'And when you're oot, can you get change for the phone box?'

'Why? Who dae you need tae phone? Gran's already here.'

'It's no for me; Lorraine wants coins tae phone her pal.'

My mam returned to Operation Nibbles as if the conversation was over.

'But ah'm here! Who else does she need tae speak tae?'

'Wheesht, keep yer voice doon or you'll wake her.'

I gritted my teeth and tugged Bimbo's lead and now that he was fully awake, he was raring to go and tried to pull me down the steps. I had to get more details from my mam. And no matter how hard Bimbo wanted to kid on he was a Husky straining on a harness, there was no way his wee body could haul my weight anywhere.

'Who did she want tae phone?'

My mam covered the plate of Ritz crackers with cling film and didn't even look up.

'Ah cannae remember. Ah think she said Paula or something.'

'Was it Pamela?'

'Aye, that sounds like it.'

'And what else did she say?'

My mam lowered her voice as if Lorraine was standing right next to her.

'Tae be honest hen, ah wisnae really listening. Noo dinnae quote me but ah think she said that she wanted tae let her pal ken that she'd be back hame early.'

I stuffed the pound note into the pocket of my shorts and yanked Bimbo down the steps. My mam shouted, 'Cheery-bye' but there was nothing cheery about today. I gave Bimbo a sharp tug on his lead and he let out a pathetic yelp. He wasn't in a cheery mood either.

The caravan was barely out of sight when Bimbo jerked on his lead and forced me into the side of the grass verge. He probably needed to crap and I didn't want the aggro of getting rid of it so I let him off his lead to run off into a clearing between a clump of trees huddled together. Bimbo spun round in circles on the chosen spot and I walked on a bit to give him some privacy. When I checked his progress, he was doing business of another kind and was humping a King Charles Spaniel, looking like he could go on as long as the Duracell bunny. At least Bimbo would go home with a holiday romance story. Through the trees, I could make out a figure as someone with a whiny Geordie accent called out *'Dinky!'* I didn't have the energy to deal with Dinky's mammy being pissed off with Bimbo for taking the opportunity for a quickie. I managed to dislodge him and release

Dinky before hauling him back on to the path. Poor Dinky hobbled off towards her mammy with tales of a dirty dawg having his wicked way with her.

I had to break into a trot to make a safe getaway and I was almost at the complex when I heard, 'Howdy partner'. What are the chances that there was more than one sad auld cowboy shuffling around the campsite? I wasn't shocked to see Johnny tip his hat at me and fall into line alongside us like a majorette at the Gala Day.

'All on your lonesome?'

'Looks like it. Ah'm trying tae get a bit of sun while it lasts.'

Johnny bent down and tickled Bimbo behind the ears. I was sure I heard him creak as he straightened up and he smelt like bed sheets that hadn't been changed for a month; he probably slept in Saddle Sore under a horse blanket.

'Just be careful. This might not be the Costa Brava but the sun's stronger than you think. That's why I wear this Stetson.'

'And there was me thinking it was 'cause you're a real cowboy.'

'A comedienne, eh? You look at me and all you see is a silly old man driving a silly looking tractor train wearing a silly cowboy hat. But that's just what's on the surface. There's a lot more going on underneath.'

'Whatever. Shouldn't you be rounding up passengers?'

'I'm on my break.'

Johnny took a seat on the bench by the path. It didn't seem like he was in a rush to go anywhere and I wasn't exactly in a hurry to get back to the caravan. I plonked myself next to him and tied Bimbo's lead to the iron leg of the bench. Johnny lifted off his hat and pointed inside; his finger was like a knotted tree root and he stabbed it at the gold letters on the label of the brown leather headband.

JOHN B. STETSON COMPANY
3 X BEAVER
KETTLE FINISH
BOSS RAW EDGE

'See that? That's the mark of quality.'

Johnny paused. I didn't know what I was supposed to say, he

seemed to be waiting for some sort of reaction. To keep him happy, I threw him a bone.

'You can tell it's a lot better quality than the crap '*Kiss Me Quick, Squeeze Me Slow*' hat ma dad bought in Scarborough last year. It was only made of velvety cardboard but this looks like a real cowboy hat.'

Johnny grinned; I must've said the right thing.

'It is indeed the real McCoy. This hat is no joke, it means business. I bet you didn't know how strong it is.'

I began to wish that I hadn't encouraged him so much. He twirled the hat gently back and forth in front of me; there was nowhere to hide. I was about to learn more.

'The toughness and water-resistance of the Stetson is legendary. In 1912, when the battleship USS. Maine was raised from Havana harbour, where it had sunk in 1898, a Stetson hat was found in the wreck.'

Johnny paused again and seemed to expect me to gasp in awe, but there were limits. I had to draw the line under how far I was willing to play along, like feeding a stray dog; it was dangerous to encourage him.

'The hat was submerged in seawater for 14 years and had been exposed to slime, mud, all sorts of filth, you name it. But when that hat was cleaned off, it was as good as new.'

Although I wasn't in any rush to get back to the caravan, I didn't fancy spending the rest of the afternoon with Johnny and his fascinating facts. Even Bimbo was looking at me with the same expression as he did when he was after a rawhide chew stick, only this time he was begging for mercy. And yet I had no choice, I was trapped and Bimbo was stuck listening to Johnny too.

'So that's why you wear a Stetson?'

'You got it kiddo. This hat's like me. It's proved itself to be strong enough to cope with life's knocks. And I've tested it to the limit. The Stetson's not a gimmick, it represents the real me.'

'Does it bother you if folk laugh at yer cowboy outfit?'

'I'm too old to care what people think about me. Maybe you believe my hat is part of a costume, like some sort of mask I hide behind? Because it's easier to pretend that you're braver, smarter and funnier than you really are if you put up a front.

Don't you think so?'

Johnny leaned back on the bench; he cocked his head like Bimbo did when you shouted *"Walkies!"*

'What you see is what you get with me. 100% real,' I replied.

'Is that so? And what's the *real* you?'

No one had ever asked me that question before and I was stuck for an answer. Johnny picked up on my hesitation.

'Your gran thinks you're pretty special. So tell me more, about the real you, whoever that is.'

'Ma gran's biased. Ah dinnae ken aboot being special. And ah dinnae ken how tae describe myself. '

I thought I only blushed in front of good looking guys, not auld codgers; it was annoying to admit that he'd cracked open a shell that I'd never realised existed.

'I can see you're struggling. I'll help you out. Tell me in three words, how would you describe the real you?'

It was too hard a challenge. I could easily fire off three random words but I wanted to make sure they were the right ones and I paused. Johnny stared me out. I held my nerve and didn't lower my eyes and I barely blinked. He wasn't going to get the better of me.

'Loyal…determined and…honest.'

'You mean funny isn't in your top three words?'

'Ah think ah'm funny but ah picked ones that no one could deny aboot me. No everybody shares ma sense of humour.'

'Really?'

I studied his face again. I couldn't tell if he was being serious or not. If I had more than three words, I'd add kind-hearted and sensitive to my list too.

'Loyal. Determined. Honest.' He repeated the words slowly as if he had to chew them into a pulp before swallowing them down.

'You've certainly made a good choice. You and I have a lot in common.'

How wrong could Johnny be? The only things we had in common were that we were in the same place at the same time. Nothing else.

'Who are you loyal tae?' I asked.

'I'm loyal to myself. I always stand my ground and don't

compromise on my beliefs. If you're a people pleaser, you'll live to regret it, trust me.'

'That's easy for you tae say, it's no as simple for me. Ah dinnae mean tae be cheeky but nobody's going tae care at *your* age. Nae offence.'

'None taken. But you're wrong. You have the opposite scenario, at *your* age you've got the world at your feet. You can do anything and go anywhere.'

'You've never met ma mam and dad!'

'So what would you do if you weren't afraid?'

'Ah'm no scared of them. But ah'm no allowed tae dae whatever ah like.'

'What age are you?'

'Seventeen.'

'It's sounds to me that you're not as determined as you think. And not as honest either.'

'What dae you mean?'

'Angela, you're an adult. Who's the one hiding behind the mask now?'

'Ah'm no hiding behind anything or anyone.'

'Fair enough, whatever you say.'

I kicked a stone at my feet. Bimbo yanked on his lead trying to chase after it. I pushed the stupid dog back under the bench; if I was being held captive by Johnny, then Bimbo wasn't going anywhere either.

'So what would you like to do if you had complete freedom?'

'Ah'd work on getting ma portfolio ready tae apply for Art School.'

'What's stopping you?'

'Ah telt you, it's ma mam and dad who're the problem. They want me tae leave school and take a crappy job in an office. In a factory.'

'And you can only apply to study art straight from school?'

'Naw, ah suppose that there might be some who aren't school-leavers.'

'Am I right in saying that getting accepted is more about talent than whether you've spent a year at school working on a portfolio?'

'Aye, what's yer point?'

'My point is that you can't use your parents as an excuse not to follow your dream. Take the office job if you must but that doesn't stop you working on your portfolio does it? And if you're as talented as your grandma thinks, then you'll get a place. Remember, you said you're determined. Prove it. Be honest too. Stop blaming other people for not getting what you want. And be loyal to your talent as an artist.'

I held my tongue as well as my breath, my cheeks puffed up and I must've looked like I was playing an invisible trumpet. I blew out the pent up air but I still couldn't speak. Bimbo's head poked out from beneath the bench and Johnny patted him gently. He seemed happy to wait for me to say something and Bimbo lapped up the attention. I was lost for words. There was a smugness round Johnny like a Ready Brek glow; he knew he'd hit me with ideas bigger than I knew how to handle.

'Ah better get back,' I said, tugging Bimbo's lead. Giving a High Five, Playing Dead and the Commando Crawl weren't the only tricks my gran had taught Bimbo; he gave me a top-class dirty look.

'You know there are over one thousand caravans on this site. On your way back, ask yourself how many are full of wannabes with unfilled ambitions. And I'd guess they'd all come up with excuses for not following their own path. Don't add to the numbers.'

Johnny tipped his hat, still playing the cowboy, as if he was about to dig the spur of his boot into his horse's side and gallop home to *The High Chaparral*, not hobble back to some dingy garage to drive a novelty tractor.

'Tell your grandma my shift's finished and the kettle will be on if she fancies a brew.'

The way she'd eyed up Johnny, I'd bet my gran fancied more than a cup of Tetleys and as sure as shit floats, she'd be down at Saddle Sore at five o'clock on the dot. She'd probably hide there until after Rita's visit. I wished I could escape from the caravan too.

Chapter Twenty Three

I slammed the coins down on the kitchen table. Surely Lorraine would hear that I'd returned and come out of the bedroom? And at least thank me for going to the arcade for change, for the second time that day.

'She's already away,' said my mam.

'Away where?'

'The phone box. She couldnae wait any longer for you. Where've you been anyway?'

'Ah was talking tae Johnny. Ah didnae ken it was an emergency and ah had tae hurry.'

'Aw that time you were blethering with yer gran's boyfriend?'

My gran looked up from her *Bumper Book of Wordsearch.*

'Boyfriend? Ah wish!'

How could an auld man be classed as a boyfriend? There had to be a cut-off point and Johnny was over the 'boy' age limit by at least fifty years. My gran and Johnny. Together. Boyfriend and girlfriend.

Senga and Johnny,
Sittin' in a tree
K-I-S-S-I-N-G
First comes love, then comes marriage
then comes Senga with a baby carriage

It was enough to give me the dry boak.

'Nae danger gran, he's all yours. And if you skip doon tae Saddle Sore at five he'll have the kettle on.'

She jumped to her feet and plugged in her heated rollers. 'Ah better get these fired up. And change intae something fresh. And put on a bit of lippy.' My gran tapped my mam on the shoulder. 'Unless you need a hand with the food?'

'Naw, you're fine. You concentrate on getting yourself dolled up,' replied my mam. 'Everything's under control.' She peeled back the cling film on the plate of Ritz crackers and rolled the plastic into a ball. 'Ah've had an idea!'

Einstein wouldn't have looked as chuffed; my mam snatched up the Primula cheese and wound it up as if she was squeezing the life out of a tube of Colgate. Every inch or so she squirted a wee dollop round the edge of the plate until the tube was only capable of cheesy farts.

'Voilà!

My mam turned to me. 'What dae you think hen?'

'Aye, it looks even better mam. You've done us proud.'

'Ah'll need tae get a shower noo though; ah'm stinking of cheese 'n' onion. In fact…' My mam rummaged under the sink and produced a can of air freshener. 'Could you run roond the caravan scooting this?'

I took the can from her like a relay baton although the race against the reek was one I couldn't win. No matter how many circuits I made round '*Home Sweet Caravan*' spraying Woodland Glade, it would still honk to high heaven. It wasn't worth arguing with her though so I began my trail of pine tree vapour until I heard a squeal.

'For Christ's sake Angela. Get that spray away fae me!' My gran fanned a copy of the *Daily Record*. 'Ah'll smell like a public toilet doused in Domestos when ah meet Johnny.'

Before I got halfway down the caravan, the spray clawed at the back of my throat; I gave the room one last squirt in the direction of Bimbo's arse and stuck the can back under the sink unit.

Like a bowl of Rice Krispies the gravel outside the caravan went snap, crackle and pop. I pulled back the net curtain: Sarah was at the wheel, Rita was in the passenger seat and Janine was in the back. As pathetic as my mam, Rita only ever took the car into Falkirk or at a push into Stirling, and she never drove on motorways.

It would take them a while to unleash Janine but I guessed my mam didn't fancy meeting them with a towel wrapped round her. I banged on the bathroom door.

'They're here!'

It was difficult to tell if my mam was having a go at Chaka Khan or Whitney's version of "*I'm Every Woman*" while soaping up. She wasn't holding back with a brave try at the high notes and had reached the chorus.

'She's fair giving it laldy!' said my gran.

I abandoned the door knocking mission and shut the living room's hopper window; our visitors didn't need to be subjected to my mam's attempt at a world class power ballad.

'You better warn yer dad as well.'

My gran took over chapping on the bathroom door until finally the water and singing stopped. I threw open my mam and dad's bedroom door.

'They're here!'

Lying on top of the duvet snoring, my dad had stripped down to his pants, with one hand behind his head and the other down his Y-fronts cupping his balls. I wondered if the pose was part of his so-called meditation routine and helped him relax.

'Ah said, they're here!'

I was impressed at how quickly my dad managed to cover himself with the duvet, right up to his ears, already tomato red.

'Jesus! Ah nearly filled ma pants!'

I'd no desire to add another image of my dad's Y-fronts full or otherwise to the one that I'd already doused in brain bleach. He poked his chin over the top of the duvet.

'What's up?'

'For the third time. They. Are. Here. Rita, Janine and Sarah so you better get dressed. Pronto.'

'Fuck!'

My dad reached his hand out from under the duvet to minesweep the pile of clothes scattered on the carpet. My gran shouted through the wall that my mam needed clothes too and I threw a bundle into the steam-filled bathroom.

There was a machine gun rat-a-tat-tat at the caravan door and all four of us held our breath. Bimbo looked freaked out too. The knocking was so rhythmic I'd swear Rita must've practised on the dashboard all the way down the M6. We froze; my mam wasn't the only one who'd watched too much Cagney and Lacey. It felt as if we should have our hands in the air, ready to face masked robbers as we cowered behind the counter at the Bank of Scotland.

'If nobody moves, nobody gets hurt!' I gave it my best shot at an American gangster accent. My lone giggle echoed off the caravan walls, the others were too slow at getting the joke. The machine gun knock fired a second round at the door.

'Just coming!' said my mam.

She took a step towards the door and we stood aside as if we were in a wedding line-up waiting to greet our guests, minus the air kisses and hugs.

'It's lovely tae see you Rita, and so sorry for yer loss Sarah. Come away in.'

The three of them edged inside, shuffling past us.

'Welcome tae hame sweet caravan,' my mam added.

No one ever spoke directly to Janine. It would've pissed Lorraine right off if she'd been here; we'd bitch about it later. I understood; I'd seen and heard it all before with her, and I was always there to support her. Pamela had no idea what being Lorraine's best pal involved and would never be able to match my friendship. It took years of effort to feel this close.

Rita coughed; between the top three candidates of cheese 'n' onion nibbles, Woodland Glade or the stubborn honk of musty caravan, it was hard to tell which aroma made her gag the most.

'Did you have a nice drive doon?' asked my dad.

'Not really. Janine had an accident, Sarah's not used to driving an estate car and cracked the bumper and I should be hosting a Scripture group meeting tonight. But we're here now after all the palaver, so where's Lorraine?'

'She went off tae phone her pal,' replied my mam. 'Take a seat, make yourself comfy.'

Everyone traipsed into the living room and one by one we squashed our arses on to the U-shaped couch, trying to settle on a slice of cushion. Only my dad didn't take a seat, he stood with his feet wide apart and his hands on his hips trying to look powerful in a room of six females, deluded as ever.

We sat there as if we were about to play pass the parcel and my dad should have his back to us, ready to press 'stop' on the cassette player. No one was singing, and there definitely wasn't a party atmosphere. Rita crossed her arms; I'd seen her in combat mode often and it was wise to take cover although this time there was no escape. I was trapped. And yet I needn't have worried, Rita didn't waste her ammo on me; I wasn't her target. Her sights were trained firmly in my mam's direction.

'And there was me thinking that she was already with her pal.

Everything will be fine you said. We'll look after her. It'll be great for her to get away. I never wanted her to go but I believed you,' said Rita.

Battle had commenced. She could ask any of our neighbours and they'd tell Rita that my mam could give as good as she gets. Only last week my mam posted a note through next door's letterbox promising to stick their wean's recorder up his arse sideways if he didn't stop practising during *Coronation Street.* Rita shouldn't look so cocky. It was tempting to shout *"Keep yer chin up but yer fists higher!"* but I didn't dare. There was no guarantee my mam would find it funny and there was every chance she'd turn on me instead.

'We have looked after her. She's just no ready tae be away fae hame,' said my mam.

'And whose fault is that?' my dad mumbled in the background.

If there had been a roll of duct tape handy, I'd have wrapped it round his chops until he turned blue. I jumped in before he did any more damage.

'You'll be needing a bite tae eat after yer journey. Ma mam has put on a lovely spread for you.'

I pointed at the display of Ritz crackers suffocating under cling film. Maybe there was still a chance for everyone to relax and rethink the mercy dash to whisk Lorraine up the road.

'And ma gran's got VIP tickets for the Clubhouse if you want tae stay overnight. There's plenty of room. This couch folds oot and you can make the kitchen table intae a double bed.'

'Aye, money cannae buy these tickets. These are for the one and only Bob Monkhouse.'

Budging her way past my dad, my gran laid the tickets out and smoothed the veneer of the table as if Rita was ready to shift the salt and pepper aside to bed down on it; she didn't even notice my mam giving her an ice-bitch glare. Rita looked at the pine effect table as if it was a cowpat.

'No thanks, we just want to get going. Sarah needs to get back for her Spiritualist meeting too.'

My gran bobbed up to the surface like a Halloween dooking apple. 'Is that the Spiritualist church in Fawkurt doon Glebe Street? A few of ma regulars go there.'

'Aye, the one next tae the shop selling Patterson's seconds,' replied Sarah, perkier by the second. 'The very one!'

The shop was part of the chain of family bakeries I worked for and it sold misshaped biscuits and stale bread. There was always a queue of gypos at the door. My gran took me to the Spiritualist church once when a star performer from Langlees was appearing and I ate an empire biscuit with cracked icing while my gran mingled before the main event.

'Who's on the night?' asked my gran.

'It's Phoenix, ah've heard he's brilliant.'

'Aye, ma pal Jeanette reached her granny through Phoenix. He'll definitely be able tae speak tae Boaby if you're in the right frame of mind. But it'll no work if Phoenix senses you're no ready.'

'How dae ah make it work?'

'Open yer heart, no just yer mind.'

'So, as you can tell, Sarah's keen to chat to Boaby.' Rita got to her feet and tapped my dad's shoulder. 'We need to get back on the road so can one of you get Lorraine for us? It's the least you can do.'

'Who rattled *your* cage?' my dad asked. Rita's hoity-toity act didn't bother my mam or dad; they were having none of it.

'Noo just hang on a wee minute Rita. It's no oor fault if Lorraine takes the cream puff if you look at her the wrong way. If she hadnae thrown a wobbler you'd still be at hame fluffing up yer cushions for yer Holy Joe pals coming roond. So dinnae blame us.'

The tension crackled like static on the bunk bed's Bri-nylon sheets. I made a dive for the foil covered sponge punctured with cheese 'n' onion toothpicks and thrust it under Rita's snout.

'Help yourself, Mrs Quinn.'

'I'm surprised there's any left.'

'And what's that supposed tae mean?' said my gran. Bimbo growled too. I hoped his snarl proved his support for me and was nothing to do with the fact that Janine had stepped on his tail as she stood up. A dark puddle at her feet began to seep into the carpet, the door opened and Lorraine rushed across to Janine.

'For God's sake, did nobody notice that she's peed herself?'

'That's all we need. Quick, where's the bathroom?'

Rita grabbed Janine's skinny arm, tight enough to bruise a

peach.

'You don't want to go in there,' said Lorraine. 'I'll take her to my room and get her changed.'

Janine shuffled past us as if her ankles were tied together. It was too late to trap any more pee; the carpet squelched, her tank was completely empty.

'Dae you need a hand?' asked Sarah. She sounded as desperate as me to feel useful and avoid the waft of warm piss rising up and tickling our nostrils.

'No thanks, there's no room to move as it is in there.'

Rita humphed and Sarah sat back down, leaving my mam to take control and produce a wet J-cloth like a magician pulling silk hankies from his sleeves.

'I'll get that,' said Rita, reaching out to grab the scrap of blue cloth. 'This carpet could do with a good clean.'

My mam's knuckles went white as she tightened her grip on the J-cloth and with a clenched jaw she bared her teeth into a forced smile.

'Dinnae be daft. You're oor guest. Sit doon and relax.'

Rita humphed again but stayed put. I eased a cheese cube and silverskin onion off a toothpick in one smooth move and toyed with the idea of using it as mini spear to lodge in Rita's eyeball. My mam dropped to her knees and scrubbed the Domestos soaked J-cloth back and forth over the shag pile. Rita turned to my dad whose head was in the fridge; he pulled out a can of Kestrel lager and sparked the ring pull sending a spray in Rita's direction. Some of it must have showered Rita but she didn't give my dad the satisfaction of taking a hankie to her face.

'Can you give us a hand with Lorraine's case?' Rita asked.

'Aye, once ah've had a drink. Look, nae hard feelings, are you sure we cannae tempt you tae stay a bit longer? The fridge is aw stocked up.'

'And no just with lager,' my mam added, getting to her feet and wringing the J-cloth out in the sink. 'Ah prepared a two course meal and nibbles for yer visit.'

'Aye, no expense spared,' said my dad, taking another glug of Kestrel and topping it off with an almighty belch.

'Excuse you,' said my mam, slapping my dad on the back of the head with the damp J-cloth.

'Why fart and waste it when you can burp and taste it?'

My dad was enjoying embarrassing Rita. I was impressed. My mam didn't share my enthusiasm; she looked like she wanted to slip down the plughole with the dirty water.

In front of Sarah was a stack of toothpicks; the silver sponge had been stripped of cheese 'n' onion nibbles and was almost spikeless. It was hard to tell if she was hungry, bored or stressed. I knew all the reasons why it was easy to fill your face without even noticing that food had disappeared off the plate.

'At least Sarah appreciates aw the effort you've went tae,' said my dad, nodding at her toothpick heap as she crunched another onion and added the stick to the pile. It reminded me of a programme I'd seen once on BBC2 where some saddo had made wee models out of toothpicks and created a toothpick city, except Sarah's set of sticks looked like a bomb had hit one of the buildings.

'They're magic. It's years since ah've had a pickle. Boaby loved onions but they always repeated on him so ah stopped buying them.'

'You get tucked in then,' said my dad.

'Are you ready to go?' asked Rita.

Sarah plucked another three toothpicks from the sponge leaving a solitary stick; Rita looked like she was the one sucking on an onion. My mam breenged into the living room, flipping cushions and peering underneath yesterday's *Daily Record.*

'You'd lose yer heid if it wisnae screwed on. What's missing noo?' asked my dad.

'Ah'm looking for ma purse.'

'Yer handbag's in the bedroom,' said my dad.

My mam marched off, Sarah chomped on the last of her cheese and onion feast and Bimbo sniffed the damp patch where Janine had peed. Rita gave Bimbo a sly tap on the arse with the toe of her shoe; my gran never missed a trick and scooped him up into her arms.

'Touch ma dog again and ah'll...'

Simultaneously, the doors to both bedrooms swung open: my mam burst out of one clutching her leatherette purse and Janine toddled out of the other wearing one of Lorraine's RaRa skirts. Janine still had on the high-necked blouse that had been underneath her flowery pinafore; she'd been taught that God made buttons to be done up, to the chin. Rita got a kick out of dictating at least one of her daughter's fashion choices.

'Didn't you have anything longer?' asked Rita, pointing above Janine's knees. Even Janine's nighties went mid-calf and the poor lassie had never been allowed to show skin. No wonder her legs were Daz-white.

'She's only going into the car. No one will see her,' said Lorraine.

Rita tugged at the bottom layer of frills until the skirt's waistband sat on Janine's hips and her knees were hidden. She nudged Janine towards the door and turned to Sarah.

'Let's get going.'

My gran squeezed past the group to dive into one of the kitchen cupboards. Out of nowhere, she magicked up a half-empty jar of silverskin onions and thrust it into Sarah's hands.

'If you pace yourself, that'll keep you going till Carlisle.'

'Wait Rita, here's petrol money,' said my mam.

My mam waved a tenner at Rita and my dad choked on his can of Kestrel, sending specks of lager flying for the second time. Rita sucked air through her teeth, rubbed the sleeve of her cardi and grabbed the handle of Lorraine's suitcase.

'There's no need,' said Rita. She hauled the suitcase closer to the door and shooed the tenner away as if it were a dirty fat bluebottle buzzing at her ear.

'Aye, put yer purse away. You're embarrassing Rita,' said my dad.

'Are you sure?' My mam kept fanning the tenner under Rita's nose.

'Of course she's sure. Rita disnae expect us tae budget for double petrol money. Isn't that right?' asked my dad.

'No need to worry, I can afford it.'

'And you make sure we aw ken it,' mumbled my gran.

My gran's comment wasn't loud, but it was loud enough. No one said a word; it's a well-known fact that trying to break an awkward silence makes it more awkward. Even Janine knew it was best to look busy, repeatedly smoothing down the frills of the RaRa skirt whilst Sarah stuck one of her used toothpicks into the jar and pierced an onion and Rita pretended she was tightening the buckles on the suitcase. Lorraine did nothing except refuse to look me in the eye; with the tip of her ponytail inside her mouth she reminded me of a cow chewing the cud.

She hadn't chewed on her hair since Fridays in primary four when we got our weekly mental arithmetic tests. It was a dead cert that Lorraine would raise her hand in answer to the, *"Who got less than 10 out of 20?"* question the teacher used to spare the blushes of the Red Group. The teacher went to the bother of naming the three maths groups with different colours although everyone in the class knew that the Red Group was the bottom group. The thickos went to see the visiting remedial teacher every Wednesday morning in the G.P. room, a pure beamer; no wonder they were called the Red Group. I spent a whole summer playing schools with Lorraine so she wouldn't be in the Red Group in primary five. She had a blackboard with a built-in clock, coloured chalks and a duster; if it was sunny we'd set up our classroom outside and the class sat on a tartan travel rug, if it rained they sat on the edge of her bed and we'd line up her teddies, dolls and Janine to be the Red Group. I was good at being the teacher: after the holidays, Lorraine moved up to the Blue Group. Just to be on the safe side, I taught Lorraine to read the answers upside down. On Fridays she would swing back in her chair and I'd angle my jotter if she got stuck. She didn't want my help these days.

'Ah think it's time you hit the road Rita,' said my dad.

'Aye, you'll want tae beat the rush hour,' added my mam.

'Very true, the sooner we're out of here the better,' replied Rita.

Lorraine didn't even give Bimbo a goodbye pat. Rita lifted the suitcase and Sarah screwed the lid on her jar of onions. Janine paused to swipe the last remaining cheese 'n' onion stick but she didn't get a chance to savour a final treat; Lorraine pushed her away from the table and propelled her towards the door.

Her wee sister coughed and a cheese cube flew through the air, minus the silverskin onions from each end of the stick, and the toothpick itself. Janine must've swallowed the whole thing and Lorraine's lurch forward wouldn't have helped.

Janine grabbed her throat and her face went beetroot with

panic. Rita dumped Lorraine's suitcase and launched herself at Janine to join my mam's frantic efforts to slap her hard on the back. There wasn't a squeal from Janine; only gurgling noises like a blocked plughole – a plunger would've been handy. Bimbo barked and Lorraine and I were paralysed as tears rolled down Janine's cheeks. Sarah's hands covered her face and she was pushed to the floor as my dad barged past to grab Janine's waist from behind.

He hoisted Janine up with a wrestler's grip and an onion bounced to the floor and rolled under the fridge to begin a new life with all the other oozy bits left to dry up and rot. There was still no sign of the missing cube of cheese or toothpick but at least Janine was able to scream; her airways were definitely free. Rita blessed herself and shouted 'Thank you Lord' with her eyes to the polystyrene tiled roof and breathing like a crank caller. But Janine's head began to shake like a horse in a cloud of midges despite Rita's tight hold on her. Above Bimbo's howling, Janine's whining and Rita's sighing we all heard my dad command me and Lorraine to 'run like fuck and phone an ambulance'.

The tension between me and Lorraine disappeared as fast as the onion under the fridge; we bolted to the door. I turned the door handle as my mam shrieked.

'Wait!'

In the confusion of a flying onion and Janine's choking fit, no one noticed that my gran had collapsed on the couch and slid to the floor. Bimbo tried to lick the pain away; she didn't move as his sandpaper tongue slabbered her from cheek-to-cheek.

'Tell them we need two ambulances!'

Lorraine took the steps two-at-a-time and we tore down the path to the main complex. There was a stitch in my side and it was impossible to keep up with Lorraine. She skidded to a stop outside the phone boxes; all three were full, and there was a queue. The run was like the scene from *Chariots of Fire*, I could practically hear the synthesizer kick in at the second verse of the theme tune. But I wasn't barefoot in a mud splattered white T-shirt and shorts, pounding through the icy sea foam in slow motion, I was bent double and panting with my hands on my knees in a disabled parking space in front of the chippy.

'It's an emergency!' Lorraine shouted at the queue as she flung open the door of the nearest box. A woman wearing more eye make-up than Siouxsie Sioux turned and tried to push Lorraine back out. I reached the phone box just in time to yank the woman out and hand the phone to Lorraine. I was too out of breath to make a 999 call but I had enough puff left to scream: 'Are you fuckin' deaf? It's an emergency! Noo piss off oot the way.'

The others in the queue hung around like one of my dad's lager farts and the woman slunk to the end of the line without a cheep. Lorraine jabbed her finger into the slot and dialed 999. I had to admit that I was impressed; it was usually me who had to take control. She explained that her wee sister and my gran needed urgent medical attention, without starting to greet. She even remembered the number and row that our caravan was on although I doubted that she was likely to forget anything about this holiday.

The ambulances passed us on our way back to the caravan and when we got to our row it was just my gran being loaded into the back, still hugging a cushion into her belly. She was conscious and managed to grab me to insist that I let Johnny know that she wouldn't be joining him for a cuppa. And to give Big Davey the VIP tickets for the cabaret if she wasn't back in time. My mam jumped into the ambulance with her as it sped off, my dad crossed his fingers and raised them in the air. Lorraine and I stood side-by-side and waved at the ambulance as if it was Boaby at the wheel of the Nut Bus on a Club trip to Carfin. Those hassle-free days seemed a long time ago.

Inside the caravan, Sarah slid the wrapper down on a strawberry ice pole for Janine to sook and Bimbo begged for a lick. They were the only calm ones. And for once it was me who was greetin' instead of Lorraine.

'Yer gran's a fighter, she'll be fine,' said my dad. He tore off a sheet of kitchen roll and I blotted my eyes.

'I hope so; one near death experience in a day is enough for anyone to cope with,' said Rita.

'Near death? Yer arse and parsley, the lassie only choked on a wee bit of cheese. It's no big deal.'

'It could've killed her!'

Rita was inches from my dad's face, close enough to spray him with spital this time.

'But it didnae kill her so there's nae point in getting aw het up aboot it. Accidents happen.'

Lorraine stepped forward, invading my dad's space as much as her mam.

'There's no such thing as an accident. My mam's right. Janine could've died.'

'Like mother, like daughter. You're a bigger drama queen than yer mammy and that's saying something!'

Sarah rubbed wide circles over Janine's back as if she was trying to wind a newborn. Janine looked up at the sound of my dad's raised voice and Bimbo took the opporchancity to run his tongue up the length of the ice pole. Sarah's nervousness was contagious; I worried about how my dad, after three cans of Kestrel, would deal with Rita and Lorraine as a tag team.

'Don't you dare stand there drunk and insult me and my family. Lorraine get your bag. Sarah, let's go. We don't need to listen to this.'

My dad nodded at the door and Sarah scrambled to her feet telling Janine to bite instead of sook on her ice pole.

'Aye, run away fae the truth. That's what's wrong with her.' Now he was pointing at Lorraine. 'Brought up tae think she's a wee princess with a holier than thou mammy. You'd get a turn at the Pavilion you're that good. But you're wasting yer time acting whiter than white with me; ah ken what you're really like.'

'D'you mean the story about the chute?' asked Lorraine.

'Chute? I don't know what you're on about,' said Rita.

'So what story is it?'

Lorraine's eyes bulged like the bullfrog I'd once dissected in biology. Forget that it can leap nine times its body length; the most interesting adaptation of the species is its skin. When the bullfrog feels threatened, it will secrete a toxin on the surface of its skin and if a predator tries to eat the bullfrog, its poisonous toxin could potentially kill its enemy. Respect. I'd bet that Lorraine envied the bullfrog's talent.

I balled up the soggy sheet of kitchen roll into my fist and pressed my nails into it. Janine crunched down on her ice pole, staining her lips strawberry red and giving her a Coco the Clown mouth. She was the only one wearing a happy-go-lucky grin.

'Ah'm talking aboot the fact that yer mammy might've been able tae kid yer daddy but go intae the Royal and any of the men at the bar could tell you the truth, there was nae immaculate conception.'

'What does he mean?' Lorraine turned to Rita. My dad kept ranting, without drawing breath, a turbo-charged lager-loosened tongue.

'Poor Tam must be black affronted. Nae wonder he never shows his face in the Royal and he has tae work away fae hame…'

'He works hard for his family and doesn't drink and gamble his wage. That's the difference between your dad and the men who prop up the bar at the Royal. Take no notice of him Lorraine, he's just jealous.'

'Jealous? Of Tam? Dinnae be ridiculous, ma wife was a virgin when she married me but Lorraine's daddy is a multiple choice question. Isn't that right Rita? Or does a trip tae confession wipe the slate and yer memory clean?'

'Don't listen to him. He's drunk.' Rita grabbed Lorraine's arm, but she didn't budge, her feet rooted into the shag pile carpet. Janine cooried into Sarah and tried to hoover up the pink watery dregs by sooking on the empty ice pole wrapper.

I said, 'Dad, leave it, will you?'

There was no need for Lorraine to hear this, not now anyway, not unless she had to. Lorraine's eyes turned full beam on me and she knew I knew. After all these years, we didn't need to use words at times like this. I said nothing and yet I said it all.

'So what's your dad trying to say about my mam?'

'Ignore him.'

'You keep telling me you're my best pal, you'd do anything for me. Prove it! Tell me the truth. It's the least you can do after last night.'

'What happened last night?' my dad asked.

'You'd be too tanked up to notice what your daughter was up to. I should never have agreed to let Lorraine come on this holiday. C'mon, let's get out of here.'

'Aye, cheerio!' shouted my dad.

Janine started greetin' and I handed her my ball of kitchen

roll. She chewed on it instead, swallowing the damp dod of paper.

Rita nudged Sarah and Janine. I grabbed the handle of Lorraine's suitcase but she ripped my hand off the leather strap.

'I asked you a question. And I'm not leaving until you answer it. You owe me.'

'Ask yer mam, no me.'

Rita had swapped her ears for a rubber pair; the Q and A session was over.

'C'mon Lorraine, let's go.' said Rita.

'Aye, ah thought you were in a hurry.'

My dad dived for the door, flinging it open as far as it would go, the hinges screeching. He raised his shoulders to his ears with his chin jutting out and arms crossed like a nightclub bouncer. 'So what're you waiting for?'

Rita stuck her chin out too, the spit of Desperate Dan with slightly less stubble, and marched towards the door with Sarah and Janine shuffling behind her. I made another attempt at taking hold of Lorraine's suitcase but she yanked it free from my grasp.

'Ah'm just trying tae help.'

'I don't need your help.'

Lorraine followed her mam, Sarah and Janine down the steps and out to the car. And I was left behind – numb with pain and shock. My dad slammed the front door and went to the fridge for another beer. Eventually I moved, and pulled the living room net curtain back to kneel on the couch with my nose to the window until it fogged up. Sarah locked the suitcase in the boot and climbed into the driver's seat, Janine was strapped in and blowing spit bubbles, Rita took up position in the front and opened her *AA Great Britain Road Atlas*. My dad squashed in beside me to have a gawk too.

'So much for Lorraine's travel sickness and needing to sit in the front. But that's typical of Rita, selective memory whenever it suits her. And Rita's got the audacity tae swan in here and say ah'm drunk? She's the one who acts like a drunk. Everybody remembers what she did. Except her,' added my dad, not letting the irony that he slurred his words spoil the effect of his profound statement.

I ignored my dad's continued rant and psychological profile of Rita as a "heid the baw" and wiped the misted glass again, but Lorraine still hadn't looked my way. Sarah stalled the engine before finally lurching off down the road. Only Janine waved goodbye.

Chapter Twenty Four

Parking at the hospital was a nightmare; I drove round the one-way circuit for over half an hour before I pounced on a space. I'd have been quicker getting the bus into Falkirk. Now that it had been fumigated and if I ignored the Axminster carpet with its wee crowns and the squelch under my feet where water leaked in from a rust-nibbled hole in the floor, I had to admit I loved having my own car. It was magic being able to pass saddos waiting at the bus stop. But I'd have to sell it or get an offer from the scrappy if I got accepted to Art School. It was a sacrifice I was willing to make; like auld folk, students were expected to use the bus and I wanted to look the part. It would be hard enough to fit in without pulling up in a clapped out Vauxhall Chevette.

The parking trauma meant that I'd missed a good chunk of visiting time and needed to hoof it as fast as I could. It was getting a bit easier to attempt to run since I'd lost a stone. If I kept away from the chippy and the icey, no one would be able to call me lard-arse if I got to climb the stairs of the famous Mackintosh building.

And yet I was a long way off not being out of puff after a sprint and was panting like a marathon runner at mile twenty. My phizog resembled a burst tomato when the door of the lift slid open and we were face-to-face for the first time since her mam rescued her from Primrose Valley. Me and Lorraine froze as if we had gone back in time and we were playing statues in the playground. Our schooldays at primary seemed a lifetime ago and although it had only been a few months since I'd last seen Lorraine, everything had changed. And nothing would ever be the same again.

She dodged past me and sprang out of the lift as if it was on fire. I stamped on a stray autumn leaf with the sole of my shoe and ground it into the floor until it could crunch no more. I let Lorraine go; there was nothing else to say. It was pointless to chase after her; she'd made it clear that she would never speak to me again.

I'd tried to phone her when I got back from holiday. If she answered she hung up when she recognised my voice, if Rita answered she let out a pathetic theatrical sigh and pleaded with me to stop pestering Lorraine; anyone would think I was some sort of paedo the way I was treated. One time, after I'd rang six times in a row, making the best use of my repertoire of dodgy accents, Rita threatened to call the polis and have me charged with harassing her family. I'd no more coins to call back; it was a bummer that Rita would think that she'd won.

Turning up at her door was no use either; Rita kept the chain on and told me this was my final warning before she lifted the phone and dialled 999. If it wasn't so sad it would've been funny. I imagined my photo in the *Falkirk Herald* in the Court Round Up feature with me found guilty of trying to be a loyal friend, and getting it so badly wrong. I was prepared to face the charges but Lorraine wouldn't give me a second chance. Rita pulled the Venetian blinds down and angled them shut when I chapped on their living room window. She slipped a camera between the slats and held it against the window; it flashed. This was real photographic evidence, and it was no joke. I took a step back and snagged my tights on a rose bush. The ladder on my tights ran all the way up to my thigh. I ripped them off and posted them through the letterbox. I took the long way home, not caring if the Proddy boys or Bandeath dugs were out on the prowl; I deserved to be battered black and blue and have the arse ripped out of my pencil skirt. It was all my own fault.

I'd fallen down a hole much deeper than the quarry and although it was tempting to try and get in touch with Lorraine again, I could take a hint. I couldn't deny it any longer – she didn't want me in her life anymore. I missed Lorraine so much that on my first week at working at OKI, I put on a fake voice that sounded as if I was gargling mouthwash and phoned in sick. Pulling a sickie meant that I could wait for Lorraine coming out of school and when she finally appeared she was arm-in-arm with Pamela. I stayed hidden behind The Frying Scotsman chip van and as if the sight of Lorraine with Little Miss Brown Nose slavering all over her wasn't enough to drive me insane, the wafts of crispy batter made me chew on my sleeve.

Weeks went by and after all the times that I'd tried to bump into her and failed, I never expected to see her coming out of the hospital lift. I couldn't understand why she was there. At a glance she looked fine to me, there were no signs of a visit to A&E and the only answer was to follow Lorraine. Even if we didn't talk, at least I'd be able to see how she really was up close but I was already late for visiting time. I pressed the button for the third floor to the Oncology ward.

My heels click clacked down the corridor; I'd bought new shoes from Chelsea Girl with my first wage packet, the same style and colour as a pair Lorraine had bought for the holiday. My feet were too wide for them; they nipped at my heels until they rubbed the skin raw and squashed my toes together letting the toenails overlap and take bites of flesh. The pain was worth it.

At the nurses' station, Staff Nurse Kavanagh was yakking on the phone. She wiggled 'Hello' with her left fingers. I could only manage to give her a nod. Even Rimmel couldn't paint a smile on my face.

Lorraine wasn't the only one who went home from Primrose Valley early. After she'd been rushed to Scarborough General, my gran was kept in overnight and moaned the whole time that she wouldn't be able to use her VIP tickets to see the Bob Monkhouse cabaret. In the morning, the doctor advised us that she was fit to travel and that it would be better to organise tests for her back home. My gran wanted to stay at the caravan for the rest of the week but my mam said the holiday was already ruined and the best thing was to cut it short and head up the road. I was glad; for once my mam was talking sense. The holiday was totally gubbed.

Before we left, my dad pulled the car up in front of Saddle Sore and my gran swapped addresses with Johnny. They agreed to keep in touch and she promised to return next summer. My dad was about to pull away when Johnny flagged the car down, leaned inside the open window and asked my dad to give him a second. He pulled out a bunch of keys and unclipped a tarnished silver Stetson from the keyring. Johnny pressed the keyring charm into my gran's palm and swore that it would bring her good luck.

The Stetson's luck didn't work beyond the M6. It turned out

that my gran had ovarian cancer and those stomach pains, running to the loo all the time and a bloated belly were the signs we all missed.

'What's for you, will no go by you,' said my gran to anyone that tried to offer her sympathy. She was having none of it and went to the bingo as usual, still rubbing the wee Stetson in the hope of hitting the jackpot with the Link-Up game. And for the first few weeks I believed that she'd fight it and win. That was until we learnt more about the 'silent killer' and that by the time the symptoms are noticeable, it's often too late.

She gave me the Stetson charm.

My gran told her clients that soon she'd be able to cross the Rainbow Bridge and pass on direct messages to their dead pets. Word got out that this was a limited offer and it was the busiest she'd ever been. But my mam said the back-to-back readings were tiring her out and we started putting folk off by telling them that her memory could only hold so many messages for deid dugs and it was already full to the gunnels. The bookings tailed off and so did my gran's energy. And there came a point, much sooner than we all expected, that she was admitted to hospital. Johnny sent a card with a drawing of a cowboy on horseback and the words,

> *"The Lord is my strength and my shield;*
> *my heart trusts in him, and he helps me."*
> *Psalm 28.7*

'If only.'

My gran couldn't manage to talk as much as she used to, she didn't have the time or energy to waste words, every sentence cost her. She'd been moved since yesterday and was now in the last room at the end of the corridor. A single room. I knew what that meant. But I needed more time. She was slipping away and I was yet to draw the perfect portrait.

Over the last few weeks, I'd thought a lot about me and Johnny's heart-to-heart when we talked about my excuses for not applying for Art School. I could hear Johnny's voice telling me to love what I do and do what I love. And I remembered his advice every time I stood at the office kettle making cups of tea for the office staff, the ones who lived, worked and would die in Cumbernauld. I could picture Johnny, in his Stetson, shaking his head in disappointment.

Every time I was handed a stack of papers to be filed.

Every time I had to stuff hunners of envelopes.

Every time I clocked out.

And every time I clocked back in the next morning.

Big Davey told my dad it was out of his hands and I wasn't able to paint the wall in the canteen as OKI didn't have a "budget for public art". And I couldn't afford the paint on my wages. There was no question that I could draw, I could paint and my art work was better than good. All I had to do was prove it. My best pal was gone and even my gran was fading in front of my eyes. I'd lost my grasp on all the things I loved and the only thing left that I had a hope in hell of holding on to was my talent for art.

I studied my gran's face, and shaded in the creases and wrinkles and the more I stared at her, the more I realised how much life went into earning each and every one of these folds of skin. My gran's face told stories, and I wondered if any of those lines had been caused by life's regrets. And if this summer's regrets would show on my face too, or if there was some way I could minimise the damage. Could I rub it all out and start again on a fresh clean page?

I stopped outside the doorway and peered inside. I needed to complete another drawing of my gran and I desperately wanted to see her.

But not like this.

Not with her shrunken body.

Not with her hair matted.

Not with her jaw slack.

Not with her stale breath.

Not with her bony knuckles.

Not with her skin jaundiced.

Not with the whites of her eyes turned yellow.

Not looking and smelling like a creature from *Alien*.

Not like this.

The body was different. And yet it was still my gran.

The click clack rhythm of my high-heeled shoes had reached its final verse and my gran's robotic head turned to face me, inch by inch, shadows deep inside her laughter lines.

'Hello stranger!'

'Sorry gran, ah had tae work late yesterday. But ah got away early today and managed tae nip intae yours and get you a fresh nightie and pants.'

'Thanks for the nightie, but ah dinnae need any mair pants hen, they're putting me in paper ones noo. Ah left ma dignity at the door when ah arrived here.'

'Is there anything else you need?'

She shook her head in slow-mo. I wished I hadn't asked her, it was precious energy wasted. And I already knew the answer, no one, not doctors or nurses, not family or friends, none of us could give my gran her life back.

I placed a cup of water under her chin. It wasn't easy to angle the straw past her cracked lips and into her mouth. Her tongue flopped out, as rough and dry as an emery board. She didn't have the strength to sook. I dipped the wee stick with the sponge on the end and dabbed it until patches of her tongue turned from dull putty grey to sugar mouse pink, almost alive again.

'So how're you feeling today?'

'Same as yesterday. But better noo you're here. How's Bimbo?'

'He's fine gran, spoilt rotten as usual.'

My gran's laughter lines went deeper still. I dragged a plastic bucket chair from the corner and pulled it up close. There was no need to tell her he was pining and he'd perched himself along the arm of the couch to keep a look-out for my gran since the day she was admitted to hospital.

'Yer pal was here tae see me.'

I sat bolt upright, wondering if I'd made sense of my gran's ghostie whisper.

'You mean Lorraine? She came tae visit?'

'Aye, she didnae stay long. She just came tae say thanks, you ken, for helping her oot. And cheerio.'

'What did you talk aboot?'

'No much, ah've no got the energy tae blether. Ah just telt her aboot Karen getting through tae the finals of that big gymnastic competition and winning first prize. She's made us aw that proud, eh?'

'Aye, but you've no tae live with her, Karen's driving us aw nuts. Gymnastics this, gymnastics that, it's aw we hear fae her.

She'd bore you tae… sorry gran.'

'Wheesht, there's nae need tae apologise.'

'Was that aw that you spoke aboot with Lorraine? Nothing else?'

'Ah cannae remember much else, just that ah gave her a wee minding. You've got the Stetson charm so ah gave her ma lucky rabbit's foot, it's no much use tae me noo. Ma bingo days are o'er.'

'Did she no mention me at aw?'

'Ah'm sorry, hen, naw she didnae. You need tae let her go too.'

I dipped my head into the carrier bag at my feet and used the hem of my gran's flannelette nightie to wipe away my tears. When my gran was told that she'd need to go into hospital, I'd never seen her look so smug. She pulled her cream leatherette vanity case out from under her bed, gave it a dust with the back of her sleeve and sprung open the lock to reveal what was stashed within its red satin guts. Like a travelling salesman, she whipped out a nightie, a pair of velour slippers, a face cloth, an embroidered hankie, three pairs of high-waister pants, a bar of Pears soap, two pairs of Pop Sox, and a packet of Fox's Glacier Mints. All of the specially chosen items were brand new; they'd been kept for 'good', waiting to be unleashed for this exact scenario. My mam said that my gran was like the battery, ever ready, and would never have had the same satisfaction if she'd died suddenly. I tried to look for the positives.

She lasted a lot longer in hospital than any of us expected and she'd resorted to wearing her washed out auld nighties. They suited her better; the new peach coloured one was too bright next to her dehydrated skin. I found one of her auld nighties easily and it gave me time to rake around a bit. The wardrobe door creaked and I pulled out the Astrakhan coat my gran had worn in the photos of my mam and dad's wedding. It weighed a ton and could stand up on its own. I tried it on and looked in the full length mirror; even after losing a bit of weight the buttons were never going to fasten, but it didn't matter. I rubbed my chin on the furry collar and strutted around the bedroom making the coat swing. I was still wearing it when I found the drawing I'd done for her birthday. I'd asked her once why she hadn't put it up in any of the rooms and she told me she didn't have any picture hooks. My gran always said, "*You can't kid a kidder.*" She was right, I'd seen a hook in the junk drawer in the kitchen, and I'd even laid it out on the bunker. But on my next visit it was gone and was back inside the drawer along with rubber bands, receipts, pens, Askit powders, scissors, batteries, razor blades, stamps, sellotape, tape measure, superglue, torch and a set of mini screwdrivers she got in a Christmas cracker.

The picture hook would never see daylight again. She hated the portrait because of all the wrinkles I'd given her; this wasn't the version she wanted me to draw, it was too realistic. I was glad she didn't have a mirror in her hospital room; she'd be chuffed with that portrait now compared to the papery skin stretched over her gaunt face.

I unzipped my new portfolio case. The money from OKI didn't go far by the time I paid my dig money and put a tenner of petrol in the car but I'd been through to Glasgow and bought myself the case from Millers. In a couple of weeks I'd have enough dosh for a set of watercolours and real sable brushes. Without Lorraine, it wasn't as if I was spending money on going to Mystique, or anywhere else.

I took out my HB pencil and sketchpad. This would be my last drawing of my gran and I'd make sure it was my best yet, the star of my portfolio. I shut my eyes. I could picture my gran, the one who always gave more than she ever took; I could see her scooping up the dead fox from the street and gently wiping its face. I remembered her using the doll's eyes to give the plastic Bambi its sight back. There were so many memories I needed to capture.

In this portrait the only lines I'd draw would be laughter lines. There was no need to record the worn out body that lay in front of me, my job was to sketch a loving face that glowed with a life well lived. It would be a portrait that did my gran justice and showed her as she was and how she will always be remembered. It would be a piece of art that she would be proud of and she'd be able to brag about *both* of her granddaughters when she went over the Rainbow Bridge. She could tell everyone she met that I was the first lassie from the scheme to go to Art School.

I was the talk of the toun.

BOOK CLUB QUESTIONS

General Questions:

1. What do you think the book is about?
2. Are there situations and/or characters you can identify with? If so, how?
3. What major emotion(s) did the story evoke in you as a reader?
4. Is the ending satisfying? If so, why? If not, why not...and how would you change it?

Specific Questions:

1. What is the significance of the title? Could it relate to more than one character?
2. The theme of friendship is explored closely in *Talk of the Toun*, and the book opens with Angela's memory of how she met Lorraine. What do you think attracted the girls to each other initially? What has kept them together all the way through school? And what has gone wrong?
3. Sitting in the café in Falkirk, Angela makes a comment that has serious moral implications. Do you agree with why she did it? Would you ever have made the same decision? Why? Why not?
4. The book is set in urban Central Scotland in 1985. How important is the setting to the story? Would the novel change in any definite sense if it was set somewhere else? How well do you think MacKinven portrays the 1980s? Can you relate to the period described and to the religious and social issues that are raised?

5. Do you feel Angela's Catholic upbringing influences the decisions she makes? Have you encountered sectarianism demonstrated by characters such as Sash? Do you feel religious tensions are still an issue in Scottish society?
6. What do you perceive as the central conflict in the novel?
7. Which do you think is the most important relationship to the plot?
8. Angela is a very complex character. Do you *like* her? What about Lorraine? Explain why, or why not.
9. What is Gran's role in the novel? Discuss the ways in which she influences Angela.
10. *Talk of the Toun* is rich with secondary characters. What is Karen's role in the novel? Rita? Janine? What about Gran's boyfriend, Johnny? In what ways do they influence Angela and progress the plot?
11. The novel is structured around a series of Angela's memories that intersperse with what is happening in Angela's present. What effect does this structure have on the story?
12. If the story were told by Lorraine, what areas of it do you think she would focus on?
13. Angela lives in a run-down council estate with her parents and sister, Karen. Lorraine lives in a private house in 'Spam Valley' with her mother and sister, Janine, whilst her father works abroad. What does the novel have to say about social class and social mobility in the 1980s? Do you think anything has changed over the last 30 years?

More Books From ThunderPoint Publishing Ltd.

Mule Train

by Huw Francis

ISBN: 978-0-9575689-0-7 (kindle)
ISBN: 978-0-9575689-1-4 (Paperback)

Four lives come together in the remote and spectacular mountains bordering Afghanistan and explode in a deadly cocktail of treachery, betrayal and violence.

Written with a deep love of Pakistan and the Pakistani people, Mule Train will sweep you from Karachi in the south to the Shandur Pass in the north, through the dangerous borderland alongside Afghanistan, in an adventure that will keep you gripped throughout.

'Stunningly captures the feel of Pakistan, from Karachi to the hills' – tripfiction.com

A Good Death

by Helen Davis

ISBN: 978-0-9575689-7-6 (eBook)
ISBN: 978-0-9575689-6-9 (Paperback)

'A good death is better than a bad conscience,' said Sophie.

1983 – Georgie, Theo, Sophie and Helena, four disparate young Cambridge undergraduates, set out to scale Ausangate, one of the highest and most sacred peaks in the Andes.

Seduced into employing the handsome and enigmatic Wamani as a guide, the four women are initiated into the mystically dangerous side of Peru, Wamani and themselves as they travel from Cuzco to the mountain, a journey that will shape their lives forever.

2013 – though the women are still close, the secrets and betrayals of Ausangate chafe at the friendship.

A girls' weekend at a lonely Fenland farmhouse descends into conflict with the insensitive inclusion of an overbearing young academic toyboy brought along by Theo. Sparked by his unexpected presence, pent up petty jealousies, recriminations and bitterness finally explode the truth of Ausangate, setting the women on a new and dangerous path.

Sharply observant and darkly comic, Helen Davis's début novel is an elegant tale of murder, seduction, vengeance, and the value of a good friendship.

'The prose is crisp, adept, and emotionally evocative' – Lesbrary.com

The Birds That Never Flew

by Margot McCuaig

Shortlisted for the Dundee International Book Prize 2012
Longlisted for the Polari First Book Prize 2014

ISBN: 978-0-9929768-5-9 (eBook)
ISBN: 978-0-9929768-4-2 (Paperback)

'Have you got a light hen? I'm totally gaspin.'

Battered and bruised, Elizabeth has taken her daughter and left her abusive husband Patrick. Again. In the bleak and impersonal Glasgow housing office Elizabeth meets the provocatively intriguing drug addict Sadie, who is desperate to get her own life back on track.

The two women forge a fierce and interdependent relationship as they try to rebuild their shattered lives, but despite their bold, and sometimes illegal attempts it seems impossible to escape from the abuse they have always known, and tragedy strikes.

More than a decade later Elizabeth has started to implement her perfect revenge – until a surreal Glaswegian Virgin Mary steps in with imperfect timing and a less than divine attitude to stick a spoke in the wheel of retribution.

Tragic, darkly funny and irreverent, *The Birds That Never Flew* ushers in a new and vibrant voice in Scottish literature.

'...dark, beautiful and moving, I wholeheartedly recommend' scanoir.co.uk

Toxic

by Jackie McLean

Shortlisted for the Yeovil Book Prize 2011

ISBN: 978-0-9575689-8-3 (eBook)
ISBN: 978-0-9575689-9-0 (Paperback)

The recklessly brilliant DI Donna Davenport, struggling to hide a secret from police colleagues and get over the break-up with her partner, has been suspended from duty for a fiery and inappropriate outburst to the press.

DI Evanton, an old-fashioned, hard-living misogynistic copper has been newly demoted for thumping a suspect, and transferred to Dundee with a final warning ringing in his ears and a reputation that precedes him.

And in the peaceful, rolling Tayside farmland a deadly store of MIC, the toxin that devastated Bhopal, is being illegally stored by a criminal gang smuggling the valuable substance necessary for making cheap pesticides.

An anonymous tip-off starts a desperate search for the MIC that is complicated by the uneasy partnership between Davenport and Evanton and their growing mistrust of each others actions.

Compelling and authentic, Toxic is a tense and fast paced crime thriller.

'...a humdinger of a plot that is as realistic as it is frightening' – crimefictionlover.com

In The Shadow Of The Hill

by Helen Forbes

ISBN: 978-0-9929768-1-1 (eBook)
ISBN: 978-0-9929768-0-4 (Paperback)

An elderly woman is found battered to death in the common stairwell of an Inverness block of flats.

Detective Sergeant Joe Galbraith starts what seems like one more depressing investigation of the untimely death of a poor unfortunate who was in the wrong place, at the wrong time.

As the investigation spreads across Scotland it reaches into a past that Joe has tried to forget, and takes him back to the Hebridean island of Harris, where he spent his childhood.

Among the mountains and the stunning landscape of religiously conservative Harris, in the shadow of Ceapabhal, long buried events and a tragic story are slowly uncovered, and the investigation takes on an altogether more sinister aspect.

In The Shadow Of The Hill skilfully captures the intricacies and malevolence of the underbelly of Highland and Island life, bringing tragedy and vengeance to the magical beauty of the Outer Hebrides.

'...our first real home-grown sample of modern Highland noir' – Roger Hutchison; West Highland Free Press

Over Here

by Jane Taylor

ISBN: 978-0-9929768-3-5 (eBook)
ISBN: 978-0-9929768-2-8 (Paperback)

'It's coming up to twenty-four hours since the boy stepped down from the big passenger liner – it must be, he reckons foggily – because morning has come around once more with the awful irrevocability of time destined to lead nowhere in this worrying new situation. His temporary minder on board – last spotted heading for the bar some while before the lumbering process of docking got underway – seems to have vanished for good. Where does that leave him now? All on his own in a new country: that's where it leaves him. He is just nine years old.'

An eloquently written novel tracing the social transformations of a century where possibilities were opened up by two world wars that saw millions of men move around the world to fight, and mass migration to the new worlds of Canada and Australia by tens of thousands of people looking for a better life.

Through the eyes of three generations of women, the tragic story of the nine year old boy on Liverpool docks is brought to life in saddeningly evocative prose.

'...a sweeping haunting first novel that spans four generations and two continents...' Cristina Odone/Catholic Herald

The Bonnie Road

by Suzanne d'Corsey

ISBN: 978-1-910946-01-5 (ebook)
ISBN: 978-0-9929768-6-6 (Paperback)

My grandmother passed me in transit. She was leaving, I was coming into this world, our spirits meeting at the door to my mother's womb, as she bent over the bed to close the thin crinkled lids of her own mother's eyes.

The women of Morag's family have been the keepers of tradition for generations, their skills and knowledge passed down from woman to woman, kept close and hidden from public view, official condemnation and religious suppression.

In late 1970s St. Andrews, demand for Morag's services are still there, but requested as stealthily as ever, for even in 20th century Scotland witchcraft is a dangerous Art to practise.

When newly widowed Rosalind arrives from California to tend her ailing uncle, she is drawn unsuspecting into a new world she never knew existed, one in which everyone seems to have a secret, but that offers greater opportunities than she dreamt of – if she only has the courage to open her heart to it.

Richly detailed, dark and compelling, d'Corsey magically transposes the old ways of Scotland into the 20th Century and brings to life the ancient traditions and beliefs that still dance just below the surface of the modern world.

The House with the Lilac Shutters: and other stories

by Gabrielle Barnby

ISBN: 978-1-910946-02-2 (eBook)
ISBN: 978-0-9929768-8-0 (Paperback)

Irma Lagrasse has taught piano to three generations of villagers, whilst slowly twisting the knife of vengeance; Nico knows a secret; and M. Lenoir has discovered a suppressed and dangerous passion.

Revolving around the Café Rose, opposite The House with the Lilac Shutters, this collection of contemporary short stories links a small town in France with a small town in England, traces the unexpected connections between the people of both places and explores the unpredictable influences that the past can have on the present.

Characters weave in and out of each other's stories, secrets are concealed and new connections are made.

With a keenly observant eye, Barnby illustrates the everyday tragedies, sorrows, hopes and joys of ordinary people in this vividly understated and unsentimental collection.

Lightning Source UK Ltd.
Milton Keynes UK
UKOW06f1236261115

263511UK00011B/184/P